THE BASE HAD BEEN PLACED ON ALERT

. . . and the situation room hummed with activity. A red light suddenly began to wink on the Six-P-Two Launch Board.

"We have an A Key indicator on the Flybaby," the technician yelled.

Like most NATO weapons, it took two keys to activate the missile for launch.

Stewart jumped up and hurried to the console just as the B Key light came on. Both keys had been activated. The missile was live now, and starting through its firing cycle. The rest of the board began lighting up. "We have a firing sequence countdown. . . ."

Tor Books by David Hagberg

COUNT-DOWN

DAVID HAGBERG

TOR

A TOM DOHERTY ASSOCIATES BOOK
NEW YORK

This novel is for Laurie

COUNTDOWN

Copyright © 1990 by David Hagberg

A Tor Book
Published by Tom Doherty Associates, Inc.
175 Fifth Ave.
New York, N.Y. 10010

ISBN: 0-812-50964-1

Library of Congress Catalog Card Number: 89-25819

Printed in the United States of America

First Tor edition: April 1991

10 9 8 7 6 5 4 3

— PROLOGUE —

NEAR EN GEDI, ISRAEL

NIGHT OR DAY—IT DID NOT MATTER THREE HUNDRED FEET beneath the desert. All was in darkness. A man dressed in Israeli battle fatigues crawled slowly through an air duct a few feet at a time. He moved cautiously lest he make a noise or stumble upon one of the many down shafts that plunged a hundred feet deeper into the bedrock.

He was sweating profusely even though the air streaming past the back of his head was cool, almost cold. To be caught here, of all places, would mean a certain and probably unpleasant death.

The man who'd been known as Benjamin Rothstein to his superiors for the past eighteen months wiped his brow with the back of his hand and continued. Fifty feet farther he began to finally see the first diffuse glimmerings of light, dull and red; flashing, he realized as he crawled closer to its source. He stopped when he could make out the square shape of the source, and he held his breath to listen. The only sounds, however, were the gentle rushing of the air-conditioning and the low-pitched rumble of some machinery.

After a few moments he continued, coming at length to a louvered opening in the air duct.

It was three in the morning. No one would be here. Nevertheless he hesitated at the louvers for a full ten minutes, listening for anything, a stray scrap of conversation, a footfall, a clink of metal against metal, the vault door opening or closing. But there was nothing.

Rothstein, whose real name was Vladimir Ivanovich Tsarev, Vladi to his friends at the Frunze Naval Academy, took a small penlight from his pocket and flashed it once on the legend marked above the louvered opening: 1-A-7. He managed a tight smile. He was actually here at the main vault. Ten incoming air vents kept the cavern cool, the air fresh. It was called negative laminar airflow. Air was pumped into the room and any air that escaped could do so only through a complex system of scrubbers, washers, and detectors. It was akin to the air system in a medical operating theater, only in reverse. In an operating room no germs could be allowed to enter. Here nothing could be allowed to escape.

The irony was not lost on Tsarev.

From a small tool kit he selected a specially designed screwdriver, and working slowly, he carefully and silently backed out the eight screws holding the louvered panel in place. He was sweating even harder by the time he was finished, and his heart hammered in his chest. His mouth was so dry he found that it was almost impossible to swallow.

Again he stopped for a long time to listen, but there were no sounds, no alarms, only the flashing red light within the vault.

"Your job will be difficult and certainly very dangerous, Vladi, do you understand this completely?" Baranov had told him what seemed like a thousand years ago.

"Yes, Comrade General," he replied.

"We have given you the knowledge and the training, and we will provide you with an ironclad background, but the rest will be up to you."

Baranov smiled, and at that moment Tsarev knew that he loved this man as he had loved his own father. He would do anything for him.

"I will make you proud, Comrade General."

"Yes," Baranov had said, rising from behind his desk at the Lubyanka Center. "You will make all of the Rodina proud."

Baranov was neither old nor young, he was ageless—a legend and an institution in the KGB. Tsarev, whom he called his little boy with the Jewish eyes, on the other hand, was very young and eager; like a little puppy at times, anxious and ready to please. Getting to Israel had been no problem, nor had enlisting in the Army been difficult. But getting this job had not been easy. The Israeli Military Intelligence security background investigation was thorough and had taken nearly a year to complete. But he was here. Baranov had provided him with a wonderful background. "Ironclad," as he had promised.

Three hundred feet above, his guard post was deserted. He had figured he had three hours maximum to find the correct air shaft, descend, enter the vault, take his photographs, and then return to duty. Nearly two hours of that time had already elapsed.

"Move, Vladi," he told himself. There were no other alternatives now.

With great care he shoved the louvered panel out into the vault, nearly dropping it in the process, then crawled through the rectangular opening, dropping nearly eight feet onto the bare concrete floor.

Laying the louvered panel aside, he glanced up at the opening he'd just come through. Not an impossible distance to reach, he decided. Then he turned around.

The vault was long and narrow; perhaps two hundred feet by thirty, with a cast concrete ceiling only ten feet above the floor. The space was more filled than he'd been led to believe it would be. The simple fact of where he was and what he was seeing took his breath away; at first with awe and then a slowly mounting fear and even anger.

The flashing red light over the main vault door, through which a narrow-gauge set of railroad tracks ran, was irritating. Why was it flashing? What did it mean?

The tracks ran the entire length of the vault. Along the walls were massively constructed steel racks on which dull gray metal cylinders, three feet in diameter and five feet long, were stacked. Even in the dim flashing light Tsarev could see there had to be at least two hundred of them.

They'd never guessed. Four or five, if any; perhaps a dozen. No more. But hundreds? The information was staggering.

He cautiously stepped across the tracks and stared toward the massive door, the red light flashing implacably, almost hypnotically. Something that somehow seemed out of place lay in a heap on the floor in front of the door.

Tsarev took a tentative step forward, then stopped when he realized what was lying there. It was a man in white coveralls, face down on the concrete floor, his right arm outstretched as if he'd been trying to reach for something.

Had there been an accident? Had the technician been trying to summon help?

Again Tsarev's eyes rose to the flashing light. It was an alarm. There *had* been an accident here. A blind panic rose up inside his chest, and he backed up a step.

"Many things can go wrong, my dear little Vladi," Baranov had said.

"Yes, Comrade General."

This time they were walking on a cold, desolate plain outside of the city of Kiev. Chernobyl was only a few miles to the north. Tsarev's training had been completed and the director of the KGB had come down to speak with him personally. It was a great honor, but Tsarev was frightened.

"What is of supreme importance is that you find out this one little thing for us, and get the information back to me. If you get photographs that would be splendid. If, on the other hand, you can only get a serial number, just one, that would be wonderful. Or, if all else fails, if you merely get to the place, see it with your own eyes, confirm its existence and its contents and get that information back to me, you will not have failed. Do you understand this?''

"What if it is not there, Comrade General?" Tsarev had asked. It had taken him the better part of an hour to summon up the courage to ask that one question.

Baranov shook his head and laughed. "It's there, my boy, oh, it's there."

Tsarev had not asked the next logical question: Then why send me to find it? Now he wished he had. Now he wished he had asked a lot of questions.

Something had gone wrong, the alarm had been raised and soon someone would be coming here to investigate. There was no time for photographs . . . in any event he understood with a sickening feeling at the pit of his stomach that photographs would be worthless. Nor was there time even for a single serial number.

He backed up another step when he spotted the technician's cart of tools and test equipment three bays down from the vault door. One of the cylinders was open, exposing its insides. Something had fallen out, smashing on the floor. It looked to him like mercury, or perhaps a small puddle of thick silver paint.

His eyes swung wildly around the cavern. He'd come this far for Baranov, he wasn't going to simply lay himself down and die like the technician. It was even possible, he thought, that whatever had killed the man would only do so within a few feet. The man had been next to the spill. He had probably dropped it himself.

Tsarev turned and hurried back to the opening in the vault wall. With fumbling fingers he hurriedly reinserted the eight screws back into the louvered panel and then tossed it up through the opening.

He was slightly sick at his stomach, the implications of which he didn't want to think too hard and too long about. Not now.

He had to get out of this place. Security would be tight above because of this alarm. If he was found missing from his post there would be questions for which he would have no good answers.

It took him three tries before he was able to leap high enough on the wall to grasp the opening and pull himself back up into the duct, slightly cutting the ring finger of his right hand in the process. But he was too frightened, too intent on what he was going to have to do to realize that he had left a smudge of blood on the concrete wall just below the duct opening, and again inside the air duct itself and on the back of the louvered panel.

He managed to pull the panel back into place and, holding it with one hand, used his special tool with the other to refasten the screws.

When he was finally finished he allowed himself just a moment to catch his breath. The nausea was steadily increasing in his gut.

"Nerves, Vladi," he mumbled to himself. "Nothing more. You're scared shitless, that's all."

He turned himself around in the narrow air duct and started back the way he had come, moving as swiftly, yet as noiselessly as he possibly could.

Now he was feeling not only the sickness, and a sense of dread, but he was feeling claustrophobic. He had been underground too long. He had to get out. Fuck your mother, but he didn't like this.

The main air-conditioning duct ran roughly east and west, the secondary lines branching off it. At three points the intake shaft ran straight up to a secured room on the surface from where fresh air was pulled in.

It was the second of these shafts that was fitted with metal rungs down which Tsarev had come. His duty post was fifty feet away at the end of the intake building.

Reaching the first shaft he nearly fell in his haste, and he was so weak with fear that it took him several minutes to calm himself enough to continue to the second shaft and start up.

Above he could see light, and now he could hear the sounds of sirens. He had to stop often in his climb. The distance up was equivalent to a thirty-story building, and he was afraid of heights. His fingers were numb and greasy with sweat on the ladder rungs. The arches of his feet ached.

Near the top he thought he heard someone calling his name, but he wasn't sure and it was not repeated. If they had come to his post and found it deserted they would be looking for him. What would he say?

Two figures dressed in thick white environment suits, big hoods over their heads, oxygen bottles strapped to their backs, stepped off the transport elevator and through the first door of the laminar lock. When the outer door was closed, they cycled the air pressure, which took a half a minute. When the pressure was equalized they opened the inner lock and stepped out into the main loading and washdown antechamber. The door to the main vault was fifty feet down the broad, low-ceilinged corridor, a red alarm light flashing above it.

This part of the chamber was clean. They hurried down the corridor where the one in the lead put down the piece of electronic equipment he'd been carrying and opened a metal panel beside the massive steel and lead door. He flipped a switch and above the door a television screen came to life with a wavering, imperfect picture. Both men could see the downed technician and beyond him the accident that had caused the alarm.

Because of the absolute secrecy of this place there were no monitor leads to the top side. Nothing that could be discovered by a snoopy referee from the International Regulatory Commission. Security was tight, but their response time to accidents such as these was of necessity very slow.

"Poor bastard," Lev Potok said.

"Dead?" the other figure, Abraham Liebowitz, asked, his voice coming over the intercom units built into their suits.

Potok was manipulating the camera controls to scan the entire vault. "Looks like it."

"It shouldn't have happened that fast. He should have had time to get out. The levels don't seem that high in there."

"High enough," Potok said. "Be my guess that he inhaled the fumes. Probably burned out his lungs."

Potok continued the scan.

"Anything else?"

"Doesn't look like it. I'll do a spot wash and we'll get him out of there. You'd better call for some help."

Liebowitz turned and went back through the laminar chamber, and telephoned from the elevator while Potok cycled the vault door. It took half a minute for the four-foot-thick door to ponderously swing open, and he stepped inside.

The technician lay on his face, his right arm outstretched. He'd gotten this far, and with the last of his strength had pressed the alarm button, and then his fingers must have brushed the vault light control, because the chamber was in darkness except for the flashing light.

Potok flipped on the main overhead lights and then bent down over the technician and carefully turned the man over on his back. His name tag read ASHER. His eyes bulged out of their sockets, and his tongue was swollen and black and filled his entire mouth. Potok had been correct in his assessment of what had happened here. Asher had made a mistake and had paid with his life for it, though it still wasn't clear to Potok what the man had been doing down here in the first place.

From a locker beside the main door he took out a containment kit and gingerly approached the spill. He sprayed a foam over the entire spill area, then laid three layers of lead film over that.

It would do until the cleanup crew arrived.

Potok went back to Asher's body. He looked down at the man. He'd seen plenty of battle casualties in his forty-one years. This one looked no better or worse than many. It was war, he told himself grimly.

What had Asher been doing down here?

Potok was ostensibly an Emergency Management Team leader. But he also held the rank of major in Mossad, Israel's secret intelligence service. He was a suspicious man by nature, and very good at his job of seeing anomalies, glitches in the fabric of human endeavor, the little out-of-place details that escaped most observers.

He turned after a moment and walked along the tracks between the storage racks. There was no evidence that anything else had been tampered with. Asher was here, had begun what might turn out to be a routine service check, and had made his fatal mistake.

But it had not been a routine check. Not at three o'clock in the morning. And not alone.

Potok took out a powerful flashlight from his suit pocket and switched it on. As he walked slowly along the tracks he shined the light over the racks, and the units they contained, as well as the floor and walls beyond.

Nothing. Everything except the spill site was clean.

At the end of the long chamber he started back, shining his light on the opposite racks and wall.

He stopped halfway, his light flashing on one of the intake air ducts. A moment later the four suited figures of the cleanup team appeared at the vault door. Liebowitz, who also worked for Mossad, was right behind them. Potok motioned for him.

Liebowitz said something to the cleanup technicians, and hurried down the tracks. Potok switched off his suit intercom and Liebowitz did the same. Leaning close so that their hoods were touching, they could talk to each other without anyone overhearing their conversation.

"What's the word topside?" Potok asked.

"No one knew he was down here other than security where he signed in."

"No one questioned him?"

"He's one of the senior techs on the maintenance crew."

"But no maintenance was scheduled?"

"No." Liebowitz glanced back at Asher's body. "Whatever he was doing, he was on his own. Sabotage?"

"If that was the case he was damned sloppy about it," Potok said thoughtfully.

"And he got what was coming to him," Liebowitz said

harshly. His mother, father, and two sisters had been killed on the West Bank four years ago.

"I want you to get back up top and find out about this one. What he was doing here, and why he was allowed to wander around on his own in the middle of the night."

"But don't make waves," Liebowitz said. It was one of Potok's favorite sayings.

"*Make* waves," Potok said.

They separated and switched on their suit intercoms. Liebowitz nodded but said nothing. He started back toward the vault door. Potok turned and shined his light on the racks, and again the beam flashed across the louvered air duct. His mouth went suddenly dry, and his heart skipped a beat.

"Liebowitz," he shouted, but before the other man could reply, Potok raced between the racks to the wall just below the vent. He shined his flashlight on it. Blood. God in heaven, it was blood.

Shining his light down the wall he could see scuff marks where someone had evidently jumped for the opening and levered himself up by the toes of his boots. He could even see where the unknown intruder had laid the louvered panel in the dust against the wall.

Liebowitz was behind him. "What is it?"

This time Potok didn't bother turning off his suit intercom. There was no time now for fine details.

"Asher had help."

"What?"

Potok shined the light on the scuff marks and on the blood beneath the louvered panel. "Someone has been here. And they've gotten out through the incoming air system."

"God . . ."

"Seal the facility! Do it now!"

"Where the hell have you been?" Sergeant Joshua Gurion shouted as Tsarev came out of the darkness around one of the air vents. The alarms had been turned off.

The sergeant seemed more irritated than angry or suspicious.

"Checking the air vents, Sergeant," Tsarev said. "The alarm . . ."

"Well, you weren't supposed to leave your post!"

"Yes, sir."

Sergeant Gurion looked beyond Tsarev to the shadows. "See anything?"

"No, sir. Everything looks fine."

This time the sergeant looked critically at him. "You sure as hell don't, Rothstein. What's the matter with you?"

"I think I'm a little sick," Tsarev said, and it wasn't a lie. He felt terrible. He could feel the sweat on his brow and his uniform was stained dark with it.

"There's nothing to be worried about," Sergeant Gurion said not unkindly. For some reason he had taken a liking to Tsarev from the beginning. "I know what you're thinking."

"It's that, but I still don't feel good, Sergeant," Tsarev said. The man was a fool, but at this moment he was a ticket out of here.

"All right, get yourself over to sick bay. I'll arrange for your replacement."

"Yes, sir."

Sergeant Gurion patted him on the arm. "You'll be okay."

"What was it, Sergeant? The alarm?"

"Nothing," the sergeant said. "And get your hand looked at, you've cut it on something."

Tsarev looked at his hand and the dried blood. "Yes, sir," he mumbled.

Outside, Tsarev got in his jeep and crossed the huge facility that was bathed in strong lights night and day. Instead of heading over to the barracks area, however, he drove directly to one of the back gates where he turned in his security badge and left the compound.

The night was extremely dark. Tsarev kept looking in his rearview mirror at the receding lights of the plant. His foot on the gas pedal was shaking, at times so uncontrollably that he had difficulty maintaining a constant speed. He was very sick to his stomach, and two miles from the facility he threw up down the front of his fatigue blouse.

He stopped the jeep and got out where he was sick again at the side of the road. When he was finished he looked back toward the facility. It sounded to him as if he was hearing another siren. But then the sound faded.

Climbing weakly back behind the wheel he forced himself to drive toward the town of En Gedi eight miles away.

When he didn't show up at sick bay they would come looking for him. "He was behind the air vents," the sergeant would say.

Twice more Tsarev was sick, but he did not bother to stop until he passed an Esso gas station a mile outside of the town. The station was closed at this hour of the morning, but there would almost certainly be a telephone inside.

He brought the jeep to a stop, made a U-turn on the narrow highway, and drove back to the station. Taking his Uzi submachine gun he stumbled across the driveway past the pumps and without hesitation shot out the lock in the front door with a quick burst.

Inside, he dragged himself across the office where he found the telephone. He picked it up, got a dial tone, and called his contact number in Jerusalem. It was answered on the first ring.

"It is there. Hundreds of them. It is there," he said.

"Have you photographs?" a man's voice asked calmly.

"No time."

"A serial number?"

"No! Haven't you heard me?" Tsarev cried. "It's there. Hundreds of them. More than we ever suspected."

"Yes, and now listen to me . . ."

An army truck screeched to a halt outside, and immediately a dozen soldiers sprang out of the back. Tsarev crashed down the telephone and rushed to the door.

He never felt the shots that killed him.

BOOK ONE

1

PARIS

PARIS WAS A MAGICAL CITY. AS LIEUTENANT COLONEL BRAD Allworth got out of his taxi in front of the Gare de l'Est and paid his fare, one part of him was sad to be leaving, while another part was looking forward to what was coming.

Hefting his B4 bag, he crossed the broad sidewalk and entered the train station's busy main concourse. He was a tall man, handsome in a rugged out-of-doors way, his stride straight and purposeful. He was a career Air Force officer and at thirty-five he figured he had a shot at full bird colonel within the year, and afterward . . . War College and his first star by forty.

The concierge at his hotel had arranged for his tickets to Kaiserslautern in Germany's Rheinland-Pfalz, so he went directly down to trackside. It was a few minutes past eleven-

thirty. His train was due to leave at midnight, getting into
the German city by morning.

He stopped at the security gate and placed his bag on the
moving belt that took it through the scanning device. Something new in the last six months. He placed his wallet and a
few francs in loose change on a plastic dish, handed it to one
of the gendarmes, and stepped through the arch.

"Your tickets, monsieur," the guard asked.

Colonel Allworth handed over his ticket as well as his
passport. The gendarme quickly flipped through them, looked
from the photograph to his face.

Technically he could travel all over Europe using only his
military ID. But because of the terrorist attacks in recent
years, American officers traveling via civilian transportation
were required to travel in civilian clothes and use their pass-
ports for identification. It had been dubbed Project Low Profile. Allworth didn't mind.

The gendarme handed back his passport and ticket, waved
an arm vaguely in the direction of the gates, and as Allworth
was collecting his money and B4 bag, the cop was checking
the papers of the next man in line.

Allworth crossed to his gate, and a porter directed him to
his first-class car. He boarded, found his compartment,
switched on the light, tossed his bag on the couch, and closed
the window shades on the corridor and outer windows.

JoAnne had flown out from Omaha with him, while their
two children stayed with her sister in Minneapolis. They'd
had a lovely thirty days in Paris and the surrounding countryside; canal barge trips, ballooning through the Bordeaux
wine country, a weekend on the Riviera, and they had relaxed with each other for the first time in what seemed like
years. Too many years. But everything was all right between
them now.

He had seen her off from Orly this afternoon. She would
be closing down their house, collecting the kids, and would
join him at Ramstein Air Force Base within the month. It
was, he decided, going to be a busy though lonely month.

Someone knocked at his compartment door.

Allworth turned. "Yes?"

"Porter, monsieur."

Allworth opened the door. An older man in a crisp white jacket smiled up at him. "May I turn down your bed for you, monsieur?"

"Not just yet," Allworth said. He pulled out a two-hundred-franc bill. "Can I get a bottle of cognac and a glass?"

"Naturellement, monsieur." The porter smiled, accepting the money. "It will be just a few minutes."

"No rush," Allworth said. Technically he was still on leave. He meant to enjoy his last day before he had to get back to work.

Loosening his tie he took off his jacket, slipped off his shoes, and opened the bi-fold door to his tiny bathroom with its pull-down sink. He splashed some cool water on his face, and drying off he smiled at himself in the mirror. SAC Headquarters at Omaha had been a career necessity. It's what brought him a step closer to the bird, and as a direct result got him his new job as missile control officer, even if he hadn't liked SAC. He was making progress, and that's all that counted.

He switched off the light in the bathroom, opened the outer window shade, and sat down on the couch. Lighting a cigarette he looked down at the rapidly clearing platform. The train would be pulling out momentarily, and for just a brief instant he felt a twinge of uncertainty.

"Comes with the territory," his father the general had told him once. "You can't move every few years without feeling dislocated. Make the service your home, then find a good woman and keep her. You'll do just fine."

Someone knocked at his door. "Porter."

Allworth opened the door and took the cognac and glass from the man, received his change, and handed him back two ten-franc coins.

"Merci."

"I don't think you'll need to turn down my bed tonight."

"No?"

"No," Allworth said with a grin.

"If you need anything else, just ring, monsieur. I will be happy to serve you."

"What time will we get into Kaiserslautern?"

"At seven, monsieur."

"Good, thanks."

"Oui."

Allworth opened the bottle and poured himself a stiff measure, then sat down again by the window as the train lurched and pulled out of the station, slowly at first, but gathering speed as they came up into the city. He laid his head back and sighed deeply, the cognac spreading its warmth throughout his body, filling him with a sense of well-being.

It had been a long haul, he thought. This was the last step before the big move. The Pentagon, Washington, a city both he and JoAnne loved. Not that they were people filled with pretensions, but they did enjoy the social whirl, being close to power. It was heady stuff for both of them.

Someone knocked at his door again, and Allworth assumed it was the porter. He went to the door.

For a brief instant he simply could not believe what he was seeing. A tall man stood in the corridor facing him, a leather bag over his shoulder. He was handsome in a rugged, athletic way. In fact Allworth thought he was looking at his own double, or a man near enough to his own twin to be startling.

"What . . ." Allworth started to say when the man raised a silenced pistol and shot him in the middle of the forehead, a huge thunderclap exploding in his head.

Inside the tiny first-class compartment Arkady Aleksandrovich Kurshin locked the door and closed the outer window shade. Working quickly, he opened his shoulder bag and withdrew a large, thin plastic sheet and spread it out on the floor. Careful to get no blood on himself or the carpeted floor he rolled Colonel Allworth's body onto the sheet. Actually the wound had bled very little, nor had the low-grain, soft-nosed bullet exited the back of the American's head. But it had killed him instantly.

Kurshin was methodical. But then he was a professional and it was to be expected.

It would be several hours before they neared the German border; nevertheless he did not waste any time. There was much to be done before he could rest.

First, he stripped Allworth's body of everything including the man's underwear, his watch, his dog tags, and his gold wedding band, carefully inspecting each item in minute detail so that not only could he make sure nothing had been stained by blood or any other body fluids released at Allworth's death, but to familiarize himself with the dead man's possessions, which for the coming forty-eight hours would be his.

Next, he removed all of his clothing, including a very expensive diamond-studded gold Rolex watch, a heavy gold neck chain, and a diamond pinky ring.

He had just a moment of revulsion as he pulled on Allworth's underwear, but he ignored his single, oddly out of place, sign of squeamishness and finished dressing in the dead man's clothing, including his watch, dog tags, and wedding ring.

He put all of his clothing on Allworth's body.

"Another, greedier, man might think to keep some of the considerable money, or perhaps some of the jewelry you will be carrying, Arkady," Baranov had told him. "After all, what use can a dead man have with such things? Besides, the first man to find his body might very well himself be a thief."

Kurshin had sat with Baranov in a café on East Berlin's Unter den Linden. He looked across his drink at the general. A rare, difficult man, he'd thought. But brilliant, and totally without conscience.

"It is part of his identification," Kurshin said.

"Exactly. We do understand each other."

Kurshin smiled. "When I steal from you, Comrade General, it will be much more than a few thousand francs and a pretty watch."

"Oh, dear," Baranov had laughed, throwing his head back. "That is rich, that is rich indeed."

Everything fit perfectly except for the shoes. His were too small for Allworth's feet. Kurshin was vexed for just a moment, but then he shrugged it aside. Allworth's shoes would be too big for him, but that didn't matter. Had it been the other way around, it would have made things difficult. So far it was the only thing they hadn't counted on.

Kurshin set the shoes aside, on the plastic sheet, and from his leather shoulder bag removed a pair of latex surgical gloves, a very sharp switchblade knife, and a small pair of pruning shears which he laid beside Allworth's body.

Kneeling next to the body, he pulled the edge of the plastic sheet up over his legs and began his work.

Kurshin had boarded the train on a French passport under the name of Edmon Railliarde, an import/export broker from Marseille. In actuality, Railliarde was a member of the French Mafia. He'd been snatched two days ago from his magnificent villa outside of Marseille and his body by now had been ground to small pieces and distributed to the fishes at sea.

Railliarde had many enemies.

Using the handles of the shears Kurshin spent fifteen minutes knocking out Allworth's teeth, destroying every bit of dental evidence that might prove he was not the French criminal, Railliarde.

Next, he clipped off the tips of Allworth's fingers, each one separating from the bloodless stump with a sickening snap. These he put in a small vial of acid he'd carried with him. This he would toss before they crossed the border.

Finally, using the razor-sharp switchblade, Kurshin removed Allworth's face, just as an animal might be skinned. This tissue, which rolled into a surprisingly small ball, went into another small container of acid to be disposed of with the dead man's fingertips.

When he was done he sat back, his stomach rumbling a little. It had been nearly twelve hours since he'd eaten last. Though there was no blood, it had been gruesome work. But necessary. Very necessary if his fiction was to hold up for any length of time.

At the window Kurshin opened the shade and looked out at the passing countryside. There wasn't much to be seen. A few lights off in the distance. They were passing through the farm country east of Paris, not too far from Châlons-sur-Marne. Perfect, he thought.

He lowered the window, the noise and rushing air filling the cabin. Tossing his shoulder bag on Allworth's chest, he wrapped the body in the plastic sheet, manhandled it up to the window, and levered it through the opening. It was gone in a sharp fluttering of plastic, and Kurshin closed and locked the window and closed the shade.

For the next twenty minutes he inspected every square inch of the cabin, the floors, the walls, and even the ceiling for any trace that a murder and mutilation had occurred here.

Satisfied at length that the room was clean, he sat down on the couch, poured a stiff measure of cognac, lit a cigarette, and started going through Allworth's suitcase, item by item, mentally cataloguing every single thing so that he would know it as well as his own possessions.

The city of Kaiserslautern in Germany's mid-section had once been a crossroads and meeting place of kings. In more recent times it had been a major resupply and staging depot for Hitler's armies. Since the war the area had come to contain the largest concentration of American Army and Air Force personnel anywhere in the world.

Arkady Kurshin stepped off the train, hefted his single B4 bag, and walked out into the bright morning's sun where he hailed a taxi, ordering the driver to take him out to Ramstein Air Force Base a few miles to the south.

There had been absolutely no trouble on the train last night. But Kurshin had known that he would pass from the instant he'd seen the look on Allworth's face when he'd opened the door.

The only real difficulty would come at the base if he ran

into someone who knew Allworth. It was possible. But the U.S. Air Force was a very large organization. And he only had to hold out for another thirty-six hours or so.

Close, he thought with an inward smile. So very close.

The cabbie was a garrulous old woman who tried all the way out to the base to engage him in conversation, but Kurshin sat back in his seat and closed his eyes. He had gotten no sleep on the train last night, and he forced himself to rest his mind for a little while. He was going to need his wits about him. But then he'd had the training. He had the intelligence. And he had Baranov's backing.

Nothing would go wrong.

Ramstein Air Force Base was a huge installation covering thousands of acres of German countryside. Much of it was underground in the old Nazi labyrinth of tunnels and storage caverns. It was the largest depot for U.S. and NATO nuclear weapons anywhere outside of the continental United States. Yet security on the base was very lax, these days.

At the main gate he cranked down his window and showed the AP on duty his ID card, and the taxi was passed through to the Bachelor Officers Quarters across base.

He paid the driver and went inside, where he signed in with the Charge of Quarters, handing over a copy of his orders.

"Welcome to Germany, sir," the young sergeant said. "Did you have a good trip?"

"Tiring," Kurshin said. "What I need is a shower, a stiff drink, and a decent steak, in that order."

The sergeant, whose name tag read LEVENSON, grinned. "Can do, Colonel, at least on the shower. You can get the drink and a good steak at the officers club just up the block."

"Sounds good."

"Have you signed in yet, sir?"

"No, I just got in."

"If you'll give me four sets of your orders, I'll have a runner take them over to base HQ for you. The commander is off the base until Monday."

Kurshin dug out the extra sets of orders and handed them over. "How about transportation?"

"I can get you a car and driver as well, soon as we get you signed in."

Kurshin grinned. The security was incredibly lax. The sergeant mistook the meaning of his smile.

"No sweat, Colonel, we aim to please around here."

"So far so good," Kurshin said, his grin broadening. And he meant it.

2

EN GEDI

HEAT SHIMMERED UP FROM THE DESOLATE FLOOR OF THE desert as the gunmetal gray Mercedes 560SE sedan fitted with United Nations flags on its front fenders appeared in the distance. Above, an Israeli Army Cobra gunship helicopter hovered at one thousand feet.

Lev Potok, seated by the open door, lowered the powerful binoculars through which he'd watched the car and shook his head wryly. It had been only a little more than forty-eight hours since the incident and already the piranhas were gathering.

"We're in a delicate position here," Dr. Moshe Ben Avral, the facility director, had told him yesterday. "We're operating what appears to the world to be nothing more than a research reactor, when in reality too many people know what is here.''

"They can only guess," Potok argued. "And if they guess correctly they cannot know for certain that this is a storage depot.''

"A guess is less damaging than a certainty?" Dr. Avral asked.

"Of course," Potok replied, his mind for just that moment elsewhere. Rothstein's background so far was coming up clean, as was Asher's. But there was no doubt that it was Rothstein who had crawled down through the intake air ducts and had let himself into the main vault. The blood on the louvered panel and inside on the floor of the air duct matched Rothstein's, and the man had received a severe dose of radiation.

So he had been to the vault and seen with his own eyes what it contained. The question was, had he had time to use the telephone in the gas station to call someone? His fingerprints were on the telephone. But had he had the time?

"We were right on his tail, Major," the team leader had reported. "He wasn't in that gas station for more than twenty or thirty seconds.''

Time enough to make a call? Potok wondered.

The shock waves of the possibility had reached the prime minister, and were coming back on them now. The depot must be moved, even though it would be impossible in under a year's time without completely blowing security.

"Then so be it.''

And now the UN's Non-Proliferation Treaty Team had come knocking at their front door again.

"Let's get back," he shouted to the pilot, and the chopper peeled off to the south.

God help us all if the secret was out, Potok thought. It would probably mean war. A war in which all the Arab States would almost certainly participate.

Dr. Lorraine Abbott sat in the backseat of the Mercedes with Scott Hayes whom she had joined in London. He was with the British arm of the NPT Inspection Service. They'd been together almost continuously for twenty-four hours. First the briefings and then the travel to Israel, and she decided that she didn't like him very much.

"A waste of time," he grumbled from where he sat slouched against the door. "They're not going to tell us a bloody thing."

Hayes was short, and dumpy-looking with long hair, a scraggly beard, and dull gray eyes. He was reputed to be a fair nuclear physicist and engineer and was a Greenpeacer, a combination Lorraine found oddly out of synch.

"At least they'll know that we're interested, and that we're keeping on top of things," she replied.

Hayes looked at her with a little smirk. "Do you think they'll bloody well care?"

Lorraine, who held her Ph.D. in theoretical physics from Berkeley, presently worked at the Lawrence Livermore Laboratories and was on call by the NPT Inspection Service as a field observer, a job which took her away from home half a dozen times each year. She was tall, slender, and attractive, with light California blond hair and wide green eyes. Her colleagues were always surprised by her chic appearance the first time they met her.

"You don't look like a physicist," they would invariably say.

Her response, if she were feeling irascible, often would be: "You do."

"They definitely care," she answered Hayes, but she didn't bother pointing out the helicopter which had just turned to the south toward the En Gedi Nuclear Research Facility a few miles off.

"So what are you going to ask them: 'Say, old chum, mind telling us where you're keeping the goodies these days?' "

Lorraine smiled. "Something like that," she said.

"Bloody hell," Hayes responded and looked out the window, a petulant set to his shoulders.

Lorraine opened her purse and with long, delicate fingers took out a cigarette and lit it, drawing the smoke deeply into her lungs. Her former fiancé, a surgeon at the UCLA Medical Center, had always been on her back about her one vice. "You're too bright for that, Lor," he'd said.

She hadn't minded, though, even if he was right; *his* one vice was his harping. No one was perfect after all.

The NPT had gotten its preliminary report that something might be amiss here at En Gedi from the National Security Agency at Ft. Meade. An unusual amount of activity had been observed from one of the KH-series flyby satellites. Photos had been sent over to the National Photographic Interpretation Center, where analysis suggested that some sort of an alarm might have been set off two and a half days ago, around three in the morning, local time.

There had been no apparent damage, no fire, and certainly no detectable radiation leaks. In addition, the Israelis had so far made no announcement about any trouble at their research reactor facility—though it would have been highly unusual for them to do so. They had been extremely tight-lipped about their involvement with nuclear energy.

Still, they had not seemed overly surprised to learn that an NPT team was being sent out to look over the situation.

Her instructions were simple, as they had been for each of her inspection trips: Keep your eyes and ears open for anything out of the ordinary.

Israel had the capacity to produce plutonium from her two research reactors, and presently she had operational one enrichment plant, one heavy water plant, and one reprocessing plant, so she also had the capability of producing weapons-grade material. The question was, of course, had Israel actually taken the next step? Had she constructed a nuclear weapon or weapons? The NPT wanted to know.

God only knew, she thought to herself as their driver brought them over the crest of a hill, the En Gedi plant off in the distance, they had the reason to build such weapons . . . their survival.

The En Gedi Nuclear Research Station was about average for a facility of its nature. The reactor itself was housed beneath a four-story fiberglass dome inside a slightly larger reinforced concrete containment building. To the east was a small venturi-shaped cooling tower. On the north side of the installation, which was enclosed behind a double line of tall electrified fences, were the various research laboratories and the main administration center. To the west were a small dispensary, dining hall, and housing units for the science and technical staff and the squadron of military guards. Syria, after all, wasn't very far away. Security here was, of necessity, very tight.

They were met at the front gate by a husky, good-looking Army officer in a major's uniform, a hard hat on his head.

"Lev Potok," he introduced himself. "I'm the Crises Management Team Supervisor. Welcome to En Gedi, Dr. Abbott, Mr. Hayes."

They shook hands.

"We understand you had a little trouble the other night," Lorraine said. There was no use beating around the bush. In that, at least, she agreed with Hayes.

Potok managed a tight smile. "It was nothing, actually. But I expect you'll want to see for yourself."

"Naturally," Hayes said sharply, and Lorraine shot him a warning glance which he ignored.

"If you will come along, then, our facility director and chief engineer are waiting to meet you," Potok said.

They had gotten out of the Mercedes. The heat at this hour of the afternoon was intense. Potok gave them hard hats, radiation badges, and visitor tags, and they climbed into his waiting jeep and were whisked across the facility to the three-story administration building.

Inside they were ushered into a conference room where two men looked up from a set of blueprints they'd been studying. One was a much older man with longish white hair, wire-rimmed glasses, and the bemused look of a college professor. He was the facility's director, Dr. Moshe Ben Avral. Lorraine had heard of him. He'd done a number of papers on the development of nuclear power sources for the third world.

"Pleased to meet you, Dr. Avral," she said, shaking hands.

The other, much stockier, much younger man, was Samuel Rosen, the facility's chief engineer. "A Brooklyn transplant," he said with a smile and a thick New York accent.

"A report has been sent along to Washington, Dr. Abbott, so we're just a little surprised that you're here," Dr. Avral said gently.

Although Israel had never signed the Nuclear Non-Proliferation Treaty of 1969 (of course at that time they had had no immediate plans for entering the nuclear race), they had come to an informal agreement with the United States to inform her ally what she was doing, and to submit to NPT inspections.

"I haven't seen that report," Lorraine said.

"Nor have I," Hayes added.

Dr. Avral nodded patiently. "No, of course you would not have seen the report. By the time it was sent, you were unfortunately already in transit."

Rosen was looking at Lorraine, an odd, almost anxious expression on his face. He was hiding something, she decided. She turned to him.

"You didn't experience much of a problem, then?" she asked.

"Not really," Rosen said. "It was a nonradioactive steam leak."

"There was an alarm," Hayes said.

"Yes. You can't believe the safety networks and backups we've got here. A valve chatters and a dozen alarms go off."

"Your team was called in?" she asked Potok, who had so far maintained a stony silence.

"SOP," Potok said. "We're dealing with nuclear energy here, Doctor. It scares a lot of people."

"Me included," she said.

There was an awkward silence, which Hayes finally filled by stepping forward and glancing down at the blueprints spread out on the conference table. "We might just as well take a look at this supposed leak, then, all right?"

Rosen and Potok exchanged a look, which Lorraine caught. Again she had the impression that they were hiding something. Perhaps something important.

"Yes, of course," Dr. Avral said, and he stepped aside to let the engineer take over.

For the next fifteen minutes Rosen went over in detail exactly what had happened the night when a steam line valve had supposedly popped loose. Lorraine stood back and pretended to study the diagrams while in actuality she was watching Potok and Dr. Avral. There was more here than met the eye. Potok was concerned and Dr. Avral was frightened.

On the way back to Tel Aviv she told Hayes that she thought the Israelis were lying.

"I don't think so," the Britisher said smugly. "That Rosen isn't bad, for a Jew. He knows his engineering."

"There was more than a simple steam leak," Lorraine said.

Hayes looked at her with renewed interest. "Are you going to put that in your report?"

"Yes."

"On what basis?"

"I don't know," she said softly. She looked up at him. "But I'm going to find out."

3

RAMSTEIN AIR FORCE BASE

KURSHIN SAT IN THE OFFICERS CLUB FINISHING THE LAST OF his steak. It was two in the afternoon. He'd taken a shower, changed into Allworth's uniform, made a brief telephone call to town, and had his driver, a young airman, take him on a brief tour of the base before dropping him off at the club. He'd dismissed the young man, but kept the car.

"Colonel Allworth?" someone said at his elbow and Kurshin looked up, an automatic smile painted on his face.

"Yes?"

"Tom McCann. I'm your number two."

McCann was a youngish-looking man with a baby face and bright red hair. He was wearing a pair of tan slacks and a light blue pullover sweater. They shook hands and Kurshin motioned him to have a seat.

"Is it captain?" Kurshin asked. He knew nothing about the man.

"Major." McCann grinned. "The OD heard you were on base and called me. The old man will be up in Berlin until Monday so I thought I'd stop by and welcome you aboard."

"I appreciate that, Tom. As a matter of fact I was going to come snooping around myself as soon as I finished lunch."

"You want to do some homework before you see the boss?"

"Something like that." Kurshin thought the younger man's expressions were boyish.

"No sweat, Colonel. Your clearance won't be posted until Monday, but if you don't mind tagging along with me on a visitor's pass, I'll give you the ten-cent tour."

Kurshin nodded. He pushed his plate away, finished the last of his beer, and looked McCann directly in the eye. "What if I was an impostor?" he asked with a straight face. "You'd give me the keys to the bank vault just like that?"

McCann's grin widened. "We got your package six weeks ago," he said. "Including your photograph. If you're an impostor, Colonel, then you're Brad Allworth's twin. Are you ready?"

"Just have to make a quick phone call," Kurshin said.

Ramstein was divided into four major sections. Near the main gate were base housing, the clubs, movie theaters, dining halls, hobby shops, class six liquor stores, and the commissary. On the east side of the base were the runways and alert hangars for the several fighter interceptor squadrons that made up the wing. To the west were the supply depots and support functions such as electrical generating plants, communications and radar squadrons, sewage treatment plant and other housekeeping functions.

Most of the sprawling wooded land area, which was enclosed by tall barbed wire-topped fencing and watched around the clock by mounted perimeter guards, served as the storage and staging area for the store of nuclear missiles including the Boeing AGM 86B Air Launched Cruise Missile, which the Air Force used, and 17 of the Army's 108 Mobile Launched Pershing II missiles.

Missile Control was housed in a cast concrete bunker constructed into the side of a hill. The situation room and operational control center were located two hundred feet back into the bedrock, impervious to anything but a direct hit with a thermonuclear device. No one felt really safe, however, as McCann explained.

"Doesn't matter how much rock you've got overhead once you know that you're their number-one target."

They signed in with the OD, Kurshin was given a visitor's pass, and McCann started toward the elevators. Kurshin stopped him.

"Let's start outside and work our way back in," he said.

McCann shrugged. "There won't be much to see."

Kurshin allowed the smile to die from his face. "In here is support. Out there is the real thing. I want to see the hardware itself, as well as the security. I want to know who's minding the store and just how good they're doing their job."

McCann stiffened slightly. "Yes, sir," he said. It was the first time he'd used proper military address.

Back outside they climbed into McCann's blue station wagon and headed on the main transport road into what appeared to be nothing more than an empty tract of woods, open grass fields here and there, and dirt tracks leading through the brush every few hundred yards or so.

Except for the paved road there was no sign that this area was anything more than some backwoods country, the dirt tracks used by forest service people, Jaegermeisters.

"What would you like to see first, Colonel, our ALCMs, or the Army's Pershings?"

They'd been driving in silence for a few minutes, the afternoon warm and very pleasant, only a few puffy white clouds overhead.

"Listen, Tom, I don't want to get off on the wrong foot here," Kurshin said apologetically.

McCann glanced at him, not sure if he should reply.

"This is an important assignment for me," Kurshin said.

"But I'm not going to be an asshole about it, if you catch my meaning."

"I'm not quite sure, Colonel . . ."

"You can can the colonel shit. The name is Brad. What I mean to say is that I'm sorry I was such a shit back there. I was out of line."

McCann relaxed, his grin back. "You had me just a little worried."

"Let's take a look around, and then get back to the club. I think by then it'll be time for me to buy you a drink."

"You're on."

Ten minutes later they reached the southern edge of the base just as a jeep with two Air Force Security Specialists drove down the dirt track that paralleled the fence. They disappeared into the distance as the fence jogged to the left.

"How often do we have a patrol past any given point on the perimeter?" Kurshin asked.

"Twelve minutes tops."

Kurshin shook his head. "That's going to have to be tightened up."

"Bob Collingwood is in charge. Do you want to see him this afternoon?"

"Monday will be fine," Kurshin said.

They turned left and headed down a gravel road that opened five hundred yards later into a clearing in which a low concrete bunker was built back into the hill. A large steel door covered the opening. Trees and grass grew on the roof.

"We have seventeen of these scattered around out here. Each contains a Pershing II."

"How about their mobile launchers, and the rigs to haul them?"

"All hooked up and ready to go within five minutes' notice or less. A couple of the teams back here can get them out in under four minutes."

"How about the teams?"

McCann smiled wryly. "There's the rub. They used to be housed back here. These days they share quarters with the Air Wing's on-duty alert crew."

Kurshin sighed theatrically. "That's going to change as well," he said. He got out of the car. "Let's take a look."

"Right," McCann said, jumping out of the car.

Kurshin went ahead to the big steel doors beside which was a much smaller personnel hatch. It was extremely quiet out here. Even the jet sounds from the distant runways were faint.

He stepped aside as McCann came up, opened a small access panel beside the door, and punched in the five-digit entry code. The hatch lock cycled and McCann pulled the narrow steel door open.

"No one else back here?" Kurshin asked.

"The patrols come around once a shift," McCann said, stepping inside and flipping on the overhead lights.

"Have they been by yet this shift?"

"They usually do it first thing," McCann said, turning. His eyes suddenly went wide. Kurshin was holding a silenced automatic on him.

"Thanks," the Russian said, and he shot McCann in the forehead.

4

RAMSTEIN AIR FORCE BASE

IN MISSILE CONTROL'S SITUATION ROOM A RED LIGHT BEGAN to wink on one of the panels.

"We have a missile bay door open indicator," the technician called from his console.

The Officer of the Day, Captain Gerry Stewart, put down his coffee and came across the room. He studied the board for a moment or two. The indicator was definitely winking. It was one of the Pershing II's.

"Try the alarm test function."

The tech flipped a switch and pushed a button that tested the validity of all their alarm systems. The lights across his board winked green, indicating the system was in proper working order. One of the missile bay doors was actually open.

Then Stewart remembered that McCann was running around out there showing their new squadron commander around, and he allowed himself to relax a little.

"Hold on to it for a minute, I think it's Tom," Stewart said and he went over to his console where he punched in McCann's car radio frequency and picked up his phone.

"Little Bird, this is Whiz Bang, you copy?" he radioed.

There was no answer.

"Anything else on the rest of the board?" he called across to the technician. The other four duty officers had looked up from their monitors.

"No, sir."

"Little Bird, this is Whiz Bang, you copy, over?"

Still there was no answer, and Stewart slowly put down his handset. If McCann had wanted to show their new CO the inside of one of the missile bays, that was well and good. They would have entered through the maintenance hatch. So why the hell had they opened the main bay doors?

He picked up the Missile Ready red phone and punched in the number for the missile bunker with the open door. The instant the connection was made, an extremely loud Klaxon would sound in the bay. Loud enough to wake the dead, he thought, though just how close to the truth he was, he could not expect as yet.

His alert crew phone buzzed, and Stewart picked it up with his left hand while still holding the Missile Ready phone with his right. "Operations OD," he answered.

"Gerry, this is Jim Hunte, we've got a missile bay open light on our board over here. Ah, Six-P-Two."

"We're showing the same thing," Stewart said. Captain James Hunte was the Army's on-duty alert crew chief on this shift. They were old friends.

"Is it an alarm malfunction?"

"Doesn't look like it. Our new CO showed up today. Tom is out showing him around. Looks like they opened the door."

"Well, raise them and tell them to close it. That's Army property, old top, remember?"

"I tried, Jim. No answer."

The line was silent for just a moment. In his other ear Stewart could hear the soft buzz indicating the missile bay Klaxon was still blaring.

"Did you try the missile bay red line?"

"I'm on it right now. It's ringing through, but there's been no response."

"All right, Gerry, no screwing around now. Should I call Colonel Collingwood or will you send someone out there to see what the hell those guys are doing?"

Stewart was an engineer out of Cal Tech. He had taken the Air Force Officers' Command Course, but he was not a decision maker unless it involved complex electronic circuitry. Interservice rivalry notwithstanding, this time he made a very bad decision.

"I'll go myself," he said.

"Collingwood could have one of his people there in a lot less time than it could take for you to drive out."

"Let's not blow the whistle just yet. It's my CO and Tom McCann."

"You're calling the shots, Gerry," Hunte said coolly. "But I don't mind telling you that the situation is making me nervous. That's an armed nuclear missile out there."

"Yeah," Stewart said. "I'll get right back to you."

"Do that," Hunte said, and he hung up.

Stewart put down both telephones and grabbed his uniform blouse. "I'm heading topside, be on TAC ONE," he told Lieutenant Hartley, his Fire Control Board officer.

He took the elevator to the surface, signed out with security, and jumped into his station wagon, peeling rubber as he pulled away from the Missile Control bunker and headed back into the staging field.

"Whiz Bang, this is OD One, any change on the board?" he radioed back to the situation room.

"That's a negative."

"Keep me advised."

The afternoon was warm. Stewart drove with the windows down. He had been in Germany for thirty months, only six more to go and he'd be rotated back to the States, a move he was looking forward to, though so far this assignment had been a piece of cake. Why now, he asked himself. He did not want to get into a fight between his new CO and Army security, but he had a feeling it was coming. Shit runs downhill, he thought wryly. And at this moment it was two lieutenant colonels, a major, and another captain versus his own two bars. He was definitely at the bottom of the hill.

He brightened a little with the thought that this could be nothing but a test of his own abilities. It was possible the new CO was pulling a little impromptu test simply to see what the OD would do about it.

If only it turned out to be that simple, he thought.

A quarter of a mile from the missile bunker he slowed down and turned onto the gravel road that led back into the woods. If he didn't know better he would have sworn that something very heavy had recently come up the road. Something with wide tires. Something very big. And his heart began to thump in his chest, a tight feeling at the pit of his stomach.

Coming into the bunker yard he slammed on his brakes and sat for a long moment. The missile bunker doors were open, and the bunker was empty. The Pershing II missile and its transporter were missing.

It was hard to keep his thoughts straight. He jumped out of the car and raced across the yard and into the bunker itself. Major McCann lay on his back, his eyes open, a small black hole in the middle of his forehead.

"Oh, shit," Stewart swore.

The transporter itself was nothing more than a flatbed truck on which the thirty-four-and-a-half-foot missile lay in its launch cradle. The tractor was a low-slung, armor-plated ten-wheeler in which the driver and normal launch crew of three rode in bucket seats. It drove like a semi truck but steered almost like a tank, capable of speeds up to eighty miles per hour on the open highway, and twenty-five miles per hour over open terrain.

Only the largest of trees or reinforced tank traps could stop it.

Kurshin barreled down the main transport road in excess of fifty miles per hour. He had timed his departure from the missile bunker so that the last perimeter patrol had passed five minutes ago and would not be back for another five to seven minutes.

He hunched forward so that he could see better through the forward Lexan-covered slits as the paved road gave way suddenly to a narrow gravel track that split abruptly left and right. The tall wire mesh fence was less than fifty yards straight ahead.

Kurshin eased up on the accelerator and downshifted so that at the moment of impact he would have more reserve power.

The transporter lurched over a big hump in the unpaved road and as he recovered, the sixty-two-ton rig hit the fence, cutting through it like a hot knife through soft butter.

He was in a line of small trees an instant later, crashing through them almost as easily as he had the fence, and then the covering fringe of forest gave way to a long, narrow field that sloped downward toward the Stuttgart Autobahn about four miles away.

Kurshin slowed the big machine even further so that he was going barely twenty miles per hour. No doubt there was a sensor on the missile bay door that would have rung an alarm in the Missile Control situation room. There were probably perimeter breach alarms as well. By now they'd know that one of their nuclear missiles was missing.

The question was: What would they do about it? From what he had seen so far, security was so incredibly lax that they might not do anything for several precious minutes.

Time was on his side.

Twelve minutes, he figured, from the moment he'd hit the fence until he was at the autobahn.

With one hand on the control column, he activated the rig's rearward-looking television cameras. He could see the path he'd taken through the woods and down the grassy field. There were no pursuers so far.

Next, he activated the skyward radar. Immediately several blips showed up on the narrow screen, but none of them seemed to be converging on his position. After a moment he decided that as incredible as it might seem no one was after him.

The hill steepened, a shallow creek crossing at the bottom before the land rose sharply upward about fifty feet to the autobahn. The big tundra tires rolled easily across the bed of the creek, the heavy trailer and eight-ton payload lurching behind him, and then he was grinding up the hill, toward the cars passing along the divided highway.

He spotted the gray Mercedes 220D parked on the paved shoulder about fifty yards to the south, and he immediately angled that way, downshifting again, crashing the gears, the big tires biting into the soft dirt, the machine giving a final lurch as it came up over the crest of the hill and crashed through the knee-high aluminum safety barrier at the side of the road.

He crossed both lanes of traffic and dipped partway down into the grassy median strip before he got the big machine straightened out.

A dark blue Fiat was suddenly there, and he crashed into the car, the big tires climbing up and over the small car, crushing it. A Citröen truck, braking hard to avoid crashing into the transporter, fishtailed, hit the median strip sideways and flipped end over end into the oncoming traffic in the opposite two lanes, bursting into flames as it disintegrated.

Kurshin skidded the transporter to a halt opposite the waiting car, the brakes locking, the big tires jumping. Traffic in all four lanes was screeching to a halt, in some cases skidding out of control, sliding down into the median, crashing off the security rail, or tailending other cars. It was pandemonium.

Two armed men got out of the Mercedes, one of them rushing back to the rocket on its trailer. Kurshin opened the door and jumped down onto the road.

"You've actually got it," Ivan Yegorov said, his eyes bright. He'd changed his name, but he was a swarthy Georgian with deep-set dark eyes.

"Cover our back," Kurshin snapped, and he hurried back to where Dieter Schey, a former East German rocket engineer, was setting up the plastique explosives around the rocket casing, about two feet forward of the recessed vanes.

Schey worked methodically as if this were his normal duty. He strapped a broad plastic collar around the forty-inch rocket, and to this he attached the separate shaped plastique charges into which he inserted a radio-controlled trigger.

He was finished within ninety seconds, and Kurshin helped him down from the trailer bed.

"Now it begins," Schey said. His eyes seemed dead, totally devoid of any human expression.

Kurshin nodded. "Everything is in readiness?"

Schey shrugged, the thinnest of smiles coming to his bloodless lips.

"Ivan," Kurshin shouted, and the three of them hurried back to the tractor and climbed inside, Yegorov getting behind the wheel.

The instant after Kurshin had closed and dogged the hatch, Yegorov slammed the tractor in gear and headed down the highway, the road banking into a long, sweeping turn, a pine forest coming up darkly on both sides of the cut through a shallow hill.

Schey took the backseat, pulling out the radio controller for the explosives, and Kurshin took the right-hand seat, studying the radio equipment for just a moment before switching to the Missile Control Squadron's TAC ONE frequency.

"Whiz Bang, this is Flybaby Six-P-Two, you copy?" Kurshin said into the microphone.

5

PARIS

KIRK COLLOUGH MCGARVEY HAD KNOWN FOR SEVERAL DAYS that someone was coming for him. Call it a sixth sense or simply the intuition of a man who had been a long time in the field, he had begun picking up signs on Wednesday outside the Louvre at the edge of the Tuileries, when he spotted someone watching him.

It had lasted only a fleeting moment. A short, nondescript man in a sport coat, his tie loose, was getting into a cab as McGarvey was coming out of the museum. The man gave a quick backward glance and then was gone.

McGarvey had stepped back into the building, remaining for a few minutes just within the doorway, watching, waiting for someone else to show up. It had been a front tail, he'd been almost certain of it at the time.

On Thursday, coming out of his apartment just off the Rue de la Fayette in the Tenth Arrondissement, he'd spotted a Mercedes sedan slowly passing, and he'd been even more certain that someone was coming. The man in the passenger seat had changed his coat and now wore no tie, but he was the same one from the Louvre.

McGarvey was a tall, well-built man with a thick shock of brown hair and wide honest eyes. Although he was in his early forties, he maintained an almost athletic physique, not because of any regular workouts—though he tried to make a practice of running a few miles each morning—but more because of the luck of some genetic draw.

He was a loner these days, more out of circumstance than out of choice. He had come out of Kansas State University more years ago than he wanted to remember and had joined the Central Intelligence Agency as a case officer. An operation that had gone sour for him in Santiago, Chile, during the Carter days had cost him his job.

They were bad times, he remembered now walking from his apartment toward the quaint Cour des Petites Écuries. To this day he remembered the face of the general he'd been sent to assassinate. The man had been responsible for thousands of deaths in and around the capital city and the only solution was his elimination. But McGarvey's orders had been changed in midstream without him knowing about it. He returned to Washington not a hero but a pariah.

He had run to Switzerland where for five years he'd maintained a relatively quiet life operating a small bookstore in Lausanne, and living with Marta Fredricks, a woman who'd turned out to be a Swiss Federal police officer assigned to watch him. Ex-CIA officers, especially killers, made the Swiss very nervous.

Across the narrow street from the Brasserie Flo, McGarvey stopped a moment to adjust his tie before he crossed and entered the restaurant's charming courtyard.

McGarvey, *pour deux, s'il vous plaît,''* he told the maitre d'.

The strait-laced Frenchman glanced over McGarvey's shoulder to see if the second person in his party was coming. "Monsieur?"

"It's a friend. He'll be arriving shortly."

"Very well."

McGarvey followed the maitre d' back through the courtyard to a pleasant table and ordered a bottle of red wine. He sat back and lit a cigarette while he waited, the pressure of his gun reassuring at the small of his back.

They were missing on Friday, but they had been there this morning down the block from his apartment. Watching. Waiting to see if he was alone, to catalogue his moves. The same man as before was behind the wheel, but someone else had been seated in the back. Because of the angle from his second-floor window he could only see the man's waist and a part of his torso, but he knew who it was and he knew what was coming. He even had a fair guess what his old friend was coming here for.

It had happened almost like this two years ago, he remembered as the steward brought his bottle of wine and opened it for him, pouring half a glass. It was a house special wine so he was not invited to taste it.

"*Merci,*" McGarvey said politely.

The steward nodded and hurried off.

It was noon and the popular restaurant was beginning to fill up. McGarvey caught the maitre d' giving him severe glances. If monsieur's friend didn't show up soon, McGarvey figured he would be asked to move to a smaller table.

Then, in Lausanne, as now, he'd been watched for several days so that his habits and routines could be established before he was picked up.

Then, as now, the moment he realized that something was about to come down he had run for his gun. It's what had ruined Switzerland for him.

"Only assassins who are still active run for their weapons," Marta had told him.

Unlike Lausanne, where after five years he had become complacent, these past two years in Paris had been different. He'd not allowed himself to lose his edge. It was simple survival, he told himself often. Because the business that had begun in Lausanne had never been finished. Not in Washington, not in Miami, and certainly not in Mexico City.

He was still out there. Waiting. Biding his time.

The familiar face and figure of John Lyman Trotter, Jr., a thin briefcase in his left hand, appeared at the entrance to the courtyard, hesitated a moment, and then said something to the maitre d', who turned.

Trotter followed the man's gaze, spotting McGarvey seated alone, and he nodded, said something else, then threaded his way between the tables.

McGarvey didn't bother to stand. He hadn't seen his old friend in two years, but the man had the same look on his face as he had had in Switzerland—one of worry and concern.

"Hello, Kirk," Trotter said. He was a tall, very thin man, all angles, with a huge misshapen nose and bottle-thick glasses. He could have been classified as truly ugly, but he'd always had a sharp mind. He had begun his career with the CIA but then had gone over to the Federal Bureau of Investigation, working his way up to an associate directorship.

"I thought it was you," McGarvey said.

Trotter sat down, laying the briefcase on his lap. Languidly, McGarvey reached out and poured him a glass of wine. Their waiter came, handed them menus, and left.

"Don thought you might have spotted him on Wednesday."

"Outside the Louvre?"

Trotter nodded.

"And Thursday outside my apartment. Not very professional."

"Professional enough," Trotter said, looking around at the other diners. "Nice place."

McGarvey shrugged. "I can watch the door from here."

Trotter managed a slight smile. "Nothing changes, does it?"

"How about you, John, still with the Bureau?"

Trotter shook his head. "I'm back over at Langley. Assistant deputy director of operations."

"Larry Danielle still there?"

"Seventh floor. He's our new deputy DCI. Phil Carrara is my boss. I don't think you knew him. He came over last year from NSA."

"A technologist?"

Again Trotter managed a slight smile. National Security Agency types were very often electronic freaks. "He's a good man."

McGarvey sipped at his wine. To this point Trotter had studiously avoided any direct eye contact. McGarvey stared at him.

"It's Baranov, isn't it, John. That's why you've come."

Trotter nodded grimly.

"He's on the move again?"

"It looks like it. Larry suggested you this time, though, not me. I swear to God. I told him that you'd had enough. That you wanted to be left alone."

"But he didn't agree."

"No."

"Why all the pussyfooting around again, John?"

"We didn't know your circumstances," Trotter replied simply.

At this point McGarvey could have been a changed man, could have turned into almost anything. They had to make certain that he was clean, and that the opposition hadn't gotten a line on him. As Trotter unnecessarily explained: "Valentin Baranov has got a very large grudge against you, Kirk. Now that he is director of the KGB he has the power to do something about it."

"You're here to save my skin, is that it?" McGarvey asked, feeling some of his old meanness coming back. His stomach was sour. It was the thrill of the opening moves of a hunt he'd been waiting for.

"To save all of our skins. The man has got to be stopped."

This time McGarvey had to smile. "What do you want this time, John? Am I to go to Moscow and assassinate the director of the KGB?"

"If only it were that easy I'd say yes." Trotter shook his

head and glanced again at the other diners. "I don't know if we'll ever really stop the man in that sense. It's become a continual mop-up operation. You know how it is."

"Yes, I do," McGarvey said pointedly. "So what's the sonofabitch up to this time?"

"We don't know. Leastways not for sure yet. But we need your help."

"Why?"

The direct question startled Trotter but he recovered nicely. "We're in over our heads, I don't mind admitting that. And you know Baranov better than any man on our side of the fence. His habits, his methods, the way his mind works."

"And your people are spotted."

"Yes."

"And if I start after him, it might draw him out. I'd be bait."

Trotter nodded. He opened his briefcase and took out a thin file folder. He handed it across and relatched his briefcase.

McGarvey opened the file folder which contained a summary of a KGB officer, with several photographs, one of them a head shot, the others obviously obtained in the field. The man was tall, good-looking in an athletic sort of way, with deep eyes that even in the photographs seemed cold, distant, and very professional.

"Formerly a Department Viktor hit man. One of the best. Baranov took him under his wing just after he returned to Moscow from the Powers thing, and the man has been busy. I've included a summary of his . . . feats."

"Who is he?"

"He's been called the chameleon, because he can be or do damned near everything. His real name is Arkady Aleksandrovich Kurshin."

"What's he done now that has you coming here to me?"

"We tracked him as far as Marseille, and it looked as if he was getting set to come up here."

"But?"

"He killed two of our people and then disappeared. Not a trace."

"He's come out to do something for Baranov?"

"Presumably. Baranov was spotted two weeks ago in East Berlin, at the same time, we believe, this Kurshin was there."

"One man . . ." McGarvey mused.

"One man," Trotter said. "He has us worried because he's . . . an assassin. The very best in the business. And when a man like him goes on the move, and then disappears, it gets us all worried. Find him, Kirk. Stop him. Find out what he's up to. And quickly."

6

ABOARD THE TRANSPORTER

ARKADY KURSHIN WAS JUST A LITTLE SURPRISED THAT THEY had actually gotten this far, though he was professional enough not to show it.

"Trust in me, Arkasha," Baranov had told him warmly that night in East Berlin.

Kurshin *could* almost trust in the man, though at this moment he knew that he was closer to death than he'd ever been in his life. He had little doubt that they would be able to pull this off, but it was afterward that weighed on his mind. Their escape. It was typical of Yegorov not to care, not to look beyond the immediacy of the situation, and the East German was such a cold fish that it was impossible ever to tell what he was thinking. But Kurshin worried about the future . . . his future.

They were racing down the autobahn, heading north at eighty miles per hour. It had been nearly twenty minutes since the missile bay doors had rumbled open and still no one had come after them, nor had Ramstein Missile Control answered their query.

Traffic was heavy, but no one passed them, so that the road ahead was clear. The speed limit even on an autobahn, this close to a city, was 120 kilometers per hour, which was about 75 miles per hour. On the opposite side of the median strip, southbound traffic moved at a normal rate. The sight of a missile transporter on the highway was nothing unusual. Germans had seen it often.

"Whiz Bang, this is Flybaby Six-P-Two," Kurshin radioed again.

Yegorov motioned toward the skyward radar. "We've got company," he said tersely.

The radar showed two strong targets incoming from the base, flying low and relatively slow. They were helicopters, Kurshin figured. He was about to key the microphone when the radio blared.

"Flybaby Six-P-Two, this is Whiz Bang. Colonel, what in hell are you doing?"

"Who is this speaking?" Kurshin asked calmly.

"For Christ's sake, stand down immediately. Do you realize what you're toting around out there?"

"I repeat," Kurshin radioed. "Who am I speaking to?"

There was a pause. "This is Whiz Bang, goddamnit. Officer of the Day, Captain Gerry Stewart. And I repeat, sir, stand down. Pull over to the side of the road immediately."

Kurshin glanced again at the tiny radar screen. The two blips appeared to be directly behind them. He keyed the radio.

"Listen closely now, Captain Stewart, because I'm not going to repeat myself, and there are a lot of lives at stake here, so I don't want you making any mistakes. Are you ready to copy?"

Again the radio was silent for a long second or two.

"We're coming up on our turn," Yegorov said beside him.

"Slow it down a little," Kurshin replied, keeping his eye on the radar screen.

"You've hijacked a missile," Captain Stewart radioed shakily. "Do you know what that means? And Major McCann. He's dead."

"Yes," Kurshin radioed back. "At this moment there are two aircraft just behind us, I assume they're helicopter gunships. Tell them to back off immediately."

"Negative," the OD shouted. "Pull over immediately, or we will destroy your transporter."

Kurshin smiled slightly. "I don't think you're going to want to do that, Captain, even if those aircraft were capable of it. We have placed fifteen pounds of plastique explosives around the body of the missile itself, twenty-four inches forward of the recessed flight vanes. If you know that missile, you will realize that should the plastique explode, it will spread the warhead's fissionable material over quite a large area."

There was no answer, nor did the blips move off.

"We have control of the explosives from within the tractor, and we mean to fire them in the next twenty seconds unless you do exactly as I tell you."

Again there was no answer.

"The clock starts now!" Kurshin said, and he sat back in his seat. He looked over at Yegorov who glanced nervously at him.

"They're not going to risk trying to take us now," Kurshin said.

Yegorov smiled thinly. "They're damned fools if they don't, considering the alternatives."

"Who the hell is this?" another voice blared from the radio.

"Your worst nightmare," Kurshin radioed back: "Fifteen seconds."

"Pull over now, or I'll give the order to blow your ass all over the highway!"

"Asses," Kurshin corrected. "There are three of us in

control of this missile, and we're about to take the next exit ramp. Ten seconds."

"This is Colonel Robert Collingwood, chief of Ramstein Security. And you listen to me, you bastard, I'm giving you five seconds to pull over or we'll blow you away."

"Seven seconds," Kurshin spoke calmly into the microphone.

Yegorov was downshifting, the big rig slowing, their exit barely half a kilometer away.

"Five seconds," Kurshin said. "Four . . . Three . . . Two . . ."

"There," Yegorov shouted in triumph.

Kurshin's eyes flicked to the radar screen in time to see the two targets peeling off left and right and gaining altitude. He breathed his first sigh of relief and glanced over his shoulder at Schey whose expression had not changed, his thumb over the electronic trigger for the explosives.

That one, he thought, would just as easily flip the switch he was holding as he would a light switch. But then, what good was a threat unless you meant to carry it out?

"Thank you, Colonel Collingwood," Kurshin radioed.

"Your transporter has a range of less than one hundred fifty kilometers, so you're not going to get very far," the security chief radioed.

Kurshin figured he was in one of the helicopters that were still behind them, but now a couple of kilometers off.

Yegorov downshifted again, the big transport shuddering as he turned off the superhighway and they rolled down the exit ramp which was marked KAISERSLAUTERN, 12 KM.

"We're not going very far, Colonel. Now listen carefully again to me."

"We're right behind you, I'm listening," Colonel Collingwood said tightly.

"We're going to bring this missile into the city, where we'll set it up on Hauptbahnhof Strasse, directly in front of the train station."

"Like hell you will . . ." Colonel Collingwood sputtered.

"I suggest for the safety of the city that you immediately see about evacuating at least the area surrounding the train station. If we should get nervous and blow the missile, there will be many casualties."

They had reached the bottom of the long ramp, and ignoring the traffic, Yegorov hauled the big transporter onto the highway leading into the city, sideswiping a small Volkswagen sedan, shoving it off to the side in a mangled heap.

"What do you want? Who are you?" Colonel Collingwood shouted.

"Clear passage into the city, for the moment. Believe me when I tell you, Colonel, that although we wish to hurt no one in Germany, we are determined and well trained."

"And then what?"

"Then we shall see," Kurshin said.

7

MARSEILLE

McGARVEY HAD TAKEN AN AIR-INTER FLIGHT FROM PARIS to Marseille on the Côte d'Azur, and a cab into town where he set up at a sleazy little hotel. Trotter agreed to remain in Paris at least through the next forty-eight hours to provide backup, especially information from the CIA Paris Station and, through their liaison services, from the SDECE—the French Secret Service.

He sacrificed stealth for speed in his search, though it wasn't likely that Kurshin was still here. And it didn't matter if he found out that questions were being asked. McGarvey wanted him to know that someone was dogging his heels.

Still, it took the better part of three hours and seven water-front bars before he came up with the name of a man who

could be bought for a few francs and a cheap bottle of wine.
Every city had such men. Marseille was no exception.

"*Mon dieu,* the Russians mind their own business here
just like the rest of us do," the old man said. He and
McGarvey were seated across from each other at a small table.
The bar was very noisy. Traffic on the nearby Canebière was
intense.

"Nothing has happened in the city in the past few days,
mon vieux?" McGarvey asked, pouring a little more wine.

The old man shrugged. "Many things happen in Marseille,
monsieur." He sipped at his wine.

McGarvey took out Kurshin's photograph and slid it across
the table. The old man looked at it for a long moment or
two, but then shook his head. *"Non."*

"You say the Russians mind their own business here, like
everyone else," McGarvey said, masking his disappoint-
ment. "Is it because of the French Mafia?"

The old man smiled slightly, his face wrinkling, his lips
parting to show his brown, chipped teeth. "There is no such
organization, didn't you know?"

"But everyone behaves."

Again the old man shrugged. "They sometimes do not."

McGarvey waited.

"A few days ago, for instance, a very bad man disappeared
to no one's sorrow. It happens, *tant pis.*"

"Who was this man?"

"Edmon Railliarde. His loss will not be mourned, let me
tell you."

"He simply disappeared?"

"Oui."

McGarvey sat back, a vague connection beginning at the
back of his mind. Trotter had called Kurshin the chameleon.
"Do you know what he looked like, this Railliarde? Can you
describe him to me?"

"Yes, of course," the old man said, glancing again at
Kurshin's photograph. "Much like this one. Of course I cannot tell his bulk from a simple photograph, but Railliarde was
a large man. A very bad man."

"And he is missing."

"Yes, but as I say no one will mourn that one."

McGarvey laid a fifty-franc note on the table, snatched the photograph, and got up. "*Merci, mon vieux*. You have been of inestimable service."

Outside, McGarvey turned away from the waterfront and hurried on foot up the main boulevard finding a public telephone box five minutes later. He placed a call to Trotter at the embassy in Paris on the Avenue Gabriel.

"I think I have a line on Kurshin," McGarvey said. "It's possible he's assumed the identity of a French Mafia boss from Marseille by the name of Edmon Railliarde." He quickly explained what he had learned.

"Are you certain about this, Kirk?" Trotter asked. He seemed oddly subdued, almost as if he were disappointed by McGarvey's news.

"Of course not, but it's a start. What's up?"

Again Trotter hesitated. "There is a developing situation at this moment in Germany. Ramstein Air Force Base. We were getting set to follow it up."

"I'm listening," McGarvey said. He had learned the hard way never to underestimate a Baranov plan. The man was as brilliant as he was convoluted and devious.

"An Army Pershing II missile has apparently been hijacked from the base."

"By whom?"

"Apparently an Air Force colonel by the name of Brad Allworth. He's got help. But what started us thinking is that Allworth was here on leave in Paris until yesterday."

"What does he look like?"

"We're getting it off the Associated Press wire. Tall, well built, good-looking, an all-American."

The connections were suddenly completed in McGarvey's head. "It's him," he shouted. "Kurshin has got that missile."

"I thought you said he took on the persona of this Mafia boss."

"Listen to me, John. I'm going to get up to Ramstein as

quickly as I can. I want you to meet me there. You're going to have to open some doors for me. But in the meantime ask the French if they have turned up a mutilated body somewhere in or around Paris within the past twenty-four hours.''

"Mutilated . . . ?" Trotter asked.

"Yeah," McGarvey said. "My guess would be that his fingerprints, dental work, and face would have been destroyed. Perhaps in an accident."

Sudden understanding dawned in Trotter's voice. "Railliarde," he said.

"He'll be carrying the man's identification," McGarvey said. "But my guess is he will be Colonel Allworth. Railliarde's body will probably never be found."

"Good lord . . ." Trotter started to say, but McGarvey had hung up the telephone and was rushing down the street to the nearest cab stand.

KAISERSLAUTERN

The silence was eerie in the Hauptbahnhof Plaza across from the large train station a few blocks north of the city center. For nearly three hours the missile transporter had remained motionless in the middle of the square where it had been carefully positioned.

"We must give them time to stabilize the situation," Kurshin explained. "I don't want some nervous sharpshooter or overzealous *polizei* opening fire."

Schey had said nothing, and although Yegorov had become clearly impatient, he too understood the wisdom of Kurshin's order. They had switched off the radio so as not to be disturbed. The three hours had also been necessary so that the means of their eventual escape could be put in place.

Kurshin had been smoking a cigarette. He ground it out on the floor and then turned up the gain on the radar set. Three blips appeared, two to the south and one north. All three of them appeared nearly stationary. Helicopter gunships, he figured.

Next he glanced at the transporter's rearward-looking television monitor. Across the square, about one hundred fifty meters away, he could see that all the streets entering had been blocked off by armored personnel carriers, uniformed police, and U.S. soldiers standing behind the barriers.

He leaned forward and peered out the Lexan-covered slits. The streets leading into the square from the north and northeast were also blocked off. In addition, he spotted at least half a dozen armed soldiers on the roofs of nearby buildings.

"We're hemmed in," Yegorov said.

"Exactly. We've no means of escape so they'll have calmed down by now," Kurshin said. He glanced over his shoulder at the East German, whose eyes were shining for the first time. He was still holding the trigger.

"Are you ready?"

Schey nodded.

Turning back, Kurshin switched on the radio. "Colonel Collingwood, this is Flybaby Six-P-Two. Do you copy?"

"That's affirmative," the radio blared immediately.

"May I assume that you have this part of the city evacuated by now, and that you have positioned only disciplined troops around the perimeter?"

"You may," Collingwood responded.

"Very good, Colonel. Within the next sixty seconds two of us will be stepping out of the transporter and we will be going back to the missile itself. Let me remind you that one of our number shall remain at all times protected within the transporter, his finger on the device that controls the plastique. Do I make myself perfectly clear?"

"You do," the Air Force security chief replied. "What are your intentions?"

"In due time, Colonel. For the moment suffice it that if anyone tries to interfere with our operation in any way, disaster will strike."

"What do you want, goddamnit?" Collingwood shouted. "Make your demands!"

"Again, in due time, Colonel. But you have my word as

an officer and a gentleman that we mean no harm to either the German or American peoples.''

''Then stand down.''

''I'm afraid that is not possible. You will understand very soon what we mean to do. I will explain everything to you at 2000 hours. But one final word of caution. We mean to raise the missile into its firing position now. But nothing, absolutely nothing will happen if you and your men show restraint. Until 2000 hours.''

Collingwood was shouting something when Kurshin switched off the radio. He turned again to Schey. ''Give Ivan the trigger. It is time for us to get to work.''

8

EN ROUTE TO KAISERSLAUTERN

McGarvey was met at Frankfurt's Rhine-Main Airport by the CIA's number two out of Bonn, a husky but studious-looking man dressed in a dark blue blazer.

"Todd Kraus," he introduced himself. "I've got a chopper standing by for you, sir."

It was a little past six in the afternoon. The airport was extremely busy but McGarvey had been passed through customs immediately. He followed the younger man across the terminal where they got in an Air Force sedan and sped to the opposite side of the field which housed the U.S. Rhine-Main Air Force Base. A Bell AH-1W Super Cobra ground attack helicopter was already warming up for them.

"We'll get you down there in under twenty minutes," Kraus said as they climbed aboard.

"In the meantime I've got a couple dozen questions for you," McGarvey said.

"Yes, sir, I expect you do. I've been instructed to brief you on the way down. Mr. Trotter is already on site."

The instant they'd strapped in, a crewman jumped aboard, closed and dogged the hatch, and went forward into the cockpit leaving them alone. They lifted off with a sickening lurch and swung left as they climbed, the helicopter taking a nose-down attitude as it rapidly picked up speed. The pilot was sparing nothing.

Kraus reached up behind him, flipped on a small overhead light, and turned back to McGarvey. He pulled a map of downtown Kaiserslautern from his jacket pocket and spread it out between them.

"I'll give you the broad strokes first," Kraus began. "A man identifying himself as Air Force Colonel Brad Allworth managed to steal a nuclear-armed Pershing missile and transporter from Ramstein Air Force Base. He drove it off the base and onto the autobahn where he was met by two other men . . . identification at this point unknown. They placed what appears to be a plastique explosive around the outside of the missile body itself, which they promise to blow if we make any threatening moves. From there they drove directly into the city of Kaiserslautern where they parked in front of the train station. They haven't moved since."

"Any casualties?" McGarvey asked.

"Major Tom McCann was found shot to death in the Pershing's missile bay."

"Anyone else?"

"Eleven German nationals were injured and three killed on the autobahn just outside Ramstein. The transporter ran over one car and touched off a chain reaction. Four of them are in critical condition in the base burn unit."

"They mean business," McGarvey said.

"Yes, sir, that they do."

"Any communications with the transporter?"

Kraus nodded. "Colonel Bob Collingwood, the man in charge of Ramstein security, has been talking with them . . .

or at least with the one who has been identified as Brad Allworth.''

"He's not," McGarvey said.

"Sir?"

"He's not Brad Allworth. His name is Arkady Kurshin."

"Russians?" Kraus asked, his eyes widening. "Sonofabitch. What the hell are they up to?"

"Whatever it is, it's not going to be pleasant, I can tell you that much. And I can also tell you that Kurshin is a pro. He'll have this entire operation figured out to the last detail, including his escape."

"Pardon me, sir, but I don't think that's possible."

"Perhaps not, but Kurshin evidently thinks so," McGarvey said. "What's the present situation?"

"As of 1630 the missile and transporter were parked, as I said, in the middle of the square in front of K-Town's main railroad station. Two men, one of them apparently this Arkady Kurshin, and another man, have been outside the transporter doing something to the missile's control units."

McGarvey nodded. "Reprogramming its guidance system, no doubt, and probably disarming the fire control officer's abort function."

"That's our best guess."

"Have they made any demands, given us any sort of a time limit?"

"No demands so far, other than to leave them alone. They've promised that they would make their intentions clear at 2000 hours."

McGarvey glanced at his watch. They had a full hour.

"But," Kraus said. "And this is the part that has everyone worried. They say they intend raising the missile into launch position."

McGarvey sat back in his seat and lit a cigarette. "Kurshin wouldn't have taken the risk of stealing a missile unless he intended launching it."

"We're hoping not, sir," Kraus said. "Collingwood seems to think that they'll make some demand and when it's met have us provide them transportation into the east zone."

"No," McGarvey said, Baranov's picture rising up in his mind. "He'll launch the missile and then make his escape."

"Launch it where, for God's sake?"

"The sixty-four-dollar question," McGarvey said, shaking his head. "What's the Pershing's range, a thousand miles or so?"

"This is a Pershing IIA. She has a range of more than two thousand miles."

"The warhead is armed?"

Kraus nodded glumly. "You can say that again. Five hundred kilotons."

"But it's a cruise missile."

"Not quite, sir. It's RADAG controlled . . . Radar Area Guidance. It's set for a latitude and longitude, and once it gets near its target the radar unit compares the returns it's getting from the ground with what's programmed into it."

"What's its target?"

"That's highly classified . . ."

McGarvey just looked at him.

"Kiev."

"They'll change it."

"They'd have to have a systems expert with them. None of ours is missing. It's the first thing we had Langley check. There aren't many men around who have that knowledge."

"Whoever is working with Kurshin does," McGarvey said. "You can bet your life on it."

ABOARD THE MISSILE TRANSPORTER

Kurshin looked up as another helicopter came in for a landing a couple of blocks away in what he was assuming was the market square they'd passed through on the way in. It made the third since he and Schey had gotten out of the tractor and climbed up on the trailer with the missile.

"How much longer?" he asked the East German.

Schey looked up from the open hatch in the missile's side.

"I was finished ten minutes ago. You asked me to stall for time."

"It's set on the new target?"

"Yes, of course, providing the data you supplied me with is correct."

"It is," Kurshin said curtly. "What about the abort mechanism?"

"Disconnected."

"At this point then, once the missile is launched there is no way for their Missile Control facility to recall it or destroy it?"

The East German shook his head. "Short of sending a fighter interceptor after it and shooting it out of the sky—an almost impossible feat—no."

"Very good," Kurshin said, glancing over his shoulder again toward the blockade at the south side of the plaza. "Button it up, let's begin."

Schey closed and relocked the small hatch on the missile's radar guidance system, and then replaced the section of outer skin he'd removed, dogging it down with a dozen flush-mounted fasteners.

"What about the plastique collar?" Kurshin asked.

"It will fall harmlessly away within the first few seconds after launch."

"There will be no effect on the missile's course?"

"None that the guidance system won't correct for."

"Good," Kurshin said, his eyes hard. He jumped down from the trailer bed and one at a time lowered the hydraulic stabilizing jacks at each corner, while Schey was connecting the four launch control umbilical cords.

If there was going to be trouble, Kurshin thought, sweating lightly, it would come now. They would be fools not to try to stop what was happening here. But then they had been fools at the base with their lack of security. This would never happen in the Rodina, not even now, though if it ever did it would shake up those pricks in the Kremlin even more than the German kid had done by flying his little toy airplane into Red Square.

Ten minutes later, Schey checked all the wires and steadying jacks to make certain everything was in order, then opened a control hatch at the side of the trailer and flipped a switch.

The Pershing missile began to slowly rise from the trailer bed.

HAUPTBAHNHOF SQUARE

"Oh, Jesus Christ," Colonel Collingwood said as the missile began to elevate from its transport trailer.

McGarvey had been looking through binoculars at the two men. The taller of them, dressed in an Air Force uniform, had turned several times, giving him a good look. He had the same bulk and general appearance as Kurshin, but his face was different. From here he looked very much like the photographs McGarvey had been shown of Brad Allworth.

He lowered the binoculars. "Blow the missile now," he said.

Trotter, who had met him when the chopper had set down, stepped back a pace and Colonel Collingwood's eyes widened.

"Is this the hotshot who was supposed to come up with the good ideas?" the security chief spat at Trotter. He looked coldly at McGarvey. "Do you know what such an action would mean? Do you know what it would do here?"

"You say the civilians have been pulled out. Clear the rest of your men except for one volunteer sharpshooter who can hit the plastique. And blow it now before it's too late."

"It would spread radioactive materials for hundreds of yards," Collingwood growled. "There would be a three-block area of no-man's-land for a long time to come."

"Yes," McGarvey said, watching the missile rise. "And probably a number of casualties. An increase in the cancer rate over the next twenty or thirty years. The news media would be on your ass. The Pentagon would probably set you out to dry. You'd be a scapegoat."

"You're goddamned right . . ."

"What do you suppose five hundred kilotons is going to do when it explodes on whatever target they've programmed it for?"

"They won't launch it," Collingwood said, but he wasn't as sure as he had been a moment earlier.

McGarvey looked at him again. "Yes they will, unless we stop them."

"Is it Kurshin?" Trotter asked.

"I don't know for sure," McGarvey admitted. "I think so, but he's wearing a damned good disguise. Had to if he was able to fool the people at the base."

"We can't destroy that missile here, Kirk," Trotter said emphatically.

Collingwood was closely watching the exchange.

McGarvey turned back to him. "If they do launch it, what's the possibility of shooting it down?"

"About one in a thousand."

Again McGarvey stared at the missile which by now was nearly at the vertical. "Well, I'd suggest that you inform your people to at least give it a try in case we fail here and that thing actually gets airborne."

That was a logic the colonel could understand. "Will do," he said, and he turned to his radioman and began issuing orders.

McGarvey raised his binoculars and slowly began to search the entire square foot by foot, from the front of the train station all the way across to the missile transporter.

It was Kurshin. He could feel it in his bones. Trotter had reported that the French police had indeed discovered a mutilated body along the railroad tracks fifty miles east of Paris. "Along the same line that Brad Allworth took to get here," Trotter had said.

That fact clinched it in McGarvey's mind. But that meant that Kurshin had had some very good intelligence information. He'd known Brad Allworth's orders, what he looked like, and what train he would be on. He also had the information needed to reprogram the missile. It was not beyond Baranov, coming up with such information. But the risks he had taken to get the data, and then so openly display that fact here like this, meant Baranov had a very large prize in mind. A very large prize indeed.

''Get the city engineer here,'' McGarvey said.

Kurshin and the other man went around to the side of the transporter, the hatch opened and they climbed inside.

''What?'' Trotter asked.

''The city engineer,'' McGarvey repeated. ''I know how Kurshin means to escape.''

— 9 —

ABOARD THE MISSILE TRANSPORTER

IT WAS COMING UP ON FIFTEEN MINUTES BEFORE EIGHT. Night had fallen, but the transporter was bathed in lights that had been hastily strung up around the perimeter of the square and on some of the rooftops. Shadows were long. Where there wasn't light, the darkness by contrast was almost absolute.

Schey had pulled the main panel from the fire control board where he had worked with a test instrument and a soldering pencil for the past half hour. He sat back and looked up, an expression of satisfaction on his face.

"There," he said. "It is finished."

Kurshin swiveled around and looked into the tangle of wires behind the panel. A small electronic device had been wired into the firing circuitry.

"Once the fire switch is thrown, the delay circuitry will

give us ten minutes to make our escape, no more,'' Schey
said.

Yegorov had been watching as well. ''What if we are
delayed?'' he asked.

The East German managed another of his pinched smiles.
''Then it will be too bad for us, because there is no way of
reversing the firing order.''

''Pull out the wires?''

Schey shook his head. ''Any tampering with the circuitry
from that point will cause the missile to immediately fire.''

Baranov had insisted that Schey be a part of the team.
Kurshin could see why now. Not only did he have the technical expertise to pull it off, but he also had nerves of steel.
Nothing seemed to agitate him. But then again he had no
love for the Jews.

Kurshin glanced at his watch. ''Put it back together and
change your clothes,'' he told Schey. He got up and went to
the back of the transporter where he pulled out the civilian
clothes that Yegorov had brought along.

The other Russian joined him, a broad grin on his face.
''Fuck your mother, but the bastards will never know what
hit them.''

Kurshin took off the uniform blouse and laid it aside. He
handed Yegorov a small mirror. ''Hold this up.''

Taking a handful of skin at the back of his neck, Kurshin
dug his fingernails in and ripped it apart, tearing it below his
shirt collar and opening his scalp all the way up the back of
his head.

Yegorov let out a small chuckle.

Pulling the hair and skin apart, Kurshin carefully pulled
the latex life mask forward off his cheeks and temples, and
then straight up from his chin, the rubber making sucking
and tearing sounds as it peeled away from his real flesh.

He'd worn the mask for twenty-four hours now and the
suddenly cool air on his face felt wonderful. Big patches of
glue and latex were stuck on his face. He cleaned these off
with a towel dipped in alcohol. When he was finished, he

took out the contact lenses that made his eyes blue, revealing his own pale green eyes.

Yegorov lowered the mirror.

They looked into each other's eyes. "It has been a pleasure working with you, Comrade," Yegorov said so softly that Schey could not hear him. "What about him?"

Kurshin's cold eyes flicked to the East German who was just finishing with the panel. "Leave him to me."

"He is excess baggage now. Dangerous to us."

Kurshin nodded. "Yes?"

Something in Kurshin's eyes, however, made Yegorov back down. "As you say," he mumbled respectfully, and they finished changing into their civilian business suits in silence.

Schey worked his way back and hurriedly changed his clothes as Kurshin went forward and sat down in the right-hand bucket seat. He turned on the radio, but waited until the other two were ready.

They looked at each other in silence, and then Kurshin picked up the microphone.

"Colonel Collingwood, this is Flybaby Six-P-Two. Do you copy?"

"That's affirmative," Collingwood's voice came back.

"Our demands are simple, but you have only sixty minutes from this moment to comply with them or we will fire the missile. Do you understand this?"

"We understand."

"First, we will require one of your Cobra gunship helicopters to land here on the square within twenty meters of this transporter. Only the pilot and copilot must be aboard. No other crew."

"Go on," Collingwood radioed, and they could hear the tightness in his voice.

"Secondly, we will require one million U.S. dollars in gold bullion. This can be arranged within the hour through the Credit Suisse Bank here in Kaiserslautern. The gold is to be loaded aboard the gunship."

"Do you realize how much that will weigh . . . ?"

"Yes," Kurshin said. "At the current rate of four hundred thirty-eight dollars per ounce, that comes out to a little less than one hundred forty-three pounds. I believe that will present no burden on your helicopter."

"I will see what I can do," Collingwood radioed. "But one hour may not be enough time."

"I sincerely hope it is, Colonel, for your sake. Believe me," Kurshin said.

There was a longish silence on the radio.

"What else?" Collingwood finally radioed.

"That is all," Kurshin replied. "At exactly 2100 hours, I and my crew shall step out of the transporter, cross to the helicopter, and the crew will fly us across the East German border. Your crew, should they not misbehave, will be allowed to return unharmed to the West. The helicopter will remain behind."

"No, you listen to me, you bastard," Collingwood shouted, finally losing control.

"No, Colonel, you listen to me very carefully," Kurshin responded calmly. "You have two further items to consider before you make your decision. The first is the plastique that we have placed around the body of the missile. It has been rewired to be exploded not only by our triggering mechanism, but also by a signal transmitted over a common military frequency. A frequency that the Cobra helicopter you are sending us is capable of transmitting on. From a long distance. If anything untoward should happen we will not hesitate to send such a signal."

When Collingwood came back on the radio he was subdued. "You mentioned two items."

"It would be most unfortunate if we were to find that any of the helicopter's electronic equipment . . . its *radio* equipment . . . had been tampered with."

"The second item, you sonofabitch."

"Yes. The second is that the missile firing control has also been rewired to a similar set of signals. We will be able to fire it from a long ways out. And, once we have left the vicinity, should you decide to make an attempt at disarming either the plastique or the missile firing mechanisms, you will be in for a nasty surprise. Very nasty.''

"Then you have made a very large mistake. That missile is targeted on a Soviet city."

"That is no longer so," Kurshin said. "We have reprogrammed its target to a city in Libya. Tripoli. Downtown."

"You're insane," Collingwood said softly.

HAUPTBAHNHOF SQUARE

"He's lying," McGarvey said.

He'd been huddled with an extremely nervous Klaus Kistner, the chief sanitation engineer for the city of Kaiserslautern. The man had been located, hauled away from his dinner, and brought unceremoniously to the square. When Kurshin came on the air, McGarvey had broken away.

"It makes sense to me," Collingwood said. "There is no reason to disbelieve him."

Trotter shook his head. "This time I'm going to have to go along with Kirk."

"There's not a whole hell of a lot we can do about it, no matter what," Collingwood shouted in exasperation. "The bastard is calling the shots. So we go along with him for now."

"He's given you an hour. Long before that time is up, that missile will be fired," McGarvey said.

"At Tripoli . . . an American nuclear missile. Christ, we'd be done in the Middle East for the next hundred years."

"Maybe Tripoli," McGarvey said, looking across at the missile. "Maybe not . . ."

"Where then?" Collingwood demanded.

"I don't know, but they've reprogrammed the missile's guidance system, in that I think he's telling the truth."

"But if he launches before the hour is up we'd have no reason to comply with his demands," Collingwood argued.

"He doesn't care about the gold," Trotter said.

McGarvey nodded his agreement. "No, a man like him wouldn't. Nor would he take the risk of something going wrong in the air between here and the east zone. We own these skies."

Collingwood was looking from McGarvey to Trotter. "Would someone mind telling me what the hell is going on then?"

"If he means to actually fire the rocket, Kirk, what's his target?" Trotter asked. "What's Baranov up to?"

"And if he doesn't need the chopper to escape, how the hell is he going to get out of there? We've got the entire square surrounded. I've got my people everywhere."

"You have the *surface* of the square covered," McGarvey said.

Collingwood glanced at the city engineer who was cowering a few feet away from them, his eyes as wide as saucers. He understood enough English to know at least the gist of what was about to happen here.

"The storm sewers," McGarvey said. "The transporter is parked directly over a sewer grate. I saw it before the light failed."

"Jesus H. Christ," Collingwood swore. "They'll have a car waiting for them a few blocks from here, and while we're waiting . . ."

"Is there a hatch in the floor of the transporter?"

"Just unplug the umbilical cords."

"Too dangerous. They might have someone watching. If we make a move to tamper with the missile from the outside they might go ahead and blow it anyway. Is there a hatch in the bottom of the transporter?"

"Yes there is, sir," an Army captain who'd been standing in the background spoke up. He came forward.

"Who are you?" McGarvey asked.

"Jim Hunte. I know that missile, sir. I'm one of the alert crew chiefs. In fact I was on duty when that sonofabitch walked off with it."

"He can disarm the missile when it's secured," Collingwood said. "In the meantime we'll cover all the sewer exits."

"No," McGarvey said. "They've still got the trigger for the plastique. And unless I miss my guess they'll be programming the missile for a delayed firing."

"Then what the hell do you want?" Collingwood shouted.

Captain Hunte wore a military .45 strapped to his hip.

"Do you know how to use that thing, Captain?" McGarvey asked.

"Yes, sir."

"Have you got the tools to disarm the missile?"

"In my car."

"Get them."

Hunte's eyes were shining. "We're going to kick some ass?"

"We're going to try to save some. Now, move yours."

"Yes, sir," Hunte snapped, and he hurried off.

McGarvey took his Walther out of its holster at the small of his back and cycled a round into the firing chamber.

"I'll start by moving my people out of here now," Collingwood said.

"No," McGarvey responded. "The moment he sees that, he'll set the missile to fire."

"Well, at least I'm going to send a few of my people with you."

McGarvey shook his head. "Just hold the fort here, Colonel," he said, and he turned and hurried off into the darkness.

Collingwood was fuming. He turned to Trotter. "Just who the fuck does he think he is?"

Trotter managed a very tight little smile. He took off his thick glasses and cleaned the lenses with his handkerchief. "You don't want to know, Colonel. Believe me."

RAMSTEIN AIR FORCE BASE

Captain Gerry Stewart was still on duty in Missile Control's situation room. He was not a smoker, but in the hours since he had discovered Major McCann's body in the empty missile bunker he had gone through nearly a pack of Marlboros.

The base had been placed on alert. The situation room hummed with activity.

A red light suddenly began to wink on the Six-P-Two Launch Board.

"We have an A Key indicator on the Flybaby," the technician called out.

The Pershing missile, like most NATO nuclear weapons, was operated on a dual key system. It took two separate keys to activate the weapon for launch.

Stewart jumped up and hurried to the console just as the B Key light came on. He stared at the board in disbelief. Both keys had been activated. Christ. The missile was live now, and starting through its firing cycle.

"Impossible," he breathed.

The rest of the board began to light up. "We have a firing sequence countdown . . ." the technician started to say, but then he stopped in mid-sentence. "It's stopped, sir," he said, looking up.

The firing sequence had stopped halfway through. Something was holding it.

Stewart turned around and rushed for his console where he snatched up his comms phone. "I want Colonel Collingwood. Now!" he shouted.

ABOARD THE MISSILE TRANSPORTER

The launch control board had come alive. For the first few moments Kurshin had thought something was wrong. The fire sequence lights had begun coming on, one at a time toward a ten-second countdown. Suddenly they stopped.

"There," Schey said, looking up. "The counter is running. In ten minutes the missile will launch."

"You're sure?" Yegorov asked, even his voice hushed now.

"Of course," Schey replied.

"Nothing can stop it?" Kurshin asked.

Schey shook his head. *"Nein."*

"Thank you," Kurshin said. He raised the pistol he'd been hiding behind his leg and shot the East German in the face, the man's head slamming backward against the bulkhead. He slipped off the bucket seat and crumpled in a heap on the floor.

Yegorov hurriedly pulled up the floor panel, and then, getting down on his stomach, reached through the opening and removed the storm sewer grate, shoving it aside. The street beneath the transporter was in deep shadow.

He looked up and Kurshin nodded.

Yegorov levered himself down into the cool storm sewer, his feet searching for and finding the metal rungs set into the concrete. When he looked up again, Kurshin handed down the trigger for the plastique.

"Just in case," Kurshin said, and he too started down into the storm sewer.

10

BENEATH THE HAUPTBAHNHOF

ONE BLOCK OFF THE SQUARE THE SIDE STREETS WERE IN darkness. McGarvey and Captain Hunte had removed the grating from the storm sewer the city engineer assured them connected with the tunnel beneath the missile transporter, and McGarvey was lowering himself into the black hole when they heard someone running down the street.

Hunte spun on his heel, yanked his .45 out of its holster, and levered the slide back.

McGarvey was halfway through the opening. He braced himself and pulled out his pistol.

"Mr. McGarvey," someone shouted from the darkness. Seconds later the figure of Todd Kraus emerged.

"It's all right," McGarvey said to Hunte. "Here," he called to Kraus.

"Christ, am I glad I made it in time," Kraus said, skidding to a halt. "You can't go through with it!"

"What's happened?"

"We just got word from the situation room at the base. The missile is in countdown mode. Both keys have been activated."

"How much time do we have?" McGarvey snapped.

Kraus was shaking his head. "No one knows, but it could happen at any second. The countdown has stopped halfway through its sequence. Once it starts again, the launch will occur in ten seconds."

"There's no way of telling if they're still in the transporter then."

"Trotter wants you back now. Collingwood is starting to pull his people out."

"They could be rigging some kind of delay circuit," Hunte said. "It would give them time to get out of there."

McGarvey thought it out, weighing the risks versus his chances of success. "Tell Collingwood to try to reach Kurshin on the radio. We can't risk sending the technicians over there until we're sure he and his people are gone." He turned to Hunte. "I'm doing this one alone."

"Like hell you are," Hunte said.

"I could order you to stay behind."

Hunte grinned. "I'm lousy at taking orders," he said. "Besides, that's my missile out there."

Kraus was looking at them, shaking his head. "You're both crazy. But I'm coming with you. There are three of them."

"No," McGarvey said. "Get my message back to Collingwood. If you want, you can stand by at the square. If we make it up to the transporter, we may need your help."

Kraus was obviously disappointed, but he nodded. "Good luck," he said, and he turned and hurried back to the square.

"I'll be right behind you, Mr. McGarvey," Hunte said, uncocking his pistol and reholstering it.

"The name is Kirk," McGarvey said, and he climbed the ten feet down into the collection vault, which was a round concrete chamber about fifteen feet in diameter. The vault itself was probably new, but the storm sewer lines radiating off at four odd angles to match the haphazardly angled streets above, were very old, constructed of brick with vaulted ceilings. The floor was covered with a few inches of water; a small stream trickled down from one of the sewer lines.

When Hunte made it to the bottom, McGarvey motioned for him to keep still as he peered into the darkness down the tunnel that led back to the square.

There was a sound. Very far away. Very distant. Hollow. As if he were hearing the scrape of shoe leather against brick.

Hunte heard it as well. He pulled out his gun again.

McGarvey cocked his ear and continued to listen. There. He heard the noises again, only this time they seemed to be receding.

"It's them," he said, climbing up into the tunnel. "They're heading in the opposite direction."

"That means the countdown clock is definitely running."

"Yeah," McGarvey said tersely, the hair on the nape of his neck crawling as he started into the darkness, his pistol in his right hand, and his left brushing the rough brick wall of the tunnel for guidance.

He'd never liked dark, enclosed spaces. When he was in high school he and some friends had explored a cave in southwestern Kansas. They'd gotten lost and it had taken them nearly eight hours in the absolute darkness to find their way out again. Standing in the open that night, he'd vowed never to get himself into such a situation ever again. But then, he thought wryly, who of us ever keeps the promises we make to ourselves?

About fifty yards down the tunnel, McGarvey thought he could see a faint glimmer of light ahead, and he stopped. Hunte was right behind him.

"What?"

"Quiet," McGarvey ordered. He'd thought he'd heard someone moving out ahead of them again, but now the tunnel was ominously silent except for the very distant sound of what he took to be a siren.

* * *

"It's a siren," Yegorov whispered.

Kurshin held up his hand for silence as he too listened. Twice he'd thought he heard another noise. Distant. He switched off the dim red penlight he carried and held his breath.

The sirens seemed to fade. He could hear water trickling somewhere, softly, slowly, but nothing else at first.

Then he heard it again, someone or something sloshing through water. Back the way they had come.

Yegorov heard it too. "Someone is back there," he said softly.

"Yes," Kurshin said, thinking it out. By now the missile's launch mode would have shown up at Missile Control. But they could not know about the delaying mechanism or how much longer before the missile launched.

"Have they figured it out then? Do they know we're gone?"

"It would appear so," Kurshin said absently. One part of him had to begrudgingly admire whoever it was coming up the tunnel. He must have a strong will. The East German said that the delaying circuit was foolproof. No way to stop the rocket from launching. How far to trust the man's judgment? There was nothing foolproof . . . nothing! Kurshin had seen the opposite to be true too often for him to believe otherwise.

He switched on his light and looked at his watch. They had eight minutes before launch. More than long enough to get clear. Schey had warned them that when the missile took off, its tremendously hot exhaust gases would rush down into the storm sewers, probably killing anyone who was within a hundred-meter radius.

He shined the light on Yegorov's face. The man was sweating lightly.

"Whoever is back there might be able to stop the launch somehow," Kurshin said.

"Then we'll destroy the missile," Yegorov said, raising the trigger.

"No," Kurshin said softly but sharply. "It must be launched. We will not fail."

"Then what?"

Kurshin listened again. The sounds of someone coming were louder. "We go back and kill them before they can interfere."

"There could be a dozen of them. More."

"I don't think so."

"But the rocket . . ."

"We go back," Kurshin said, pulling out his silenced Graz Buyra automatic. It was a very large, ominous-looking weapon. A KGB Department Viktor assassination device. "Now."

Yegorov was obviously torn between his fear of being roasted alive, and Kurshin whose ruthlessness was well known within the KGB.

"I have no desire to be caught down here when the missile is launched," Kurshin said. "But I have even less desire to return to Baranov a failure."

Yegorov nodded. He pulled out his silenced pistol. "Then let's do it quickly, Comrade, so there will be time for us to get clear. I don't wish to become anyone's martyr."

"But softly, Ivan," Kurshin said, once again dousing his penlight and pocketing it. "If we can hear them, it's a safe bet they can hear us."

Being careful to make as little noise as possible, Kurshin started back the way they had come. Within thirty meters they had come to an intersection. Above, a dim light showed through the grating. Kurshin stopped a moment to search his memory of the sewer blueprint he'd studied. The lines all interconnected.

He turned back to Yegorov. "You head straight toward the transporter. I'll take the right-hand tunnel. I believe it will circle around. If I can get behind them, we will have them in a cross fire."

"Just remember where I will be standing."

"Yes," Kurshin said. "And you had better be standing there, Ivan."

* * *

Twice more McGarvey stopped to listen, but the tunnel was silent. Either the Russians were by now out of earshot, or they too had stopped to listen. McGarvey had heard them, had the Russians heard their pursuers?

The light grew brighter in the tunnel ahead, until McGarvey stopped at the vault beneath the transporter. He could see that the grate above had been removed, and he could see up into the interior of the transporter itself, red and green lights flashing from the instruments on the launch consoles and radar screen.

Hunte was just behind his right shoulder. He whispered in McGarvey's ear. "If we're standing here when that bird launches, we'll be cooked meat."

McGarvey nodded, but he was still listening. Had he heard a sound up the tunnel to his left?

"What are we waiting for . . . ?" Hunte started to say, but McGarvey backed up against him and shook his head.

Hunte's eyes narrowed. He was getting jumpy.

McGarvey led him a few feet farther back into the tunnel. "I think they've come back," he said, his voice barely audible.

Hunte glanced toward the vault.

"We'd be sitting ducks, do you understand?"

Hunte nodded.

"I want you to go back down the tunnel for about fifty feet as quietly as you can. Then turn around and run like hell back here."

"You're going to try to flush them out?"

"Something like that. Now go. I don't know how long we've got before that missile will fire."

Hunte turned and disappeared into the darkness, making absolutely no noise. McGarvey waited for a couple of moments, then turned and edged back to where the tunnel opened into the vault beneath the transporter. Remaining in the shadows he checked to make sure his pistol was ready to fire, and brought it up, steadying it against the greasy damp brick wall.

For a long time nothing seemed to be happening. Once again in the distance McGarvey could hear a siren from the streets above. It would take Hunte a minute or so to get into position and start back. Kurshin had lied about wanting the helicopter and the gold, and he had almost certainly lied about the intended target. But where, if not Tripoli? The new Pershing had a range of more than two thousand miles. That covered a lot of territory, all the way from the British Isles to parts of the Middle East, including some important oil fields. Was that Baranov's game? Interrupt the industrial West's major supply of crude? It was certainly possible.

The radio in the transporter above blared.

"Flybaby, Six-P-Two, this is Colonel Collingwood, do you copy?"

There was a movement in the tunnel to the left, as if someone had taken a step backward. McGarvey stiffened.

"Flybaby Six-P-Two, this is Collingwood, talk to me, you sonofabitch."

Whatever the Air Force colonel was or was not, if he was still in the square, McGarvey had to admire his guts.

"The chopper is ready and your gold is on its way," Collingwood's voice boomed in the collection vault.

Hunte was taking too long. McGarvey started to turn when he heard the distinctive soft plopping sound of a silenced pistol shot.

There was a flash of movement from the collection vault. McGarvey turned back in time to see a large burly man leaping out of the left tunnel, a big pistol in his right hand, a small black box in his left.

McGarvey fired twice, the first shot catching Yegorov in the chest, the second in the side of his neck, bursting his carotid artery, the bullet deflecting off a bone, and finally destroying his throat. The big man crashed backward against the concrete wall, and the triggering device fell into the water.

The tunnel was suddenly silent.

McGarvey turned around and dropped to one knee, his pistol up, but the darkness behind him was absolute.

Almost too late he realized that he was outlined by the

light behind him, and he dove forward at the same moment
something plucked at his sleeve and he heard another silenced
shot.

He fired twice down the tunnel. At this point he didn't
think there was much fear of hitting Hunte. The captain was
probably dead.

Again the tunnel was in silence. Even the sirens topside
had stopped.

McGarvey started to edge forward, keeping to the far left
wall.

Something moved ahead of him, and he fired two more
shots into the darkness, quickly scrambling to the right side
of the tunnel as two answering silenced shots were fired.

McGarvey held his breath to listen. There were no sounds
ahead. He concentrated on the darkness, his gun up, ready
to fire the moment he spotted the pinpoint of a muzzle flash.

"We're running out of time, you and me," he called softly
into the darkness.

Another silenced shot was fired, the bullet ricocheting with
a whine off the brick wall. The flash was to the right.
McGarvey aimed slightly left and squeezed off a shot, then
quickly shifted sides to the left and immediately back to the
right.

There was no answering fire.

"Who are you?" a voice came from the darkness, speaking
English with a flat midwestern accent.

McGarvey could not pinpoint the voice. He turned his head
left so that his own voice would bounce off the opposite wall
of the tunnel. "Are you sure you want to know, Arkady
Aleksandrovich?"

"You have me at a disadvantage."

"Yes," McGarvey said. "You and Comrade KGB Chairman Baranov. He and I are old friends, you know."

McGarvey thought he heard a splash of water straight down
the tunnel, but then there was silence.

He waited ten seconds and then started forward.

"I'm coming for you, Arkady," he said.

Still there was silence.

Forty feet farther down the tunnel he came to a body. It was Jim Hunte. McGarvey could tell from his uniform, and the tool kit slung over his shoulder. He felt the man's body, his fingers discovering a small amount of blood and a bullet wound on his face just above the bridge of his nose.

Christ! In the dark!

McGarvey leapt to his feet. "Kurshin," he shouted, his voice echoing and reechoing off the tunnel walls and ceiling. "Kurshin, you sonofabitch, I'm coming for you!"

There was no answer.

McGarvey turned on his heel and, mindless now of the noise he was making, raced down the tunnel toward the collection vault. There had been three of them. Two were accounted for. The last one was probably long gone by now. There probably was little or no time left before the launch.

In the collection vault McGarvey snatched up the electronic trigger that Yegorov had dropped, and stuffing it in his pocket climbed the metal rungs up the side of the vault and pulled himself into the transporter.

If need be, he told himself grimly, he would destroy the rocket if it actually started to lift off.

A slightly built man dressed in civilian clothes, blood streaming down his face, was bunched up beside the bucket seat in front of the firing console. He rolled over and groaned.

McGarvey nearly shot the man before he realized that he was no threat, and was probably very near death.

Lights were flashing all over the fire control panel in a bewildering sequence of reds and greens and ambers. Whatever was happening was occurring at an increasingly rapid pace.

"Answer me, you bastard," Collingwood's voice boomed from the radio speaker.

McGarvey found the radio console at the front right seat and yanked the microphone off its hook.

"This is McGarvey. I'm in the transporter. The Russians are dead or gone, and so is Hunte. This thing looks like it's ready to launch, get someone over here on the double."

He threw down the microphone, undogged the main hatch,

swung it open with a metallic clang, and turned back to Schey, gently turning the man over on his back and straightening out his legs. The man's eyes fluttered open.

"There isn't much time," McGarvey said. "Do you understand?"

Schey's eyes seemed to come into focus and he looked up at McGarvey.

"Your friends are dead. How do I interrupt the firing sequence?"

The East German managed a tight little smile of triumph.

"It's over," McGarvey said. "You've lost. How do we shut this goddamned thing down?"

Schey's eyes closed and he gave a big shuddering gasp. At first McGarvey thought he was dead, but the man's breathing steadied out.

McGarvey got to his feet as the first of Collingwood's people showed up at the hatch.

"I don't know what to do," he shouted. "This thing is on a countdown."

The first technician through the hatch shoved McGarvey aside and quickly scanned the board. The second man came through and crowded in beside him.

"They've got a timer on it," he snapped, pulling a screwdriver out of his pocket. The other man did the same and together they unfastened the dozen screws holding the firing control panel in place.

The first man gingerly lifted the panel away from the console, stretching out the wires beneath. They both sucked air a second later.

"Twelve seconds," one of them said.

The other was pawing through the wires. He looked up. "It's on a failsafe," he said.

"Impossible," the other man replied.

"This sonofabitch is going to launch in another ten seconds, and there isn't a fucking thing we can do about it."

McGarvey had backed up to the hatch, other technicians and security people crowding around the transporter.

The two technicians at the console leapt up and bodily

shoved McGarvey out the door. ''Clear the area, this sonof-abitch is about to launch!'' one of them shouted.

Everyone scattered. McGarvey rushed around to the side of the transport trailer, the umbilical cords snaking out from the tractor to an electrical panel beneath the missile.

Baranov had planned something. Whatever it was, it would be brilliant and devastating. What?

He had taken a huge risk not only by having Kurshin and the others steal the missile, but by so openly displaying the depth of his intelligence information.

Whatever target they had programmed the missile to hit would be important. London? Paris? Where?

The technicians and security people were halfway across the square. Someone was shouting.

The delay circuitry was failsafe, the technician had shouted. McGarvey pulled out the trigger for the plastique.

The seconds were ticking. No time. Christ, there was no time!

He tossed the trigger to the pavement and stepped forward to the four umbilical cords. Each was connected to the firing panel by a thick electrical plug. McGarvey grabbed one of the large cables and yanked it out of its socket.

There were a lot of sirens. He yanked the second plug and the third. His time had run out. Ten seconds had to have elapsed.

He yanked the last plug out of its socket at the same moment a big spark jumped from the contacts to the side of the trailer, and nothing happened.

For several long seconds McGarvey stood there, his knees weak, his heart hammering in his chest. But nothing had happened. Nothing!

11

CIA HEADQUARTERS

"THE SONOFABITCH JUST PULLED THE PLUG," PHIL CAR-
rara, deputy director of operations, said, his voice tinged with
a bit of awe.

"At that point he didn't have anything to lose," Trotter
replied.

"Except his life."

The two of them had ridden up to the seventh floor and
when they stepped off the elevator they crossed directly to
the DCI's conference room adjacent to his office. It was
a few minutes before eight in the morning, but Trotter,
who'd gotten no sleep on the military jet over, was still on
European time where it was early afternoon yesterday. He
was dead tired.

They were met in the anteroom by the director's security

people. Trotter turned over his pistol before they were allowed inside.

The room was long and broad, big windows looking out over the new section of headquarters which had just been completed the year before, and beyond, the rolling wooded hills of the old Bureau of Public Roads property.

The DCI, Roland Murphy, who had retired from the Army as a major general to take the assistant directorship, was hunched over the long conference table looking at a series of maps and photographs. He was a very large man, with a bull neck, beefy arms, and thick eyebrows over deep-set eyes. He'd taken over as DCI two years ago after the death of Donald Powers.

With him at the table were Lawrence Danielle, the new deputy director of central intelligence, and Howard Ryan, the Agency's general counsel. In contrast to Murphy, Danielle was a small man with a permanently pinched expression on his face, and a voice that was so soft listeners often had to strain to hear him. He'd worked his way up through the ranks over the past twenty years, and had even served as an interim DCI a number of years ago before Powers had been hired for the job, and again for a short period before the president had talked the general into taking over the helm.

Ryan was relatively new to the Agency. Like Carrara he had come over from the National Security Agency. He was an extremely precise man, whose father ran one of New York's top law firms. "This sort of excitement is better for the blood than corporate law," he was fond of saying. And he was sharp.

They all looked up when Trotter and Carrara entered the room and approached the long table.

"You look like hell," Murphy rumbled brusquely.

"No sleep on the flight over, General," Trotter said. "I just got in, as a matter of fact."

"Coffee?"

"Yes, sir."

Ryan went over to the sideboard to pour him a cup from

the silver service. Trotter's eyes strayed to the maps and photographs.

"Has Phil briefed you on the latest?"

"No, sir," Trotter said, looking up. "Just that there have been some new developments overnight." Actually Carrara had told him that this was a council of war.

"That's the understatement of the year," Murphy said, shaking his leonine head. "I've got to see the president at nine-thirty, which gives us just a little over an hour to figure out what the hell we're going to do."

Ryan came back with the coffee and handed it to Trotter.

"Thanks," Trotter said. "What's happened?"

"First things first. What about this free lance of yours, McGarvey? Is he all right?"

"Disappointed. He's on his way back to Paris by now, I suspect. We had no reason to hold him."

"Kurshin just disappeared into thin air?" Danielle asked, his voice soft.

Trotter nodded glumly. "By the time we got everything sorted out, he was long gone. No trace whatsoever except for the latex mask he had worn. We found it along with Brad Allworth's uniform in the transporter."

"We have a confirmation that the body the French police found along the railroad tracks outside of Paris was Allworth," Ryan said. "He was shot in the forehead at close range. Nine-millimeter slug. Almost certainly a Graz Buyra. The SDECE has been very cooperative."

"Well, I'll tell you one thing. McGarvey saved our asses," Murphy said. "In a very big way."

"Sir?" Trotter asked.

"The technicians pulled that Pershing apart overnight. Its guidance system was reprogrammed just as you expected. But the target profile was not for any city. No one could make any sense of it until they pulled the flight coordinates out of the inertial guidance system."

"Where?" Trotter asked.

Murphy glanced down at a message flimsy on the table.

"Latitude thirty-one degrees, five minutes north, and longitude thirty-five degrees, twenty-four minutes east. Too far north and east for it to be Tripoli." He turned the map around so that Trotter could see it, and he stabbed a blunt finger at a spot along the southern edge of the Dead Sea. "En Gedi," he said. "More specifically the Israeli nuclear research facility eight miles from the town."

Trotter didn't understand, and it was evident on his face.

"What is it?" Danielle prompted.

Everyone was looking at him. Trotter felt as if he were on stage, his audience waiting for his next line.

"From where I sit that doesn't make much sense," he said.

"Go on," Murphy ordered.

"Israel has two such installations in addition to their facilities for enrichment and reprocessing of nuclear fuels, as well as at least one heavy water plant."

"Get to the point."

Trotter glanced at the map. "We're fairly certain that this was the big operation we were expecting from Baranov. Kurshin is his handpicked man. Frankly I don't think he'd bother with a simple research reactor."

"Why?" Danielle asked.

"For one thing, he placed Kurshin in a high-risk situation. He wouldn't have done that for such meager pickings. In the second place, by reprogramming that missile he's tipped his hand that he's got a damned good pipeline either into the manufacturer of the guidance system . . ."

"Goodyear," Ryan interjected.

"Yes. Either that or into the Pentagon itself."

Danielle and Murphy exchanged glances.

"The Pentagon," the DCI said.

"Do we know who it is?" Trotter asked.

"Not yet, but the list is narrowing."

"But don't you see, General, that's my point. Whatever the KGB has got going in the Pentagon, and of course we've long suspected something like this, Baranov wouldn't tip his hand merely to destroy one of Israel's two research reactors."

Murphy sighed deeply and shook his head. "No, he wouldn't."

"There's more?" Trotter asked.

"You bet," Murphy replied. "Four days ago an NSA satellite picked up what was believed to be an alarm situation at the En Gedi facility. It was turned over to the Non-Proliferation Treaty Inspection Service. They sent two of their people over to have a look; one of them coincidentally was Lorraine Abbott who has done a little work for us in the past. The other was a Brit."

Trotter said nothing.

"Scott Hayes, the Brit, reported that he was satisfied that the Israelis were telling the truth. Apparently a leak in one of the steam valves. Nonradioactive."

"Dr. Abbott didn't believe them?"

"No. As a matter of fact she's still over there snooping around. She's convinced they're lying. She has a feeling that whatever happened was a hell of a lot more important than a simple steam leak."

"Why?"

"She's being watched by the Mossad, and the Israelis have all but ordered her out of the country. The clincher came out at the facility, though. She and Hayes were shown around by a man who identified himself as a Crises Management Team leader. Lev Potok. He's Mossad."

"What are they hiding?" Trotter asked.

"Something important enough for Baranov to go after it," Murphy said.

"We think that Israel has a stockpile of battle-ready nuclear weapons," Ryan said.

"We've suspected that for some time now. But there's been no proof . . ." Trotter stopped. "En Gedi?"

Murphy nodded. "That's our best guess."

"Then the Russians know about it. Baranov would have to be sure about his information to take such a risk."

"And he won't stop," Murphy said.

"No."

"You and McGarvey are our resident Baranov experts,"
Murphy was saying.

Trotter was thinking ahead of the DCI. Baranov would
certainly not stop with one failure. He would keep at it until
he succeeded. With Israel's nuclear capability destroyed there
would be no stopping an all-out—Soviet-backed—attack.
This time the Arabs would probably succeed, and the entire
region would join the Soviet bloc—oil and all.

"The ball is in your court," Murphy said.

"Why not tell the Israelis what we know?"

"So that they could prepare themselves?" the DCI asked.
Trotter nodded.

Murphy shook his head. "No good. We're in a very delicate balance over there, you know that, John. Almost anything could tip the scales one way or the other, and there'd
be an all-out shooting war. It's a gentleman's agreement
between us. Call it a politically necessary fiction. If we ac-
knowledge to Israel that we know they have battle-ready
nuclear weapons, they will be forced into doing something.
They would have to for their own sake. Just as we would be
forced into demanding they dismantle those weapons."

"Which they would not do," Trotter said.

"No," the DCI agreed. "As I said, the ball is in your
court."

"I don't know if McGarvey will agree to it."

"Convince him," Murphy said. "But his primary mission
is going to have to be confirming that the Israelis actually do
have nukes, and that they're stored at En Gedi."

"We're going to spy on our allies?"

"It's a tough world."

PARIS

Kurshin held the telephone tightly to his ear as the secure
connection to Moscow via the embassy's satellite communications link was completed, and Baranov came on the line.
He did not sound happy.

"What are you doing in Paris?"

"I failed," Kurshin said simply. He was calling from a telephone booth at the end of a narrow side street off the Rue de la Fayette in an area of nice apartment buildings.

"Yes? What about the others?"

"I disposed of the East German as you directed me to do. But Ivan was shot to death in the sewers." Kurshin's grip tightened on the telephone receiver. The man had come to the second-floor window across the street.

The line was silent for a long time, but Kurshin didn't really mind. He was content for the moment to watch the man in the window above looking down at the street. He was evidently searching for something or someone. Here I am, Kurshin muttered to himself.

"Tell me everything that happened, Arkasha," Baranov was saying. "How did they know about the sewer? Did Schey say something to someone? Perhaps one of his friends?"

"I don't know, but there were two men in the sewers. One of them was wearing an Army uniform. Captain's bars. But the other one . . ." The window curtains fell back and the man above was gone.

"Yes?" Baranov prompted.

Kurshin turned back to the telephone. "The other one knew my name."

"Impossible."

"Nevertheless it is true. And he knew your name. He said that you and he were old friends."

"All that in a dark sewer? You talked to him then. You perhaps became friends? So much so that you decided to spare his life? What, Arkasha? Tell me, I am listening."

"I tried to kill him, and yes we had that discussion. But he was very good. He was willing to wait there in that tunnel with me to die when the rocket took off."

"Which it did not. And you cannot tell me what this one looked like."

"Oh, yes," Kurshin said. "I did not leave the area. When I came up to where the car was waiting I drove immediately back to the square, to see . . . if he was successful."

"He was."

"Yes, he was," Kurshin said, the thought still terribly rankling. "He came out of the transporter and pulled the umbilical cords from the missile. Schey told us the launch was impossible to stop. But this one did it with his bare hands."

There was a low, harsh sound on the telephone. Kurshin almost thought the KGB director was chuckling.

"It must have come within a split second of the firing impulse, but the missile did not launch."

"You got a good look at him?"

"Yes, I did, Comrade Chairman. A very good look. It is a face I shall never forget." He looked up. The man had come back to the window. "In fact I am looking at him again this very moment, and as soon as I hang up I shall kill him."

"What?" Baranov suddenly screamed. "You are in Paris . . . you're calling from outside the embassy?"

"Yes," Kurshin replied, the first inkling that he had made a mistake coming to him.

"Describe him to me," Baranov ordered.

Kurshin did.

"You say you are looking at him now? Can he see you?"

"I don't think so," Kurshin said. The man had gone again from the window. "No, he is gone now."

"Then hang up the telephone, you idiot. The man you have described is Kirk McGarvey. And since you have already come up against him and are still alive, you may consider yourself extremely lucky."

"But . . ."

"Get out of there now, Arkasha. We will meet twenty-four hours from now in the usual place. But go before it is too late."

—— 12 ——

JERUSALEM

THE SOVIET UNION MAINTAINED NO EMBASSY IN ISRAEL, AL-
though they had been one of the first nations to recognize
Israel's legitimacy as a state in 1948. Instead, their affairs
were looked after by the Soviet Interests Section of the Hungarian Embassy, a situation that was starting to come apart.

For the past seventy-two hours, telephone calls in and out
of the embassy had been closely monitored from the King
David Hotel a block away. It was early afternoon. The other
technicians were taking a break.

Abraham Liebowitz, headphones on his ears, looked up as
the tape recorder automatically came on. "It's him again,"
he said.

Lev Potok had been gazing out the window of their seventh-
floor suite, thinking about Lorraine Abbott and her meddling.

He turned and hurried over to Liebowitz, taking the headphones from him.

". . . June thirtieth, yes I understand," the same voice as before was saying. He spoke English with a Russian accent.

"It is vital now that a very close watch be kept, you understand this?"

"Yes."

"We are to be advised of any unusual activity in or around the target facility. Of course you can well understand the need to keep our . . . friend advised of such happenings."

"Yes," the Russian said.

Potok glanced down at the tape machine. The call was outgoing from the embassy. The man giving the instructions was obviously Hungarian. He was at the embassy, the other one was somewhere within the city.

Liebowitz was on the other telephone speaking with their technician at the telephone exchange. He looked up. "We have the first three digits," he said. "They are the same as before."

Potok nodded. They had picked up half a dozen calls like this one from the embassy to the same voice. So far, however, the calls had been as brief as they had been enigmatic, allowing the telephone people to trace only the first two or three digits of the number being called.

"Now more than before this has become an extremely important project to him," the Hungarian said. "Especially after our German failure."

"Yes, I understand this. Everything will be as you ask," the Russian said.

Potok held the earphones tighter. What German failure? he wondered. And what was the significance of the date in June? That was barely two weeks away.

Liebowitz held up four fingers. The telephone system within Israel used only six digits. They were close now.

"If something comes up you will use the normal contact procedures unless it is an emergency, and then you know what to do."

"Certainly," the Russian said. "But there may be others involved now, so we must be very careful."

"We're well aware of the delicacy, just you be aware of the importance."

Liebowitz held up five fingers. He was grinning.

"Enough," the Russian said. "I will hang up now. But it is you who must keep me advised of any changes."

Hold on, Potok said to himself.

"You forget yourself . . ." the embassy speaker said, but the other one interrupted him.

"Don't tell me my job. If there hadn't been a failure we would be finished here. Don't forget your position." The connection was broken.

"Damn," Potok swore, yanking the earphones off his head, but Liebowitz was smiling triumphantly, and holding up six fingers.

"We've got the sonofabitch," he said. He turned back to the telephone. "Yes, go ahead," he said. He quickly scribbled an address on a pad of paper. "We owe you guys a dinner," he said. "A big dinner." He hung up, ripping the paper off the pad and handing it to Potok.

"It's an apartment on King David Street not two blocks from here! Second floor in the rear!"

Potok grabbed his jacket, tore out of the room, and was halfway down the corridor by the time Liebowitz came running after him. The elevator was on the ground floor so they took the stairs, pounding down them two at a time.

On the ground floor they turned right and raced out to the rear parking lot.

"Drive," Potok ordered, jumping in on the passenger side. He yanked the radio handset from its hook as Liebowitz got in behind the wheel, started the engine, and peeled rubber out of the parking lot.

"Central, this is Cold Shoulder Operation, we need a backup immediately," Potok radioed. He read the address off the paper.

"We'll have someone there within ten minutes," the radio

dispatcher at Mossad's communications center on Hamara Street in Tel Aviv said. They would probably be sending either local civil police or possibly someone from Knesset Security, but it didn't matter. Potok wanted backup in case something went wrong.

"We're going in first, so tell them to watch out for us," Potok shouted.

"Will do."

Traffic was heavy, nevertheless it took Liebowitz just under two minutes to make it to the apartment building where he screeched to a halt half up on the sidewalk.

Potok pulled out his gun and entered the building, Liebowitz, his gun drawn, right behind him. An old woman had come out of her ground-floor apartment.

"Get back," Potok warned as he headed up the stairs.

The woman, startled, stumbled back into her apartment and slammed the door.

Another door slammed upstairs and someone came running down the hall.

"Watch out," Potok shouted as he lurched left, flattening himself against the cracked, dirty plaster wall.

Two shots were fired from above, the bullets smacking into the wall just above Liebowitz's head.

Potok shoved forward and fired three shots in rapid succession. A car horn honked out on the street and someone shouted something from below, and then the apartment building fell silent.

"You can either throw down your gun right now, or come out of here feet first," Potok shouted. "But you're not getting away."

He glanced back at Liebowitz crouched below him on the stairs. After a moment he nodded, and girding himself leapt up the last few steps into the narrow corridor.

A figure of a man was just disappearing around the corner at the end of the hall when Potok snapped off a shot, the bullet hitting the man in the back of his left leg just behind his knee. He cried out and crashed to the floor.

Potok rushed forward and coming around the corner he

dropped into a shooter's stance, both hands on his pistol trained on the center of the man's forehead.

The Russian was short and squat with thick dark hair and narrow pig's eyes. With one hand he was holding his leg, in the other was a big pistol. He was looking up at Potok, a thin sneer on his lips. He started to raise his pistol.

"Is it worth it, Comrade?" Potok said evenly.

Liebowitz was just off his left shoulder. In the distance they could hear a lot of sirens. The Russian's eyes flicked to him, and after a tense moment he shook his head and slumped back, letting the gun slip from his hand.

Potok stepped forward and gingerly kicked the gun out of the Russian's reach.

"Call an ambulance," he told Liebowitz. "But keep everyone else out of here. We don't want to disturb any evidence of this one's drug dealings, do we?"

LOD AIRPORT

It was late evening and in the past three hours they had made very little progress.

The bullet had been removed from the Russian's leg, his wound patched up, and he had been taken immediately to the military side of Lod Airport outside of Tel Aviv. AMAN, Israel's Military Intelligence Service, had of course agreed to cooperate with the Mossad and had lent the use of one of the prisoner interrogation units. The building was off on its own and absolutely secure.

A search of the apartment had turned up nothing more than the Russian's forged Israeli passport under the name of Norman Katz. But Mossad files across town had come up with his photograph and a brief dossier identifying him as Viktor Nikolaievich Voronsky, a minor KGB legman who had last been spotted working in Damascus. He had apparently disappeared from view six months ago, but he had been considered of such minor importance that no search had been made for him.

Voronsky sat in an ordinary wooden chair across the table from Liebowitz. He had been given no drugs for his wound, and it was evident on his face that he was in considerable pain.

Potok leaned against the door on the opposite side of the small smoke-filled room. So far they had not revealed the fact that they knew Voronsky's real name, or that they had been monitoring his telephone conversations for the past three days.

"Just your name," Liebowitz started again patiently.

"I've told you a hundred times, you bastards, my name is . . ."

"Voronsky," Potok interrupted from where he stood.

The Russian's head snapped up, his eyes opening wide for just a moment, but then narrowing. He shrugged and sat back in his chair.

"So, fuck you," he said in Russian.

"And your mother," Potok replied in the same language.

Again surprise showed on Voronsky's face.

Potok came forward, pulling the extra chair around so that he could straddle it, his arms draped over the back. "Viktor Nikolaievich, you are in very deep shit at this moment. But I suppose you know that."

Voronsky shrugged. "Deport me."

Potok smiled. "Oh, no, Niki, it is not going to be that easy, unless of course you wish to cooperate with us."

"I'm a spy, if that's what you want. I will be exchanged within thirty days in any event. We have a number of your friends rotting at this moment in Damascus. You can't believe the conditions . . ."

Potok smiled gently again. It stopped the Russian. "Ah, but you should ask some of your PLO terrorist friends what our internment camps are like."

The Russian looked to Liebowitz. "I demand to speak to someone from my interest section in the Hungarian Embassy," he said.

Liebowitz spread his hands. "Seems to me that you've already done enough talking with them, Comrade Voronsky."

"What are you talking about? What is this?"

"We're gangsters, Niki," Potok said. "Isn't that what you've been calling us for the past ten years or so?"

"Then I demand to speak with your supervisor. I want these proceedings recorded." Voronsky glanced at the tape recorder set up on the table.

"Just a few questions," Potok said. He nodded at Liebowitz who switched on the tape machine.

"*. . . June thirtieth, yes I understand,*" Voronsky's voice came from the speaker.

Liebowitz reached out and switched off the machine.

"Let's begin with that date, Niki. June thirtieth. What is going to happen on that day? Something very bad for Israel?"

Voronsky reared back as if he had been slapped, the sudden movement hurting his leg, and he nearly cried out in pain. "Sonofabitch . . . I demand my rights."

"What rights?"

"Under Israeli and international law . . ."

Potok was shaking his head. "Israeli law applies only to Israeli citizens. Not you, Niki. And we do not recognize your so-called international law. But then neither do you. Here you are completely beyond any law. June thirtieth."

Voronsky shook his head.

Liebowitz shifted the tape forward.

"*. . . advised of any unusual activity in or around the target facility.*"

"The target, Niki, is it going to be attacked on June thirtieth? Is that it?" Potok asked. He nodded for Liebowitz again.

"*. . . Now more than before this has become an extremely important project to him. Especially after our German failure.*"

"Who is this man spoken of, Niki? And what German failure? What happened in Germany?"

Voronsky was still shaking his head.

Potok got up from his chair, withdrew his pistol, cocked the hammer, and, before Voronsky could move, jammed the barrel into the side of the Russian's head. Liebowitz jumped up and tried to stop him. It was part of the routine.

"Nyet," the Russian cried.

"Talk to us, Niki. It is all we ask."

"Lev," Liebowitz said urgently.

"If you don't want to watch, then get the hell out of here, but I'm going to blow this bastard's brains all over this cell unless he talks to me."

"Lev!" Liebowitz said again, pulling Potok aside. "Outside. Now."

There was something in Liebowitz's tone, in the expression on his face, that penetrated. Potok stepped back, and nodded. Something was wrong. It wasn't part of the script.

Outside the cell, the door closed, Liebowitz was shaking. "The German failure they talked about. I know what it is."

"Yes?"

"It was on the news, for God's sake. But it didn't mean anything to me until just now. I swear . . ."

"What?"

"The terrorists at Ramstein Air Force Base. They stole a Pershing missile. Set it up downtown."

Potok suddenly did see it all, and he could feel the blood draining from his face. "En Gedi?"

"Yes," Liebowitz said. "They know! The bastards know, and they're going to try again . . ."

There was a tremendous crash and the sounds of something breaking from within the cell.

Potok clawed the door open in time to see that Voronsky had smashed the tape recorder on the floor and had a long, jagged shard of plastic casing in his right hand.

"No," Potok shouted, leaping forward, but he was too late.

Voronsky in a last desperate act drew the edge of the plastic shard across his neck, once, twice, a third time, blood spurting everywhere as he sliced through major arteries, and his breath suddenly giving a big slobbering gurgle as he actually managed to cut through his windpipe.

13

TEL AVIV

McGARVEY HAD ARRIVED AT TEL AVIV'S LOD AIRPORT shortly before six in the evening. At seven sharp he paid off his cabbie and strode into the Uri Dan Hotel, his single leather overnight bag slung over his shoulder.

On the flight over from Paris he had asked himself a dozen times why he had agreed to Trotter's assignment. And each time he came up with the same answer: Baranov. It was an unfinished business for him. The Russian would not give up so easily. And since Kurshin had disappeared, it was a safe bet that he would be involved in whatever else happened.

"Baranov's handmaiden perhaps," an extremely strung-out Trotter had said. "But Kurshin in his own right is a very accomplished man. A very dangerous man."

"So I understand," McGarvey said dryly.

They had met this time at a small anonymous sidewalk café on the left bank. It was noon and the place was crowded. No one paid any attention to them.

"They'll try again. I don't know where or how, but I do know the target."

"Not Tripoli?"

Trotter glanced around at the other patrons in the café and at traffic along the busy Boulevard St. Germain. "En Gedi," he said softly.

"In the Middle East somewhere?" McGarvey asked. He'd never heard of the place.

"Israel. South shore of the Dead Sea."

"What's there?"

Again Trotter hesitated. "Ostensibly a research reactor."

"Ostensibly?"

Trotter leaned forward. "Kirk, this is top-secret information. If you open your mouth at the wrong time or place they'll have your ass."

McGarvey said nothing.

"We think it's a weapons stockpile."

"Nuclear?"

Trotter nodded.

"Then it's true after all."

Again Trotter nodded.

McGarvey looked away, across the boulevard as a truck rumbled past. "It's something Baranov would go after."

"We think so," Trotter said. "We'd like you to stop him."

McGarvey had managed a tight smile and looked back at his old friend. "And what else, John?"

"We're not sure about the stockpile theory. We want you to confirm it."

"How?"

"You can start with Dr. Lorraine Abbott."

The Uri Dan, right on the beach, was one of Tel Aviv's largest and best hotels. Crossing the big lobby McGarvey automatically scanned the mostly casually dressed people coming and going, immediately picking out a small, dark-complected man in shirtsleeves obviously watching a tall, good-looking blonde woman seated alone in the cocktail lounge.

He had only briefly glanced at the woman, but as he came up to the desk he looked back again.

"Sir?" the desk clerk asked politely.

"McGarvey. Reservations have been made."

The clerk punched his name into the reservations computer, looking up a moment later. "Kirk McGarvey?"

"Right."

"Yes, sir, we have your reservation. And a package has arrived for you from your embassy. If I may see your passport, sir?"

McGarvey handed it over. His gun and a few other things had been sent ahead in the diplomatic pouch. "Do you have a Dr. Abbott registered here?"

"Yes, sir."

McGarvey motioned across the lobby to the open cocktail lounge. "I haven't seen her in years. Is that her over there? The blonde?"

The desk clerk gave him an odd look, but then nodded. "Yes, sir, that is Dr. Abbott. If you would just sign here, please."

McGarvey had his bag sent up to his room, and with his package in hand angled across the lobby toward the cocktail lounge, passing the man in shirtsleeves, who looked idly up at him.

McGarvey stopped. "You know, pal, it's considered impolite to stare."

The man just looked at him, and McGarvey turned and continued across to the lounge and around the railing to Lorraine Abbott's table.

She looked up at him, a questioning expression on her face.

"You don't look like a physicist," he said.

Her eyes widened slightly, and her nostrils flared. "Neither do you."

McGarvey laughed. "That's because I'm not. May I join you?"

"I think not," she said, starting to gather her purse and rise.

"I bring you greetings from the general."

She stopped. "The general?" she asked.

"Roland Murphy."

It took her just a beat to catch her breath. "Then someone *is* listening," she said, sitting back.

"Yes, they are. May I sit down?"

"Of course," she said absently. "I don't think I caught your name."

"McGarvey. My friends call me Kirk." He reached across the table and they shook hands.

"Mine call me Dr. Abbott," she said. "What can I do for you, and the general, Mr. McGarvey?"

"First of all, are you aware that you're being watched?"

She nodded over her shoulder. "I think his name is Larry. Mossad. They've been back there ever since . . ."

"En Gedi," he finished the sentence for her.

"Yes," she said, looking at him with renewed interest, her right eyebrow raising. "But if you know the significance of that, then you must have come here to tell me something."

McGarvey decided that she was a lot like his ex-wife Kathleen; outwardly haughty and self-assured, beautifully coiffed, made up and dressed, which he thought might be nothing more than a cover-up for a slight inferiority complex. Women were not supposed to be physicists. At least not beautiful ones.

"Do you read the newspapers, Doctor? Watch television news?"

The questions startled her. She nodded.

"Then you are aware of what happened recently in West Germany. The business concerning a terrorist attack on a Pershing missile?"

"I think I may have seen something or other," she said vaguely, still not catching his drift.

"The missile had been reprogrammed to strike En Gedi."

She sucked in her breath, a little color coming to her lightly tanned high cheeks. "Why?"

"I was hoping you could tell me that," McGarvey said. He leaned forward in his chair. "What do you think is going on out there?"

She glanced over his shoulder toward where the Mossad legman had been seated, but he was gone. McGarvey had spotted him leaving a minute ago.

"He's run off to report that you're having a drink with a so far unidentified man," McGarvey said. "But I asked you a question."

"I don't know what you're talking about, Mr. McGarvey, or whoever the hell you are. But I think this conversation has gone as far as it's going to go."

"The general is waiting for your call, Doctor. But please do it quickly. I think we're not going to have much time here."

She hesitated, obviously torn between wanting to believe he was who he presented himself to be, and reluctance to discuss these highly secret matters so openly.

"Let me tell you first," McGarvey said. "We think that the Israelis have hid in or very near their nuclear installation at En Gedi their entire stockpile of battle-ready nuclear weapons. And we think that the incident our satellite picked up last week may have involved a Soviet penetration of that secret."

"Oh, Christ," Lorraine Abbott said.

"Yes," McGarvey replied. "Oh, Christ."

BOOK TWO

───── 14 ─────

TEL AVIV

DARKNESS HAD SETTLED OVER THE EASTERN MEDITERRA-
nean and with it came the lights of Tel Aviv, a city of 350,000
people, twenty percent of whom were Arabs who lived in an
uneasy harmony with their Jewish masters.

In a third-floor office of a surprisingly small and unpre-
possessing building in a courtyard off Hamara Street, Lev
Potok sat back from his desk and rubbed his burning eyes.
He had been working steadily for the past three hours trying
to put everything together in his report to Isser Shamir,
director of the Mossad. But the situation wasn't clear in his
own mind, so how could he make anyone else understand?

The suicide of Viktor Voronsky in the interrogation cell
weighed heavily on his mind. It had been a mistake on his
part leaving the obviously distraught Russian alone, even for

a few moments. But what in God's name had motivated the man to such a desperate act? There were forces here, he told himself, that were much greater than any of them had any reason to suspect.

Spying and espionage were one thing, but on arrest most spies were professional enough to understand that most likely they would only spend a few months or perhaps a few years behind bars before an exchange was made, and they were repatriated.

Voronsky, though, had apparently killed himself so that he would not be broken under interrogation. But who was the master, who had been pulling his strings to such an extent? The Russians he had known were dedicated, but unlike many Arabs they were not fanatics.

Lighting a cigarette, he looked at the half-finished page in his typewriter. They had come up with a date barely two weeks from now, but they had no concrete idea what it meant.

The Hungarian Embassy was involved, directly or indirectly, but the telephone messages had been cryptic and could have meant anything. Even an upcoming trade agreement.

Liebowitz's speculation that the so-called *German failure* mentioned on the telephone had something to do with the aborted hijacking of the Pershing missile several days ago was just that—speculation.

The pieces of the puzzle seemed to want to come together, almost of their own volition. But it was like building a complicated piece of machinery without blueprints, without even a firm idea what the machine was supposed to do.

Someone knocked on his door, and he looked up in irritation as Liebowitz stuck his head inside.

"Larry just came up. I think you'd better listen to what he has to say."

"What's she done this time?" Potok asked. Larry Saulberg was one of the team assigned to keep a watch on Lorraine Abbott's movements. So far she hadn't done much except remain in her hotel, reading the steady stream of NPT documents and reports that had been coming to her out of Washington twice daily. They had not been able to tamper with the letters for fear they would tip their hand even more than they already had. It was a delicate balance.

"She's got a gentleman caller."

"Is it that prick Hayes back again?"

"No," Liebowitz said. The man had a flair for the dramatic.

Potok pulled the paper out of his typewriter, placed it in a file folder with the rest of his report, and put the entire thing in his desk drawer. He nodded when he was ready, and Liebowitz stood aside.

Larry Saulberg was a small, dark, intense man who'd immigrated with his parents from Kenya about fifteen years ago. He had absolutely no sense of humor, but he was like a hound dog with his steadfast devotion to his job. He'd even changed his name to one that sounded more Jewish.

"Who is watching her at this moment?" Potok asked.

"Chaim," the little African said, his obsidian eyes bright.

"What have you got for me?"

"At seven this evening a man showed up at the hotel where he registered and had his bags sent up to his room. He received a package from the desk, and then went directly to Dr. Abbott who was seated in the lobby cocktail lounge where he introduced himself and sat down."

"Yes, and who is this man?" Potok demanded. He glanced at the wall clock. It was well past eight-thirty. "And why didn't you report this sooner?"

"He is registered under the name of Kirk McGarvey on an American passport; he has a long-term French visa along with a lot of others," Saulberg reported. "The reason for the delay is I wanted to make sure who he was before I came up here to you. The package he received at the desk was sealed with a diplomatic stamp."

"Why didn't you just stick with him?" Potok asked. There was something else. There was always something else.

"Because he had me made from the moment he entered the hotel," Saulberg said. "He even came over to me and told me that it wasn't polite to stare."

Potok suppressed a grin. Saulberg was deadly serious, as

was this entire business. McGarvey was most likely just another NPT courier. "Go on."

"I ran him through our files," the legman said.

"Yes?"

Liebowitz, who had stepped in behind Saulberg and had closed the door, handed over the file folder he'd brought with him. "He came up with this, Lev."

"Well, who is he?" Potok asked, opening the file.

"A former CIA case officer," Saulberg said softly. "Who is almost for certain an assassin."

Potok's eyes shot up from McGarvey's photograph, something clutching at his gut. "What?"

"Not only that, Lev," Liebowitz interjected. "We have it on good authority that he has been in Germany."

"Recently?"

"Yes."

Isser Shamir, known as Isser the Little, was a tiny barrel-chested man who stood barely five feet, and whose head seemed almost ludicrously too large for his body. His longish white hair was always in disarray, his wide dreamy eyes seemed always to be half-closed as if he were drifting, but his mind was absolutely sharp. First class. Like a computer, his friends said; like a steel trap, his enemies countered.

He looked up from reading Potok's hastily finished report. "There is confirmation that McGarvey was in Kaiserslautern during the incident with the missile?"

"Not one hundred percent," Potok admitted. "Liebowitz telephoned a friend on the police force, who said that a man matching McGarvey's description was there. In fact, it was he who may have disarmed the missile."

"And now he has come here," Shamir said gently.

"Yes, sir. Meeting with Dr. Abbott."

"It makes one wonder who he has come here to assassinate."

"That part has not been confirmed," Potok said. He sat forward. "But it has made me ask if there is any connection between the hijacked missile and En Gedi."

Shamir nodded. "That too makes for interesting speculation, Lev. What is your assessment in light of what you learned from the telephone intercept and your interrogation of this Russian?" He tapped a finger on Potok's report. "You don't say here."

With Isser the Little you never speculated. You either had the facts, and all of them, or you admitted up front that you didn't know. Now he was asking for a guess. Potok, for all his years in the service, felt just a little uncomfortable. But then the stakes were so high that they couldn't afford not to consider any and every possibility, no matter how farfetched.

"I have a feeling that Rothstein and perhaps Simon Asher were working for the Russians. Their contact was Viktor Voronsky. I think that the Russians know about En Gedi, I think that the hijacked missile was somehow reprogrammed to strike there, and I think that they are planning to try again on June thirtieth."

Shamir was nodding sadly. "What about Dr. Abbott and the NPT?"

"I think she suspects but doesn't know."

"And Mr. McGarvey?"

Potok nodded. "He knows. He would have gotten it from the reprogrammed rocket's guidance system."

"That makes him a very dangerous man as concerns Israel's safety."

"Yes, sir."

"What's he doing here?"

Potok shook his head. "I don't know."

"Nor do you wish to hazard a guess?"

"Not this time."

"I see," Shamir said. "Well, then, find out."

"How far may I take it?" Potok asked, keeping even the slightest inflection out of his voice.

Shamir didn't seem surprised by the direct question, but then Potok had never known the man to show surprise. "If he knows, as you say, from the reprogrammed missile, then the Americans know."

"Yes, sir."

"But they have said nothing. Perhaps he has been sent as an emissary."

"Would they have sent such a man as him on such a mission?"

Shamir shrugged. "Perhaps."

"Then he has come as a friend."

Again Shamir shrugged. "Which places you in an extremely delicate situation. Fully as delicate as Israel finds itself in. Friend or foe, I suspect that soon enough the entire world will be privy to our little secret. It is up to us to keep it a secret for as long as possible, and then to safeguard what we have from attack. Whatever it takes."

After Potok left, Shamir sat for a long time staring out of his fifth-floor window toward the lights of the Shalom Meir Tower a few blocks away. It was the tallest building in Israel. A beacon, he thought, not only for hope as it had been designed, but now for guided missiles as well.

Years ago, or was it centuries, he sometimes wondered, he had come to this city when it was mostly a collection of whitewashed homes, churches, mosques, and a few synagogues, all lorded over by the British. The future then had been very uncertain, as it had again seemed so in 1948 when their fight for independence had come.

So many lives lost, so much blood spilled on both sides, so much senseless destruction, and now it threatened to happen again.

Shamir was an ardent student of history. It seemed at times like these that we were indeed doomed to repeat our mistakes. If the Russians took over the Middle East, this part of the world would surely sink into the dark ages. Sanity and reason would be lost for a very long time to come.

Harry Truman, or had it been one of his successors, had been correct when he'd prophesied that the advent of nuclear weapons meant the abolition of all-out war. No one in their right mind would begin a war that could go nuclear.

But if those weapons, as terrible as they were, no longer existed, what would hold back the horde?

He turned after a long time, picked up the telephone, and started to dial a Washington number, but before the connection was made he hung up. He and the general went back a long way together. But he decided that he didn't want to hear a lie from a friend. He would rather find out the truth himself.

EAST GERMANY

The skies were overcast across much of central Europe. When Arkady Kurshin stepped from his plane and crossed the tarmac into East Berlin's Schönefeld's Airport it was very dark and raining, a chill wind blowing from the northwest. The weather matched his mood. He'd come so close in Kaiserslautern that he'd almost been able to taste his success.

With a growing disbelief he had watched McGarvey simply pulling the plugs on the missile. Even now it was difficult to believe.

Again in Paris he had come close. It would have been so easy to wait until dark, then sneak into McGarvey's apartment and kill him.

This far away the hate still burned strong within him.

On the basis of his Soviet Russian diplomatic passport, one of several he carried, he was passed through customs with no delay. Outside a car and driver were waiting for him. He tossed his single bag in the back and climbed in the front.

The driver, dressed in civilian clothes, said nothing as he pulled out into traffic, nor did he seem inclined to speak, so Kurshin sat back in his seat with his own morose thoughts for the twenty-minute drive out to Friedrichshagen on the Grosser Müggelsee.

Their intelligence about En Gedi was ironclad, Baranov had assured him, as was their information from the Pentagon. Had McGarvey not interfered, the rocket would have launched, and by now he would be on his way back to Moscow a hero, instead of here with his tail between his legs.

"You understand," Baranov had said before Kurshin had crossed the border into Western Europe, "that the price of our failure will be steep. They will know that I have a penetration agent working in their midst.''

''I will not fail, Comrade General,'' Kurshin had promised.

But he had failed. And perhaps this very night he would get his nine ounces—a Russian euphemism for a nine-millimeter bullet in the back of the head.

They skirted the small residential town and on the northwest side of the lake took a narrow dirt track down toward the water's edge, the hills steep here, the pine trees very thick. They were stopped three kilometers off the main road by a pair of KGB guards armed with the new AK74 assault rifles equipped with night vision scopes.

Kurshin had to present his papers. As one of the guards held a flashlight on his face, the other one got in back, opened his suitcase, and took his gun.

''You're late,'' one of them said.

''His plane was delayed,'' the driver explained.

The flashlight was withdrawn and the rear door was slammed. One of the guards was speaking into a walkie-talkie as they continued up the road toward dim lights just now visible through the trees and rain.

Kurshin shifted in his seat so that he could feel his left leg just above the ankle with the toe of his right shoe. The small .32 caliber automatic was still secure in its holster.

Fuck your mother, he thought, using the national expression of disgust, but he wasn't going to let himself be gunned down so easily. If need be, he would kill Baranov and make his escape.

The narrow road opened onto a broad gravel driveway that led up to a large house, almost a mansion, rising out of the side of the hill. They parked in front. Kurshin got out of the car and started to reach in for his bag.

''I'll get that for you,'' the driver said.

Kurshin shrugged and went up to the house, the front door opening for him. Inside the main stairhall he gave his coat to another burly man in civilian clothes, who laid it over the back of a chair and started to pat him down, but Baranov appeared at the head of the broad stairs.

"That will do, Gregori," he said.

The guard stepped back.

"Come, Arkasha," Baranov called down, his voice soft and congenial.

Kurshin went up the stairs and at the top Baranov embraced him, holding him tightly for a long moment or two before kissing him. Then arm in arm they went down the corridor and into a study, a big fire burning in the fireplace across from a comfortable grouping of heavy chairs and couches. The room was book-lined and pleasantly warm.

"Cognac or vodka?" Baranov asked.

"Vodka," Kurshin replied.

Baranov waved him to a seat while he poured their drinks. "It is too bad about Germany, but we are not finished yet." He turned, smiling. "Unless of course you mean to give up and return to Moscow, or perhaps shoot me to death with that little ankle gun of yours."

Kurshin was startled, but he didn't allow it to show.

Baranov laughed as he came across the room and handed him his drink. "Didn't I tell you once, Arkasha, to trust in me? I have friends everywhere. How else do you think I could get out of Moscow unobserved? You simply cannot believe the pressures and restrictions placed on the shoulders of the director of KGB." He laughed again. "But the job has its compensations, and so will you, as you shall soon see."

"Comrade?" Kurshin asked, confused. He felt as if he were sitting next to a high-tension wire. The slightest wrong move on his part and he would be dead.

"You are going to kill McGarvey for me—and for yourself as well, I suspect—and afterward you are going to strike En Gedi, only this time your method will be so spectacular, so completely unexpected, that they will be talking about you for many years to come. With respect, Arkasha. And fear."

15

TEL AVIV

AT FIRST ORRAINE BBOTT WANTED NOTHING TO DO WITH
McGarvey. As she said, he could have been anyone with
some inside knowledge. Even Mossad trying to trick her into
revealing the extent of her own information.

"If I were a Mossad agent, it would have been an extraordinary admission on my part, telling you about En Gedi,"
he'd said.

"If it's true," she'd countered.

"That's what I'm here to find out."

They had left the cocktail lounge early, and McGarvey had
gone up to his room where he cleaned up and changed clothes.
A few minutes before nine he went up to her seventh-floor
room and knocked on the door.

"I want to tell you one thing," she said, letting him in. "I am no spy."

"Neither am I," McGarvey said and he motioned for her to keep silent. For a moment or two she had no idea what he was trying to tell her as he gestured at the ceiling, the drapes, the television set, and the telephone, but then she caught it.

"The room is probably bugged," he mouthed the words.

She nodded her understanding.

"Are you ready for dinner?" he asked out loud.

She was dressed in a simple dark skirt and white silk blouse, sandals on her feet, and only a slight amount of makeup to accent her high cheekbones and wide eyes. She looked freshly scrubbed, almost but not quite innocent. She nodded a little uncertainly. "Here in the hotel?" she asked.

"I thought we'd go for a walk first. It's a nice evening. Afterward you can buy, last time in San Francisco it was my treat, remember?"

She shot him an angry look, but got her purse. They picked up their tail as they crossed the lobby to the front doors, and outside they walked across the broad driveway and headed back into the city, the night pleasantly cool with a nice breeze from the sea.

"Did you call the general?" McGarvey asked when they were well away from the hotel. Traffic was still fairly heavy. The city smelled of car exhaust and something else, something almost exotic.

"No. I didn't think it was too smart under the circumstances."

"They're probably going to kick both of us out of the country by morning," McGarvey said. He didn't bother turning around to see if their tail had followed them from the hotel. He knew the man had. Instead, he kept his eye on the passing cars and trucks, because he had even less doubt that he had been made from the moment he'd shown up at the hotel. The Mossad would be frantically trying to figure out what the hell he was doing here.

Lorraine bridled. "I'll be damned if I'll let them," she snapped. "I'm still an NPT representative, and there are still questions about the incident for which I've received no satisfactory answers."

"This is their country, Dr. Abbott," he said. "And they consider themselves at war. If they want you to leave Israel you'll have to go." He looked closely at her. She was angry, but he could see just a little fear and uncertainty tinged in her eyes. Trotter had told him that she'd done a little work for the Company. But it had mainly been of the variety of keeping an open eye and reporting what she saw. "If and when they ask you to leave, I want you to go without an argument."

She stopped short and faced him. "Who the hell do you think you are?" she demanded.

"At this point, someone who is trying to save your life, Dr. Abbott," he said firmly.

She was taken aback. Her mouth opened.

"There have already been half a dozen lives lost," he told her. "And if you get in the way they won't hesitate to pull the trigger, no matter who you represent . . . or how pretty you are."

This last stung. "Goddamnit . . ." she started to protest angrily, but McGarvey took her arm forcefully and they continued down the street.

"Now, just what is it I'm supposed to be looking for out at En Gedi?" he asked.

"Air vents," she said after a moment. "And the equipment for a laminar airflow installation. If they're storing weapons out there, they'll probably be deep underground." She looked at him. "They'll shoot you."

"I'll take my chances."

"You're crazy if you think you can just sneak in and look around."

"It's called a finesse," McGarvey said. "Now let's get to a very public restaurant. You and I are going to have a loud argument."

EN GEDI

McGarvey pulled the small dark blue Fiat he had stolen from a side street in Tel Aviv to the side of the road and doused the lights. Below in the valley about two miles away was the En Gedi Nuclear Research Station, lit up like a small town along the shore of the Dead Sea. A faint wisp of steam came from the one small cooling tower. Even from this distance he could see some activity within the compound.

If the weapons were stockpiled down there, the Israelis would have been fighting a difficult battle from day one. If they guarded the place too heavily, it would call attention to the fact that something more than research was going on. If they were too lax, it would invite penetration.

Lorraine had put on a convincing performance, raising her voice so loudly that everyone in the restaurant had stopped and looked at them.

She had jumped up and started to leave, but he managed to grab her arm. Immediately she whirled around and slapped him in the face. "You sonofabitch," she shouted, and she stomped off.

McGarvey threw down enough money for their bill and hurried out after her, but she was already halfway down the street. "Then go, bitch," he shouted, and he turned and stormed off in the opposite direction.

In the first sixty seconds the Mossad team who had been watching them was confused. This wasn't what they expected at all. McGarvey had been easily able to shake the one man who'd split off to follow him, had doubled back to an area of apartment buildings, finding the Fiat, and headed out of the city.

His cheek still stung, and he reached up to rub it, a faint smile coming to his lips. He had told her to go directly back to the hotel and start packing without a word to anyone. He hoped that she had done just that.

He had been told a long time ago that if getting in the back door was impossible, you could always try the front door. The trick was in coming up with the key.

Trotter had wanted him to confirm the existence of the weapons stockpile here. Going through the back door could get him killed, so he'd been provided with a key. It had come with his weapon in the diplomatic pouch.

He pulled the plastic NPT Inspection Service badge out of his pocket, clipped it to his lapel, and switched on the headlights. He pulled away from the side of the road and headed down into the valley.

For most of the way he drove slowly but steadily, keeping the car in a straight line. It was getting late, nearly midnight, and there was no other traffic on the road.

At the bottom the highway curved south. A broad road led east for two hundred yards to the research facility's main gate. Anything that moved on the highway in the vicinity of the entrance road would be carefully monitored. Guard towers rose every three hundred yards or so from the inner fence.

As he neared the access road, McGarvey sped up a little, then stabbed on his brakes as he swung the car left, nearly running it off the highway. When he finally got the car straightened out, he turned onto the entrance road and shakily drove toward the main gate, swerving from side to side, alternately hitting his brake and the accelerator.

Two men came out of the gatehouse and watched him. A second later one of them hurried back inside while the other stepped around the barrier and started to wave his arms.

McGarvey slumped over the wheel at the last moment and let the car roll slowly the last few yards, crashing it gently into the fence, his head bouncing off the wheel and then lying on the horn.

Someone was shouting something, and a moment later the car door was yanked open and he was pulled away from the steering wheel. He let his eyes flutter.

"Heart . . ." he stammered. "It's my . . . heart."

Already there were four or five armed guards surrounding the car and others coming from the compound on the run.

Hands were fumbling at the plastic badge on his lapel. McGarvey opened his eyes and looked up into the concerned face of a young soldier.

"Please help me," he whispered. "My heart . . ."

"It's all right, take it easy now," the soldier said. He shouted something in Hebrew over his shoulder. McGarvey thought he caught the English letters NPT, and the guard turned back to him. "An ambulance is coming. Just take it easy. Do you have any medicine with you?"

"No . . . nothing," McGarvey whispered, trying to grab for the young man's tunic. "Help me . . ."

"Easy now," the soldier said. He took McGarvey's NPT badge and handed it out to one of the other soldiers, who said something in Hebrew.

Within ninety seconds the ambulance, siren blaring and blue lights flashing, came from within the facility, eased through the gate, and pulled up alongside McGarvey's car.

"I don't want to die," McGarvey whispered.

"You'll be okay now," the soldier said. "Just lie back and relax."

The soldier moved aside as two ambulance attendants rushed over. One of them opened McGarvey's shirt and listened to his chest with a stethoscope.

"It hurts," McGarvey whispered.

"You got chest pains?" the attendant asked. "Your heart sounds good."

"Christ, it hurts . . . hard to breathe."

"Let's get him to the clinic," the attendant shouted.

With the help of the other attendant and one of the soldiers, they eased McGarvey out of the car, placed him on the gurney, and started to strap him down, but he struggled up against them.

"No . . . God no . . . !"

"All right, no straps," the attendant said, and they rolled him over to the ambulance and put him inside. One of them got in the back and the other hurried around front and climbed in behind the wheel.

As they started to move, the attendant placed a blood pressure cuff on McGarvey's left arm. McGarvey could see out the windows as they passed through the inner gate. He reached around to the small of his back, grabbed his gun, and, pushing the attendant back, sat up, bringing his pistol out.

"I don't want to kill you," he said.

16

EN GEDI

THE AMBULANCE ATTENDANT STARED OPENMOUTHED IN stunned disbelief as McGarvey yanked off the blood pressure cuff and swung his legs over the side of the gurney.

"If you cooperate with me, I promise that no one will get hurt."

The driver had no idea yet that anything was wrong. The attendant with McGarvey hadn't uttered a sound.

"Take off your uniform," McGarvey said urgently. "Now."

The attendant hurriedly began unbuttoning his white tunic as McGarvey twisted around, opened the door to the cab, and placed the barrel of his pistol at the base of the driver's head. He could see through the windshield that they were approaching the dispensary. At the restaurant, Lorraine had drawn him a quick sketch map of the facility. The air vents and airflow equipment, if they existed, would most likely be located somewhere in the vicinity of the secondary power-generation building. She had vaguely remembered something from one of her early inspection tours. There would be procedures, she'd been told, should the reactor building itself ever have to be sealed. The people inside would need an emergency air supply.

"There has been an accident in the air vent building," McGarvey said softly.

The driver jerked as if he had been shot. He started to turn around but McGarvey jammed the gun harder against his neck.

"I don't want to kill you or your partner, but I will unless you cooperate with me completely. Do you understand?"

The driver was swallowing hard, but he nodded. The attendant with McGarvey had the tunic off and was removing his trousers.

"Slow it down and turn here."

"I don't know what you're talking about," the driver stuttered. "What air vent building? I don't . . ."

"I think you do," McGarvey said. "It will be a big building near the power generators."

"It's G-3 between the reactor building and the cooling tower," the attendant in back said. "For God's sake, do as he says, Misha."

The driver had slowed down. They were barely twenty yards from the back of the dispensary. He said something in Hebrew.

McGarvey cocked the Walther's hammer. "Now," he demanded.

"Yes, yes, I'm doing it," the driver cried, and he slowed even further as he hauled the ambulance around in a tight circle.

"Cut the siren," McGarvey ordered.

The driver did as he was told.

"Nice and easy now. And I don't want you to stop for anything, anything whatsoever, do you understand this?"

"Yes, sir."

McGarvey turned back to the other attendant who was now sitting in his shorts and boots. "I want some surgical tape and a packet of gauze," he said.

As the attendant was rummaging in the ambulance's supplies, McGarvey pulled off his jacket and donned the white tunic, buttoning it up over his shirt, while keeping an eye on the driver.

It wouldn't take very long now for security to realize that something was wrong and issue an all-out alert.

The attendant's trousers were a little small, but they were baggy so he was able to pull them on over his own trousers. He got up from the gurney and made the attendant take his place, lying face up.

"We're coming up on it now," the driver called back. "Fifty meters."

"Can you drive inside the building?"

"I don't know."

"Try," McGarvey said. He turned back to the other attendant and quickly strapped him down to the gurney, stuffing a wad of gauze into the man's mouth, and then taping more gauze over his face as if he had been severely injured. The ambulance was beginning to slow down again. He grabbed a stethoscope, looped it around his neck, and then crawled forward into the seat next to the driver. The man was highly agitated, his eyes bulging practically out of their sockets with fear.

So far the alarm had not sounded. But it wouldn't be much longer now.

They were approaching a large, three-story metal building, two squat stacks rising five feet above the flat roofline. There were no windows, but on the front and side walls were large service doors, both of them closed, flanked by smaller doors.

The building could have housed almost anything and was probably used as a warehouse for parts and equipment even if it also housed the laminar airflow equipment that Lorraine Abbott had described for him.

"They would have to hide it out in the open so that no

one from the NPT Inspection Service would know it for what it was,'' she'd said bitterly.

"But you had no reason to be suspicious."

She smiled wanly. "You forget, that's our job. But I guess we were blinded by the fact that Israel was operating a research reactor that we all thought was a fuel breeder." She shook her head. "Which it is, of course. But we never thought to look for evidence of a weapons stockpile."

"That's what I'll try to find out," he said.

"Goddamnit, they'll shoot you," she insisted again.

He had grinned. "If they do, it'll prove that whatever they're trying to hide is damned important."

"You're crazy."

"I've got a job to do," he'd said.

"Pull up at the front service door," McGarvey told the driver. "And hit your siren."

The driver nervously swung the ambulance around and stopped in front of the door. He flipped the switch for the siren, the bellowing whoops echoing and reechoing off the buildings.

A man in battle fatigues came out of one of the smaller doors.

"We have an emergency," McGarvey instructed the driver, jamming the barrel of his gun into the man's side.

The driver hung out the open window and said something in Hebrew. The soldier, who was armed, shouted something back. McGarvey jammed the pistol harder into the driver's side and the man shouted something else.

A moment later the soldier went back into the building, and the big service door began to open.

"What did he say?"

"He said he knows of no emergency here. But he will admit us, only just within the loading area. He has to get his sergeant."

"All right, listen to me now," McGarvey said. "We're going to drive right through the loading area, all the way to the back of the building if we can get that far."

"They'll open fire . . ."

"Not at an ambulance. Besides, my gun is a hell of a lot closer to you than theirs. Do you understand me?"

The young driver was torn between two choices, both of which frightened him half out of his mind. But what McGarvey said was true. He nodded.

When the door was three-quarters open the soldier beckoned for them to drive through.

"Now," McGarvey said.

The driver jammed his foot to the floor and the ambulance shot forward past the startled soldier into the cavernous building. Big lights hung from the ceiling illuminating the front third of the interior which was obviously used as a storage area. Tall crates were stacked, in some cases nearly up to the rafters, on long pallets that formed rows and lanes. To the left they passed four jeeps and two canvas-covered trucks, backed up against the wall, and then the lane swung sharply right, deeper into the bowels of the building, darkness closing around them.

McGarvey reached over and shut off the ambulance's siren, and suddenly he could hear a loud Klaxon blaring. Within the building. The alarm had definitely been raised.

They sped past what appeared to McGarvey to be electrical distribution cabinets, something Lorraine had said he might see, and then the lane suddenly turned left again, the driver nearly missing his turn. The ambulance skidded, slamming sideways into one of the cabinets with a huge shower of sparks, before the driver regained control.

The lane immediately opened into a broad, dimly lit area where what appeared to be a series of wide air vents jutted from the concrete floor.

"Bingo," McGarvey said.

Two soldiers in battle fatigues came out of the shadows in a dead run, their Uzi submachine guns unslung.

The driver slammed on the brakes, hauling the ambulance around to the right, sending it into another skid at the same moment the soldiers opened fire.

"Down," McGarvey shouted, pulling the terrified young driver below the level of the windshield that erupted in a shower of glass.

The ambulance shuddered to a complete stop against one of the air vents, knocking it askew. McGarvey shoved open his door and leapt out, keeping low as he raced around the half-crumpled vent into the darkness.

"Don't shoot! Don't shoot!" he shouted as he ran.

A burst of automatic weapons fire ricocheted off the concrete floor ten feet behind him.

McGarvey pulled up behind another of the air vents, yanked open the screen that covered the intake, and stuck his head inside. The darkness was unfathomable. But he could hear machinery running, and he could definitely feel that the vent was drawing air down into the shaft, not the other way around.

The warehouse was suddenly in silence as the Klaxon was cut off. To the left he heard someone running, and then he stopped. Someone shouted something in Hebrew, and another man farther away answered. More soldiers were pounding in from the front of the building.

McGarvey figured he had less than a half a minute remaining. He had found most of what he had come looking for. But not all of it.

If the weapons are stockpiled underground, they will be very deep. Perhaps two hundred feet or more, Lorraine Abbott had told him.

He ejected a round from his Walther, and then stuffing the gun back in his pocket, he dropped the bullet down into the air shaft, cocking an ear to listen for when it hit bottom, counting the seconds silently.

Five seconds later he heard the faint clatter as the bullet hit bottom. Three hundred feet, give or take, he calculated. Deep. Deep enough for a weapons stockpile.

Now was the time to save his own life. He turned away in time to see the stock of an Uzi swinging in a tight arc toward him but not in time to protect his head as it connected with a sickening crunch and he went down.

17

CIA HEADQUARTERS

IT WAS JUST SIX IN THE EVENING WHEN TROTTER DECIDED there was little else he could accomplish from his office. So far they'd heard nothing from McGarvey, but then he hadn't expected much of anything this soon.

Turning off the light in his third-floor office he got his briefcase and stepped outside. His secretary had left a half hour earlier and the corridors were already settling down for the night shift.

Three doors down, he punched in a five-digit access code which admitted him into the Operations Center. There the OD monitored all incoming calls and messages for operations that were currently on the critical list. It was his job to make a preliminary evaluation and then contact the proper section if an immediate follow-up was needed.

Trotter had cut his teeth in this section in the early days, and still maintained an interest in the case officers who were assigned OD duty. He made it a point to stop in on a regular basis to talk with them, get to know them on a personal basis. Besides, he was worried about McGarvey. Not so much for the man's physical safety, he'd shown that he was capable of taking care of himself, but because of the kinds of hell McGarvey always seemed to leave in his wake. This time they were dealing with a sensitive ally.

Tom Dunbar, the early shift OD, looked up from his console when Trotter came in. He was a no-nonsense Harvard graduate who at the age of thirty had already shown his mettle and finesse in two important foreign postings. He would be rotated to the Russian Desk within the next few months preparatory to an assignment in Moscow. The big one.

"Slumming tonight, John?" he asked.

"I'm on my way home. Maybe put on a steak, have a couple of beers," Trotter said. He'd lived alone in a big house across the river since his wife had died several years ago. In actuality he intended to have a glass of wine and perhaps a sandwich and then go to bed.

"Sure, rub it in. I'm stuck here until midnight, and I've got to be back first thing in the morning for a physical."

"No rest for the wicked," Trotter quipped. "Anything yet on Standhope?"

STANDHOPE was the computer-generated operational name for McGarvey's assignment to Israel. But it was in the blind. Only a very few people within the Agency actually knew the details. This number did not extend to the OD, who merely worked from a short list. If anything at all came in he had a list of four people to call: the general, the Agency's general counsel, the DDO, and of course Trotter.

"Nothing in the last half hour," Dunbar said. "Was there anything from last night that I should know about?"

Trotter shook his head. "Probably not. It's just getting started."

"Your baby?"

"In a manner of speaking. Anyway, I'll be home if anything does come up. I'd appreciate a call no matter what.''

"Sure thing," Dunbar said. "Enjoy your steak."

"Thanks, I will," Trotter said, and he left, taking the elevator down to the ground floor, turning in his security badge with the guards at the door and heading across the parking lot to his car.

It was always like this, he thought, during the first critical hours of an operation. This time, however, it was worse because not only were they spying on a friendly nation, they were using a free lance to do it. The general had never really answered his direct question of what the Agency's position would be if the operation were to fall apart. "We'll see" was the best he'd been able to get.

He had just reached his car when someone came running across the parking lot from the main entrance.

"Mr. Trotter. Hold up, sir," the man called out. He was one of the security people from the front desk.

Trotter automatically reached up to his lapel to see if he had forgotten to turn in his badge, but he remembered that he had.

"It's the general, sir," the guard puffed. "He wants you upstairs on the double."

Something clutched at Trotter's gut, and he hurried back across the parking lot.

"I just received a call from Lorraine Abbott," the DCI said when Trotter walked in.

Howard Ryan, the Agency's general counsel, was seated across the desk from Murphy.

"Has McGarvey made contact with her?" Trotter asked.

The DCI motioned him to a seat next to Ryan. "Yes, and she sounded plenty upset."

"It's just two in the morning over there, what's happened?"

"Possible big trouble for us," Ryan answered.

"Evidently he's on his way out to En Gedi," the general said. "Dr. Abbott told me that he arranged a little show for their Mossad tails and managed to break free."

It sounded like Kirk. "And she hasn't heard from him since?"

"That's right," the general said. "He left several hours ago, and she thinks there is a very good possibility that he was arrested or even shot."

"Surely she wasn't calling from a hotel phone?"

"No. A public phone on the street. They might come up with the number, but they won't get any further than that."

"Well, we gave him the assignment," Trotter said. "It's going to be up to us to get him out of there if he is in trouble."

The general's eyes narrowed. He was in one of his dangerous moods. "You explain it to him, Howard."

"We're going to have to deny him if he was actually arrested while on military property," the counsel said.

"Goddamnit . . ." Trotter started, but Murphy held him off.

"He's armed, I assume," Ryan said.

"We sent it over in the diplomatic bag. But remember what he did for us, and the Israelis, in Germany. Let's just not forget that now. And we did send him on this assignment, after all. We owe him, sir."

"What do you suggest?" the general asked coolly.

"You're personal friends with Isser Shamir. Call him."

"And tell him what?"

"That a mistake has been made and we'd like our man back, in one piece."

"He'll naturally ask what McGarvey was doing at En Gedi."

"Lie to him," Trotter said with a straight face.

The DCI and Ryan exchanged glances. "Short of that, John. Let's say that there was some compelling reason that made such a call impossible. Then what?"

Trotter almost asked what could be so compelling, but he held the question in check. "Short of that, I would suggest that we take this over to the President. Immediately this evening. He can call the PM. They owe us. They started spying on us first."

The general had been hunched forward over his desk, his

shirtsleeves rolled up, exposing his thick forearms. He leaned back now, settling his bulk into the big leather chair. He nodded.

"Let's say we get him out of there, John. What's next?"

"Knowing McGarvey, if he actually got into the facility, he will have found out what we asked him to find for us. If it's positive, if he can confirm the existence of their weapons stockpile, then we go ahead with our original plan. It's a safe bet that Baranov won't back off."

Again the general and Ryan exchanged glances.

"You're talking about bait here, aren't you," Ryan said softly.

It was the same thing McGarvey had said. And it was true, of course. But it was the business.

"I'm talking about using a resource to its best advantage," he said without blinking.

The DCI nodded again. "If he was identified in Germany, they'll pull out all the stops to get him."

"Yes, sir."

Again the DCI glanced at Ryan. "I'll see what can be done. But maybe we've made a mistake. Maybe we should have told the Israelis that the Pershing had been targeted on En Gedi."

"It would have tipped our hand," Ryan said.

"Springing McGarvey isn't going to do us, or him, much good either."

TEL AVIV

Lorraine Abbott sat in her darkened hotel room chain-smoking cigarettes and looking out across the dark Mediterranean. Although it was a clear night the horizon was an indistinct blackness. Way out at sea she thought she could see the lights of some slow-moving ship, but then it disappeared, her night vision destroyed as she lit another cigarette.

For the tenth time she told herself that she had done the right thing by telephoning Murphy on the special number he had given her more than three years ago. He had sounded noncommittal—of course, it was an open line—but he had told her to return immediately to her hotel and sit tight. He would look into things and get back to her.

California just now seemed like a long way off. Her first mistake had been sticking it out here in Tel Aviv. She had won points with Mark O'Sheay, the NPT Inspection Service operations director, but she hadn't accomplished a thing by remaining.

Her second mistake had been listening to McGarvey. He was an arrogant, conceited, macho sonofabitch. That had been her first impression, and nothing that had happened since had changed her mind.

And he was a spy. Not her variety, not simply an eavesdropper or an observer, but a legitimate gun-carrying spy. A James Bond in Rambo warpaint. It made her sick to think that she had gone along with him. Not only had he seriously jeopardized her position here in Israel, it was possible that she would be asked to resign from her NPT position, which, though it wasn't crucial to her career, provided her with . . . what?

She turned that thought over in her mind. Burnout, her department head called it. "You can jaunt off all over the world from time to time. It's better than reading science fiction. Recharges your batteries."

What if they had shot him, the same thought that had driven her to call the general invaded her consciousness again, and her hand shook as she stubbed out the cigarette in the overflowing ashtray.

Someone was at the door. She thought she heard a key grating in the lock. She turned around at the same moment the door burst open, snapping the chain, and an instant later the room lights came on.

Two men, guns drawn, were standing there.

Lorraine had raised a hand to her mouth in shock, but she found that she couldn't do anything else, not even cry for help.

Two other men crowded into the room, one of them checking the bathroom, and the other looking in the closet, the chest of drawers, and even under the bed.

"Dr. Lorraine Abbott?" one of the gunmen asked in English.

She nodded, finally finding her voice. "Who are you?"

"Military Intelligence, Doctor," the gunman said. "You are under arrest."

"Arrest? My God, on what charge?"

"Espionage."

A pale blue Volkswagen camper van was parked at the edge of the beach across the street from the Uri Dan Hotel. Two young clerks from the Hungarian Embassy were in the front, making out, his hand beneath her sweater, cupping a breast.

In the back, Arkady Kurshin was watching the hotel's front entrance through binoculars. McGarvey was currently away from the hotel. He'd been seen leaving earlier in the company of a so far unidentified blond woman. The woman had returned soon afterward, had left once, and had come back again.

"Who is she?" he'd asked the man seated next to him.

"I don't know yet," Aleksei Piotrovsky, KGB's number-two man in Israel, said. "But I do know those pricks who came up in that gray Mercedes."

"Mossad?"

"No, AMAN. The question is, what the hell are they doing here at this hour of the morning?"

It could be because of McGarvey, Kurshin thought. The moment they'd been informed that he was here in Tel Aviv, he had flown directly from his hotel in Rome where he'd been waiting for further word from Baranov.

"There can only be one reason for him to be in Israel at this point," Baranov had explained. "It's because of the Pershing. They know we were going after En Gedi. He's come to find out for himself."

"Either that or tell the Israelis."

"I don't think so," Baranov had replied. "But it gives you the easy opportunity to take him out. Don't miss."

"Here they come," Piotrovsky said.

Kurshin raised his binoculars in time to see the four AMAN plainclothes officers emerge from the hotel. They had brought the blond woman with them, her hands held curiously stiff behind her back.

It took him several seconds to realize that she was handcuffed. They had arrested her. He lowered the binoculars again. What had they stumbled across here? And where was McGarvey?

"I want to know who that woman is, within the hour," he said.

Piotrovsky glanced over at him and swallowed. This was one man, he thought, who was to be placated at all costs. "Yes, Comrade," he said.

18

THE WHITE HOUSE

ROLAND MURPHY HAD BEEN IN PLENTY OF TOUGH SPOTS IN his life, but he'd never been known to walk away from a fight, or hang his head in submission no matter how he had conducted the battle.

This was the day, however, when the shit was very likely to hit the fan. He had taken a calculated risk, and it was about to come back and bite him.

It was just seven-thirty. The president had agreed to see him in his study. He rose from behind his desk when Murphy came in. He was a large man, who like the general preferred rolled-up shirtsleeves and loosened ties and had some years ago served a brief term as director of the CIA. He was a no-nonsense man. "Harry S told his people that the buck stopped at his desk. I tell mine that this is where the bullshit stops!''

"We have a developing problem on our hands, Mr. President, that could turn into something very political.''

"You wouldn't be here at this hour of the evening if it wasn't serious, General,'' the president said wryly. "Coffee?''

"I'd prefer something a little stronger this time.''

The president's thick eyebrows rose. "This *is* serious,'' he said. He poured them both a good measure of Jack Daniel's.

Murphy knocked his back, set the glass down, and then extracted a group of satellite reconnaissance photographs from his briefcase and laid them out on the desk.

The president set his whiskey aside, picked up a large magnifying glass, and hunched over the photographs, studying each one carefully. "En Gedi?'' he asked.

"Yes, sir. These were taken shortly after midnight, local time. They showed up on my desk an hour ago.''

"They're having another alert over there?''

"Someone may have been injured. That's an ambulance at the main gate in the first frames. It headed for the dispensary, but then made a turn and went back across the facility, entering what we have been identifying to this point as a warehouse.''

"To this point?'' the president asked.

"We now believe that the building may contain something else. Something that might point to another purpose for the facility's existence.''

"Namely as a weapons depot?''

"We now believe that is very likely.''

"The Russians know about it, as well, otherwise they wouldn't have pulled that jackass missile stunt,'' the president said, shaking his head. "You know, General, I've been behind this desk for one hundred sixty-three days, but it only took half that long for me to lose my capacity for surprise.'' He glanced down at the photographs. "This is no coincidence.''

"No, sir, it is not," Murphy said. "But I'm afraid I've made a mistake that could cost us."

"Welcome to the club," the president said not unkindly. "What sort of a mess have we gotten ourselves into this time?"

Murphy extracted a thin, buff-colored file folder from his briefcase. It was stamped top and bottom Top Secret, a pair of orange stripes diagonally across the cover, beneath which was stamped the legend: STANDHOPE. He passed it across to the president, who made no immediate move to open it.

"We believe that the previous En Gedi incident may have involved a penetration of the facility by the Russians, which led them to hijack the Pershing."

"Yes, we've gone over that."

"We also have very good reason to believe that the Russians have a knowledgeable source within the Pentagon. Someone who would have had the data about the Pershing's Radar Area Guidance system."

"The one you are calling Feliks."

"Yes, sir," Murphy said, girding himself. "But the impetus for our investigation is and always has been whether or not the Israelis are in actuality maintaining a stockpile of battle-ready nuclear weapons. At En Gedi, or anywhere else for that matter."

"Your rationale for believing that Valentin Baranov is personally involved."

"Yes, Mr. President."

"He brought down your predecessor. Is this a vendetta?"

"No, Mr. President, it certainly is not," Murphy said, careful to keep his voice as inflectionless as possible, letting the meaning of his words convey his anger.

"Sorry, Roland," the president said. "But get on with it."

"We need to know what is going on at En Gedi."

"You have sent someone there?" the president asked sharply. "And you think he has been arrested?" He glanced again at the photographs.

"It's most likely that he has been arrested, yes, Mr. President."

The president stared long and hard at him. But when Murphy started to say something, the president shook his head. "Wait."

He put on his glasses, opened the STANDHOPE file, and began reading. It took him less than five minutes; like Jack Kennedy, he was a speed reader. When he looked up and took off his glasses, there was an angry set to his mouth.

"Yes, General," he said. "You definitely have made a mistake. I would never have authorized this."

"Then we would have been stopped in our tracks. Baranov is almost certainly going to try again." Murphy had decided that no matter what happened he was not going to back down. Presidents came and went, the problems remained. If he wanted the resignation of his DCI, he would have it, but Murphy was not going to cower.

"I could have your ass for this," the president said coldly. "But I'm probably just as guilty. I should have telephoned Peres and told him about the Pershing. So you see, General, you are not the only one to make a mistake."

No answer was expected.

"What do we do about it, Roland?"

"I need your authority to call Isser Shamir and tell him what we know," Murphy said.

"The timing is off, he'll know that."

"I'll lie. We weren't certain until this moment."

"You want him to release McGarvey, a lone ranger who is in possession of Israel's most vital state secret?"

"Yes, sir."

"Why should he do that for us?"

"Because of Baranov's continued threat. We mean to set McGarvey after Feliks with the hope that it will force Baranov's hand and pull Arkady Kurshin out of hiding. At the very least it may delay another strike against En Gedi, possibly giving the Israelis enough time to move their weapons."

"You'll invite the Mossad to participate in this investigation?" the president asked.

"Naturally," Murphy said, although until this moment the thought hadn't occurred to him.

"We have our sensitive secrets as well, Roland," the president said with a dangerous edge to his voice.

"It will be a tightly controlled operation."

The president closed the STANDHOPE file and sat back in his chair. He finished his drink. "McGarvey was involved with Baranov the last time, wasn't he?"

"Yes, sir."

"Baranov would naturally have a grudge against him."

Murphy nodded.

"If the Russians succeed this time the entire Middle East could fall. At the very least the entire region would become embroiled in an all-out war." The president gathered up the photographs and STANDHOPE file and handed them back to Murphy. "You have my authorization, Roland. Make your call to Shamir. Let's just hope that this doesn't blow up too badly, because a lot of people will start getting killed."

CIA HEADQUARTERS

Isser Shamir was an extremely early riser. Murphy knew that for a fact. The two of them went way back together, and when they'd both been promoted to head their respective secret intelligence services, they had continued their warm relationship. Shamir had even been Murphy's house guest on a visit to Washington a few years ago. He was up every morning before five, making his own tea and then taking a long walk.

Even so, Murphy held off calling until well after ten o'clock, making it after six in the morning in Tel Aviv. He wanted Shamir to be well rested and wide awake.

He telephoned Shamir's blind number. The director of the Mossad answered on the first ring, and Murphy would forever be left with the impression that the man had been waiting for the call.

"Do you know who this is?" Murphy asked.

"Yes," Shamir answered.

"Let's go over."

In this instance, the Israelis were using American-made telephone encryption equipment, as they had begun to do nearly ten years ago, like the secret services of a half-dozen other allies.

"Good morning, Isser," Murphy said when the switch had been made. "Can you hear me all right?"

"Yes, just fine, General. How is the weather in Washington?"

"It's warming up."

Shamir chuckled. "Here as well."

There was no doubt in either man's mind that they were speaking about the same subject, and it wasn't the weather.

"There has been another incident at En Gedi," Murphy said.

"We were hoping for cloud cover, but then we cannot have everything."

"I'd like to propose a trade," Murphy said, getting right to it.

"Yes, I am listening."

"I will give you some information, and then you will give me something of equal importance." At this point there was no ironclad guarantee that McGarvey had been arrested, or, if he had that he was still alive. But all the signs pointed toward something happening out there at the same time Lorraine Abbott had said he was there. If there was one thing Murphy did not believe in, it was coincidences.

"We always appreciate anything that you can do for us," Shamir said noncommittally.

"You were aware, of course, of our recent troubles in West Germany involving a nuclear-armed Pershing missile."

"Of course."

"We've just learned that the rocket had been reprogrammed. Its target, which it would have almost certainly reached had it actually been launched, was En Gedi."

"I see," Shamir said, and even in those two words Murphy could hear the man's surprise.

"The man who stopped the launch, at great risk to his life, was one of our people."

"A true hero."

"His name is Kirk McGarvey. And at this moment he is there in Israel."

"Yes, we know this."

"We need him back in Washington, Isser."

"What is he doing here, General?" Shamir asked pointedly.

It was time now, Murphy thought. To every operation came moments of truth, sometimes so stunning they seemed larger than life.

"We *know,* Isser. He was sent to confirm . . ."

"To spy on Israel, is that what you are telling me? Is that what you meant to say? Is that exactly your meaning now?"

"Let's stop screwing around," Murphy snapped. "Here is the deal."

"I'm listening."

"The Russians broke in out there and almost certainly know what's going on. It's the only reason they would have gone to such extraordinary lengths, to steal a Pershing and reprogram it. The operation is, we believe, being handled by Valentin Baranov, and he won't stop, you know this. We also believe that he has an agent highly placed within the Pentagon. We would like McGarvey back here to find him. We would be willing, under the circumstances, to make this a joint operation. It would be to both our interests."

The line was silent.

"Do I make myself clear?"

"Perfectly, General," Shamir said distantly. "I will have to take this up with my . . . superiors. I assume you have or will be doing the same?"

"The president is waiting for a call from Mr. Peres, if it comes to that. But I believe we can handle this among ourselves."

"I will see what can be done," Shamir said. "But there will be at least one condition that we will insist upon. The NPT must be kept out of this. Completely."

"I don't understand . . ."

"Dr. Abbott was arrested earlier this morning by AMAN on a charge of espionage."

"Oh, Jesus Christ," Murphy swore softly.

"If you say so," Shamir said.

19

TEL AVIV

THE ROOM WAS LARGE, THE BARE WALLS AND CEILING WHITE-washed, the floors tiled so that sounds seemed sharp and angular. McGarvey sat in a chair in the middle of the room. His five interrogators sat behind or perched on the edge of a long table, facing him.

It was dawn finally and his head was splitting. He suspected they were in a Mossad safehouse somewhere in or near Tel Aviv. From time to time he could hear the sounds of traffic, and once he thought he might have heard a ship's whistle from a long way off.

Lev Potok got up and came over to McGarvey. He had been the toughest of the interrogators, his face was now screwed up in a grimace of disgust. "You are an assassin,

McGarvey, this much we know for certain. What we would like to know is who you planned on killing out there.''

"No one," McGarvey said softly, relaxing, saving his strength. By now Lorraine Abbott would have realized that something had gone wrong and would have called the general.

"Then what were you doing with an NPT identification badge and a gun? Can you tell me this?''

"Not yet," McGarvey replied, giving the same answer he'd given all night. It would be up to the Agency to decide what to tell the Israelis. He had gotten the information they'd wanted.

"Not yet," Potok said. "It is a bullshit answer. What does this mean?''

"You'll find out in due course.''

Potok suddenly swung around and slapped McGarvey in the face with his open hand, the blow rocking McGarvey backward, nearly tipping the chair over.

"Talk to me, you bastard, or you'll never leave this room alive," Potok shouted.

McGarvey shook his head to clear the fuzziness. He reached up with his right hand and touched his upper lip. His fingers came away bloody.

"I'll tell you this much," he said. "If you do that again, *you* won't leave this room alive.''

Potok wanted to come after him, McGarvey could see that much in his eyes. But there was something else there as well, and it wasn't fear.

"Lev," one of the men at the table said gently.

Potok turned away and went back to the table, where he hesitated for a moment, but then turned around again to face McGarvey. He leaned against the table.

"We know quite a bit about you, McGarvey," the Israeli said, calm again for the moment. "For instance, we know that you once worked for the CIA, and that you were, until a couple of years ago, in retirement in Switzerland. What has happened since?''

"I moved to Paris.''

"Yes, and what were you doing in Germany just last week?"

McGarvey said nothing.

Potok shook his head. "We have reason to suspect that the Pershing missile which you so valiantly disarmed was aimed at us. For that we thank you. We are not the enemy."

"If you know or have guessed that much, then you know that I'm not the enemy either."

"Then why did you come to Israel, Mr. McGarvey? You came to spy, I think, and not to kill anyone. But why? Are you a free lance these days, or has the CIA rehired you?"

"I can't tell you that yet."

Potok threw up his hands in disgust. "You are treading on exceedingly dangerous grounds with us. In Israel we shoot spies."

"We might have to start shooting yours then as well," McGarvey retorted. It had been Israel's big embarrassment that their operation to steal U.S. cruise missile plans had been discovered by the FBI. It had been called a "maverick" operation by Jerusalem, a statement that no one believed, but that everyone could live with.

Potok was getting worked up again. "Everybody out of the room," he ordered.

The others looked up at him in surprise.

"We can't do that, Lev," one of them said.

"That's a direct order, Abraham; you know what's at stake here. Out. All of you!"

The man started to say something in Hebew, but Potok cut him off.

"Now!" he shouted.

"All right," the man said, and he got up and left the room with the other three without a backward glance.

When the door closed Potok managed a tight little smile. He reached over and shut off the tape recorder. "Now it is just you and I."

McGarvey did not want to hurt the man who was only doing his job the best he knew how. His back was against the wall. Twice in barely a week Israel's most important secret had been compromised. First by the Russians and now by the CIA. But McGarvey wasn't going to simply sit back and take whatever the Mossad wanted to do to him. He tensed.

"Tell me about your relationship with Dr. Abbott, are you fucking her?" Potok asked, the question completely unexpected.

"What are you talking about?

"She was under surveillance. When you and she pulled your little trick so that you could break out, she was arrested. Right now her main concern seems to be your well-being."

McGarvey was careful to show no reaction. Had she had the time to call the general? If not, it would be up to Trotter to realize that something had gone wrong and to blow the whistle. But that could take time.

"She has nothing to do with this," he said.

"Ah, your concern is equally touching. But the fact of the matter is that she does have something very much to do with this. Enough for our charge of espionage against her to stick in court. But I asked you a question. Are you fucking her?"

"Up your ass."

Potok snatched up a pistol from the table and pointed it directly at McGarvey's head. "One question. Yes or no?"

"You will have a hard time justifying my death, Major Potok," McGarvey said, revealing for the first time that he knew who and what Potok was.

"You were shot trying to escape."

"No," McGarvey said. He folded his hands on his lap and crossed his legs.

Potok cocked the pistol's hammer, his aim never wavering. "How does it feel to have the tables reversed, assassin? No one will mourn your passing, I think."

The door opened. Potok's gaze shifted beyond McGarvey. Liebowitz said something in Hebrew, his tone definitely urgent.

Potok seemed to waver.

Liebowitz said something else.

Slowly Potok's gun hand came down. He uncocked the

pistol, looked bleakly at McGarvey for several long seconds, and then left the room.

MOSSAD HEADQUARTERS

Potok sat in stunned silence across the desk from Isser Shamir. What he had just been told confirmed their worst fears and suspicions. The Russians definitely knew about En Gedi and they were going to destroy the place at all costs. June thirtieth was the date.

"As I said before, Israel is in a delicate position," Shamir continued. "We cannot bring diplomatic pressures to bear without admitting the truth."

"All the work . . . all the years, the security."

Shamir shook his leonine head, his eyes sad. "Haven't you learned by now that trying to hold a secret is more difficult than trying to hold water in your hands? Ultimately impossible."

"Then the weapons must be moved."

"I agree. But this will take time, which you and Mr. McGarvey will provide for us."

Potok sat forward. "What?"

"The Russians apparently have a source within the Pentagon, someone the CIA has code-named Feliks. You and Mr. McGarvey are going to return to Washington to find this leak and plug it."

Potok was shaking his head in disbelief. "I don't understand . . ."

"The information that the Russians needed to reprogram the Pershing missile to strike En Gedi came from this Pentagon source."

"Surely they won't try to steal another missile," Potok argued. "Every American installation in the world will be watching for just such an attempt."

"Perhaps you are right, Lev, perhaps not. The real issue, however, is somewhat more complicated. Valentin Baranov has planned this strike. Your Mr. McGarvey stopped him two years ago. Once he learns that McGarvey is again trying to interfere with one of his operations, the Russians will almost certainly go after him.''

"He will be a marked man.''

"Yes, but a man not to be underestimated. Once the Russians are drawn out, it will be up to the two of you to stop them.''

"I'm to work with him, then?''

"For him,'' Shamir corrected. "It is a strange world, isn't it?''

JERUSALEM: THE HUNGARIAN EMBASSY

Kurshin could hardly believe his ears. He was seated in the embassy's basement communications room where he had come to find out about the American bitch, Lorraine Abbott, and now he was being told that she and McGarvey had left Israel.

"You are sure?'' he asked.

"Yes, Comrade,'' Piotrovsky said. "I watched them board the flight for Paris.''

Why? Kurshin asked himself. First McGarvey had disappeared. Then the woman had been arrested, and now the two of them were on their way to Paris. It made no sense.

"Can you get aboard that flight?''

"No.''

"Then we will have lost them!'' Kurshin screamed.

"Pardon me, Comrade, but we do have resources in Paris. It should be a simple matter to trail them from there.''

The bastard was correct, of course. But Kurshin still could not get rid of the vision of McGarvey pulling the Pershing's plugs, just as he might have unplugged a night light.

They were not going to Paris, though. It was just a way point for them. Kurshin was almost one hundred percent convinced they were returning to Washington.

"Make certain they do not go into Paris. They'll probably be switching planes. For Washington. Do you understand?''

"Yes, Comrade."

"Once they have left French soil your job will be done."

Kurshin slammed down the telephone. Within twenty-four hours, forty-eight at the most, they would be dead. Both of them. He would see to it himself.

20

WASHINGTON

They'd switched planes at Paris's Orly Airport and as on the first leg of the trip, Lorraine Abbott maintained an uneasy silence. They traveled first class, and crossing the Atlantic she managed to get a few hours' sleep or at least pretended to.

She was angry that she had been pulled into this situation against her will, and now it would probably mean that her career would be sidetracked. The moment they got home, she'd told him even before they'd left the ground at Lod, she would go directly up to the NPT Inspection Service's office at the UN in New York, make her report, and then try her best to forget the ugly incident had ever occurred.

The pilot switched on the 747's No Smoking and Fasten

Seatbelt signs, and McGarvey gently nudged her. Her eyes came open immediately, and she glared at him.

"We're coming in. Put on your seatbelt," McGarvey said.

She glanced out the window before she did as he told her. He studied the back of her head for that moment. She had a right to be angry, he thought. He had placed her life, and certainly her career, in jeopardy. Even though she was an NPT field inspector whose job it was to find out such things, her knowledge of what was really happening at En Gedi placed her in danger. He was going to have to ask Trotter to have the Agency do something for her. At least until this business was taken care of.

At least she had called the general before her arrest. It's what had started the wheels in motion.

Potok had not returned, but an hour after he had left, McGarvey's personal belongings had been returned to him, and he had been driven directly to the VIP lounge at the airport. They'd picked up his bag from his hotel. About his gun no one would comment.

Lorraine had shown up a couple of minutes later, just as surprised to see him as he had been to see her.

"Are you all right?" he had asked when they were alone for just a second or two.

"No thanks to you," she'd snapped, her eyes straying to the thick bandage on his head.

"What did you tell them?"

"Nothing," she said. "Because that's exactly what I know." She turned away.

It was just two in the afternoon when they touched down at Dulles Airport, and McGarvey went with Lorraine down the jetway into customs. A young man in a three-piece suit directed them away from the counters, and through a door that led directly out into the terminal.

"We have a car waiting for you," he said. "Will either of you be needing medical assistance?"

"Who are you?" McGarvey asked pointedly, before Lorraine could say anything.

"Oh, sorry, sir," the young man said. He dug out his Agency identification. His name was Stanley Barker. "Mr. Trotter sent me out to pick you up."

"That's just fine," Lorraine said. "Now if you will just excuse me, I've got to see about a flight to New York."

"I'm sorry, ma'am," Barker said, a little embarrassed. "But my instructions were to pick up both of you."

"I demand . . ."

"Ma'am, Mr. O'Sheay is waiting for you. He asked me to assure you that all of your questions will be answered."

"Mark is here, in Washington?"

"Yes, ma'am. In the area. I have a car just outside."

She looked at McGarvey, a smug little grin of satisfaction on her lips. McGarvey figured she was going to get her answers, but they probably would not be ones she would care to hear.

Crossing the terminal McGarvey spotted at least three men who were probably FBI surveillance people, and he allowed himself to relax for the first time since they'd left Israel. All the way across he'd gotten the uncomfortable feeling that the operation had been too loose. They had simply been kicked out of the country and left to fend for themselves. Considering the nature of his assignment, and the fact that they were carrying around in their heads the literal future of Israel, he had expected to be shadowed. But until now he had picked out no one.

Outside, a dark gray Taurus pulled up. Barker got in the front, and they got in the backseat. McGarvey spotted at least two surveillance cars, one in the rear and one in the lead.

Barker turned in his seat as they pulled away from the curb. "Your bags will be brought along shortly, not to worry," he said.

"Where are we going?" McGarvey asked.

"Falmouth."

"What?" Lorraine asked, sitting forward. "That's in Virginia."

"Yes, ma'am, about fifty miles south of here."

"Goddamnit, you said that Mark O'Sheay would be meeting us."

"He's down there waiting for you," Barker said. "Believe me, Dr. Abbott, this is for the best. You'll understand once it's explained to you."

"Has anyone been spotted coming in?" McGarvey asked.

Barker looked at him through lidded eyes. He finally shook his head.

"We don't think so. Leastways, we haven't spotted any unusual activity. If they're there, they are good."

"You can count on it," McGarvey said, relaxing back in his seat and lighting a cigarette.

Lorraine had followed the exchange. "What's going on?" she cried. "You bastards, someone tell me what's going on."

"Yes, ma'am, as soon as we get there."

"And stop calling me ma'am," she screeched.

FALMOUTH

The safehouse was on a ninety-acre farm a few miles outside the small town, the Rappahannock River bordering the property to the south. The house itself was a two-story colonial built on the crest of a hill with a clear view in three directions. The access road wound up from a secondary highway through a thick stand of trees that at times formed a canopy over the narrow road. General Accounting actually owned the place, but the FBI's Witness Protection Program had been the most recent users.

They parked in front and went up the sloping pathway to the broad porch. Before they went inside McGarvey turned and looked back down the road. The cars that had come from the airport with them had peeled off and were nowhere in sight. The afternoon was warm and lovely. The countryside seemed peaceful.

Inside the foyer they were met by a well-dressed man with startlingly blue eyes and a slightly disdainful expression.

McGarvey had never met him, but he pegged the man almost immediately as a lawyer.

"Any trouble?" he asked Barker.

"No, sir."

From somewhere McGarvey thought he could hear the murmur of a conversation. A bulky man in a khaki shirt and trousers, hunting boots on his feet, stood at the head of the stairs. When McGarvey looked up at him, he moved off. He was armed with an M16 and he looked serious. Whatever had happened or was about to happen here, they were definitely taking it for real.

The blue-eyed man spoke. "I'm Howard Ryan, general counsel for the Central Intelligence Agency, and you must be Dr. Abbott." He stuck out his hand, but Lorraine ignored it, her right eyebrow rising slightly.

"Would you mind telling me what is going on here, Mr. Ryan?" she demanded. "If it's no trouble, that is."

"Of course," Ryan said smoothly. "Would you like to freshen up before we get started?"

"No. Is Mark O'Sheay here?"

Ryan nodded. "Yes, he is. If you'd like we can go in now. They are waiting for you."

"It's been a long trip, don't screw with me," Lorraine said crudely.

Ryan's gaze shifted to McGarvey. "You can wait in the living room, we'll be with you in a half hour."

"I don't think so," McGarvey said.

"That's an order, Mr. McGarvey . . ." Ryan started to say, but Trotter had come to a doorway at the end of the stairhall.

"It's all right, Howard. We'll see them both."

McGarvey and Lorraine went back to the study, where Trotter was waiting.

"Hello, Doctor, I'm John Trotter, I'm also with the Agency. We have someone here whom you know." He stepped aside.

A fat, academic-looking man with pince-nez was just rising from his seat at a long table.

"Mark?" Lorraine gave a little cry and she went in.

McGarvey was right behind her. He could see that O'Sheay was angry and disturbed.

"Now," Trotter said, coming in with Howard Ryan, who shut the door and locked it. "We have a lot to talk about, and very little time, I'm afraid, to do it in."

21

THE SAFEHOUSE

NOW THAT SHE WAS WITH AT LEAST ONE FAMILIAR, FRIENDLY face, Lorraine Abbott had regained some of the confidence she had lost when she'd been arrested in Tel Aviv. "What's going on here, Mark?" she asked her boss. "Have they told you yet?"

"If you'll just have a seat, Dr. Abbott, we can get started," Trotter said. "We have a lot of ground to cover."

"I will not," Lorraine snapped at him. "Mark, can we get the hell out of here? Now?"

O'Sheay shook his ponderous head. "Not just yet," he said. "Listen to the man."

McGarvey had remained standing by the door. She shot him an angry look. "I've listened to about as much as I want to listen to. My lab will be expecting me."

"We have taken the liberty of informing them that you are on an extended assignment with the NPT," Trotter said.

"You what?"

"Please, Dr. Abbott, if you will just have a seat, I'll explain everything to you."

"Goddamnit . . ."

"Sit down," McGarvey said. "The man is trying to save your life."

"I don't . . ." she started again, but then she nodded and sat down, O'Sheay next to her, and Trotter and Ryan across the table. McGarvey remained standing.

"Before we begin, it is my duty to inform you, Dr. Abbott, that these proceedings are being videotaped, and that the subjects that will come under discussion are classified top secret. You may not divulge what has happened here with anyone outside of this room unless you are instructed to do so by proper authority."

Ryan passed a single-page document and a pen across to her. "If you have understood what Mr. Trotter has just told you, please sign this; it outlines the penalties for noncompliance under the National Secrets Act."

The color left her face.

"I've already signed it," O'Sheay said.

"But the NPT . . ."

"Has been cut out for the moment. Just sign it, Lorraine."

She did it, and pushed the paper back to Ryan, who put it in a file folder. She was subdued. McGarvey felt a little sorry for her. She was a smart, beautiful woman, but she had been playing an amateur's game until now. Her education wasn't going to be pleasant to watch.

"On June ninth of this year you were dispatched by the Non-Proliferation Treaty Inspection Service to investigate an incident at the En Gedi Nuclear Research Station," Trotter began.

Lorraine nodded.

"Along with a British scientist, Scott Hayes, you did so. Mr. Hayes was apparently satisfied with what he was shown.

We have seen his report. But you were not. Can you tell us why?''

Again Lorraine appealed to O'Sheay for help, but he nodded for her to answer the question.

"I felt they were hiding something," she said. Her voice had lost its harsh edge.

"Hiding what?"

"Mr. McGarvey has already briefed me."

"We'll get to that, Doctor. What did you think the Israelis were hiding?"

"I didn't know at the time, but the man who met us at the gate was Lev Potok. I happen to know that he is a major in the Mossad."

"After your inspection tour was completed, why didn't you return home and make your report?"

"I talked to Mark and told him that something funny was happening, and asked him to send out whatever material he could on the research facility. Construction and start-up information, that is."

"You were looking for something specific?"

"Yes."

"Could you explain that to us," Trotter gently prompted.

"I thought there was a possibility that the Israelis were hiding fissionable material somewhere within or beneath the facility. Specifically weapons-grade material. There is certain equipment . . . certain things they would have to have done in order to maintain such a depot."

"Did you find anything in your document search?"

"I wasn't sure at the time. There were certain airflow installations that supposedly were to be used in a reactor room emergency. I thought it was possible they could be used for something else."

"The equipment is there," McGarvey said.

Lorraine looked up at him. "You saw it? You were actually inside?"

"Not in the weapons vault itself. But the laminar airflow equipment was there, laid out about the way you said it might be. And the air shafts are deep. Perhaps three hundred feet."

She nodded thoughtfully. "Judging from their reaction, you must have struck a nerve."

Trotter hadn't turned to look at McGarvey, he'd kept his eyes on Lorraine. "Your conclusion then, Doctor, from everything you've seen and heard concerning En Gedi?"

She glanced at Mark. "If you mean to ask, do I believe the Israelis are storing nuclear weapons at En Gedi, I can't answer you. If you want to know do I think it's possible, I do. Very likely, in fact."

Now Trotter turned around to face McGarvey. "The good doctor says you briefed her, Kirk."

"I told her everything," McGarvey said.

"Everything?" Ryan snapped.

"Yes."

"Well, that tears it," Ryan said in disgust. "You had no goddamned brief . . ."

McGarvey overrode him. "Her ass was hanging out on the line. I was either going to tell her nothing, or I was going to tell her everything. And that, Counselor, was my studied decision as a field officer whose own ass was on the line."

"Under the circumstances I have to agree with Kirk," Trotter said.

Lorraine's eyes were bright. "Why am I getting the feeling that I'm not going to like what's coming next?"

"It's for your own protection, Doctor," Trotter said. "Believe me, if there was any way, any way at all of doing this any differently we would."

"What are you talking about?"

"You are going to have to stay here, for . . . a few days, perhaps a little longer."

"Bullshit," she snapped, jumping up. "I'm not going to be kept a prisoner in my own country. In the first place I've done nothing wrong, and in the second place I have two research grants and two teams I'm currently supervising."

"I'm sorry."

"Mark, for God's sake," she cried.

But O'Sheay was again shaking his head. "There's not a thing I can do about it, Lorraine, I'm sorry. I'd rather do without your company for a few days or even a month than forever.''

''And they will kill you if they find you, Dr. Abbott,'' Trotter said.

''Who is they?''

''That isn't necessary to know at this moment,'' Ryan said.

''The Russians,'' McGarvey interjected.

Ryan thumped his fist on the table. ''Listen here, mister, I've had enough of your prima donna crap.''

McGarvey ignored him. ''It will be the same people who reprogrammed the Pershing to strike En Gedi. They know what's there, and they won't stop.''

''Trotter!'' Ryan demanded in exasperation.

''Let's step outside for a moment, Kirk,'' Trotter said. ''Please.''

''I'll talk them into getting you a computer, maybe flying some of your programs out here, if that'll help. But no matter what, you're going to have to remain here out of sight for as long as it takes.''

She was shaking her head in amazement. ''I don't believe this.''

''Believe it,'' McGarvey said. He turned, opened the door, and went out into the stairhall where he lit a cigarette.

Trotter and Ryan were right behind him, and Ryan was fuming.

''That was quite a performance in there!''

''Counselor, why don't you stick to counseling and let me stick to spying,'' McGarvey told him. He turned back to Trotter. ''They're there, John. I'm as convinced as I can be without having actually seen the weapons themselves.''

''Are you all right?'' Trotter asked.

''Just fine. She saved my ass by getting to the general before they picked her up. She's got fine instincts.''

''She'll be okay here, Kirk. You're coming back to Washington with me this afternoon.''

McGarvey shook his head. ''Leave me a car, and I'll drive in tomorrow morning. It's been a long forty-eight hours. I can use a few hours' sleep.''

"Everything is all right here," Trotter said.

"I'm sure it is. I'll be even more sure in the morning. What are we going to do now? Baranov won't back off, and Kurshin is still floating around out there somewhere."

"You're going after FELIKS," Trotter said. "We'll brief you in the morning."

"Have your people developed a short list?"

"Not as short as we'd like, but you'll have a decent head start."

"I'll see you in the morning."

"Sure," Trotter said. "We'll leave you the Taurus."

Ryan had held his silence, listening to the exchange. "I think it would be better if you came back with us now, McGarvey."

"I don't," McGarvey said, starting to turn away.

"What, are you fucking her already?"

McGarvey swiveled smoothly on his heel, grabbed a handful of Ryan's shirt front, and half lifted him off his feet. "That's the second time I've been asked that question, and frankly I'm getting tired of it. Have you seen my dossier, Counselor?"

Ryan was able to do little more than squeak an affirmative.

"Then you know what I am," McGarvey growled. "And didn't your mama ever tell you not to piss off a killer?"

It was nearly midnight. The light wind had died and the evening had become warm and humid. McGarvey stood on the side porch in the shadows watching the gravel road as it disappeared down into the woods toward the highway.

Trotter had left four FBI officers here to watch after Lorraine Abbott's safety. So far he had picked out three of them. One in an old pickup truck just down from the barn, another just off the road, a flash of his white face briefly visible in the starlight, and the third had actually lit a cigarette farther down in the woods.

"I want to thank you," Lorraine Abbott's voice came from the open window just behind him and to the left.

"Go to bed, Doctor," McGarvey said.

"The name is Lorraine."

McGarvey smiled to himself. "I thought your friends called you Dr. Abbott."

"None of them have any balls."

He had to laugh. "Now you sound like one of the boys."

"Did you ever know a physicist who wasn't?"

"Not one who looks like you."

22

CIA HEADQUARTERS

IT HAD BEEN A LONG TIME SINCE MCGARVEY HAD BEEN TO the headquarters building. The last time he'd left in disgrace and had packed himself off to Switzerland. It was odd coming back like this.

Driving up the broad road from the main gate where Trotter had left him a grounds pass, he could see that the new section of the main building had been completed. The Russians, it was said, were adding on to their Foreign Operations Building on the Circumferential Highway outside of Moscow. When that building had been constructed in 1972 it had been a nearly exact copy of CIA headquarters. It was a safe bet that their new addition would closely resemble the CIA's. Spying was a big business, and the KGB admired the Americans' way of doing it.

He parked the Taurus in the visitors' lot and walked across to the main entrance of the building, where he signed in and was searched with a metal detector.

Trotter himself came down a couple of minutes later to fetch him. "Has she settled down?" he asked on the way up to the seventh floor.

"She's still grumbling, but she's beginning to understand. How about O'Sheay—do you think he'll blow the whistle?"

"No," Trotter said.

McGarvey hadn't thought so either. The man had been cowed. But they had probably made some sort of a deal with him. After all, his job in a large measure depended on National Security Agency spy satellites. The NPT Inspection Service would be hard pressed to do without the KH-11.

"How about her computer?"

"Barker will have it to her by this afternoon. We're just waiting for some of her research materials to come in from California." Trotter looked at him. "She'll be all right out there, Kirk."

"Any word on Kurshin?"

"No, he's gone to ground again."

"If he's found out about her, he might try something."

"That's why you're here," Trotter said.

"We want him to come to Washington, after me."

"Which he will do, once you start poking around Baranov's main source."

"He's pretty good, John."

"Yes he is, but now we know his target."

"And he knows that we know," McGarvey said.

They had to sign in with the seventh-floor security people, where they were again subjected to a metal detector search before they were allowed across the corridor and through the glass doors into the huge outer office of the CIA's director.

Lawrence Danielle was just coming from his office adjacent to the general's, a pleasantly neutral expression on his face when he spotted McGarvey.

"Hello, Kirk. Welcome back."

They shook hands. Danielle had headed the review board which had recommended McGarvey's dismissal. McGarvey was surprised at his own self-control now. He had done a lot of thinking, though, and years ago he had come to the conclusion that it had been time for him to get out anyway. It didn't matter that Danielle had made the decision for him.

"This go-around it's just a part-time job."

"Yes, well, they're waiting for us inside."

The DCI's secretary buzzed them through and they went into the general's vast office with its magnificent view of the rolling hills to the southwest. Howard Ryan and another man were seated across from Murphy, who rose from behind his massive desk.

"Kirk McGarvey, I assume," the general said.

"Yes, sir," McGarvey said, crossing the room and shaking his hand.

"I don't believe you've met Phil Carrara, our deputy director of operations."

"No," McGarvey said.

Carrara got to his feet and they shook hands. "A hell of a job you did for us in Germany," he said.

"I had help."

"Yes, it's too bad about Jim Hunte. He was a good man from what I understand."

"Yes, he was."

"I believe you know Howard Ryan, our general counsel," the general said.

Ryan didn't bother to rise nor did McGarvey even look at him. "Yes, sir, we've met."

In the awkward silence that followed, Murphy waved them to the three vacant chairs. It was an odd little group, McGarvey thought. But then the need-to-know list for this operation would have to be kept very small. Washington was a town filled with ears, and Baranov had his share of them. A basic assumption of every secret intelligence service was that the enemy almost certainly had his own people on the payroll. Not very often the Kim Philbys, but certainly the odd reader or analyst here and there. Ultra-sensitive operations of necessity were often top-heavy with brass.

"I've read John's overnight report, which included Dr. Abbott's assessment of what you found at En Gedi," the general said. "And I think we're all agreed here—and the president concurs—that the Israelis do have battle-ready nuclear weapons, that they are stored beneath En Gedi, and that the Russians know about it and will certainly make their next attempt to destroy the facility on June thirtieth. That gives us eleven days."

The date was something new. But McGarvey kept a poker face. "Not enough time for the Israelis to move the depot and maintain any kind of security."

"No, nor have they confirmed or denied the real purpose of En Gedi. I have spoken with Isser Shamir, and the president with Prime Minister Peres. They're angry, of course, that you got as far as you did, but when we explained our position—fully explained it—they agreed to your release. Contingent on two things."

"The first would be that the NPT Inspection Service was to be cut out of the deal," McGarvey said. "What about the second?"

"That you're to have help on this one," the general said. He glanced at Trotter.

"Mossad?"

"Yes," the general said. "I want you to understand something up front, McGarvey. I think you handled Germany brilliantly, but I think you fucked up at En Gedi. It was a damned fool stunt that could have gotten you killed, and certainly pissed off our only ally in the Middle East who is worth a damn."

"I got what I was sent to get," McGarvey said. He'd expected the little morality speech.

"I also want you to understand that the reason your name came up in the first place was because of the way you handled yourself two years ago."

McGarvey leaned forward. "Let's cut the bullshit, Mr. Director," he said. "We all know why I've been brought back into the fold. I'm to be used as bait for Baranov and his trigger man, Arkady Kurshin.''

Ryan started to say something, and Danielle was hiding a little grin, but the general held them off.

''All right, we'll cut the bullshit, McGarvey. You make me nervous, and it's not because you're a maverick who wants to do things his own way, but because you are an assassin. Very probably you are unbalanced, and certainly you are dangerous.''

''You're most likely right, General, but at the moment I'm needed,'' McGarvey said, surprised at the hurt he was feeling. This was like coming back from Vietnam all over again. He touched his face, remembering the spit.

''Yes, you are. But if you want out you have my word that no one on this side of the Atlantic will ever bother you again.''

''I'm along for the ride.''

''Why?'' Murphy asked him point-blank.

Why indeed, McGarvey wondered. He didn't know, it was as simple as that. Or was it? What *did* he believe in? Truth, he supposed. Justice, though he hadn't seen much of it in his life. Honor? Was that it?

''It's a job,'' he finally said.

The general grunted. He tossed a fat file folder across the desk to McGarvey.

''We want you to find Feliks for us, and we hope your doing so will draw Arkady Kurshin out of hiding before the thirtieth. He'll try to kill you, of course. We want you to kill him first.''

''And afterward?'' McGarvey asked, not yet reaching for the file.

''Go back where you came from.''

Carrara, who had done most of the actual briefing on the FELIKS file, rode down to Operations on the third floor with Trotter and McGarvey.

''There has already been a lot of fallout on this one,'' he said. ''NATO has been raising hell about our security, and the president has a tight lid on the entire mess. And it's a mess. We're all under a lot of pressure here. With the addition of the Israelis, it's made things doubly difficult.''

"It's the business," McGarvey said, getting him off the hook for the general's comments.

"Yes. John will take it from here. He'll set up your cutout procedures and security arrangements. Good luck.''

"Yeah," McGarvey said. "Thanks.''

"He's a good man," Trotter said as Carrara headed down the corridor to his own office.

McGarvey turned to him. "They all are," he said. "Or at least most of them start that way.''

"I'm sorry about upstairs . . .''

"Don't be, John. Murphy knows what he's talking about. Possibly the only man in this town who does. Nothing has changed.''

Trotter just shook his head.

"Let's go meet my Mossad partner, maybe he'll be willing to tell me how we've suddenly come up with such a specific date.''

"Not here. From this point on we're keeping both of you at arm's length from the Agency. Murphy's orders. We've got a place set up for you in Georgetown. It should be okay for a few days, maybe longer. At least we've got secure phone lines in and out.''

"Anything on the opposition yet?''

"No, but watch yourself.''

"Are you coming over?''

"No. But I'll give you a contact number and physical handover procedures.''

"They'll try again.''

"No doubt of it, Kirk, no doubt whatsoever. Just take care of yourself, and when it's over I'll see that you're treated right. I promise you that, Kirk. I swear to God.''

"Sure," McGarvey said.

23

GEORGETOWN

THE SAFEHOUSE WAS A THREE-STORY BROWNSTONE A COUple of blocks from Georgetown University in a nondescript but obviously expensive neighborhood.

McGarvey had parked his car by the Naval Observatory and had taken a cab past the place, watching for anything or anyone out of the ordinary. But he had seen nothing. Still, his instincts were telling him that Kurshin was very near. He could almost taste it in the air.

Paranoia? he wondered. With age and experience sometimes comes overcaution. He was back on the hunt, and only Trotter, it seemed, was minding his back door. And exactly what *fallout* had Carrara been talking about? As with every operation he'd been involved in, the unanswered questions were a legion in the beginning, among them the participation of the Mossad.

"We're helping them out, Kirk. Naturally they'd insist on inserting one of their own people into the operation," Trotter had explained.

"We're talking about a Soviet penetration agent somewhere within the Pentagon. That covers a lot of territory."

Trotter had nodded glumly. "We all know it, but your arrest put us against the wall."

McGarvey said nothing.

"It'll be up to you to see that they don't get into too much mischief . . ."

"For Christ's sake, John, we've been around too long for that kind of crap. Talk to me. Murphy must have safeguards."

"Yes, he does."

"If they get in my way someone could get hurt."

"I know," Trotter said. "In this my hands are practically tied, Kirk. I'll do what I can to keep them off your back, but when it gets down to the last analysis, it'll be up to you to make peace with the Mossad."

McGarvey hadn't bothered asking what he'd meant by that; he figured he'd be finding out soon enough.

He got his car from the Naval Observatory, parked it on a narrow side street a block away from the safehouse, and went the rest of the way on foot, reasonably certain, at least for the moment, that he had not been followed.

Mounting the steps at three in the afternoon, McGarvey had the impression that he was passing from one time zone into another, and no matter what had come before, once he crossed the threshold there would be no turning back.

He let himself into the stairhall and stood in the shadows for a few moments listening to the sounds of the house. They would be alone, Trotter had assured him. "Complete privacy. Hash out whatever it is you two have to hash out there, inside the safehouse, away from prying eyes and ears, and then do your job."

Lev Potok, wearing khaki trousers and a light V-neck sweater, appeared at the head of the stairs.

"You," McGarvey said, once again amazed at his own self-control.

"There's some cold beer up here. I think you and I are going to have to get some things straight between us before we get started."

"You bet," McGarvey growled, starting up the stairs.

He followed Potok down the hall into the long, narrow living room, with large bowed windows that looked down on the street. A white noise generator had been attached to the windowpanes so that conversations could not be picked up from outside.

"When did you get to Washington?" McGarvey asked.

"Last night."

"Have you been briefed?"

Potok had stepped into the small utility kitchen. He came back with two beers, handing one to McGarvey.

"Yes. I was allowed to read the Feliks file." He shook his head. "This man has been very damaging to you, I think. And to us."

"Who briefed you?"

"Howard Ryan. He is your Agency's general counsel, I believe . . ."

"I know the man," McGarvey said. He went to the window, parted the curtains, and looked down at the street. Normal traffic, nothing out of the ordinary, but there was something. "Who knows you're here?"

"The prime minister. My boss. A few people in travel and historical section . . ."

"And the Russians."

Potok started to object, but then he nodded. "You are probably correct."

"Your service is just like any other . . ."

"You've made your point," Potok said. "But before we start, let me apologize for . . . Lod."

"You were doing your job."

"Yes. But·would you have tried to kill me had I slapped you a second time?"

McGarvey turned away from the window where he had been studying the Israeli's reflection in the glass. "Yes."

Whether it was the answer Potok had expected or not, it didn't show on his face. "I see."

"Like you said, we've got a few things to get straight between us. You are working for me on this project. I won't lie to you, nor will you lie to me. The first time it happens, I'll have your ass on a plane back to Israel."

"Fair enough, within certain limitations," the Israeli said cautiously.

"Whatever your instructions were, the Pentagon will not be a Mossad supermarket."

"Understood."

McGarvey stared at him for several long seconds, trying to work out in his own mind exactly how he felt about working with the man. He was a professional, otherwise he wouldn't have been sent here. Was that enough?

"We have a lot of ground to cover," McGarvey said. "I'm going to ask you a question, for which you'll give me the truth. And then you can ask me a question, which I will answer truthfully."

Potok nodded, the caution still in his eyes.

"There was an incident at En Gedi, which the NPT investigated. It was picked up by our KH-11 surveillance satellite. We believe that the Soviets penetrated you. Is this correct?"

"Yes. His name was Benjamin Rothstein."

"Where is he now? Do you have him?"

"He is dead. Where is Dr. Abbott at this moment?"

"In a CIA safehouse about fifty miles from here. The NPT has been cut out of this operation until it's over. At that time it'll be up to the politicians to negotiate some sort of a deal." McGarvey had perched on the edge of the couch. "We know what is stored at En Gedi."

Potok's jaw tightened.

"Now, tell me exactly what happened out there with Rothstein. I want to know everything."

The Israeli glanced at the windows. "If I cannot?" he asked.

"Then our association ends here and now. I won't work with you."

"Is this place bugged?"

"I was told it was not."

"Did you believe them?"

McGarvey shrugged. It was hard sometimes to know exactly what he believed. "I don't think either of us has much choice. They know a hell of a lot more than they've told either of us. But we've got a job to do."

"Yes," Potok said. "We have a job to do and it will not be pleasant. Nor do we have much time."

"No."

"We were penetrated twice," Potok said. "The first time by Rothstein, who was almost definitely a Russian, and the second time by a nuclear technician named Simon Asher."

"Rothstein was in the vault? He saw the weapons?"

Potok was very uncomfortable. "Yes. He managed to get clear of the base, and we think that he managed to call his contact with the information."

"What about Asher, did he escape as well?"

"No. Nor have we found a Russian connection yet. In fact, he was born in New York City and educated here in the States."

"What happened to him?"

"He died of radiation poisoning," Potok said. "Our scientists say that he was attempting to install an . . . initiator into one of the weapons. But he made a mistake, spilled radioactive material, and died."

"When did this happen?"

"At the same moment Rothstein was in the vault."

"That doesn't make any sense," McGarvey said half to himself. What the hell was he being told? "If Rothstein was working for the Russians, to confirm the existence of your weapons stockpile, then why was Asher down there trying to destroy the place?" He looked up. "That's what he was trying to do, wasn't it?"

"Yes. Maybe it was a safeguard. The Pershing missile would be sent if Asher had failed. But . . ."

"What?" McGarvey said, sitting forward.

"We have been monitoring the telephone lines from the Hungarian Embassy for some time now. We have a new technique that allows us to do this without being detected, no matter how sophisticated their telephone equipment is. There were a series of telephone calls between the Soviet Interests section of the embassy and a man we arrested a few days ago. They discussed the failure in Germany, and they said that another attempt would be made on June thirtieth."

It was the date, finally.

"What about this man?"

"His name was Viktor Voronsky. A KGB field officer who had until a few months ago been seen in Damascus. It is possible that he was Rothstein's contact."

"He's dead?"

"Unfortunately. He committed suicide. But, no mention was made of Asher's attempt to destroy the facility."

McGarvey nodded. "Then something else is going on. But it's Baranov. It's the way he works."

"My turn," Potok said. "There were three men who hijacked your Pershing missile."

"Arkady Kurshin, whose file I've brought for you. He managed to escape. And it'll be he who is going to make the next attempt. Ivan Yegorov, who I killed. And an East German rocket scientist by the name of Dieter Schey."

"What happened to him?"

"He'd been shot in the head, probably by Kurshin, and left there to die. We have him here in Washington. He's alive, but not conscious."

Potok's mind was racing, McGarvey could see it in his expression. "In order to get to Arkady Kurshin we must uncover Feliks."

"Who almost certainly is Baranov's source for technical

information," McGarvey said. "Of the sort Kurshin would have needed to operate the missile."

"Information that their rocket scientist needed to operate the missile," Potok took the thought a step forward. "If we therefore make an announcement that Dieter Schey is alive and well, angry that his own people left him for dead, and that he is willing to cooperate with us in naming his Pentagon source, Kurshin will come after him. Schey will be the bait."

"Something like that," McGarvey said. "But there's more."

"Yes?"

"Kurshin will be coming here to kill me as well."

"Why?"

"I stopped him in Germany."

"There's more?"

Again McGarvey nodded. "It's a long story, Lev, one I'm going to have to tell you on the run. But it goes directly back to Baranov. The man has got a price on my head."

THE FALMOUTH SAFEHOUSE

The four-seat Ranger helicopter came in low from the southwest for the third time in the past half hour. FBI agent Tom Sills watched it through binoculars from the edge of the clearing by the driveway. He could see the pilot and three other men, one of whom had a pair of binoculars raised to his eyes.

Sills keyed his walkie-talkie. "Goddamnit, it's the same bird. Have we gotten anything out of the FAA yet?"

"Just got off the blower with them," Bert Langerford radioed from the house. "Registered to Bekins Real Estate Company out of Alexandria."

"Well, I don't like it."

"They're showing property, Tom. Do it all the time."

"I said I don't like it," Sills barked. "On this pass the sonofabitches were scoping us. Call operations and have them send a couple of men over to Alexandria—wherever that chopper took off from—and check these guys out."

"Christ, we're supposed to be keeping this low-key."

"Do it now, Bert, goddamnit!" Sills snapped. He laid the walkie-talkie down and watched the helicopter as it disappeared to the northeast. He had been a field agent for a long time, long enough to trust his hunches. And he had a bad feeling about this one.

24

SOVIET EMBASSY: WASHINGTON

WHEN ARKADY KURSHIN WALKED INTO THE *REFERENTURA*, the most secret section within the embassy and the one in which KGB matters are discussed, there was an immediate electricity in the air.

In the eighteen hours he had been here he had galvanized the entire KGB staff into his own personal weapon. But then his credentials were beyond question; even the ambassador deferred to him. He was a Baranov tool, and Baranov was one of the most powerful men in the Rodina at this moment.

Boris Antipov, the KGB *rezident*, seated at the end of the long table, was fidgeting with some papers. He looked up with a start.

"Good evening, Boris Nikolaievich," Kurshin said pleasantly enough. He glanced at the other two men seated around the table. They were Yuri Deryugin and Mikhail Lakomsky, the Washington operation's best case officers. Either one of them could have easily passed for an American. Their English was perfect, as were their bearing and manner and dress.

"Have you found her?" Kurshin asked, standing at the end of the table, his powerful hands splayed out in front of him.

"Yes," Deryugin replied. "As you know, we managed to trace her transfer out of Washington as far as the Falmouth area, where we had to back off for fear of detection."

"Yes?" Kurshin replied, holding his impatience in check.

Deryugin glanced at his partner. "We arranged to take a helicopter tour of the area this afternoon with a real estate firm. We found her at a farmhouse a few miles outside of the town, right along the river."

"You actually saw her?"

"No. But the house is being guarded by at least three FBI agents. They're even wearing their blue windbreakers with FBI stenciled on the back."

"But you didn't see her face."

"No, Comrade. But she is there all right. I don't think they are playing games."

Kurshin thought about it for a moment or two, and then nodded. They were almost certainly correct. "Were you spotted?"

"Yes."

Kurshin waited for the explanation.

"It won't matter. Such flights are very common over the area. We were merely a pair of businessmen looking for investment property. Even if the FBI checks . . ."

"They will."

"Yes, Comrade, *when* they check they will find that we work for Xavier Enterprises here in Washington. It is a blind company, of course. They will learn nothing."

"Excellent work, Yuri Ivanovich," Kurshin said. He glanced at his watch. It was just 7:30 in the evening. "Do you foresee any problem getting in there and killing her?"

"When?"

"Tonight."

The two field officers again exchanged glances. "No, Comrade."

"Will you require more people?"

"No."

Kurshin allowed a slight smile to play across his lips. He admired competence. If McGarvey wasn't out there, and he didn't think McGarvey was, they would succeed.

"Do it," he said.

The *resident* was clearly agitated. Kurshin turned to him.

"Do you have a problem with this, Boris Nikolaievich?"

"I have many problems, Comrade Colonel, which is part of my job. As far as killing an American citizen here on American soil, there will be repercussions, of course. There is no way of predicting how severe their countermeasures will be, but they will happen."

"If it is traced back to us."

"It will be," Antipov said, not willing to back down. He too was very good at his job, and although he had an abiding respect and even fear of Kurshin, he had his own brief. Secretly he was one of the men within the KGB who thought Baranov was a madman and would someday bring them all down. Of course he never voiced his opinion . . . or at least not that one.

Kurshin was beginning to lose his patience. "You have read the directive."

Antipov nodded. "An extraordinary document."

"Yes," Kurshin said coolly. Baranov had sent the directive ahead of him, giving Kurshin extremely broad powers and authority. In short he was not to be refused anything, anything at all. Not by the ambassador, and certainly not by the *resident*.

"There is a possibility that Xavier may already have been penetrated."

"But we are not certain?"

"No."

"Then no matter what happens, it would take the FBI time to connect our attack with the helicopter overflight and therefore Xavier and back to us."

"In all probability, yes."

"By then this mission will be once again off American soil," Kurshin said, giving his first hint that what was happening here in the Washington area was only a small part of a much larger and more important whole. Important enough to require the killing of Dr. Abbott.

"But I will not be," Antipov said softly.

Kurshin's eyes narrowed, causing the *rezident* to flinch, but still the man did not back down.

"As you know, Comrade Colonel, Hammerhead is our most important source here in Washington at the moment," Antipov said.

Second most important source, Kurshin thought, without giving voice to the extraordinary secret Baranov had shared with him. He didn't know the agent's real name, only his code name and the fact he was of utmost importance. He merely nodded.

"I will arrange, as you asked, for you to meet with him. But under the circumstances I do not believe this would be wise."

"Why?"

"In all likelihood it would compromise not only us but him."

"This meeting is extremely important, Comrade Antipov. Extremely important. I trust you passed my message to him?"

"Yes, but under the circumstances . . ."

"What circumstances?" Kurshin shot back dangerously. He had been out on the streets all day trying to get the flavor of the city. He had even walked past the White House, where he'd stood by the fence gazing at the seat of power. It had given him a chill, which he had found somehow annoying.

Antipov opened one of the file folders in front of him and passed it down the table. "I take it that you have not seen a television or radio news broadcast this afternoon."

"What is this?" Kurshin asked, without looking down at the open file.

"Transcripts of several news broadcasts. We monitor them on a daily basis, of course. These are from the six o'clock news programs. I think you should read them."

Kurshin did not want to be trifled with. His failure in Germany still rankled. Nothing could go wrong this time. Nothing. He wouldn't allow it. With a great effort of will he tore his eyes away from the *rezident* and began reading the transcripts, the top one from Peter Jennings's ABC television report.

After a few seconds he looked up.

"The one they are talking about must be Hammerhead, Comrade Colonel," Antipov said. "They know."

That wasn't what had struck Kurshin. Another name leapt off the page at him. A name impossible to believe. He was back in the transporter.

Nothing can stop it?

Schey shook his head.

Nein.

Thank you.

The pistol was coming up, Kurshin could feel it in his hands, the metal warm, smooth to the touch, the weapon comfortably heavy. Sure. He had shot the East German in the face. He could not have survived.

"It is a lie," he mumbled.

"Then it is a lie extraordinarily damaging to their position, Comrade Colonel. With it they have given away their only advantage . . . that they suspect there is a penetration agent *within the Pentagon*."

Kurshin went back to his reading, quickly scanning the text—English on the left, Russian on the right—through the rest of the ABC report as well as the half a dozen others that had been monitored. He was looking for one name other than Schey's, but it wasn't there. Nevertheless, he thought, looking up at last, this was McGarvey's doing. Baranov had told him all about the man, about his early days with the CIA, about his Swiss girlfriend, about his parents and the ranch they had left him. Even Kurshin had thought it was incredibly callous of McGarvey to have sold off the property. The man was now living off the interest the money provided him. But land was far more important than money.

"Have you an emergency contact procedure with Hammerhead?" he asked.

Relief showed on Antipov's face. "Yes. I'll make contact immediately. And I'm going to recommend that we pull him out of there before it is too late."

"No," Kurshin said softly, a plan already forming in his mind.

"But . . ."

"There are things here that you do not understand, Boris Nikolaievich. Important things. More important even than Hammerhead."

Antipov threw up his hands in despair. "He has been a loyal source. We must pull him out."

"Contact him immediately. Tell him that it is essential that we meet this evening, but that we will meet in another place."

"I won't do this . . ." the *rezident* started to say, realizing almost immediately that he had stepped over the line.

"You will," Kurshin said gently, and he could read the surprise on Antipov's face.

"Yes, I'll do as you say, Comrade Colonel," Antipov agreed. "But it is my duty to warn you that you may be walking into a trap. If this Dieter Schey has named our man, or at least given them the information they need to track him down, they will be waiting for you."

Kurshin flipped the file folder closed and straightened up. He glanced at the two field officers. "You have your assignment."

Both men got to their feet.

"If there is any trouble, get out immediately. You have a usual route out of here?"

"Across the Mexican border," Deryugin said.

"Dr. Abbott must die tonight. That is your top priority.

There will be no other considerations. Do I make myself clear?"

"Perfectly, Comrade Colonel."

"Go," Kurshin said, and the two men left the *referentura*. He turned back to Antipov. "You believe that this may be a trap?"

"Yes, I do."

"Good, then let's help them spring it," Kurshin said. "By the way, who is this Hammerhead?"

"He is an Air Force colonel. Works directly for the Joint Chiefs as a weapons strategist. He knows every single weapon within the American military system. All services."

"A gold seam."

"Yes," Antipov said.

"It's a shame," Kurshin mumbled, but didn't say any more.

25

BETHESDA NAVAL HOSPITAL

"THERE ARE EIGHT OFFICERS AND TWO CIVILIANS ON THE list of suspects," McGarvey said as he and Potok took the elevator up to the fourth floor. "If they are watched too closely, Feliks will either skip or dig in, and we will have lost."

"I agree, but you are taking a very large risk, making such an announcement and then pulling off all surveillance," Potok said. "We don't know if Kurshin will make contact."

McGarvey looked at him. "He will, but first he'll come here to take care of Schey. He made a mistake with the Pershing, and another with Schey. He'll come to finish the job."

"And we will be waiting for him."

"Yes," McGarvey said. "But we're going to take him alive, if at all possible."

Potok shrugged. "From what I've learned about this man, I don't think that will be so easily accomplished."

"We'll try."

They were met at the nurses' station by Dr. Julius Rabbinoux, the naval physician in charge of the ICU where the East German rocket scientist was being kept. He was a dark-haired, thick-eyebrowed little man with a swarthy complexion and piano player's hands.

"Are you the jackasses responsible for pulling off the security people from this floor?" he said without preamble when McGarvey showed his FBI identification.

"Just the replacements, Doctor. How is he doing tonight?"

The doctor stared at them for a long time. When he spoke his head bobbed up and down as if he were a boxer waiting to slip a blow. "Stable, but not much change."

"Has he regained consciousness?"

"There are moments," the doctor said. "He's still alone in there, no other patients; I assume that's still the drill."

"Yes, it is. But I'm going to be up front with you, Doctor. There may be trouble coming our way tonight."

Dr. Rabbinoux bridled. "Then I'll have the Marines up here right now . . ."

"No," McGarvey said. "That's not going to be possible. But you may pull your staff off this floor."

"I don't know what kind of goddamned stunts you people are pulling, but this is as far as it goes," the doctor snapped. "I'm getting my security people up here on the double."

McGarvey took a pen from the doctor's pocket and reached out for the clipboard he carried. He jotted a number across the top of the patient report form and handed the clipboard back.

"Do you recognize this number?"

"No, should I?"

"It's the White House."

"Crap."

"Someone is standing by for your call," McGarvey said. It was the number Trotter had given him.

The doctor's eyes widened. He finally nodded. "I'll make that call," he said. "In the meantime I want you to stay out of the ICU."

"Make the call, Doctor, and then get your people off this floor."

Dr. Rabbinoux turned and stalked down the empty corridor. The two nurses behind the desk turned away and suddenly busied themselves.

"We'll lock the elevator out as soon as the floor is cleared," McGarvey said softly. "Check the east stairs, I'll take the west."

Potok nodded and headed down the corridor. McGarvey went to the opposite stairwell, opened the door, and looked down into the well. It was quiet, and smelled of cement dust and a faint hospital odor. "Come on," he told himself. "He's here and waiting for you."

Taking the stairs two at a time, he went down to the third floor and looked out on the corridor as a nurse was just turning the far corner. This was one of the recovery wards. Kurshin, when he came, would be passing this way, he suspected. Another visitor to see a friend. He was called the chameleon. He would blend in.

Closing the door, he again listened for sounds, any sounds, as he pulled out his gun and checked the load, but there was nothing. Potok had brought the gun over with him and had handed it over at the Georgetown house.

"Not a very good weapon, I think," the Israeli said.

It was a Walther PPK, lightweight, flat, reasonably accurate and fairly jam proof. At one time it had been the weapon of preference in the British Secret Intelligence Service. McGarvey had selected it as a young man because he had had a feeling for the traditions of the business. By the time he understood it wasn't the best choice, he had become too proficient with it to change. It was an old friend.

"Not an assassin's gun."

"No," McGarvey had said, and neither of them had taken that line of thinking any further.

He hurried back up the stairs and reentered the fourth-floor corridor as Potok was coming from the east stairwell. He was shaking his head.

"Nothing."

It was a little after nine. "It's too early yet. He'll wait until the hospital settles down for the night."

"Unless he's coming in as a visitor," Potok said. "He could be in the building already."

"I don't think so."

Potok looked at him closely, but said nothing. He was professional enough to respect another professional's hunch.

One of the nurses had left, the other was behind the counter. She put down the telephone.

"Who else is on this floor tonight?" McGarvey asked her. Her name tag read LEVIN.

"Patients?"

"Yes."

"Only ICU-4A," she said. Schey's name had never been used, only his bed number in the fourth-floor ICU. The other patients had been moved at the request of the FBI. The hospital director had not liked it, but he had gone along.

Dr. Rabbinoux got off the elevator a minute later. He didn't look happy. He motioned toward the elevator. "They need you in Six-ICU, stat," he told the nurse.

"What about . . . ?"

"I'll stay with him," the doctor snapped.

She gathered up her purse, came around the counter, and took the elevator up.

"Maybe you should have gone with her, Doctor," McGarvey said.

"He's my patient."

"As you wish," McGarvey replied. He re-called the elevator and, using the key he'd been supplied with, locked the car from opening on this floor.

All that was left were the stairwell doors, both of which could be seen from the glass doors that led into the ICU.

"Now, let's go see the patient," McGarvey said.

"I don't want you endangering him," Dr. Rabbinoux said.

"Believe me, Doctor, we're just as interested in keeping him alive as you are. But I'd like to see him. You can be right there with me."

"I don't know who he is, nor do I want to know . . ."

"He is an East German, Doctor, who worked for the KGB. He and his two friends hijacked a nuclear missile from one of our bases in Germany, reprogrammed it to strike a spot in Israel, and nearly succeeded in firing it."

"Jesus Christ," Dr. Rabbinoux said, half closing his eyes. "Did you shoot him?"

"One of his friends did it. The KGB. It's how they operate."

"They're coming here? The KGB? To finish the job?"

"We think so."

"Sick. All you bastards are sick."

"You're wearing the uniform, Doctor, or had you forgotten?"

Dr. Rabbinoux wanted to make a sharp retort, but he held himself in check. "No," he said finally. "I have not."

"May I see him now?"

"Yes."

"Watch the stairwells," McGarvey told Potok. The Israeli too wanted to protest, but he understood the validity of McGarvey's order, and he nodded.

ALEXANDRIA

Trotter sat in his study, the lights out, the door to the living room open so that he could hear the Mahler symphony playing on the stereo system. He was drinking a glass of white Zinfandel and smoking his first cigarette in seven months.

There had been times in his long career, waiting for the telephone to ring like now, that he had wished for something to happen. His call to arms, as he termed it. Action was better than inaction. Movement was better than remaining station-ary. This time, however, he wanted nothing to happen. At least not yet.

Was he getting old? Slowing down? Or had he simply become more of a realist who understood that in this danger-ous world no news was almost always good news?

The telephone rang, and it was a mark of his expectations that he didn't flinch. He finished his wine, put the glass down, and picked up the telephone on the third ring.

"Yes?"

"This is Special Agent Tom Sills, I have been authorized to call this number."

"Yes, go ahead," Trotter said, keeping his voice even. His heart was beginning to accelerate.

"You know who I am and where I'm calling from, sir?"

"Yes, I do."

"Well, sir, we've got a possible situation developing out here. I thought I'd better give you a call."

"Is the house secure?"

"Yes, sir, for the moment. But we were overflown three times this afternoon by a civilian helicopter operated by Be-kins Real Estate in Alexandria. A team went out there to talk with the pilot, who told us that he had shown some property to two men from Xavier Enterprises, a Washington com-pany."

"Go ahead."

"Sir, that company is flagged by our Counter Intell people. It's a Russian front organization. Most likely KGB."

"Damn," Trotter swore half to himself. "You say the property and the subject are secure?"

"Yes, sir."

"Just hold on, I'll come out there myself. Should be able to make it within the hour."

"Shall I call for help?"

"Not yet. Just keep your eyes open."

"Will do, sir."

Trotter broke the connection and dialed the Georgetown

safehouse but there was no answer. Next he called the White House number McGarvey had been given as a contact.

"Trotter," he said when the man answered it. "Run down McGarvey and Potok. Tell them there may be something developing at Falmouth. I'm on my way down there now."

26

THE PENTAGON

THE JOKE WAS THAT LT. COL. BOB RAND WAS AT FORTY-one the world's oldest computer hacker. But of the nonmalicious variety. Once, on an evening two years ago, a number of his friends were at his house in Arlington Heights when he tapped into the bank's computer system for a captain from the Strategic Planning Pool. With a few touches of his keys he transferred an even one million dollars into the captain's checking account.

For a few hours the captain was rich. In the morning, before the bank reopened, Rand retransferred the money out of his account, leaving the bank officials in happy ignorance.

In the main, however, Rand was a loner, had always been a loner, taking his solace in his studies. He had become, at

thirty, one of the youngest lieutenant colonels in the Air
Force, a rank which ten years later he still held, not because
he didn't deserve a promotion but because his superiors understood that Rand was in the perfect job. To promote him
would be to lose him.

He had always been a man with a bitter edge. The world
had passed him by in looks—he was very short, with a thin,
almost emaciated torso, a ridiculously oversized head, and
watery, myopic eyes—it had passed him by with women—
who would not look twice at him—and even the Air Force
had passed him by with promotions.

But he had become a defector in the beginning not because
of any dislike for his own government, but merely for, he
liked to think, the ultimate in hacking. He told the Russians
what they wanted to know about U.S. weapons systems, and
in the doing gained rare insights into what the Soviets were
most frightened of.

Because of his unique, intimate knowledge of the enemy's
fears and weaknesses, he had become the Stephen Hawking
of strategic weapons planning.

But now, for the first time in his life, he was frightened.
It wasn't a game any longer, and someone was watching him.
He had tried two months ago to tap into the FBI's computer
system, but had failed to come up with anything specific about
himself, except that the Bureau believed there was a Soviet
spy within the Pentagon whom they had code-named FE-
LIKS, after the cat he supposed.

Over the following weeks he had come to believe that he
was *the* FELIKS they were searching for, and he understood
that there was no simple way out for him.

Tonight he was convinced of it. It was nearly ten in the
evening. He sat in his tiny office in one of the sub-basements
of the Pentagon staring at his computer screen.

Normally he was home by six in the evening, when he
would check his computer message service. If he was going
to be late, he would bring up his home system on his office
machine to see if anything was waiting for him on the amateur
network. This evening he had forgotten until now.

There was a message, from a man he knew only as Dr. Jo, at TS Industries in California's Silicon Valley. A complicated series of formulae filled his screen, describing the effects on a computer's bubble memory system as it began to reach absolute zero, where all electrical resistance disappeared. In reality it was a message from his Soviet control officer.

By running the formulae through a complex series of transformations, Rand could come up with a date, time, and grid reference for the city of Washington.

The date was today, and the time was 2230, barely a half hour from now. Rand pulled up the street map of Washington, overlaid the grid reference, and picked out the meeting location.

It was odd, he thought, meeting in a hospital parking lot, but then their meetings had been held at odder places: the Lincoln Memorial, Union Station, Gallaudet College.

No way out, he thought again. He had gotten a kick out of the movie. But in real life things like that simply didn't happen. He'd gotten the latest information they'd wanted, it was stored now in his home computer, and he would give it to his control officer tonight. But he was also going to give the man something else. Something the Russians simply couldn't refuse.

Erasing the incoming message, Rand shut down his computer, pulled on his uniform blouse, and, briefcase in hand, took the elevator up to the security gate.

"Working late tonight, Doc?" one of the guards said as Rand turned in his security badge.

He managed a tight smile and a shrug, laid the briefcase on the counter and opened it. Besides a few computer magazines, and a couple of nonclassified reports, there was a Police Special .38 revolver in a standard military issue holster.

"You going partridge hunting?" the guard asked a little too sharply.

Again Rand managed a little smile. "They want me to qualify by Monday, but I haven't shot the damned thing for two years. Figured I'd go to the range." He pulled out the orders he had worked up for himself, directing him to the range officer for pistol qualification on 26 June.

The guard relaxed. "Watch out you don't shoot your foot."

"They'd probably qualify me on the spot," Rand quipped. "It would be the first thing I'd ever hit."

Outside in the parking lot, Rand tossed his briefcase into the passenger seat of his panel van and got in. Swiveling his seat toward the back he flipped on the van's computer system, which was connected by cellular telephone to his house, and within seconds the data the Russians had requested from him was being transferred onto a floppy disk.

Reaching over, he opened his briefcase, took the pistol out of its holster, and laid it on the seat next to his right leg.

Oh, yes, he thought, smiling. He was definitely going to give the Russians something they couldn't refuse. When the disk drive stopped, he swiveled forward, started the van and pulled out onto the highway.

BETHESDA NAVAL HOSPITAL

Arkady Kurshin stood in the corridor a few feet from the emergency room watching the elevator going up. His car was parked just outside, and no one had given him a second glance as he had entered the hospital through the staff entrance.

He was dressed in surgeon's blue scrubs, including the booties and cap.

Schey was in the fourth-floor ICU. He had gotten that information easily from the hospital switchboard.

The elevator passed the third floor but instead of stopping at the fourth continued up to the fifth. He had punched the buttons for both floors.

They had the elevator blocked on four, which left two stairwells, both of which would be watched. They wanted him to come here. They were waiting for him upstairs. McGarvey was waiting for him. He could almost feel the man's presence in the air.

There had been no other special security from what he had been able to see. But the fourth floor would be different.

Turning, he walked back down the corridor, passed through the emergency room, and stepped outside into the still warm evening. Checking his watch he saw that it was nearly ten-thirty. HAMMERHEAD would be arriving at any moment.

He crossed the parking lot, stopping in the shadows between a Ford and a van about thirty feet from his own car as a pair of headlights entered the parking lot from the far end, and slowly started down the back row.

HAMMERHEAD had worked out the contact procedures himself some years ago. He was given the meet time and place over his computer message network. A car would be waiting for him with its dome light on. They had used four different color cars: white, blue, red, and black, and license plates from the District of Columbia, Maryland, Virginia, and Delaware. Each plate began with the same letter: P. Rand was searching now for the white Mercedes with its dome light on and the proper license plate.

At the end of the first row the van turned down the next, passing beneath a light, giving Kurshin a brief glimpse of a lone man behind the wheel.

The van passed the Mercedes, stopped, backed up, and then pulled into the adjacent parking place. The headlights went off, the driver's side door opened, and a man stepped out.

Kurshin, carrying his medical bag loosely in his left hand, stepped out of the shadows and approached Rand who looked up nervously and backed up a step.

"Good evening," Kurshin said pleasantly.

Rand's eyes flicked from his medical garb to the black bag. He nodded. It was obvious that he was very frightened. A gold seam, perhaps, but an amateur ready to explode.

"Damn," Kurshin suddenly swore. "Looks as if I've left my dome light on. Probably run down the goddamned battery."

"It would take at least twenty-four hours to do that," Rand answered automatically.

"It's only been out here fifteen hours."

"Then you'll be okay."

"Yes, I guess I'm safe."

Rand was shaking his head. "Who the hell are you? I've never seen you before. Where is Thomas?"

Thomas, for the past couple of years, had been Antipov himself.

"He sends his greetings," Kurshin replied. "You must know by now that the situation is becoming dangerous for you."

"You're goddamned right I know it. They're calling me 'Feliks the Cat,' for Christ's sake. Can you imagine that? I got it off the FBI's machine. Christ."

"Do you have something for me?"

"You're damned right I do," Rand said. He was working himself up. "But this time I want something in return."

"Is this information valid? It has not been compromised?"

Rand waved the questions off. He pulled out a three-and-one-half-inch floppy disk from his pocket and held it in his left hand. His right hand was in his trousers pocket. His nostrils were flaring and his eyes were very wide.

Something was drastically wrong here. Kurshin's gut tightened, but he held himself in check.

"This is our information?"

"Everything you asked for. Current to the next twelve days and untraceable. I mean totally in the blind."

"You mentioned something in return."

"I want out," Rand said.

"What do you mean?"

"I want you to take me to Moscow. I'm going to trade you this data for my passage."

"I don't think that's possible . . ." Kurshin started to say when Rand suddenly pulled the .38 Police Special out of his pocket and cocked the hammer.

"Then I'll bag me a goddamned Russian spy," Rand shouted.

Driven purely by instinct, Kurshin batted the pistol away. Rand's finger jerked on the trigger and the gun went off. Kurshin pulled out his silenced Graz Buyra from the waistband of his scrubs and fired one shot point-blank into Rand's face. As the man was flung backward he fired his gun again, the noise shockingly loud in the parking lot.

"Those were gunshots," McGarvey shouted, racing out of the ICU.

He and Dr. Rabbinoux had been standing beside Schey's bed near the window. When the shots were fired, McGarvey had looked down into the parking lot. But there was nothing to be seen.

Potok had drawn his gun.

"Somewhere outside," McGarvey snapped.

"He knows we're here, and he's trying to draw us out," Potok said.

They were in the outer office. Dr. Rabbinoux snatched the telephone. McGarvey grabbed it from him. "Get the hell out of here now, Doctor," he yelled.

"That's my patient in there . . ."

"Not for the moment. I'm telling you to get out of here. Go to your office and stay there, no matter what you hear."

Dr. Rabbinoux stepped away from them uncertainly, then turned and hurried out into the corridor, and disappeared.

"I'll take the west stairwell," McGarvey said. "You stick it out here. Anyone comes through either door, shoot them."

"What about Schey?"

"I don't give a shit about him. He's served his purpose. It's Kurshin down there, and he's waiting for me."

"Watch yourself," Potok said, but McGarvey was already racing down the corridor.

The stairwell was silent. If anyone was coming up they were making absolutely no noise. McGarvey switched the Walther's safety to the off position and started down, taking the stairs two at a time but making as little noise as possible. At the bottom of each course he leaned well over the steel railing which gave him a clear shot at the next two courses below. Nothing moved. No one was there.

On the third floor two nurses were talking at their station, and on the second an attendant was pushing a man in a wheelchair through a set of swinging doors. Nothing out of the ordinary.

At the bottom, McGarvey pulled out his FBI identification, clipped it to his lapel pocket, and stepped out into the corridor.

A knot of people had gathered near the front desk, staring and gesticulating down the broad corridor toward the emergency room entrance.

Two Marine guards came pounding up the hall, and when they spotted McGarvey, they split up, dropping into shooter's stances.

"Halt! Halt!" one of the Marines shouted as McGarvey started to turn toward them.

He raised his hands above his head so that his gun was in plain sight. "FBI!" he shouted.

The Marines were well trained but they were young and inexperienced. They hesitated, their weapons trained on McGarvey. Behind him he could hear that the people who'd been standing near the front desk were scattering, trying to get out of the line of fire.

"Look at my badge," McGarvey yelled. "I'm FBI!"

One of the Marines straightened up and cautiously approached, his eyes switching nervously from McGarvey's gun to the badge on his lapel.

"I'm Special Agent McGarvey. FBI. You can check it out, but we heard shots down here."

"Call Captain Schiller," the Marine called back to his partner. "On the double."

The other Marine jumped up and rushed down the corridor back into the emergency room.

"What the hell happened?" McGarvey demanded. "I heard two shots, somewhere outside."

The Marine was still uncertain. "We'll just wait . . ."

"Goddamnit," McGarvey shouted. "You people know what's going on up on the fourth floor. It's why I'm here. Now what the hell happened out there?"

The Marine finally backed down a little. He lowered his weapon, and McGarvey slowly lowered his hands.

"It's an Air Force officer. He was shot out in the parking lot."

"Who did it?"

"We don't know, sir. He apparently drove up, shot the officer and drove off. The police have been notified . . ."

"How did you know this, exactly? Did you see it yourself?"

"No, sir. It was the doctor who . . ."

"What doctor?"

"A surgeon, I think. Blue scrubs. He saw everything, called for the emergency room team, and got him inside."

"Christ," McGarvey swore. "It's him!"

"Sir?"

"That doctor is the killer! He's Russian! KGB!" McGarvey pushed past the Marine and raced down the corridor to the emergency room.

The kid caught up with him almost immediately. Together they burst through the swinging doors and into the waiting room filled with people.

"He's in here," the Marine shouted, swinging left and rushing into the examining room area.

McGarvey was right behind him.

A team of doctors and nurses were working frantically on a man lying flat on his back on an examining table. Kurshin was not among them. The Air Force officer had been shot in the face.

"Where is the doctor who brought this man in?" McGarvey shouted.

One of the nurses looked over her shoulder at McGarvey and the Marine standing there, guns in hand, then glanced at the team members and shook her head. "I think he's on seven getting an operating room ready," she said and went back to her work.

Arkady Kurshin nodded tiredly at the three nurses on the fifth-floor duty station as he picked up the telephone and dialed the three-digit number for the fourth-floor ICU. Rand's blood had splattered the front of his scrubs. It made him look as if he had just come from an operating theater.

"Tough night, Doctor?" one of the nurses asked.

"You wouldn't believe it if I told you," Kurshin said, injecting a note of deep tiredness into his voice.

The nurse smiled solicitously and moved off so that he could have a little privacy for his telephone call. It was ringing.

Potok answered. Kurshin did not recognize his voice, but he knew it wasn't McGarvey.

"This is security," Kurshin snapped, keeping his own voice just low enough so that the nurses couldn't hear what he was saying. "We've got him on the second floor."

"What? Who is this?"

"Security, goddamnit. The Russian, we've got the bastard cornered on the second floor. Is McGarvey there?"

"No, he went down just a couple of minutes ago."

Shit, Kurshin swore to himself. "Well, we need help, goddamnit. Either find McGarvey or get your ass down here on the double."

"What about Schey?"

"We've got the goddamned Russian cornered, didn't you hear me?" Kurshin snapped. The nurse was looking at him. He smiled tiredly, and she gave him a knowing look.

"On my way," Potok said.

"Good," Kurshin said and he hung up the telephone. The elevator was still on the fifth floor. Except for McGarvey's absence, his luck was holding. But if the bastard had gone downstairs, he would know by now what was going on. There still could be a chance.

"The nights keep getting longer," the nurse said.

"Isn't that the truth," Kurshin replied and he went down the corridor and stepped out into the stairwell. He could hear someone rushing down the stairs below as he pulled out his gun and hurried down, his bootied feet making absolutely no noise.

The fourth-floor corridor was deserted. Nothing moved, there were no sounds.

Kurshin hurried down the corridor, his every sense alert that this was a trap.

He pushed open the ICU doors and went into the unit itself. Schey was the only patient. He had regained consciousness, and his eyes were open. He spotted Kurshin and he went wild, thrashing around in the bed, pulling IV tubes out of his arms.

"You were a mistake, Dieter," Kurshin said softly in German. He raised his gun and shot the East German in the face. Above the bed, the heart monitor went flat and began to whistle in a steady tone.

Turning, Kurshin walked back through the ICU and out into the corridor at the same moment Dr. Rabbinoux was emerging from his office.

"Who called you up here?" Rabbinoux started to ask.

Kurshin raised his pistol and shot the doctor in the face at a range of less than twenty feet, the man's head snapping back, his eyes and nose filling with blood, and his body slamming backward against the wall.

McGarvey. He wanted McGarvey. It was the entire reason for coming here like this tonight. The bastard had sent up the signal: Here I am, come and get me. Dieter Schey, your little East German expert, is here. Bait. Come if you can.

"Well, I came," Kurshin mumbled in frustration.

Reaching the stairwell he heard the first-floor door slam open and someone start up the steps. More than one person. At least two, perhaps more.

He wanted McGarvey, but he had another job to do. As much as it rankled, he was professional enough to realize that if he remained here to fight it out, he would lose. There was no way of going up against them all. At least not this time . . . perhaps.

Kurshin turned and hurried noiselessly back up to the fifth floor, where he flashed the nurses another tired smile. The elevator was still on this floor. He punched the button, the doors opened, and he stepped aboard.

"Have a good evening," he said pleasantly.

"You too, Doctor," the nurse said.

* * *

McGarvey with the two Marines right behind him held up at the fourth-floor door, opening it carefully. "Potok," he started to shout, the word dying on his lips as he spotted Dr. Rabbinoux's body lying in a pool of blood.

He slammed open the door and ran down the corridor, again holding up at the ICU door. The Marines were right behind him. McGarvey motioned for them to back him up, and he shoved his way into the room, sweeping his gun right to left, keeping low, moving fast.

Schey was dead, shot in the face at close range.

"Christ!" McGarvey swore.

"Sir," one of the Marines shouted from the corridor. "Out here!"

McGarvey spun on his heel and raced back out of the ICU. Potok had just come through the east stairwell door. The Marine had a gun on him, Potok's hands raised above his head.

"Where the fuck did you go?" McGarvey shouted. "You bastard!"

Potok was shaking his head.

McGarvey turned on the Marine. "He's on the loose. Have this building sealed. Immediately!"

"Yes, sir!" the Marine snapped, but McGarvey had the feeling that they were too late. Once Kurshin was free, God only knew what would happen next.

27

THE FALMOUTH SAFEHOUSE

TROTTER HAD USED HIS CAR PHONE TO CALL AHEAD TWICE. Each time FBI Agent Tom Sills had assured him that nothing had happened yet, but that they were keeping their eyes open.

Turning off the secondary highway he hurried up the narrow gravel road three-quarters of a mile to the house. His windows were down. The night was very dark under a slightly overcast sky, and the air smelled heavy. It would probably rain soon, he thought.

Fifty yards before the road opened into the clearing, his way was blocked by a battered blue pickup truck and he had to stop. He reached beneath his coat and pulled out his pistol, thumbing the safety off.

"It's me," he called out softly. "John Trotter."

The beam of a powerful flashlight off to his left suddenly illuminated the interior of the car, blinding him.

"It's him," a voice said from the darkness.

He heard the static and crackle of a walkie-talkie. A second later the flashlight was switched off, and Agent Sills approached the car.

"You made good time, sir," he said. "Sorry about the light, but we had to make sure."

"No problem," Trotter said. "Everything is still okay here?"

"So far so good," Sills said but he seemed a little embarrassed. "I'm sorry, sir, but I called for backup. It's very dark out here and there's no way the four of us will be able to cover every approach."

They had wanted to keep this operation as quiet as possible, but the man did have a point, and Trotter conceded it. "You're right, but I want the extra hands kept away from Dr. Abbott. Officially she is just another body in the Witness Protection Program."

"Yes, sir."

"They don't even have to know she is a woman."

"No."

"Move your truck now and tell them I'm coming up to the house. I want to talk to her."

"Will do," Agent Sills said.

Yuri Deryugin and Mikhail Lakomsky lay on the floor of the dark woods a few meters down from where the blue pickup truck was parked. They were dressed in black night fighter coveralls, their faces blackened. Each of them was armed with an AK74 assault rifle equipped with infrared spotting scope. In addition they each carried a suppressed .22 caliber automatic pistol, a razor-sharp stiletto, and a wire garrote capable, in the right hands, of completely severing a man's head from his body.

They were both experts, KGB Department Viktor graduates, whom Baranov had handpicked for advancement.

For the past hour since penetrating the property's outer

fence, they had reconnoitered all the approaches to the house, spotting the three FBI agents, one by the pickup truck, one just within the woods down from the clearing, and the other on the east side of the house. They assumed there would be at least one other agent within the house, in addition to the man who'd just shown up.

They had been close enough to overhear most of the conversation between Sills and Trotter, so they knew that they would have to get in and out soon, before the reinforcements arrived.

Deryugin motioned for Lakomsky to hold up. The other man nodded and took aim on Agent Sills's back with his rifle.

It was very quiet. Even so, Lakomsky could hear absolutely no noise as Deryugin crept forward toward where Agent Sills was backing the pickup truck into place.

Sills got out of the truck. He was dressed in a blue windbreaker and dark blue baseball cap. He carried an M16 rifle, which he slung, barrel down, over his shoulder as he stepped off the road, and hid himself behind the bole of a larger tree, barely one meter from where Deryugin lay perfectly still.

Slowly, the Russian rose up from the darkness behind Sills. He held the garrote loosely in his two hands, and as he took a single step forward he raised it up over his head.

Sills never really knew what happened. One instant he was standing behind the tree looking toward the driveway, and in the next something incredibly sharp was around his neck, and his world began immediately to grow gray and soft.

"We think there may be some trouble coming our way," Trotter told Lorraine Abbott. They sat in the pleasantly furnished living room across from each other. Agent Bert Langerford had stepped out into the stairhall to let them talk.

"Is it the Russians?" she asked. She hadn't gotten much rest in the past few days, and it was beginning to show in her eyes, which were red and puffy.

"We think so," Trotter said. "I'm not going to lie to you. But I think you will be safe here for the moment. We have some more people coming in to help out tonight. And in the morning we'll be moving you to another place."

She was watching him, her nostrils flared. "You *think* there may be some trouble. You *think* they may be Russians. You *think* I'll be safe here for the moment. What, Mr. Trotter, do you *know*?"

"That you are a very important woman, Dr. Abbott," Trotter said tiredly. "And that the Russians want you dead."

"Why, in God's name? What have I done to them?"

"You got in their way."

"How?"

"By helping Kirk McGarvey."

"Damn," Lorraine said in frustration. She jumped up and went across to the heavily draped window, hugging herself as if she were cold.

"Please don't open the curtains," Trotter said.

She spun on him. "Are they here now?"

"It's possible."

"Then what?" she demanded.

Trotter didn't understand the question. "Doctor?"

"If they come here tonight and try . . . and fail. Then what happens to me?"

"As I said, we'll be moving you to a new safehouse."

"I mean afterward. How long is this going to keep up?"

"I don't know," Trotter admitted. "But not very long."

"It's already been too long," Lorraine snapped. "Far too long."

28

BETHESDA NAVAL HOSPITAL

"IT WAS KURSHIN ON THE TELEPHONE," POTOK SAID. He and McGarvey stood back as the FBI's forensics crew worked with two computer experts from the CIA's Technical Services Division, going over Rand's van.

There were police and military security people everywhere, and more were coming. They could hear sirens in the distance.

"Yeah," McGarvey said. "And now the sonofabitch is gone." It rankled, and it was all he could do to hold his anger in check. The man was good. Almost too good, as if he had gotten information from another source.

"If I had stayed . . ."

McGarvey shook his head. "He would have found another way in, or he would have killed you."

An APB had been put out, and police in a twenty-five-mile radius were looking for Kurshin. But no one had actually seen him leave the hospital or seen what kind of a car he was driving.

The Soviet Embassy was being watched, but it wasn't likely he would go back there. He'd had this all worked out in the beginning. Rand's meeting him here like this was nothing more than a convenience for him. All of his ducks had been lined up in a neat little row.

"What I can't figure out is what happened here. The shots you heard were fired from Rand's pistol."

"He was on Trotter's short list, and he was smart enough to figure that we were on to him. He probably came here demanding that Kurshin get him out of Washington. When Kurshin refused he pulled out a gun."

"The poor bastard never had a chance," Potok said.

McGarvey looked at him. He was starting to come down, and a deep tiredness seemed to be closing in. But there was something else. He was missing something. Kurshin had known what the setup was on the fourth floor. How? Who knew besides Trotter?

Don Lillianthal, one of the CIA technicians, broke away from the others searching Rand's van and came over to where McGarvey and Potok were standing. He was young, in his early twenties.

"It's all there," he said. "Hell of a setup. State of the art. The man definitely knew his shit."

"What have you got for us?" McGarvey asked.

"It's hard to say, Mr. McGarvey. What he's got in there is an IBM XT, but jazzed up with some of his own circuitry, and wired directly into a cellular telephone. Which means he could tap into his own home system, which I'm sure is a doozy, and in turn tap into any computer network in the country . . . hell, probably the entire world."

"Any physical evidence that he turned something over to the Russians?"

"Only in a negative sense, sir," Lillianthal said. "One of his disk readers was empty."

"Which means?"

"It might mean nothing. But for a man like Dr. Rand, he'd almost always be running one program or another. We found plenty of disks in the van."

"Anything classified?"

"Almost certainly," Lillianthal said. "That'll be up to the Pentagon to decide, they know their own shit better than I do. But the point I'm trying to make, sir, is that it's possible that whatever information he'd wanted to pass over to the Russians was contained on the disk he took out of the reader. He just bought the farm before he had a chance to reload."

"How much information is on one of those things?" McGarvey asked.

"A lot."

"Enough, let's say, to reprogram an intercontinental ballistic missile?" Potok asked.

Lillianthal grinned. "Hell, sir, there's enough room on that type of disk to *build* an ICBM."

Potok turned away, his jaw tight. McGarvey knew what the man was thinking. June thirtieth was less than two weeks away, and almost certainly Kurshin had the data he needed for the second attack. But what data? Rand was an expert on virtually every weapons system within the U.S. and NATO arsenals. That was a lot of dangerous territory.

"Thanks," McGarvey told the kid. "We'll get out of your hair now."

"No sweat. We'll have something put together for you first thing in the A.M. We're heading over to his house now."

"That's it for us now," Potok said when Lillianthal had gone. "Truly, I am sorry that this did not work out."

"It's not over with yet."

Potok shrugged. "It is for me. Now I must call my embassy, and in the morning I will return home. We have much work to do."

"I'll see what I can do from this end," McGarvey said. "It may not be much."

"I think you will go after Kurshin. I think that you will not let that go so easily, but it has nothing to do with Israel. It has only to do with you."

"If I come up with something . . ."

"Then you will contact me, or you will not. We'll see."

A Montgomery County patrol car pulled up, and the cop called to them from the open window. "Mr. McGarvey?"

McGarvey turned around. "Yes?"

"Been trying to find you for the last half hour, sir. You're supposed to call two-eight-seven on the double. Sounded urgent."

It was the extension Trotter had given him. "Hold on," he told Potok. "Can I call out on your radio?" he asked the cop.

"Yes, sir," the cop said.

McGarvey went around the car and got in on the passenger side as the cop contacted his central dispatch. He handed the microphone to McGarvey, who radioed the telephone number.

It was answered on the first ring. "Good evening, the White House."

The cop's eyes widened.

"Two-eight-seven," McGarvey said.

The connection was made a second later. "Yes."

"McGarvey."

"There may be a developing situation at Falmouth. Trotter is on his way there now."

McGarvey's grip tightened on the microphone. "How long ago?"

"Sixty-five minutes."

"Call him and say that we're on our way."

"Yes," the man said and the connection was broken.

"Can you get me a helicopter?" he asked the cop. "Now?"

"Yes, sir. On the hospital roof. Five minutes."

"Do it," McGarvey snapped and he jumped out of the car.

Potok had heard the entire exchange. "He made his contact, took care of Schey, and now he's after Dr. Abbott?"

"Looks like it," McGarvey said. "We just might have the bastard after all."

* * *

Arkady Kurshin lowered his police-band walkie-talkie, a thin smile coming to his lips. From where he stood on the roof of the hospital building he had a clear sight line down into the parking lot.

The game he was playing was dangerous, and he knew it. If he lost now, his life would be forfeit. Baranov would see to it. The entire project rested on his decision and his ability to carry it out.

But the timing was tight. It depended upon who would show up first, McGarvey or the helicopter.

Kurshin was still dressed in his blue hospital scrubs. He moved away from the roof edge and in the shadows pulled off the bloodstained clothes, bundled them up and stuffed them behind an air-conditioning vent. Beneath, he wore a short-sleeved khaki jacket, khaki trousers, and soft boots.

He had reloaded his automatic on the way up to the roof, and he checked its action as he moved directly across to the helicopter pad on the north side of the building, low red lights outlining the landing circle. From where he crouched in the darkness behind the main air-conditioning equipment house he could see the elevator door to his left, and the helicopter pad directly ahead.

Trotter was assistant deputy director of operations for the Agency, and a longtime friend of McGarvey's. Baranov had described him as a capable administrator and more than a fair cop. Something had spooked him into going out to Falmouth. Kurshin figured it was probably the helicopter overflight this afternoon. Antipov was probably right, the Americans had discovered the true nature of Xavier Enterprises.

Again, Kurshin had the thought that he was backing himself into a trap. He had the data they needed, so why hadn't he turned and left the hospital when he'd had the chance? By now he would have been long gone. On his way back to Rome where his team would be gathering.

McGarvey. He had eyes now only for that man. He could still hear the American's voice clearly in his mind from the sewer tunnel beneath the streets of Kaiserslautern. He could still see McGarvey disarming the missile. And he could still feel the incredible surprise and anger that had overcome him at that moment. The bile then as now tasted bitter at the back of his throat.

He had been staring at the elevator indicator—the car was still on the ground floor—when he suddenly could hear the distant sound of an incoming helicopter. He looked up and searched the sky, finally finding it coming fast from the northeast. He glanced at the elevator indicator again; still the car remained downstairs.

Time. It always was just a matter of timing.

The helicopter, with police markings on its tail, quickly loomed large overhead as it slowly came in for a landing, centering on the pad and swinging around in a tight little circle before settling in.

Hiding his gun behind his right leg, Kurshin ran across to the helicopter, keeping low. The pilot was alone in his machine. As Kurshin approached he popped open the door.

"Mr. McGarvey?" he shouted over the noise of the rotors.

"No," Kurshin said. He raised his pistol and shot the cop in the face, careful to aim above the microphone in front of his lips, and below the rim of his helmet. The cop's body was shoved to the side against his restraints, and then slumped forward.

Kurshin looked over his shoulder. The elevator indicator was on the second floor and starting up now!

Shoving his pistol in his belt, he quickly unharnessed the cop's body, manhandled it out of the helicopter, and dragged it across the roof, dumping it in the darkness behind the air-conditioning house. He unstrapped the helmet and pulled it off the cop's head. Only a small amount of blood had spattered the inside of the helmet which Kurshin quickly wiped off with his handkerchief, and as he raced back to the helicopter he pulled the helmet on.

He scrambled into the machine, strapped himself in, and plugged in his headset. A split second later the elevator door opened, and two men stepped out, one of them McGarvey.

They rushed across the roof to the helicopter as Kurshin reached over and popped open the rear door, then turned back to his instruments and control column.

This machine, he decided, wasn't much different from the larger Hind trainers he had learned on.

"We have to get down to Falmouth in a hurry," McGarvey said, climbing into the rear seat.

"Yes, sir," Kurshin replied. "Exactly where do you want to go?"

"I'll tell you on the run. Now get us out of here."

— 29 —

THE FALMOUTH SAFEHOUSE

IT HAD TAKEN YURI DERYUGIN A FULL FIFTEEN MINUTES TO make his way through the dark woods to the edge of the clearing. He had sent Lakomsky across the dirt road to approach the house from the east. Between them they would be able to cover the entire clearing and three sides of the large farmhouse.

Standing behind the bole of a large tree, the Russian raised his rifle, activated the infrared scope, and slowly scanned the clearing left to right. Images appeared pale gray and ghostly, but nobody could hide in the darkness.

A very bright light bloomed in his scope from the edge of the woods about fifty yards to Deryugin's left, momentarily overpowering his scope and blinding him. For a second or two he wasn't sure what he had seen. Gunfire, an explosion? But there had been no sound.

The light breeze was blowing in his face, and the images in his scope cleared about the same moment he smelled cigarette smoke. One of the FBI agents had actually lit a cigarette. In Deryugin's mind the action was extremely stupid, unprofessional. They were expecting trouble, and yet this man could not control his petty vice.

The agent's body was partially hidden behind brush and small trees, but Deryugin had a clear sight line on his head. At this distance he would have preferred a torso shot, and under normal conditions he would have moved in closer to get it. But there were others coming. He had heard the other agent tell Trotter so.

There was no time.

Deryugin settled the rifle's crosshairs on the FBI agent's ear, then raised his aim slightly to compensate for the effect the Kevlar silencer would have on the path of the bullet and squeezed off a shot, the noise audible perhaps for as far as twenty yards.

The agent disappeared, his body crashing into the brush. For just an instant Deryugin thought he might have missed, but there were no other sounds in the woods, and he knew that he had not. The agent was down and dead.

Again the Russian carefully scanned the clearing and the house, left to right. He caught a movement in the woods across the driveway, lost it, then picked it up again, a dark figure moving silently. It was Lakomsky getting into position.

From the helicopter they had spotted a man on the east side of the house. Lakomsky would be in position to see him at any moment now.

The walkie-talkie he had taken from Sills's body crackled to life. "Hank?"

Deryugin pulled it from his pocket and put it to his ear.

"Hank, for Christ's sake, was that you making all that goddamned noise over there?"

It would have to be the agent on the east side of the house. Apparently he had heard the body crashing into the brush, but had not heard the silenced shot.

"Tom, you copy?"

"What the hell is going on out there?" another voice radioed.

"Is that Bert?"

"Yeah, I'm in the front hallway. Now what the hell is going on out there?"

"I heard a noise in the woods, and now I can't raise Hank or . ..." The agent's voice was abruptly cut off in mid-sentence by a distinctive short, sharp sound and the radio was silent.

Deryugin knew what he had heard. Lakomsky had shot him. The sound was that of a high-powered rifle bullet hitting a human skull.

"Mays, you were cut off," the agent from inside the house answered.

Deryugin keyed the walkie-talkie. "Christ, I think Mays and Hank are both down. We've got troubles out here."

"Who is this?"

"Tom," Deryugin replied, muffling his voice a little.

"Goddamnit, Sills, where the hell are you?"

"I'm coming up the road from the truck. Should be to you in a couple of minutes, maybe less."

"Are we under attack?"

"I think so . . ." Deryugin radioed, cutting himself off before finishing the sentence. He dropped the walkie-talkie to the ground and raised his rifle, aiming at the front door of the farmhouse.

"Sills?" the agent in the house radioed urgently. "Sills, goddamnit."

At this point, his first objective accomplished, Lakomsky would have moved farther south so that he could cover the rear exits from the house.

Sixty seconds. Deryugin was going to give the agent inside the house that long. No more.

Less than ten seconds later the front door of the house

opened. The lights inside had been switched off; nevertheless Deryugin could see the figure of a man just inside.

He waited patiently.

The FBI agent came out of the house a moment later in a dead run, momentarily catching Deryugin off guard. But the Russian was a professional and extremely well trained.

He led the man off the porch, and twenty feet from the house, he squeezed off a shot, hitting the man high on his torso, literally lifting him off his feet.

Bert Langerford's M16 fired a quick burst as he went down, but he was dead before he hit the ground.

Deryugin lowered his rifle. Now there was only the woman and Trotter, left inside.

Moving fast, he stepped around from behind the tree and zigzagged across the clearing toward the house.

Langerford was down and a dark-suited figure was racing across the clearing from the woods.

Trotter, standing a few feet inside the stairhall, led the man with his pistol and fired off three shots in rapid succession. The figure went down, rolled twice, and fired two shots, the bullets smacking into the wall behind Trotter.

A silenced rifle, Trotter had time to note, as he dove left. His heart was hammering in his chest. Somehow they had managed to take out all four agents. There was no telling how many of them were out there. But Sills had said he had called for reinforcements. If they could only hold out here for a little longer.

Lorraine Abbott was at the head of the stairs. Langerford had told her to hide herself somewhere upstairs, but she had turned back when she'd heard the M16 firing.

Deryugin fired a third shot, the bullet shattering a section of banister a few feet below where she stood.

"Get back," Trotter shouted up at her.

He started for the stairs when the back door burst open, and Lakomsky's big frame suddenly filled the doorway. Trotter snapped off two shots, both of them hitting the Russian in the chest, driving him backward.

Deryugin fired a fourth shot from the front of the house. Ignoring it, Trotter took the stairs up two at a time. Lorraine had shrunk back against the corridor wall, her eyes wide with fright. Grabbing her arm, he roughly hauled her the rest of the way down the hall to the attic door, which he yanked open. The narrow stairs led up into the darkness.

"They've come here to kill me, haven't they," Lorraine whispered. She was very frightened.

"Yes, but I've managed to kill one of them, and I may have wounded the one out front."

"There's probably more than two of them."

"Possibly," Trotter admitted. "But the FBI is sending someone else out here. They should be arriving very soon."

"Can we hold out that long?"

"We're going to try, Doctor, believe me," Trotter said. His weapon was a six-shot .38 caliber revolver. He'd already fired five times. "For now I want you to go up to the attic, find the darkest spot, and hide yourself. No noise, no sounds, nothing. And I don't want you coming out of there until you hear my voice or McGarvey's."

"He's coming here?"

"I left the message for him. Now get up there. No noise."

She looked at him for a long moment, then turned and headed up the stairs on the balls of her feet.

As soon as she had disappeared into the darkness, Trotter closed the door and headed back down the corridor to the stairs, stopping just at the end of the corridor.

Nothing moved below in the stairhall. The front door was still open.

Turning, he hurried silently back down the corridor and went into one of the front bedrooms, where he cautiously approached the window and, parting the curtain slightly, looked down into the clearing.

Langerford's body still lay in the gravel driveway, but the Russian was gone. Where was he, and how many others were out there?

There was no telling when Sills's reinforcements would

show up, or if McGarvey had gotten his urgent message. Until then it would be up to him to hold out here. His first task would be to find more ammunition for his weapon, or take the rifle from the dead Russian in the back hall.

"Put your gun down, Mr. Trotter," someone said from behind him.

Trotter stiffened and started to turn.

"I will kill you unless you do exactly as I say."

Trotter weighed his chances, which at the moment were practically nil. The man behind him was almost certainly a Russian Department Viktor type. Highly trained, highly motivated.

"We don't do things like this on each other's territory," he said.

"Your gun. Drop it."

"If you know my name, then you know who and what I am. If you kill me, the political repercussions could even bring a man such as Baranov down."

"I have no time to argue with you. Either drop your gun this instant or I will kill you."

Trotter had absolutely no doubt the man meant what he was saying. Time, it was all he needed.

Slowly he bent over and laid the .38 on the floor, and straightening up he stepped away from it and turned around. The Russian was tall and very well built. His weapon was equipped with the latest night spotting scope, and silencer, which explained their effectiveness.

"Where is Dr. Abbott?"

"The FBI is sending reinforcements out here. They will be here momentarily."

"Yes, I know this," Deryugin replied calmly. "So you will either take me to Dr. Abbott or I will kill you and search the house myself."

Trotter shook his head. "You will either kill me now or then, so it doesn't matter."

"No. I don't mean to kill either of you. My orders were to come here, kidnap Dr. Abbott, and take her to Fredericksburg, where an airplane is waiting to take us to Mexico City. If you cooperate, I will bring you as well. You would be quite a prize in Moscow.''

Was the man telling the truth? Probably not, Trotter decided. An assassination was infinitely easier than kidnapping. There would be no need for them to take the latter risk.

Again it came down to a question of time.

''She's in the basement.''

Deryugin's eyes narrowed. ''I think she is up here somewhere.''

''As soon as the shooting began, I sent her downstairs. I came up here to see what was happening outside. High ground.''

Deryugin was weighing the possibilities, Trotter could see it in the man's eyes.

''We will go to the basement. If you are lying I will kill you.''

Trotter nodded. ''I think we've already established that.''

They had followed Interstate 95 out of Washington, skirting Falmouth along the Rappahannock River which brought them in from the rear of the ninety-acre property on which the farmhouse was perched.

At first they nearly overflew the place. There were absolutely no lights showing from the house. They came around in a tight circle, and McGarvey finally spotted Trotter's car parked behind the FBI's blue van.

''There,'' McGarvey shouted, leaning forward. ''Set us down in the clearing at the front of the house.''

Kurshin nodded. ''Yes, sir.''

McGarvey sat back and studied the pilot's neck and shoulders. The voice. There was something vaguely familiar about the man. He hadn't gotten a very good look at him because of the helmet he wore, and the rush they were in. But all the way down something kept nagging at the back of his mind.

''Kirk,'' Potok suddenly shouted.

McGarvey turned to him. They were barely a hundred feet off the ground now. Potok was pointing down. There was a body lying about thirty feet from the front of the house, FBI stenciled in yellow letters on the back of his dark blue windbreaker.

"Get us down now," McGarvey shouted. "And then call for backup."

"Yes, sir," Kurshin replied.

McGarvey pulled out his Walther, checked the action, and switched the safety off. The instant the helicopter's skids touched the gravel driveway, he popped the hatch and he and Potok scrambled out, separated and raced up toward the house.

Behind them the helicopter rose up a few feet and sideslipped all the way across the clearing, where it set down just at the edge of the woods.

It was a good move, McGarvey thought, getting the machine out of the line of fire. But he didn't have time for that now.

Potok reached Langerford's body first and turned it over. "He's dead," he called out.

McGarvey nodded and pointed up toward the house. The front door was open.

Together they raced the rest of the way up the driveway, mounted the three steps onto the porch, and stopped on either side of the door, their guns up and at the ready.

They exchanged a look, and McGarvey rolled left, leaping into the stairhall, sweeping left to right as he ran. He pulled up at the bottom of the stairs.

In the dim light filtering in from outside he could see another figure lying in a heap in the back corridor. This one was dressed in black.

Potok came in a moment later, flattening against the opposite wall. For a moment they remained in position, listening. But the house was absolutely still.

"Trotter," McGarvey shouted. There was no answer.

They were too late. While Kurshin had been running them around in circles at the hospital, he had sent his people out here to kill Lorraine.

"We'll start upstairs," he said.

"They may still be here, Kirk," Potok said softly. "That body out front was oozing blood. He cannot have been dead for more than a few minutes."

"I hope you're right," McGarvey replied. His gut was tight, and a rage threatened to engulf him. Control, he told himself. It always came down to that.

The upstairs corridor was in nearly complete darkness. McGarvey started up the stairs, slowly, softly, his every sense straining to detect a noise, a movement, anything that would indicate someone was waiting above.

At the top he stepped into the deeper shadows along the wall and cocked his ear. Had he heard something? Perhaps above, in the attic, a floorboard creaking.

"Hold up," he whispered softly to Potok who was a few steps down.

The Israeli stopped.

"John?" McGarvey called out. "Lorraine?"

There was a definite movement above in the attic, and then someone was coming down the stairs at the end of the corridor. McGarvey dropped back and brought his gun up, aiming into the darkness.

A door banged open.

"Kirk?" Lorraine Abbott cried. "Oh, God, is it you?"

"Here," McGarvey called to her.

She came the rest of the way down the corridor in a rush, and suddenly she was in his arms, crying and laughing. For just a second or two, McGarvey kept his gun up, but then he allowed himself to relax, and he led her to the head of the stairs.

"There was shooting, and I think they killed all the FBI agents. I can't believe you're here. It's over."

"Are you all right?"

"Frightened, but I'm okay." She spotted Potok and stiffened.

"What about John? Where is he?"

Her eyes suddenly went very wide. "Oh, my God, Kirk. You haven't found him?"

"What is it?"

"The basement," she stammered. "I heard them from up here."

"Heard who?"

"One of the Russians. He wanted to know where I was hiding. John told him I was down in the basement. They're still there."

Potok spun around and dropped low so that he could see down into the stairhall. He shook his head.

"Stay here," McGarvey whispered urgently to Lorraine. "It was a police helicopter that brought us in. The pilot has called for backup."

"Kirk, it was the Russians in a helicopter this afternoon. That's how they found us."

"It's all right. No matter what happens stay here," McGarvey said. He hadn't really listened to her.

She nodded, her eyes wide.

Potok started down the stairs, McGarvey a few feet behind him. Suddenly there was a shuffling below.

"Kirk," Trotter cried out.

A burst of automatic weapons fire raked the stairwell. The Israeli took at least three hits in his legs, and he pitched forward, tumbling down the stairs.

"Now!" Trotter shouted again.

McGarvey was down the stairs in time to see Trotter desperately struggling with a black-suited figure who was trying to bring his bulky rifle around again.

He snapped off three shots as he scrambled past Potok, the first going wide, the second hitting the Russian in the neck and the third smacking into the side of his head, spinning him around against the wall, where he collapsed.

"Are you all right?" he shouted back at Potok who was struggling to sit up.

"I'll live," the Israeli said, gritting his teeth in pain.

"John . . . ?" McGarvey started to ask when another burst of automatic weapons fire raked the stairhall, this time from the rear corridor.

Trotter took at least one hit in his hip, the force of the bullet slamming him backward off his feet.

A blindingly hot and heavy blow struck McGarvey in his side, shoving him to the left, as he fired two shots at a khaki-suited figure in the back doorway.

He hit the floor and rolled over and over toward the wall as the firing went on and on.

It came to him in a split instant then; their pilot in the khaki jacket, his familiar voice, there on the roof of the hospital waiting for them. It was Kurshin. It had to be!

He fired three more shots in desperation, but the doorway was empty.

"Kurshin!" he shouted at the top of his lungs. "Kurshin!" He tried to struggle up, but it was hard to move, and it seemed as if the stairhall was becoming even darker than before. "Kurshin," he shouted again.

In the distance he thought he could hear sirens, a lot of them, but that was impossible, he thought, sinking back on the floor.

Again he had failed.

The sirens were much closer now, but then they were drowned out by the sounds of the helicopter lifting off.

He had failed, but so had the Russian.

There would be a next time, he thought as the darkness settled in over him. There definitely would be a next time.

BOOK THREE

—— 30 ——

ROME

Arkady Kurshin walked along the tree-lined pleasant Via San Domenico, hate riding on his shoulders like a
powerful dark cloud. He limped slightly from his wound, but
it had been nearly six weeks since Falmouth and he was almost
completely recovered.

It was early evening. Traffic downtown had been snarled
up, as usual, making it difficult for him to meet his rendezvous
schedule and still take his usual precautions. His face was
different now, though, as was his hair, his clothing, and
his manner of speaking. Here he was a Frenchman visiting
Italy.

At the corner across from the Hotel Aventimo, he stopped
to light a cigarette. There wasn't much traffic, but down the

block music came from the open doors of a small café, and a young couple strolled arm in arm beneath the street lamp, disappearing around the corner.

A large, swarthy man, dressed only in slacks and an open-collar shirt, stepped out of a dark doorway up from the hotel and looked pointedly across the street at Kurshin.

If he looked right or left, it would mean that the rendezvous wasn't safe. He did neither, and Kurshin went across the street.

"You were not followed?" the lookout asked. His voice was soft; nevertheless he spoke in Italian in case someone was listening.

"Of course not," Kurshin replied. "My people are here? All of them?"

"Yes, and it has become a real bitch keeping them out of trouble. You know how the navy is."

"We'll be gone soon."

"Not soon enough."

Kurshin gave the lookout a hard stare. He could have broken the man in two with his bare hands, the impertinent bastard. But then respect was such an ephemeral quality. Baranov had let the word float down subtly that one of his handpicked few had erred. It would be up to him to rebuild his reputation, but if he failed this time Baranov would completely wash his hands of him.

The lookout caught something of that from Kurshin's eyes and he backed down. "They are waiting for you upstairs. Will you leave tonight?"

"Thank you for your help," Kurshin said, ignoring the man's question.

"Yes," the man said. "Will you or the others be needing anything else?"

"Our transportation has been taken care of?"

"There is a camper van in the garage. It won't attract any attention, the roads are filled with them these days."

"And the boat?"

"Waiting for you in Naples. The provisions are already on board, as is the paperwork."

"And the other items?"

"On board as well."

The lookout was actually the number-two man behind the KGB's Rome *resident*. A good and competent man was how Baranov had described him. He had made the arrangements for the hotel, their transportation, and the boat in Naples without knowing any of the other details of the operation. He had not been told that the men upstairs were naval officers, but then it would have been easy enough for him to deduce that fact simply by the way they talked and behaved themselves.

"There will be no track here in Rome," he assured Kurshin. "Good hunting."

"Thank you, Yuri Semenovich. Your contribution will not go unnoticed."

Kurshin turned, walked the rest of the way down the block, and entered the hotel, which looked almost like a small villa. Small and very private. The desk man was not on duty and the tiny lobby was in semidarkness. He took the narrow elevator up to the third floor and as he softly slid the iron gate back he heard a low burst of laughter from the room at the end of the corridor. Carefully he moved closer. He could hear them talking inside, though at first he couldn't make out the words.

Someone said something, and again there was laughter.

"You're goddamned right," another of them said clearly.

Competent and dedicated men, and all of them English speakers. A rare combination for a Soviet naval officer.

Kurshin knocked once at the door and all sounds from within ceased. A moment later he knocked twice, and the door was opened a crack. The room was in darkness, a clubroom odor of cigarette smoke, vodka, and male bodies wafting out.

He pushed the door the rest of the way open and stepped inside. Someone to his left closed the door and the lights came on, leaving Kurshin blinking at the six officers each pointing a silenced Makarov automatic at him, and he managed a slight smile.

"Good evening, gentlemen," he said in English. "Either shoot me or offer me a drink. Frankly I'd prefer vodka."

There was a camaraderie within the military services, especially the navy, that was completely alien to Kurshin. He had to force his bonhomie. He had almost always worked alone. This time, of course, it would have been completely impossible.

"Search him," one of the men said. They all were dressed in ordinary street clothes.

One of the others laid his pistol down and quickly frisked Kurshin, coming up with his Graz Buyra. He stepped aside.

"Now, drop your trousers."

Kurshin's eyes narrowed, though he understood the reason.

"Now," the officer snapped.

Kurshin did as he was told. He had taken the bandage off the wound high on his thigh. It was puckered and an angry red color.

One of the others stepped a little closer and looked at the wound. "It's real," he said.

The first officer lowered his gun. "Well, I don't think the Americans would shoot one of their own people just to infiltrate us."

"Captain Makayev?" Kurshin asked, pulling up his trousers.

"At your service, Comrade Colonel," Captain First Rank Nikolai Gerasimovich Makayev said, and they shook hands "When do we get out of here?"

"Tonight," Kurshin said, looking at the other five men. "I have a camper van parked a couple of blocks from here. We'll be leaving in singles and pairs, so we won't attract too much attention to ourselves."

"Our orders?"

"Not until we're at sea."

Captain Makayev nodded. It was a sensible rule that they all understood, though they had not been told very much about this assignment, other than that it would be extremely dangerous, but that those who returned would be well rewarded. Each man in his own way was in very great need of such rewards.

"Now introduce me to the others, Captain."

Makayev nodded. "You've already met my executive officer, Captain Second Rank Gennadi Gavrilovich Fedorenko."

He was the officer who had patted Kurshin down. He seemed very self-assured. They shook hands.

"And our ship's doctor, Avenir Akimovich Velikanov."

He and Kurshin shook hands.

"That wound of yours should be covered, Colonel," he said.

"I'll let you see to it once we're out of here," Kurshin said. The doctor was an alcoholic, but he was competent enough for what he had to do, which after all would not involve *saving* lives.

"Our nuclear engineer, Captain Second Rank Ivan Pavlovich Abalakin. Our missile man, Lieutenant Aleksei Sergeevich Chobotov, and our boy genius sonarman, Lieutenant Aleksandr Ivanovich Raina."

Kurshin shook hands with them as well.

"You all have experience on Alpha-class boats?"

"Yes, sir," Captain Makayev said, his eyes shining. "And we're anxious to get to work."

"There'll be plenty of it for you to do, Captain, believe me. And very soon."

31

THE ISLAND OF SÉRIFOS

McGARVEY STOOD ON A WINDSWEPT ROCKY PROMONTORY looking out across the azure Aegean Sea toward the mainland fifty miles to the northwest. He was winded and sweating under the fierce Greek summer sun and the breeze felt good on his legs and bare torso.

He was running five miles a day now, up and down the craggy paths around the tiny rock-strewn island. A dozen families of Greek fishermen lived in a tiny village on the north side of the island, leaving him in relative isolation on the south side where he had taken up residence in an abandoned lighthouse.

For the past few days he had known that someone would be coming. He had felt it in his bones. It was a common feeling for him, which had saved his life on more than one occasion. He had picked out the small hydrofoil boat while it was still eight or ten miles out, by its long, creamy wake. Now it was barely a mile off the ancient stone dock in the village below. He had been brought here to this island the same way a month ago, and now someone was coming to him.

Unconsciously he touched the healing scar on the small of his back to the right of his spine. Kurshin's bullet had destroyed one of his kidneys and it had been removed that night in the Bethesda Naval Hospital. He had nearly bled to death on the operating table, and still a weakness would come over him at the odd moment.

But he had been lucky, once again. How long would that hold?

Turning, he started down from the crest of the hill toward the lighthouse two miles away, running lightly so as not to jar his back, but easily because it felt good to be alive and functioning again.

At first an old woman had come up from the village to help tend to his wound and cook his meals. But after the first week he had hiked across the island, showing up at the small taverna. After that he had been left alone; going into the village only once a week for food, newspapers, and other supplies.

A week ago the doctor from Síros on his monthly rounds had come up to see him, pronouncing him reasonably fit for light exercise. But by then he had already been running every day.

The lighthouse was perched on a sheer cliff that dropped ninety feet to the sea. A narrow path led to a stone bridge across to it.

Inside, McGarvey wiped off his face with a towel, and in his bedroom pulled out his Walther automatic, checked its action, and went back outside, across the bridge, and up the path beyond where it branched off toward the village.

It was just noon, and his stomach was rumbling. With all his work, and the fresh sea air and his daily swims before dinner, he had built up a healthy appetite. But who was coming? Only a very few people knew where he had been taken. But as on that night at the hospital, he had the feeling that Kurshin had another source of information. Someone other than FELIKS in the Pentagon. Someone in the Agency.

He climbed farther up the hill where he took up a position from which he could see the village path. By now the hydrofoil would have landed, and if someone were coming up here to him, they would be showing up soon.

Paranoia, the thought came to him as it often had over the past few years. Mistrust. Suspicion. Once he'd thought he knew something about honor, but in this business the opposite seemed true just as often.

A lone figure appeared at the crest of the hill and started down the long side, moving slowly, awkwardly. He was dressed in dark slacks and a light-colored shirt, but it wasn't until he got a little closer that McGarvey could see he walked with a limp and was using a cane. He knew who it was.

Stuffing the pistol in the waistband of his shorts, he scrambled down the hill and went back up to the path. Trotter was just coming around the corner, and he stopped as McGarvey came up.

"I saw the boat coming in, but I didn't know who it was," McGarvey said.

Trotter's eyes went to the pistol. He nodded. "How are you doing, Kirk?"

"Better. You?"

"They gave me a plastic hip. We'll see how it turns out." Trotter glanced up toward the lighthouse. "Anyway, I'll be back in the office on Monday."

"There's been nothing in the papers about En Gedi."

"No," Trotter said. He nodded toward the lighthouse. "Let's go inside. It was a long hike up from the village. I'd like to sit down."

"Sure," McGarvey said, leading the way. There was an awkwardness between them that he was having difficulty getting a handle on. He could usually anticipate his old friend, this time he didn't know.

They sat on the stone veranda overlooking the sea.

McGarvey brought out a bottle of retsina wine, bread, olives, sausages, and feta cheese. On this side of the island the afternoons were pleasant.

"You hit him, you know," Trotter said.

"Kurshin?"

"Yes. We found blood at the back doorway, and then across the clearing to where the helicopter was parked. We found it back in Alexandria with a lot of blood in the cockpit."

The Agency had debriefed him in the hospital but had refused to answer any of his questions.

"No sign of him from that point?"

Trotter shook his head. "He definitely didn't return to the embassy; the Bureau was watching the place around the clock."

"Then he's disappeared again."

"He hasn't been spotted anywhere. Not Moscow, not East Berlin."

"What about the other two men at the house?"

"Baranov's Department Viktor people. Some of the best. They're both dead, of course."

"What's been done about it, John?" McGarvey asked. "Until now we haven't done anything like that on each other's turf. At least not directly as a KGB operation."

"I don't know," Trotter admitted. "Ultimately that's the president's decision."

"But?" McGarvey said sharply.

Trotter hunched his shoulders as he sipped his wine. He looked out to sea again. Other islands dotted the horizon.

"I owe you my life. Kurshin would have killed us all."

"But he accomplished his objective. He got to Rand and most likely he got the information he'd come for."

"We're not so sure, Kirk. The reason you haven't read anything about En Gedi is because absolutely nothing has happened. June thirtieth came and went without incident. For all we know Kurshin could be dead somewhere. And maybe Rand's disk is with his body."

"Any idea what was on it?"

"No."

"What about the Israelis?"

"I don't know that either. Our lines of communication have been severely curtailed. But I do know that Lev Potok will be all right, again thanks to you."

"Which leaves Baranov," McGarvey said, beginning to understand finally. "The reason you've come here."

"Not the only reason, Kirk," Trotter said, turning back to him. "I came here to thank you, and to see how you were getting along. Whether you know it or not, or care to admit it, you at the very least delayed their plans, and possibly even destroyed them."

"Still, there's Baranov. Always Baranov."

Trotter nodded glumly. "The general asked me to come speak with you . . ."

"Authorized you, John," McGarvey said a little crossly. "Let's get our terminology straight right at the beginning."

"Yes. Authorized."

"No bullshit now. Tell it to me straight. What is it you want? Exactly."

"There is going to be a Law Enforcement conference in East Berlin in seven days. The heads of the police forces from every country in the Warsaw Pact will be there. So will Baranov."

"Along with half the KGB to guard him."

"We have come up with a copy of his itinerary."

"No mean trick . . ."

"We have our sources as well, Kirk, you know this. At any rate there is a possibility, just a possibility, of taking him out."

"And Murphy is authorizing such a mission?"

"Not yet," Trotter said. "He's going to the president with it. But first he wants to know if you would be willing to take it on." Trotter's eyes narrowed. "I am your friend, whether or not you want to believe that, and I'm telling you up front that the Agency will give you all the backup it can . . . but only to the point that you enter Germany. After that you would be on your own. I mean *totally* on your own. If you

were caught we would be able to prove that you were unbalanced, and that your action was totally yours."

"Why this now? Why the sudden change of heart?"

"The man is insane, and Gorbachev either won't or can't
do anything about him." Trotter leaned forward. "The man
is consolidating his power, Kirk. He has most of the military
establishment behind him now. The old guard who believe
that Gorbachev has gone too far."

"When do you need my answer?"

"If he goes ahead with En Gedi, and he is successful, we
think he means to take over the entire Middle East."

"When?"

Trotter sat back again. "Soon, Kirk. The conference begins
in seven days and the general still has to go to the president
with it."

"Why me?"

"Again I won't lie to you," Trotter said. "But the answer
should be fairly obvious. You're the right man for the job.
It would be a vendetta, something everyone concerned would
understand."

"I appreciate your honesty," McGarvey said. He got up
and went into the house where he found a pack of cigarettes
and lit one. It was his first since he had come to the island.

Assassins were meant to assassinate. His sister would say
that he was finally developing a conscience. It was war,
wasn't it? Kill or be killed. Each time the call to arms came,
he had more and more difficulty in accepting his role.

Until now.

Vengeance will be mine, the Lord said. But he wasn't
living in the modern world.

Trotter had come to the veranda door. McGarvey could
feel his presence behind him.

"All right," he said, without turning. "I'll do it."

"We'll brief you in Athens on Tuesday if we get the green
light. But we'll have to keep you at arm's length, you understand this?"

"Yes," McGarvey said tiredly.

There was a small silence.

"Are you up for this, Kirk? I mean if the president gives us his go-ahead."

McGarvey shrugged. "How do any of us know whether or not we're up to something, unless we actually do it."

Again there was a silence.

"I'll get back then," Trotter said. "But I brought someone with me."

McGarvey turned around. "Who?"

"Lorraine Abbott."

"Why?"

"Because she insisted."

"Take her back with you, I don't want to see anyone now."

"She doesn't know about this, of course, and she mustn't . . ."

"Take her back with you, John, I mean it."

"I can't."

32

THE ISLAND OF SÉRIFOS

McGarvey put on a shirt and walked back to the village with Trotter. They didn't say much to each other on the way over, both of them lost in their own thoughts.

The afternoon sun beat down with a vengeance, the interior of the island extremely hot, and they were sweating freely by the time they made it across. Most of the men were out with the fishing fleet. The village had a deserted air to it.

Lorraine Abbott sat at an outside table in the taverna just across from the dock. The only boat was the long, sleek hydrofoil that had brought her and Trotter over from Lávrion on the mainland. She was in the shade, but the mass of her blond hair made it seem as if she were under a spotlight. She wore a short khaki skirt and military blouse with epaulets, a thin gold chain around her long, delicate neck, and simple tortoise-shell sunglasses, which she took off when she spotted them coming across the dusty square.

"Hello, Kirk," she said, her voice soft, mellifluous.

McGarvey hadn't heard anything like it since he had come to this island, in fact not for years, since his ex-wife. His own reactions were disturbing to him. Excess baggage is the bane of any field officer. Hadn't that been drummed into his head? Wasn't it true?

"What are you doing here?" he asked a little more harshly than he had intended.

"I came to see you."

"No," McGarvey said, shaking his head. "Go back on the boat with John. Return to the NPT."

"I'm no longer with the service."

"Then return to your lab, Doctor."

"I'm on a leave of absence."

"Not here," McGarvey insisted. "You don't belong anywhere near me. You can't know how close you were to being killed. Christ, this is not polite society." He turned on Trotter. "Tell her, John. Take her back with you."

"I tried," Trotter said, spreading his hands.

"I hope to Christ someone is still watching her."

"The Bureau is taking care of it."

"Then why isn't she at the safehouse?"

Again Trotter spread his hands.

"I signed a release," she said. "I won't be cooped up any longer."

"Then they'll try again to kill you, and this time they'll probably succeed."

"Not as long as I'm with you."

McGarvey's jaw was tight. "You can't know how wrong you are, Doctor. How terribly, tragically wrong you are. Go away from me. Leave now while you still have the chance."

"No."

"I'm leaving here in a few days."

"Then I'll come with you."

"That will be impossible, Dr. Abbott," Trotter said.

She looked from McGarvey to him. "You're sending him out again?" she asked incredulously. "You can't be serious."

"I can't say anything more, you know that," Trotter said.

"The man was nearly killed. He lost a kidney, for God's sake. Are you all crazy?" She turned again to McGarvey. "Tell him, Kirk . . ." she started, but something in the look in his eyes stopped her.

"Now, will you go back with John?" he asked.

"No," she replied firmly. "If you're leaving in a few days I'll stay here until then."

"You don't owe me anything," McGarvey said, raising his voice.

"Yes I do. I owe you my life. But I didn't deserve that remark. I'm here because I want to be here."

"Why?"

Her eyes were wide just then, and she blinked. "Because . . ." she started.

McGarvey just stared at her.

"Because I have nowhere else to go," she finished her sentence.

It was late evening. The air had cooled down as it did every night, and a soft breeze blew across the veranda at the lighthouse.

They had remained in the village taverna until the fishing fleet had come in, and then had had a simple dinner and listened to the concertina player and watched the men dance.

All through the evening they had avoided touching each other, and for the most part their conversation had been desultory. Not once did they bring up what had happened to them since Israel, or that he would soon be going back into the field.

On the way up the path in the darkness, she slipped and nearly fell, so that he reached out and grabbed her arm to steady her. The contact had been electric for both of them, nearly taking McGarvey's breath away.

She was like his ex-wife Kathleen, in many respects—in

a certain haughtiness, in her makeup and her intelligence—
yet she was different. She was softer around the edges, more
sincere, even little-girl-like at times. It was confusing.

He had taken a shower, and he stood now in his robe
smoking a cigarette and staring out across the dark sea,
listening to the waves against the rocks below, and won-
dering what was happening to him. He had come a long
way since Santiago, and in many ways an even longer distance from his life in Switzerland, and then Paris. Light-
years, in fact.

The question was: Where was he going? But then, that was
the question everybody asked themselves. He didn't know if
there could ever be any good or accurate answer. You just
took it as it came, a step at a time.

She came from inside and stood beside him. He could smell
her pleasant, clean odor and see her from out of the corner
of his eye, but he did not turn to look at her.

"It's very beautiful here," she said after a time.

"Yes, it is."

"But it's odd, somehow. There's a strange flavor to it.
Maybe it's just the Greeks, but it feels very, very old. Almost
as if we were living in a graveyard. Do you know what I
mean?"

McGarvey had felt almost the same thing. "I think so."

"When I was a little girl, thirteen or fourteen, I think, I
went back to the Midwest to visit some of my cousins. There
was a county fair we all went to one night. Ferris wheel,
bumper cars, Tilt-a-whirl, cotton candy, foot-long hotdogs,
all that. And there was a palm reader, an old woman in a
tent at the end of the midway. My cousins teased me about
it, but I had my palm read. It was something that just hit me
at the time."

McGarvey finally turned to look at her. She was dressed
only in a short silk nightgown with thin straps. From the dim
light inside he could see that her complexion was slightly
flushed. Her chest rose and fell too fast, as if she were trying
to catch her breath.

"What did she tell you?" he asked, his voice nearly catching at the back of his throat.

She turned to him and smiled a little uncertainly. "I don't remember all of it," she said.

He said nothing.

"She told me that I would fall in love, but that my life would be difficult."

"Why?"

"Because he would be a dangerous man. But she told me it would be all right, that he would be there to protect me."

"Why?" McGarvey asked softly.

She shook her head. "I don't know."

He took her in his arms then, and as she came to him she sighed deeply as if she had finally been able to take a deep breath, as if finally she were out of danger. He had tried to tell her, but she hadn't been ready to listen then, and he was of no mind now to repeat his warning.

They kissed deeply, and afterward he picked her up and carried her inside to the big bed upstairs.

THE WHITE HOUSE

"Where is he at this moment?" the president asked.

"On a small Greek island about fifty miles off the mainland," the DCI Roland Murphy said. They were alone in the president's study. "It's isolated out there, which gives us pretty good control over the situation."

"Has he given you his answer?"

"Yes, Mr. President, he has. John Trotter went out to talk with him. He said he'd do it."

"Even under the strict conditions you imposed on him?" the president asked. "Once he enters Germany we totally divorce ourselves from him?"

"Yes, sir."

After a beat the president shook his head. "I don't like

this, General. In fact I like it even less than your last operation.''

"I didn't think you would. But you said yourself that Gorbachev no longer has any real control over Baranov. And it's not inconceivable that an accident could happen and Baranov would rise to power.''

"We lived through the specter of another KGB chief becoming party chairman.''

"Baranov is an entirely different animal, Mr. President. We've been suffering from his handiwork for too long now.''

The president leaned forward. "If we make him a target, you'll be a natural for retaliation.''

"Yes, sir, I've taken that into consideration.''

"Could it be pulled off?''

"If it was anyone else other than McGarvey, I'd say he'd have a less than fifty-fifty shot at it. But with him . . . he has a habit of doing the impossible.''

"We've treated him shabbily.''

"He is an assassin, Mr. President.''

"Yes," the president said, nodding thoughtfully. "But have you stopped to ask what that makes us?''

Murphy let the remark pass. "I need your go-ahead, Mr. President.''

"They'd crucify me.''

"Yes, sir. But you've never seen the report. This conversation is not being recorded. And McGarvey will be kept at arm's length throughout the entire operation.''

"What about afterward? Assuming he is successful.''

"We keep him at arm's length.''

Again the president hesitated for a beat.

"You're a tough man, General.''

"It's a tough business, Mr. President," Murphy said. "Do I have your authorization?''

"Only to put everything in place," the president said. His eyes bored into the DCI's. "I want you to listen very closely to me now, because I don't want any mistakes. You can put your people into place, but the trigger will not be pulled until you get word from me. Under no circumstances will Mc-Garvey assassinate Baranov until you have personal word from me.''

"It'll put him in a nasty spot. He could be left hanging . . .''

"As you said, General, this is a tough business.''

33

THE MEDITERRANEAN

THE U.S. LOS ANGELES-CLASS ATTACK SUBMARINE *INDIANA-polis* ran submerged, two hundred feet beneath the surface of the dark sea on a course of 210 degrees out of Sixth Fleet Headquarters at Gaeta, Italy. She was one hundred miles offshore in a run-and-drift mode in which she would make fourteen knots for a half hour, and then shut down to drift for the next half hour.

She had been in the eastern Med for the past two weeks, taking part in a naval exercise with the *Nimitz* and her support group, called LOOKUP. The Soviets had become active in the region recently and the exercise was designed to test their willingness to remain in the area, based on their battle group strengths coming through the Bosporus.

The mission completed, *Indianapolis* was heading back to

her patrol station, code-named ROUNDHOUSE, off the Italian coast for further orders.

She had made it nearly six hours early and had gone into her run-and-drift mode to give the sonar operators some more practice. They had picked up a couple of ships on the surface, identifying both as freighters. There were no other submarines in the area, and they would have been very surprised had there been.

Commander John D. Webb, J.D. to his friends, looked at his watch. It was twenty minutes until two in the morning, local time. He switched on the light over his bunk and sat up, wiping the sleep out of his eyes. At forty he was beginning to burn out on submarine duty. This was his fourth boat and she was a beauty, but his thoughts lately had begun to turn more and more to Norfolk where he and his wife Lois had a small house, and to the sub school at New London, Connecticut, where he had been offered a teaching job.

Time now, he wondered as he got up and used the small head, to call it quits? Lois certainly wouldn't fight him. Their marriage had survived this long against the adversities of a navy career. Time now to reap some of the benefits.

Slipping on his shoes, he walked next door to the officers' wardroom where he poured himself a cup of coffee, and then headed forward to the attack center, passing the sonar room where the duty supervisor and one of the kids were playing a game of chess. They both looked up as the captain passed.

Lieutenant Earl Layman, his executive officer, had just shown up; he had the conn with another officer and six enlisted men.

"Just about time to get the mail," Webb said, ducking through the hatch.

Layman looked up from the chart table. "Good morning, Captain. We're back on station."

He and Webb had served together for nearly five years now. Layman was next in line for his own boat and he deserved it. The two of them were almost exact opposites in every respect. Where Webb was short, dark, and husky, Layman was tall, pale, and lanky. Webb had graduated from

Kansas State with a degree in engineering, while Layman had graduated first in his class from Harvard as a mathematics major. Webb was a pragmatist, Layman was an idealist. But their differences never got in the way, in fact they were complementary.

"Best damned skipper and exec combination in the entire Navy," Admiral Wannover, CINCSUBATLANT, called them.

Webb picked up the telephone. "Sonar, conn, what's it look like out there?"

"Nothing in the past hour, Skipper."

"All right, Tommy, keep your ears open, we're heading up." Webb put the telephone down. "Earl, bring the boat up to periscope depth."

"Aye, Captain, bringing the boat up," Layman responded.

"Reduce speed to five knots and come right to zero-zero-five degrees," Webb said softly.

"Reducing speed to five knots, coming right to zero-zero-five, aye."

The problem with submarines had always been communications. While they were submerged the only effective means of contacting them was through either the ELF (Extremely Low Frequency) or VLF (Very Low Frequency) systems.

The former was based in Wisconsin and could transmit to submarines anywhere in the world, even subs that were as deep as a thousand feet. The problem with the system was its speed. It took fifteen minutes to transmit a single three-letter code group. And communications were only one way.

With the VLF system, an updated C-135 aircraft flying at thirty thousand feet over a sub's patrol station would trail an eight-mile-long wire antenna. But again communications were slow and only one way.

The alternatives were communications buoys either sent up by the submarine, or dropped from a passing ship or aircraft, or for the submarine to come to periscope depth and raise her satellite antenna. The latter systems, however, exposed the submarine to detection.

Lieutenant j.g. Robert Hess, the ELINT (Electronic Intelligence) officer, popped his head around the corner from his cubicle. "Are we going upstairs, Skipper?"

Webb turned to him. "On our way up, Bob. Have you got something for us?"

"Negative. But if we have the time, I'd like to put up the ECM mast. We can use the practice."

The Electronic Counter Measures mast, like the boat's two periscopes, could be raised or lowered. It contained three directional antennae and two omni-directional arrays. Anything transmitting electronic energy within a hundred miles of their position was detectable with the system.

"Permission granted. But we're not going to be long."

"Aye, aye, Skipper," Hess said, ducking back.

It took another three minutes to reach periscope depth, where Layman leveled the boat, and the satellite antenna and ECM mast were raised.

"We have an uplink," the radioman reported.

"Send our ready-to-receive," Webb ordered.

"Aye, Captain," the radioman replied, and he activated the high-speed burst transmitter that sent the *Indianapolis*'s identification code, position information, and the ready for reception signal in less than a quarter of a second.

One second later the complete message was received, and the printer chattered into life.

280301ZJUL
TOP SECRET
FM: COMSUBMED
TO: USS INDIANAPOLIS
A. LOOKUP TERMINATED AS OF DAY AND DATE.
B. PROCEED COMSUBMED INST. 1733.4 AREA
OF PATROL AS ASSIGNED ODRS.
C. REPORT AS NECESSARY.
XX
EOM
280302ZJUL
BREAKBREAK

"They could have said thanks, job well done, or something," Layman said when he read the message.

Webb smiled. "What'd you expect, Earl? Two more weeks we'll be back in port. Not so rough."

Layman had to grin as well. "That's what we're out here for."

"Right," Webb said. "Lower the masts and take us down."

"Hold on a second, Skipper," Hess called from his cubicle.

Webb turned and stepped around the corner. "Got something?"

"I think so," Hess said. He was listening intently to a pair of earphones. "It sounds like . . . like a mayday, but very faint. Broken up. Sometimes garbled."

"A long ways off?"

"No, sir," Hess said, looking up. "Close." He turned a couple of knobs on his console. "My DF puts him a couple of hundred yards out."

"What else?"

"Nothing, sir. Just the very faint SOS. Sounds like his batteries might be just about gone."

The *Indianapolis* was equipped with the BQQ-5 passive/active sonar suite. There had been no reason for them to go active in the past twenty-four hours. They had missed the target above, apparently because the boat was dead in the water.

Back in the attack center Webb picked up the phone. "Sonar, conn."

"Aye, conn."

"We have a target on the surface, fairly close, and probably stationary. Ping it once for range and bearing, give it five seconds and ping a second time for movement."

"Aye, Skipper."

A moment later everyone aboard the ship heard the lone pong as the sonar went active.

"Range one hundred seventy-five yards. Relative bearing, 175 degrees."

The second pong sounded throughout the ship.

"She's dead in the water, Skipper."

"Search periscope," Webb said. The larger of the two periscopes rose up and broke the surface of the night sea. At first he couldn't see much, so he dialed in the image intensifier and suddenly he could see the white tops on the waves.

A small pleasure boat wallowed in the seas. She showed no lights or any activity on deck. Webb made a quick 360-degree sweep to check for any other ships or aircraft, but there was nothing.

"Looks like a small cabin cruiser," Webb said. "Dark. Nobody in sight."

He flipped another switch on the periscope's control panel and the image of the small boat appeared on a small television screen to the left.

"Still getting that SOS, Bob?"

"Yes, sir," Hess called out. "But it seems to be getting fainter. Her batteries are going fast now."

The *Indianapolis*'s patrol station and her position at any given moment, like that of any other U.S. missile or attack submarine, was top secret. By surfacing now they would be giving themselves away. But then they could not simply ignore the code of the sea.

Webb picked up the telephone. "Communications, conn."

"Aye, conn."

"Get a message off immediately to COMSUBMED. Tell them we've detected an apparent SOS from a small private cabin cruiser. We're surfacing now."

"Aye, Skipper."

"Surface the boat, Earl," Webb said. He punched another button on his phone. "Quartermaster, conn."

"Aye, conn."

"We're coming to the surface, Tony. Looks like we're receiving an SOS from a small cabin cruiser. She's showing no lights, no activity on deck. Get together a boarding party. Better bring Davidson with you."

"Aye, Skipper."

"And, Tony?"

"Yes, sir?"

"Take along your sidearms."

"Yes, sir," Lieutenant j.g. Tony D'Angelo, the boat's quartermaster, said, "we're on our way."

34

THE MEDITERRANEAN

THE SEAS WERE RUNNING ONLY TWO OR THREE FEET SO THAT the *Indianapolis*, whose main deck was barely on the surface, provided a stable platform. Quartermaster Tony D'Angelo, Medic Chief Petty Officer Robert Davidson, and Petty Officers Charles Markham and Don Gilmore scrambled out of one of the aft maintenance hatches.

D'Angelo—a tough, beefy Italian from Brooklyn—raised binoculars to his eyes and searched the sea behind them, almost immediately picking out the cabin cruiser barely one hundred yards away now. She was long and sleek, more like fifty or fifty-five feet, he figured. Probably worth a half a million at least. A definite pussy wagon, like only the Italians knew how to build.

Markham and Gilmore had pulled out the rubber raft and it inflated with a noisy hiss as they tossed it over the side.

"All right, lock it up," D'Angelo said.

Markham closed the access hatch and a seaman below dogged and sealed it.

"You copy, Tony?" D'Angelo's walkie-talkie crackled.

He looked up at the bridge on top of the sail. Webb and Layman were looking down at him.

"Aye, aye, Skipper," he radioed back.

"Watch yourself."

"Yes, sir."

The night was warm, but the sky was overcast and the sea was very dark. The submarine showed no lights, and rowing away from her D'Angelo got the impression he was looking back at some prehistoric sea monster, which except for her lineage, she was.

Twenty-five yards away from the cruiser, he was able to pick out her name on the stern. He radioed back to the *Indianapolis*. "I can see her name now, Skipper. The *Zenzero*, out of Naples. Means ginger, the spice."

"Any damage evident?"

"Negative. No sounds of machinery, no lights, nothing. She's definitely dead in the water."

"Any signs of activity on deck, or through the windows?"

"Negative, Skipper," D'Angelo radioed. "Wait just a minute, we're going around to the port side."

They came around the stern of the cruiser. Markham was in the bow of the rubber raft. "The boarding ladder is down, Lieutenant."

D'Angelo could see it. He also spotted empty davits amidships. "Skipper, their boarding ladder is down, and one of her runabouts is missing. Looks like she might be abandoned."

"Hold up there," Webb radioed back.

They came up alongside the ladder and Markham secured a line to it.

"Tony, we're still receiving the SOS, but it's very faint now. Someone is definitely aboard."

"We're starting up."

"Just a second, we're doing a radar sweep. We may be able to pick up that missing auxiliary."

The rubber raft rose and fell on the swell relative to the much bigger cruiser. D'Angelo cocked his head to listen, but there were absolutely no sounds on the gentle night breeze. Absolutely nothing.

"All right, we've got it," Webb radioed. "We're painting a small target about eight miles out and heading almost directly south. Probably trying to make Sicily."

"What do you want us to do here, sir?"

"Go ahead and board her, find out what's going on."

"What about the auxiliary?"

"We'll message COMSUBMED, they can contact the Italian coast guard," Webb radioed back. "Don't worry, Tony, we won't leave them."

"Aye, Skipper. We're going aboard now."

Markham scrambled up the ladder first, D'Angelo right behind him, and then Gilmore and Davidson. The cruiser was laid out with a large foredeck, a much smaller afterdeck, with the main saloon taking up most of the ship's length. A ladder ran from the afterdeck up to a large, covered flying bridge. Everything about the aluminum-hulled vessel was rich and finely finished.

D'Angelo pulled out his .45 automatic and led the way aft, where an open sliding glass door led into the well-furnished main saloon. The interior of the ship was in complete darkness.

Gilmore pulled out a flashlight and shined it around the interior. Nothing seemed to have been disturbed.

"We're inside now, Skipper. Everything looks fine."

"No sign of anyone yet?" Webb radioed.

"Negative."

"Tony, the signal has just about died. Check out the radio room first, and then make a quick sweep through the entire boat, including the engine spaces. COMSUBMED wants us out of here on the double."

"Aye, Skipper," D'Angelo radioed, and he stuffed the

walkie-talkie in his pocket. "Charlie, check the engine room. Don, you take the cabins belowdecks. Doc and I will find the radioman."

Markham and Gilmore took the stairs below, as D'Angelo and Davidson went forward through the saloon, past a small but efficient-looking galley to port, and what appeared to be a well-stocked pantry to starboard.

The owner's stateroom opened straight ahead. To the port was a big head with a bathtub, and to starboard a narrow, closed door was marked RADIO ROOM.

D'Angelo raised his pistol and slowly pushed the door open. He was beginning to get spooked. Something all of a sudden didn't seem right to him, though he didn't know exactly why.

The radio room was crammed with electronic equipment. A few lights shone on one of the consoles, and the very faint sound of the Morse code SOS message came through one of the speakers. But there was no one there.

"What the hell?" D'Angelo said, stepping the rest of the way into the tiny compartment and shining his flashlight over the equipment.

A small tape recorder had been plugged into one of the transmitters. It was sending the message.

"What's going on . . ." Davidson started to ask when they both heard the sliding glass doors in the saloon close softly.

The medic spun around. D'Angelo shoved him aside and rushed down the passageway.

Something popped and began to hiss angrily to his left. He turned at the same moment his entire body was gripped with an incredibly painful spasm.

"Charlie . . ." he screamed, grappling for the walkie-talkie in his pocket, but he was falling, an impenetrable darkness descending over him.

Arkady Kurshin, dressed in black, crouched in the darkness of the *Zenzero*'s afterdeck, counting slowly to ten. Dr. Velikanov crouched behind him.

"Now," Kurshin said softly. He pressed a button on a

small transmitting device, and the cruiser's air-conditioning units rumbled into life.

He counted another ten seconds and hit the button again, shutting off the air-conditioners.

Checking over the rail to make certain the submarine had not moved, and that no other boat was coming across, he pushed open the saloon door and went inside.

D'Angelo, his eyes open, his tongue protruding from his mouth, lay on his side in the middle of the big room. Davidson lay crumpled in a heap in the passageway just behind him.

"Get started, we don't have much time," Kurshin told the doctor. He turned and hurried down the stairs belowdecks. Gilmore was dead at the foot of the stairs, and Markham's body lay half in and half out of the doorway that led into the engine room.

He seized Gilmore's body beneath the armpits and dragged him up the stairs, dumping him in a heap in the middle of the saloon.

The doctor had his bag open and the equipment he needed laid out beside him on the carpeted floor. He had already opened D'Angelo's jacket and shirt and had cut away the dead man's undershirt, exposing his broad barrel chest.

"Tony, what's going on over there?" D'Angelo's walkie-talkie blared.

Ignoring it, Kurshin hurried back downstairs, where he grabbed Markham's body and dragged it back up to the saloon.

Dr. Velikanov had opened a twelve-inch gash in D'Angelo's gut. The wound was bloodless although some of the dead man's body fluids were seeping out. The smell was horrific.

"Tony, for Christ's sake, what's going on over there?" the walkie-talkie crackled. "Do you copy?"

As the doctor continued with his gruesome task, Kurshin yanked open the jackets and shirts of the other three sailors, cutting their undershirts open with his own knife.

"How much longer?" Kurshin asked.

Dr. Velikanov was already sewing up the gash in D'Angelo's gut, using coarse thread and big running stitches. He glanced up, his jaws tight, his eyes narrow. "Five minutes and this butchery will be done."

"Tony, this is Captain Webb. I want you out of there now!"

Kurshin scrambled over to D'Angelo's body and pulled out the walkie-talkie. He keyed it and, holding the unit well away from himself, screamed hoarsely.

"Christ . . . Christ . . . Skipper, we've got a fire started over here . . . there are . . . dead bodies everywhere . . . God, it's . . . horrible . . ."

"Tony, is that you? Tony, get the hell out of there, now, it's an order!"

"Skipper . . . this place is . . . about ready to blow . . . oh, God . . ."

"Tony! Tony!" the walkie-talkie blared, but Kurshin switched it off and tossed it down on the floor.

Dr. Velikanov was just about finished with Davidson. Kurshin hurriedly rebuttoned D'Angelo's shirt and jacket and dragged his body out onto the afterdeck, making sure he kept well below the level of the rail.

The beam of a searchlight suddenly swept across the ship. Kurshin waited until it had passed, and then dragged the body forward and dumped it over the side into the rubber raft.

By the time he got back to the saloon, Dr. Velikanov was finished with Davidson and was halfway through with Markham. Whatever the man was, he was efficient. Kurshin dragged Davidson's body onto the afterdeck and dumped it overboard. The searchlight was still playing over the cruiser.

"You've got two minutes," Kurshin said, hurrying again below decks. In the engine room he used a hacksaw to cut the fuel lines to both engines and then started the pumps. Diesel fuel began spurting out all over the place.

Setting an incendiary fuse for five minutes, he tossed it down on the floor and then set the other charges to blow five seconds later. He rushed back upstairs.

Hurriedly he rebuttoned Markham's shirt and jacket and dragged the body outside, where he dumped it over the rail.

"Ahoy the vessel *Zenzero*, this is the U.S. Navy," an amplified voice rolled over the water from the *Indianapolis*. "Stand by to be fired upon unless you immediately signal your identification."

"It's done," Dr. Velikanov shouted from the saloon.

Kurshin rushed inside, helped him rebutton Gilmore's shirt and jacket, and together they dragged his body out onto the afterdeck and around to the port side, where they dumped it down into the rubber raft on top of D'Angelo's body.

"You have thirty seconds to comply, *Zenzero*," the amplified voice boomed from the sub.

Kurshin yanked open a compartment door across from the boarding ladder, pulled out a rubber raft canister, and dumped it over the side, the raft immediately popping open and inflating with a hiss. Next he pulled out a waterproof equipment bag with its own flotation collar and dumped it into the water.

He hustled the doctor down the ladder and bodily shoved him into the sea. Pulling out his knife he cut the painter holding the *Indianapolis*'s rubber raft to the ladder and shoved it away with his foot. He jumped into the water and in a few powerful strokes reached the equipment bag, which he hauled up into their own raft, and then clambered aboard himself. As he was shipping the oars, Velikanov climbed aboard, and they headed away from the cruiser, keeping it between them and the submarine.

The raft was black, as were their clothes. They were completely invisible to radar, and twenty-five yards out they would be invisible to anyone aboard the sub.

An explosion suddenly shattered the night, and flames roared out of the saloon door.

35

THE MEDITERRANEAN

THICK BILLOWS OF OILY SMOKE, BACKLIT BY THE FLAMES raging through the *Zenzero*, rose two hundred feet into the night sky. Captain Webb, shaking with barely suppressed rage, was watching through binoculars from the bridge atop the *Indianapolis*'s sail.

Layman and three others had taken another rubber raft across. This time they were armed with M16s. He had ordered them to shoot anyone on sight.

"Bridge, communications," the bridge speaker blared.

Webb hit the talk switch. "Bridge, aye."

"Skipper, COMSUBMED wants to know if we require any assistance, and they're asking for an update."

"Tell them that there's been an explosion and fire aboard the cruiser and that we may have casualties."

His walkie-talkie squawked into life. It was Layman. "Skipper, we just fished Markham out of the water."

"What kind of shape is he in, Earl?"

"He's dead."

Webb was stunned into silence for just a beat, but then his anger rose up around him again as a fire brighter and hotter than that consuming the *Zenzero*. He hit the comms switch.

"Communications, bridge."

"Aye, bridge."

"Have you sent out that message yet?"

"It's in the machine now, Skipper . . ."

"Belay that," Webb shouted. "Send instead, stand by."

"Yes, sir."

Webb keyed his walkie-talkie. "Any sign of the others, Earl?"

"I don't know, Skipper. We've spotted something floating low in the water on the port side of the cruiser, we're heading over there now."

"Any sign of life aboard?"

"Negative, negative. If anyone was aboard, they're sure as hell dead by now."

"What happened to Markham? Was he burned?"

"No, sir," Layman said, and Webb could hear the strain in his voice. "No burns, no blood that I can see, no injuries. His eyes are open, and he's just dead."

Besides the lookout, the only other person on the bridge was the Second Officer, Lieutenant Kenneth Woodman. He was a young man who would someday make a good skipper. He knew the boat, he got along well with the men, and he knew how to take orders.

Webb turned to him. "I want you to get below. Help Owens set up the dispensary for casualties. I don't know how many, or what shape they'll be in, but I suspect it'll be bad."

"Aye, Skipper," Woodman said.

"And, Ken."

"Yes, sir?"

"Not a word to the rest of the crew. Understand?"

"Aye, aye."

Woodman went below. Webb keyed his walkie-talkie again. "What's your status, Earl?"

"Hold on, Captain, we've got another body in the water."

Webb raised his binoculars and searched the waters around the furiously burning cruiser, but he couldn't spot Layman's raft. They had already gone to the opposite side of the *Zenzero*.

"My God, Skipper, it's Davidson. He's dead too. Just like Markham. He's not been burned or injured in any way that I can see, and his eyes are open. Skipper, it looks like he's . . . like he *was* in pain."

"What about the other object you spotted floating in the water?"

"We're on our way over to it . . . but it's hard to get much closer . . . it's damned hot . . ."

Webb keyed the comms switch. "Bob, what are we showing on radar?"

"Still clear, Skipper," Hess came back.

"What about that auxiliary? Are you still painting her?"

"Yes, sir. She's about ten miles out now, but she seems to have slowed down."

"Same course?"

"Yes, sir."

"Keep an eye on her, Bob. Anything electronic coming from her, let me know immediately."

"Aye, Skipper."

"It's our boat, Skipper," Layman radioed.

Webb keyed his walkie-talkie. "How about D'Angelo and Gilmore?"

"Dead, just like the others. But it looks as if they were dumped into the raft, Captain. Gilmore is lying on top of Tony, as if someone . . . tossed him."

"Listen to me, Earl. Is there any possibility, any possibility at all, that anyone could still be aboard that cruiser?"

"Negative, Skipper. You can't get within a hundred feet of it. Nothing aboard is alive."

"Do you see anyone else in the water, any other bodies, another rubber raft?"

"Negative."

"Get back here on the double," Webb said. Again he keyed his ship comms. "Plotting, bridge."

"Plotting, aye."

"I want a best possible course and speed to the auxiliary that radar is painting to our south."

"We going to stay on the surface, Skipper?"

"Yes," Webb said.

"I'll have it in a second."

"Quartermaster, bridge."

"Quartermaster, aye."

"I want four men at the after loading hatch. Our people are on their way back, and they're going to need some help."

"Aye, Captain."

"Conn, bridge. I want Boyle up here on the double."

"Aye, aye, Skipper."

Webb again raised his binoculars. He could see Layman and the others heading back now, the other raft in tow. He keyed his walkie-talkie. "Earl."

"We're on our way back, Skipper."

"There'll be someone at the after hatch to help you. I want Tony and the others brought immediately forward to the dispensary. I'll meet you there."

"Yes, sir."

Third Officer Lieutenant j.g. Ernie Boyle came up through the hatch. He was young, barely in his mid-twenties, but he was already as good as any other officer aboard.

"You've got the bridge, Ernie," Webb told him.

"Aye, aye, Skipper."

"Keep an eye peeled. Earl and the others will be loading through the after hatch. I'll be in the dispensary."

"Yes, sir," Boyle said, and Webb clambered down into the boat.

Kurshin had angled them away from the cruiser. One hundred fifty yards out from the *Indianapolis*, he stopped rowing and looked back. The submarine showed no lights and was visible only as a vague black shape against the overcast sky.

"Is this far enough?" Dr. Velikanov asked. "They might send someone to look for us." He was clearly agitated.

"They're busy gathering their dead, Doctor," Kurshin said as he unzippered the waterproof equipment bag. "They'll be taking them aboard soon, I expect."

"Such a terrible waste. They were just young boys."

Kurshin gave him a hard look. "This is war."

"Yes," Velikanov said, nodding. "What we are doing could very well precipitate the nuclear holocaust."

"You received your orders, Doctor. But the choice was yours. And to this point you have carried out your duties very well."

Velikanov shook his head. "Too well," he mumbled.

Kurshin had pulled the AK74 out of the bag. Quickly he attached the image-intensifying night scope and loaded the heavy assault rifle.

He brought it up to his shoulder, keyed the scope, and slowly scanned the submarine from bow to stern, images coming through the eyepiece in shades of bright gray.

Two men were on the bridge atop the sail. One of them had a pair of binoculars and was looking out to sea in the opposite direction. The other man was looking down at the aft deck.

Near the stern the last of the bodies was lowered through an open hatch. Two of the sailors remained topside to deflate the rubber rafts so that they could be brought back aboard. Even at this distance Kurshin could see by the way they moved that they were very angry.

The captain, however, would be containing his own anger. Most of the boat's 127-man crew would still be unaware that four of their comrades were dead. The submarine would not be at battle stations yet. The interior spaces would not be sealed. Nor would the ventilation systems be isolated. There was no need for it.

Kurshin checked his watch. He had set it in the timer mode.

So far thirty-six minutes had elapsed since Velikanov had begun his work. The timing was critical.

"You are certain that you made the insertions in the proper order?"

"Yes," the doctor said softly.

"Then we don't have long to wait."

"How long?"

"Less than four minutes now," Kurshin said, once again raising his rifle and sighting on the bridge. "Start rowing, Doctor, I would like to be closer."

Webb was in the dispensary with Woodman and Medic Second Class Justin Owens when Layman and Anders carried D'Angelo's body inside and laid it on the operating table.

"Christ," he said, bile rising at the back of his throat.

D'Angelo was in rictus, his tongue protruding. His eyes were open and his face held an expression of horror or extreme pain.

"Are the others like this, sir?" Owens asked, bending over D'Angelo and studying his eyes. The kid was huge, he had played football in high school, but he had a gentle touch.

"All of them," Layman replied, looking at Webb.

"Where are they, Earl?" Webb asked softly.

"Officers' wardroom."

Owens was looking up.

"What is it, Justin?" Webb asked.

"Skipper, I've only read about this. Saw a film. But unless my guess is way off, I'd say it was gas."

"Gas? What kind of gas?"

"Nerve gas. Labun, or something like that." Owens turned back to D'Angelo's body. "He's got the symptoms. No apparent wounds or other trauma." He felt the base of D'Angelo's skull, his neck, and chest.

"Dispensary, conn, is the skipper back there?" the comms speaker squawked.

Webb turned and hit the switch. "Webb, here."

"Sir, COMSUBMED is pressing. They want to know our situation."

"Tell them to stand by. What's the status of the auxiliary to our south?"

"Looks like she's dead in the water now, sir."

"Have you got that intercept course plotted?"

"Aye, aye, sir."

"Jesus Christ," Owens swore, and Webb turned around. The medic had opened D'Angelo's shirt. A huge gash had been cut in the quartermaster's gut and had been roughly sewn up. Webb could hardly believe his eyes. Layman's mouth had dropped open, and one of the crewmen who had helped carry the bodies aboard stood in the doorway shaking his head.

"Skipper?" the speaker blared.

"Stand by," Webb snapped, keying the comm. "What the hell happened, Justin?"

"Christ, I don't know, sir. Someone cut him open and sewed him back up."

"Is that what killed him?" Layman asked.

"I don't think so," Owens said.

"Check the others, Earl," Webb said.

Layman brushed past the crewman and hurried the few steps to the wardroom.

"Open him up," Webb ordered.

Owens was breathing through his mouth, and his face was red. "Yes, sir," he said.

He pulled on a pair of rubber gloves and got a scalpel from the autoclave. Carefully he began cutting the running stitches in D'Angelo's gut, one by one. His hands were shaking.

Layman came back slamming the flat of his palm against the bulkhead. "Every one of them, Skipper. They cut them open and stitched them back together, like fucking stuffed turkeys."

"Someone was aboard that cruiser," Webb said.

Layman looked up, sudden understanding dawning in his eyes. "You're goddamned right they were. When they were done, they dumped Tony and the others overboard, set the cruiser on fire, and got the hell off the ship. Probably a rubber raft, so we wouldn't paint them on radar. And they would have kept the cruiser between us and them until they got far enough out so that we couldn't see them."

"That auxiliary to our south will come back for them," Webb said.

"But why . . . ?" Layman started to ask, but Owens shouted something as he jumped back away from the operating table and dropped the scalpel to the deck.

Webb spun around. The wound in D'Angelo's gut was fully open. Something had been stuffed inside his body. Webb got the impression that it might be a cylinder of some sort. Eight or ten inches long, perhaps a couple of inches in diameter.

All of a sudden he knew!

"Gas . . ." he shouted. The cylinder in D'Angelo's body made a popping noise and began to hiss furiously.

36

THE MEDITERRANEAN

KURSHIN'S WRISTWATCH BEEPED SOFTLY AT THE FORTY-
minute mark. They had gotten within one hundred yards of
the submarine.

"Stop rowing," he told the doctor, and he raised the AK74
to his shoulder, scoping the boat from stern to bow. The after
hatch had been closed, as he expected it would be. There
was no sign of any activity on deck, nor was the boat showing
any lights.

Slowly raising his aim up the broad sail, he could see the
officer and lookout as before. One had his back toward them,
the other was looking this way.

The small rubber raft bounced and moved on the small
seas, the targets weaving in and out of the scope's field of

vision. But he had made successful shots in conditions far worse than these.

His watch beeped again after twenty seconds at the same moment the lookout's head was centered in the reticle of the assault rifle's scope. He squeezed off a shot, the noise shockingly loud on the quiet sea.

The seaman's body was shoved forward against the rail, his head exploding in a mass of blood, bone, and gray matter.

Immediately Kurshin shifted his aim slightly left as the officer started to turn and rear back. He squeezed off a second shot, driving the officer forward and out of view beneath the level of the armor steel coaming.

If something had gone wrong in the dispensary aboard, the alarm would be sounded now, but as Kurshin kept his aim on the bridge there was no movement aboard the boat, no sounds, no lights, nothing.

After a full thirty seconds he lowered the rifle.

"The boat is dead," he said softly. Even he was impressed and moved by what they had done and by the ease with which they had accomplished it.

"The boat itself is of no real interest to us, Arkasha," Baranov had told him. "Although there are certain technical and design specifications our people would like you to learn for them, we cannot risk starting a war over it."

"These boys you are giving me are going to want to keep him. Will they be able to contain themselves so that they can operate the boat?"

"That will be up to you. But believe me, they are capable."

"Five men and a drunken doctor . . ."

"And you, Arkasha. Do not fail me . . . this time."

Kurshin glanced over at Velikanov. The man's lips were half parted and he seemed to be mumbling something. Aboard the cruiser he had been frightened and then disgusted. Now he was neither, he was in awe.

"It's time," Kurshin said softly.

The doctor blinked and looked at him.

"We have no idea what messages they passed to their fleet

command headquarters. We must be out of here within the hour.''

Without being told to do so, Velikanov took up the oars and began rowing them toward the submarine, lying dark and menacing in the water.

Already the flames aboard the cruiser had begun to die down. The ship was listing a few degrees to starboard. Within the next few hours she would probably be at the bottom of the sea, though it didn't really matter; there was nothing aboard now to connect her with the KGB. The nerve gas and cylinders were American made. They had been stolen more than a year ago from the Dugway Proving Grounds in Utah. Nor was there anything to connect them in Naples, if the KGB's Rome *resident* had done his job correctly.

Kurshin had been aboard Soviet submarines before, but he was still impressed by the sheer size of the American boat floating in the water, her black sail rising up out of the broad, gently sloping hull.

The submarine was slightly low at the stern. Kurshin directed Velikanov to approach the boat well aft of the sail so that they would be able to climb aboard. Forward she was too high out of the water, her hull too sharply sloping for them to get up on the deck.

Minutes later they bumped gently against the *Indianapolis*'s hull, the waves shoving them half up on the deck. Kurshin scrambled aboard with the raft's painter and his AK74. Dr. Velikanov passed up the equipment bag, and then clambered on deck himself.

For a long beat Kurshin just stood there in the darkness. He cocked an ear to listen, but there were no sounds. Taking out his knife, he pulled the rubber raft up a little higher on deck, and then sliced the fabric with a loud pop. The little boat, almost completely deflated, floated away. They were committed now.

Slinging the rifle over his shoulder and hefting the equipment bag, Kurshin hurried forward, Velikanov right behind him, passing beneath the broad hydroplanes jutting out from the side of the sail.

There was no access into the submarine without help from inside, except from the bridge deck. Kurshin laid down his rifle and pulled a grappling hook and line from his equipment bag. Standing back, he tossed the hook up over the top of the sail, the grapples clanging loudly against the steel plating, scraping against the coaming, and then coming free.

Kurshin gathered up the line for a second try and tossed the hook up again. This time it caught. He tied the tail of the line to the equipment bag.

Unzippering his black jumpsuit, he checked to make certain his pistol was ready to fire and free in its holster strapped against his chest.

"Can you make it up this line?" he asked the doctor.

Velikanov looked up. The sail rose more than twenty feet off the deck. He nodded. "I think so."

"Give me a couple of minutes to check out the boat, then come up."

Again the doctor nodded.

"A couple of days and you will be on your way to Moscow."

"Or dead."

Kurshin nodded. "Yes," he said, and he started up the rope, hand over hand, his nonskid soles adhering easily to the sail's plating.

Near the top he reached up over the coaming and hauled himself the rest of the way into the narrow two-man forward bridge well.

The lookout lay crumpled in a heap, most of the side of his head destroyed. There was blood everywhere, but the officer was gone, the hatch down into the boat closed.

Kurshin looked down at Velikanov who was staring up at him, and then scanned the length of the submarine. No one else was there. All the hatches remained closed.

He had hit the man. He'd seen that clearly in the scope. The officer had been knocked off his feet. He was certain of it.

"There is a body up here, Doctor," he called down. "When you come up, bring it aboard."

"Just one?" Velikanov asked.

"Yes," Kurshin said, and turning back to the job at hand he spun the hatch wheel, counterclockwise all the way to its stops. The wounded officer had somehow managed to get below and close the bridge hatch. If he had had the presence of mind to dog it there would be no easy way to get inside. There wouldn't be time. Soon fleet headquarters in Gaeta would be sending out an aircraft to find out what was happening.

Time, it always came down to time. And luck.

The hatch came open easily, counterbalanced on a hydraulic cylinder, the odor of machine oil and electronics wafting up to him.

The interior of the boat was bathed in red light. There were a thousand places for a man to hide himself below. If he was armed, it could take hours to flush him out. Hours they did not have.

But the officer was wounded. Kurshin pulled out a flashlight and switched it on. Blood was nearly invisible in red light, but under his flashlight beam he could see a trail of it down the ladder, and at the bottom a pool of it where the officer had probably fallen and lain for a moment or two.

Replacing the flashlight in a zippered pocket, Kurshin pulled out his gun and started slowly down the ladder into the boat, taking care to make no noise so that he could hear any movement from below.

At the bottom he stepped over the pool of blood, swinging his gun left to right.

He was in the attack center just forward of the control room. Numbers and images continued to flash across equipment panels and computer screens, and somewhere aft some sort of an indicator was beeping softly.

Two bodies lay on the deck, and a third was slumped forward over an equipment console. He could see through the open hatch into the control room where at least four other bodies either lay on the deck or were crumpled forward against their electronic panels.

Taking his flashlight out again, he switched it on for just

a second or two, long enough for him to pick out the trail of
blood leading aft through the attack center and the control
room. He shut it off and started aft, stepping carefully over
the bodies.

Third Officer Lieutenant j.g. Ernie Boyle knew that he was
bleeding to death and was desperately in need of medical
assistance.

He had thought he was dreaming when Finney's head suddenly exploded, and then something slammed into his back
between his shoulder blade and neck, shattering his collar-
bone. But it was nothing by comparison to what he'd felt
when he'd managed to get below.

So far as he could tell, everyone aboard was dead. How
it could have happened he had no idea. There was no blood,
no obvious injuries, but they were all down.

He had made his way back through the control room into
the comms center, but he had not been able to make his eyes
focus or his hands to work well enough to operate the emergency communications equipment.

The *Indianapolis* was under attack. He knew that much.
But by whom, or to what purpose, he couldn't know.

Help, it was the one thought that kept running through his
head. He would have to contact COMSUBMED and tell them
what was happening. But first he had to stop his bleeding,
or he would die.

He stood just within the tiny dispensary, his breathing
erratic, his back and shoulder on fire, spots dancing in front
of his eyes, trying to make some sense out of what he was
seeing now.

Boyle had been born and raised on a farm in northern
Minnesota. Like most young men in the upper Midwest, he'd
learned to hunt with his father and uncles. He'd shot his first
deer when he was fourteen, and his father had made him gut
it out himself, getting well bloodied in the process. But he'd
never seen anything like this before.

The captain, exec, and their medic lay crumpled in a heap
on the deck. Tony D'Angelo lay on his back on the operating

table, a big gash in his belly. A slim metal cylinder jutted half out of his guts.

Boyle forced himself to step over the exec's body and stumble over to the supplies cabinet where he found a big box of gauze pads. With bloody fingers he managed to yank out a huge wad and press it against the massive wound in his shoulder. The bullet had entered his back, and had exited the front, tearing a three-inch hole in his chest above his lungs.

Someone moved in the corridor. Boyle spun around, nearly falling down with dizziness because of the sudden motion. For some reason in his semidelirium he thought it was Second Officer Lieutenant j.g. Woodman. They were friends.

"Ken?" he mumbled, lurching forward to the door.

Tripping, he fell up against the bulkhead, a tremendous pain raging through his body, stunning him awake, and he staggered backward.

Everyone aboard was dead. Ken Woodman would be dead as well. The *Indianapolis* was definitely under attack. Whoever it was, they were aboard now.

The exec had a .45 automatic strapped to his hip. Boyle dragged himself to where Layman lay on his side and fumbled the weapon out of its holster. It seemed to take him forever to get back to his feet, lever a round into the chamber, switch the safety off, and turn around.

A large man, dressed all in black, stood in the doorway. He held a big pistol in his right hand, a flashlight in his left.

"What happened here," Kurshin demanded, his English perfect.

Boyle was confused again. The .45 was pointed directly at the big man's chest, his finger was on the trigger. But the enemy wasn't supposed to ask what was happening.

Suddenly it came to him. COMSUBMED knew they were in trouble. They had sent help.

"Are you a SEAL?"

Kurshin smiled gently. "Yes. Is your skipper dead?"

"I think so . . ." Boyle mumbled and he turned away,

to look at Captain Webb, when he realized his terrible mistake.

He started to turn back when a tremendous thunderclap burst in his head, and he was falling, falling, and the darkness came.

37

THE MEDITERRANEAN

DR. VELIKANOV STOOD JUST WITHIN THE ATTACK CENTER when Kurshin appeared from aft. His face was pasty in the dim red light, and his hair was plastered back with sweat from the exertion of climbing the sail.

"I heard a gunshot," he said timorously.

"It was the officer from the bridge. I'd only wounded him."

"Now he is dead."

"Yes, Doctor, now he is dead, as is everyone else aboard except for you and me."

Velikanov was looking at the downed crewmen. He was shaking his head. "And now what, Comrade Colonel?" There was blood on his hands.

"Begin clearing the bodies out of this space, the control

room, the sonar and radio rooms, the officers' wardroom, and the galley.''

''Where shall I put them?''

''In their bunks.''

''Where will we sleep?''

''We won't,'' Kurshin said. He brushed past the doctor and hurriedly climbed back up through the interior of the sail to the bridge deck, where he hauled up his equipment bag.

The fire aboard the *Zenzero* was all but out, and the cruiser's list was becoming more pronounced. She was also down at the bow. Not long now, Kurshin thought. He pulled out a portable radio from his equipment bag, switched it on, and keyed the transmit switch.

''Yes,'' he said in English.

''Here,'' a voice came back.

''Now,'' Kurshin radioed, and he switched off the set without waiting for a reply, stuffed it and the grappling hook and line into his bag, and lowered himself through the open hatch, closing it behind him and dogging it shut.

Velikanov had already removed two of the bodies from the attack center. Kurshin laid down his bag and dragged the third body back through the control room, passing the doctor as he was coming forward.

''Most of them are already in their bunks.''

''Just the night watch was on duty,'' Kurshin said. ''At any rate we will have help in a few minutes.''

''The others are coming now?''

''Yes. I'll be aft, continue with your work,'' Kurshin said, and he dragged the seaman's body past the open door to the comms center just as the printer came to life with five bells, indicating a top priority, most urgent message. He ignored it. The message would be from Sixth Fleet Headquarters at Gaeta. They would be anxious to know what was happening out here.

He dumped the man's body with the others in the dispensary, then stepped back to the open door of the officers' wardroom where the other three bodies into which they had implanted the Labun canisters had been left.

One at a time he dragged them across the narrow corridor and into the dispensary.

When he was finished he was sweating lightly. He checked his watch. It was coming up on three in the morning. It had been less than ten minutes since he had given Captain Makayev the signal that everything was ready here. The auxiliary was capable of making twenty knots in these light seas, which put them another fifteen or twenty minutes out.

Over the past weeks while he had been on the mend in a Rome hotel, he had studied in great detail the information Rand had provided them, information which had also been sent to Moscow for Captain Makayev and the others. Included on the disk was the boat's complete physical layout, as well as information on her mechanical, electronics, and weapons systems, and her patrol station, called ROUNDHOUSE. In the Soviet Navy no mere lieutenant colonel, no matter his family connections, would have been privy to such devastating information. In that respect, at least, Soviet military operations were much more secure.

The *Indianapolis* was very large as submarines go, over three hundred fifty feet long and displacing nearly seven thousand tons when she was submerged. Driven by a water-cooled nuclear reactor, she was capable of speeds of around forty knots. In addition to her complement of 533-millimeter SUBROC antisubmarine missiles, antiship missiles, and Mark-48 torpedoes, she carried two varieties of the TLAM Tomahawk cruise missile, one of which was loaded with 200-kiloton nuclear warheads for deployment against land-based targets.

She was a powerful, expensive, and important weapons system. One the Americans would certainly fight for.

"But we will give her back to them, Arkasha," Baranov had said. "Because there is simply no way for us to get her out of the Mediterranean without detection. We're bottled up."

But the Mediterranean was a very big body of water. And deep, where secrets could be hidden for a very long time.

Forward, in the radio room, Kurshin pulled the bodies of the two radio operators out into the corridor. Velikanov was just dragging a body out of the control room. He looked up and their eyes met. He seemed on the verge of collapse.

"When you're finished, take these forward," Kurshin said. "I've taken care of the officers' wardroom."

Velikanov nodded, disappearing through the attack center hatch toward the crew accommodations forward of the sail.

If anyone fell apart, he would be the first to go, Kurshin decided. The man would have to be closely watched.

The radio room was a tiny equipment-filled space. A bank of three teleprinters was built into the forward bulkhead. One of them was connected to the satellite transceiver on which the *Indianapolis* had been communicating with Sixth Fleet Headquarters. Kurshin cranked the message off its roller.

280354ZJUL
TOP SECRET
FM: COMSUBMED
TO: USS INDIANAPOLIS
A. CONTINUATION RESCUE OPERATION
AUTHORIZED ONLY IF IMMEDIATE LOSS OF
LIFE IS PROBABLE.
B. IMPORTANT NO CIVILIAN PERSONNEL BE
ALLOWED ABOARD.
C. IMPORTANT YOU IMMEDIATELY REPORT
YOUR PRESENT SITUATION.
D. ITALIAN COAST GUARD REPORTS
LIBERIAN-REGISTERED M.V. LORRELL-E HAS
DETECTED SOS AND IS ENROUTE YOUR
POSITION. ETA 0430z. RESCUE OPERATIONS
WILL BE TURNED OVER TO THEM ASAP.
WHAT THE HELL IS GOING ON OUT THERE,
J.D.? KENNY SENDS.
XX
EOM

280355ZJUL
BREAKBREAD

"Fuck your mother," Kurshin swore half under his breath. Four-thirty Z—Greenwich mean time—was three-thirty by his watch. They had less than a half hour before the Liberian ship would arrive.

Stuffing the message flimsy in his pocket, he stepped out into the corridor. "Speed it up, Doctor, we've got company coming," he shouted as he rushed into the attack center and took his portable radio from his equipment bag.

The doctor was just coming back from the crew quarters forward. "What? What is it you were shouting?"

"There's a civilian ship on its way to us. Should be here in less than a half hour. We're going to have to be out of here by then, so hurry up with those bodies."

"I don't know if . . ."

"Do it," Kurshin said, the force of his expression taking the doctor back a pace.

"Of course."

Kurshin turned and hurried aft through the control room, past the radio and sonar rooms, the dispensary, and finally through the equipment spaces, and missile storage area where he pulled up short for just a moment. The *Indianapolis* carried eight Tomahawk missiles, four of which were nuclear-armed. Even nestled in their storage racks, their flight fins retracted into the casings, the missiles looked deadly. The raw power here was awesome even to Kurshin. The bodies of three crewmen on the deck heightened the effect.

But there was no time.

Continuing aft he passed the nuclear reactor itself, only one body crumpled in front of a control panel. Most of the power plant was contained in sealed units or behind hatches labeled with the danger-radiation symbol. He came to the access chamber for the after loading hatch. Two seamen were crumpled on the deck. Ignoring them, Kurshin climbed up to the hatch, undogged it, spun the locking wheel, and popped it open.

Immediately he could smell the sea and the still smoldering *Zenzero*, and hear the waves washing up against the hull.

Pulling himself up on deck, he switched on the portable radio. "Code three," he spoke into the microphone.

"Understand," Makayev's voice came over the speaker.

It was their prearranged code that they were on the verge of detection and time was of critical importance. Makayev would be driving the auxiliary as hard as humanly possible through the choppy seas.

Kurshin turned and scanned the horizon, almost immediately picking out the white steaming light of the approaching Liberian freighter low on the horizon to the southeast, nearly the same direction Makayev and the others were coming from.

He debated warning them, but by now they had almost certainly spotted the lights themselves. Makayev, he'd been assured, was a highly competent submarine driver. He knew what was at stake here. And he knew what it would take to dive the boat and get away.

There was nothing left for him to do on deck. Makayev and the others would either arrive in time, or they wouldn't. At this point the question was academic.

Climbing back down into the boat, Kurshin left the after hatch open and hurried forward, where he began removing bodies from the crucial control and reactor room spaces.

Five submariners, a drunken doctor, and an assassin. Even now he didn't think it was possible.

38

COMSUBMED OPERATIONS

CAPTAIN KENNETH REID STOOD JUST WITHIN THE DOORWAY
to the communications center, sipping a cup of coffee.

"Nothing yet?" he asked.

Chief Petty Officer Sally Powell looked up from her console and shook her head.

"But we've still got the downlink?"

She glanced at her board. "Yes, sir. Unless they've got a malfunction aboard, they should be receiving us."

Reid was a worrier, had been all of his life. Barely in his forties, his expressive face already showed stress lines, especially around his eyes and mouth. His blood pressure was on the high side of normal for a man his age, and his cholesterol level had gone through the roof with his assignment to Italy. Just now the base doctor was on his ass.

"I'll be in my office for a minute, buzz me if anything comes in," he said, putting his cup down on top of one of the consoles.

"Aye, sir," the chief radio operator said. She looked up. "Do you think anything is wrong?"

"I don't know," Reid said, but he was developing a very bad feeling about this one. He walked down the corridor to his office and telephoned the CINCMED, Admiral Ronald DeLugio, at his home north of Gaeta.

"Admiral, we still haven't gotten any reply from the *Indianapolis*. We've got our downlink, but there's been nothing since their last nearly an hour ago."

"What about that Liberian freighter, Ken? How close is she?"

"Should be on the scene within the next few minutes. I've held off communicating directly with her."

"No, I don't want you doing that yet. J.D. is a good man, could be he's just got his hands full. What else have we got in the area?"

Reid glanced up at his status board. "Not a thing within a few hours. I've got an Orion standing by on the apron. Could be out there in under twenty minutes counting roll time."

"All right, listen up, Ken. We're going to stop screwing around on this one. I'm on my way in. In the meantime, query J.D. one more time. Tell him it's imperative that he report his status. You can put the Orion up, but just for an overflight unless she detects trouble, then she's authorized to stay on station."

"Will do, Admiral."

"One more thing, Reid," Admiral DeLugio said.

"Yes, sir?"

"Call our ASR crew in. Have them standing by."

The suggestion took Reid momentarily aback, even though he'd had the same thought himself. Just now the ASR 21 *Pigeon* was in port from her support mission on LOOKUP. She was designed for submarine rescue.

"Will do, Admiral," he said.

"Anything comes up, Ken, anything at all, call me enroute. I should be there within fifteen minutes."

"Yes, sir," Reid said and he hung up.

Back in the communications center he scratched out a quick message and handed it to Sally for transmission. He had marked it with the Z designator for a flash message. If nothing else it certainly would get Webb's attention.

```
Z280417ZJUL
TOP SECRET
FM: COMSUBMED
TO: USS INDIANAPOLIS
A. MOST URGENT YOU IMMEDIATELY
REPORT YOUR STATUS.
B. ORION P-3C ENROUTE YOUR POSITION.
TALK TO ME, J.D. KENNY SENDS.
XX
EOM
280418ZJUL
BREAKBREAK
```

Reid picked up the phone and called Lieutenant Commander Morris Segal, the on-duty Air Operations Officer. "Morris, this is Ken. I want you to send that Orion up now."

"No word yet?"

"Not a peep. DeLugio is on his way in. He says to have your people report back, but that they're to stand by on station only if there is an indication that Webb might be in some sort of trouble."

"You got it," Segal said. "But it won't be light for another couple of hours yet, won't be able to do much until then."

"I know," Reid said. "We've got the *Pigeon* standing by, just in case."

"Jesus," Segal said. "That bad?"

"I haven't a clue, Morris. I just hope to Christ we won't be needing her."

Kurshin had just dragged the body out of the reactor auxiliary control room when he heard the distinctive metal clang of the after hatch being closed. Pulling out his pistol he stepped through the hatch into the machinery spaces forward of the reactor, and held up in the shadows.

After a second or two he could hear them coming forward. Their voices were hushed, almost subdued, yet he could hear their excitement. An act of this sort would be totally unprecedented, Baranov had warned him.

"There will be no room for error, Arkasha. No room."

"Yes, Comrade General," he'd replied. "I have no wish to take a one-way ride."

"No." Baranov had smiled. "I have other great things for you. Do not fail me."

Captain First Rank Makayev stepped through the hatch. Kurshin moved forward, placing the barrel of his pistol against the man's temple before he could react.

"The code," Kurshin said softly.

Makayev shrugged away from the gun and looked into Kurshin's eyes. "That freighter was right on our ass, Colonel. So unless you want to serve her crew tea and blinis you'd better let us get to work."

There weren't many men whom Kurshin admired, but he was beginning to like Makayev already. He lowered his gun, switched the safety to the on position, and holstered it.

"The after hatch is sealed?"

Makayev grinned. "There are no screen doors on a submarine. How about forward?"

"The boat is ours, and ready to go."

"Then let's get the hell out of here," Makayev said. He turned back to his crew. "Aleksei, get started with your baby. I want her ready to go within the hour, just in case we have to bail out."

"Yes, Comrade Captain," his missile man snapped.

He turned to his *starpom* (executive officer) and sonar man.

"Gennadi, take Aleksandr forward, get him set up on sonar, and then check the board for diving status."

They brushed past Kurshin and hurried forward to the control room, leaving only the nuclear engineer, Captain Second Rank Ivan Pavlovich Abalakin.

"You're our most important crewman, Ivan Pavlovich," Makayev said. "Think you can handle this monster?"

Abalakin shrugged and smiled, though it was clear he was extremely nervous. "I have studied the systems, Comrade Captain. The Americans have designed most of their controls to work on automatic function. I will manage."

"Good," Makayev said, clapping him on the shoulder. "We shall keep the ship's comms open at all times. We will talk to each other."

Abalakin turned and went into the reactor auxiliary control room, and Makayev and Kurshin started forward.

"Have you ever steered a submarine, Comrade Colonel?" the captain asked.

"No, but I've been aboard one of our Alfa-class boats," Kurshin said.

"Ah, she is a good boat, but much smaller than this one, and cruder too, I think. But this morning you will be our helmsman. I hope your hand is steady."

Passing the sonar room, Lieutenant Raina had already donned the earphones and was fiddling with the controls on the center console.

"Watch that freighter, Aleksandr Ivanovich, and anything else in our vicinity," Makayev said.

The kid looked up and nodded.

Makayev's *starpom*, Captain Second Rank Gennadi Gavrilovich Fedorenko, was busy at work when they entered the control room.

"How does it look, Gennadi?"

"The information we were provided was good, Niki. Very good. She's not so different from our boats. Same board."

"Status?"

"All green, we're ready to dive," Fedorenko said, his eyes shining.

Makayev studied the control room's layout for just a moment, then motioned Kurshin toward the helm. "Just like driving an airplane, Comrade Colonel. Turn the wheel right and we go right. Push it forward and we go down. Make only small motions."

He hit the ship's comms. "Prepare to dive the boat. Ivan, how do we look?"

"Ready to give you turns for maximum speed, Captain."

"Stand by," Makayev said. "Aleksandr, what's our friend doing out there?"

"I put him at eight thousand meters," the sonarman said. "Nothing else in our vicinity."

Makayev turned to his *starpom*. "Dive the boat, Gennadi. Take us to one hundred meters, on a course of two-zero-five."

"Aye, Skipper."

"I'm ringing for one-fourth forward," Makayev said. "Colonel, push your wheel forward, to five degrees down planes. The indicator is just over your head."

COMSUBMED OPERATIONS

CPO Sally Powell suddenly sat forward and flipped a couple of switches on her console. Reid stood on the balcony just behind her.

"We've lost the downlink with *Indianapolis*," she called out.

Reid stepped forward, gripping the rail so hard his knuckles turned white. "Has she submerged?"

"I don't know," she said, looking up at him. "We've just lost her."

39

ATHENS

THEY LAY IN EACH OTHER'S ARMS WATCHING THE SUN RISE outside their hotel window. The last few days had been like a dream, unreal, events moving around them as if they did not exist in the world.

McGarvey turned to look at her. She had let her hair down and it spilled across her pillow, framing her delicate face and neck. Her breasts rose and fell with each breath, the nipples still hard from their lovemaking.

"It's almost time to get ready," he said softly.

She looked at him, then reached out and touched his lips with her fingertips, a wan smile barely creasing her mouth. "I know."

"They've set up a safehouse for you outside of San Francisco. I want you to go there."

"There's someone I have to see in Washington first."

"The general?"

She nodded.

"He won't tell you anything about me."

"I don't expect he will, but that won't stop me from asking." Her eyes opened a little wider and she propped herself up on her side. "It's the Russian. He got away and you're going after him. That's it, isn't it?"

"Don't do this . . ."

"Just tell me that much, Kirk, please. I deserve it." She laid a hand on his chest. "I promise I won't make any trouble. I'll go out to California and wait. For however long it takes."

He disengaged himself from her, swung his legs over the edge of the bed, and got up. He padded over to the bureau where he lit a cigarette from his pack, and then went to the window. He could just make out the cathedral and old metropolis. So much old and consistent history here, he thought, whereas his own history was short and anything but coherent.

"Is he that important to you, Kirk?" she asked from the bed.

She was talking about Kurshin, who was after all nothing more than a handmaiden, nothing more than a tool, while McGarvey was thinking about Baranov. Was the man that important after all—to him or to the geopolitics that Trotter had been spouting?

Often he'd asked himself that question, but he'd never come up with a really satisfactory answer, no matter who the target was.

If Hitler had been assassinated long before he had come to power, would someone even more monstrous have risen in his stead? Perhaps a more intelligent man who would have recognized the contribution that German Jews—especially Jewish scientists—could have made to the war effort. Had Einstein been a loyal Third Reich subject (he did love his country) would Germany have developed the atomic bomb first?

We'd made plans to assassinate Fidel Castro using Mafia

hit men. That had backfired, and Kennedy had been killed instead.

We all but gave our approval when the Shah of Iran was overthrown, but a monster had taken his place. Had Khomeini been killed in Paris, who would have taken over in his stead?

McGarvey would forever remember the men he had killed. Their faces were burned indelibly into his brain. Had their deaths made the slightest difference?

He hoped so, but he thought not.

"Kirk?" Lorraine said.

"Get dressed, I'll take you out to the airport."

"Don't do this."

"I don't have any choice," he said softly. "None of us do." Someone had said that to him. She was dead now. One of Baranov's legion of victims. He wanted to tell Lorraine about her. He had tried to warn her, but she wouldn't listen. None of them ever did.

"Get dressed," he said again.

He heard her getting out of bed and coming across the room to him. He waited for her touch, but it never came. She turned and went into the bathroom, leaving him alone again, as he had been for most of his life.

Turning, he stared at the bathroom door as the water began to run in the shower. He didn't want it to be the same with her. Not this time. Not ever again.

Lloyd Yablonski was a big, red-faced Polack from Philadelphia who had followed John Trotter to the CIA from the Bureau. He met them in the TWA terminal at the East Hellinikon Airport a few minutes after eight.

He and Lorraine shook hands when McGarvey introduced them. "So, you're to be my baby-sitter?" she asked.

Yablonski grinned broadly. "The pleasure is all mine, Doctor, believe me."

Lorraine smiled despite herself, instantly warming to the man. She sincerely hoped that he wouldn't get into too much trouble because of what she was planning on doing. But nothing was going to stop her. Nothing.

"Any troubles on the way over?" McGarvey asked him.

"No, sir. You?"

"We're clean. She wants to stop in Washington."

"Yes, sir. She's to be the director's guest for a day or two before we head out to Frisco."

"Watch yourself."

Yablonski nodded. "You too, sir."

"I don't know how long I'll be," McGarvey said, turning back to Lorraine.

She could see the tension in his eyes. He was gone already. In the field, she thought the term was. "Don't do this, Kirk, please."

"Take care of yourself," he said abruptly and he walked off.

Lorraine watched him head toward the exit. It was now or never, but then she'd never had any trouble being decisive.

"Do you have any aspirins?" she asked Yablonski.

"No, I don't. What's the matter, Doctor, do you have a headache?"

"Splitting. Would you get me some? I'll check my bag through and meet you at the ticket counter."

Yablonski hesitated.

"I would appreciate it. Really."

"Sure," he said, and he headed toward the shops on the mezzanine.

Lorraine waited until he was lost in the crowd, and then sprinted across the ticket hall in the same direction McGarvey had gone.

Outside, she was just in time to see him pulling away in a taxi, and she shoved her way past a couple starting to get into the next cab, and scrambled into the backseat, slamming the door.

"I want you to follow that taxi," she told the driver. "The one that just pulled out."

"What, madame," the driver sputtered. "That is impossible . . ."

Lorraine had pulled a hundred-dollar bill out of her purse.

"Twice this if you don't lose him. This is not illegal, I promise you, but it is very important to me."

The driver hesitated only a moment longer, then snatched the bill from her hand and pulled out into traffic.

Trotter's safehouse was a whitewashed three-story building with a roof garden just off Askilipiou Street northwest of the city center and not far from the thickly wooded Lykabettos. The entrance was at the head of the stairs off a small, pleasantly sunny courtyard.

"Did she get off all right, Kirk?" Trotter asked, letting him in. Trotter still walked with a cane.

"She wasn't happy, but Yablonski seemed competent."

"He is."

"I'm counting on you, John. No screwups with her safety this time."

They had moved into the living room at the rear of the house. Trotter's attaché case lay open on a large coffee table. He'd brought a pistol; it lay as a paperweight on a sheaf of file folders. A street map of East Berlin and its environs was spread out over half the table.

"Have you had your breakfast yet, Kirk? Do you want some coffee?"

"When do I go over, John?"

Trotter looked at him for a long moment. It had always been like this between them at the beginning of an assignment. In the old days McGarvey had thought his friend was afraid of him. He had come to learn, however, that Trotter was afraid *for* him.

"Tonight."

"That's a long time for me to hang out over there. The conference doesn't start until Friday."

"Baranov flies in from Moscow on Thursday night. Eight o'clock. There's to be a reception for him and the police chiefs at the Horst Wessel Barracks. Should break up sometime after midnight when Baranov will be taken by chauffeur-driven limousine to his own little retreat outside of Friedrichshagen on the Grosser Müggelsee. We just found out about that spot. Himmler used it during the war.''

''It will be guarded, I assume.''

''Heavily,'' Trotter agreed. ''But the place is very isolated. It's possible for you to come up from the lake. A small boat will be provided on the south shore, along with the equipment you'll be needing.''

''The shoreline will be watched.''

''Oxygen rebreathing gear.''

''What about the weapon?''

''Two actually,'' Trotter said, and he hesitated again. ''An AK74 assault rifle with an image-intensifying scope, and a suppressed Graz Buyra.''

''The boat is Russian made?'' McGarvey asked.

Trotter nodded.

''And the underwater gear?''

Again Trotter nodded.

''Russian weapons.'' McGarvey shook his head. ''What about my papers?''

Trotter took a thick manila envelope out of his attaché case, opened it, and withdrew a well-used passport. Even before he handed it over, McGarvey could see that it was a Soviet diplomatic passport.

He opened it. His photograph stared up at him. His hair was cropped short, and was slightly graying, and his eyes were a deep green. His appearance had been altered only slightly, but the effect was as startling as the name. Arkady Aleksandrovich Kurshin.

McGarvey looked up. Trotter handed him some letters, a few old photographs, an envelope with a few hundred rubles, a Russian-made comb, a handkerchief, and Kurshin's red-covered KGB identification booklet.

''You are putting me out on a limb.''

''It's the only way, Kirk,'' Trotter said. ''Or at least it's a way. No questions will be asked.''

''What if I'm picked up?''

''Your passport is diplomatic.''

"But they will believe I am a Russian."

"Naturally. It would be too risky for you otherwise. Kirk, I want you to know that the need-to-know list on this operation is very small. Only half a dozen people."

McGarvey laid the documents on the coffee table and went to the sideboard, on which he had spotted a bottle of cognac along with the coffee service. He poured himself a stiff measure of the liquor, drank it down, and poured himself another.

"But you want me in place forty-eight hours before the hit, John," he said.

"We have an apartment and even a car for you."

"Why such a long time? A lot can go wrong."

"We're going to disavow you should anything go wrong. That comes from the top."

"We've already gone through that. Kurshin's identification will prove to them, if I'm caught, that I was working alone. He's beat me twice, this is a vendetta. But why do you want me in place so early?"

"We don't have approval for the operation yet, Kirk. It's as simple and as complicated as that."

McGarvey turned around. "Murphy hasn't gone to the president yet? Or are we going to isolate the White House?"

"He's gone to the president, but he hasn't given us the green light."

"Then we wait until then . . ."

"You're to be in place . . . fully in place first. He wants your situation to be completely stabilized before he gives his go-ahead."

"Why?"

"I don't know."

"Yes you do. John, talk to me."

Trotter shook his head.

"I can think of only one reason for doing it this way. You suspect a traitor in the CIA. Christ, it can't be happening again. Not after all that we've gone through."

"He may have been there all along. We don't know."

"At this point only the president, Murphy, and you know

why I'm going in so early. But everyone else knows that I'm going in."

"You don't have to do this . . ."

"No safety valves for getting me back across if everything blows up. I understand this. But what about afterward?"

"If you get out clean, you'll be taken care of. It's all I can promise you."

"How will the green light be transmitted to me?"

"Radio Berlin One. The special request show. We've prepared a key phrase."

"Baranov will be expecting me."

"Probably. But he won't know where or when the attack will come."

McGarvey thought about it for a moment, weighing the pros and cons, the risks versus the benefits. He nodded. "When do I leave?"

"You have a noon flight to West Berlin. You'll take a cab across."

40

USS *INDIANAPOLIS*

MAKAYEV WAS DRIVING THE *INDIANAPOLIS* HARD TO THE southwest toward the Strait of Sicily and the Malta Channel which would put them in the eastern Mediterranean.

At speeds near forty knots the submarine was noisy. But as Makayev explained, their first obligation was to get as far away from the hijack site as possible in the shortest time.

"Sixth Fleet Headquarters obviously knows something is wrong. We've seen that from the messages they sent. They will already have instituted the first elements of their search."

"But they will not find anything," Kurshin replied.

"On the contrary, Comrade Colonel, they will of course find the *Zenzero* and the auxiliary boat that we used."

"That ship is probably at the bottom of the sea by now."

"No matter, they will find it. But all of that will take time.

They cannot believe that their submarine and crew of more than a hundred twenty men has been hijacked."

Dr. Velikanov had been pressed into service as cook. He had brewed some tea and made sandwiches, and was bringing them forward. He stopped short and nearly dropped the tray he was carrying at the mention of the crew. His reaction was not lost on any of them in the control room.

"There was no other way, Doctor," Makayev said gently from where he stood with Fedorenko at the chart table.

"They were kids, most of them."

"I know, but that is past."

"When you live close to the grave, you can't weep for everyone," Velikanov said, quoting an old peasant proverb. "Is that what you are saying to me, Nikolai Gerasimovich?"

"Where are they, what have you done with them?"

"They are mostly in their bunks," Kurshin said from where he still sat at the helm.

Velikanov put the tray down. "We will come very near to Sicily. Let's surface and take rubber rafts ashore. We can go home, leave this boat for the Americans to find."

"That's not possible."

"You are the skipper of this vessel, Niki. Please. They were just boys. This could start the nuclear holocaust . . ."

"I am not the president to give this order, Doctor."

"No," Velikanov said sharply, his voice rising. "Nor did the president give such an order. It was the KGB. You know this!"

"Yes it was," Kurshin said. This was the trouble he had been expecting. He'd hoped it wouldn't come so soon.

"It's Baranov. He's insane. He'll kill us all!"

"Relieve me at this wheel," Kurshin snapped.

Makayev hesitated a moment, his gaze switching from Velikanov to Kurshin.

"Now," Kurshin insisted.

Makayev nodded for Fedorenko to take over. He took the starboard wheel. "I have the helm," he said softly.

Kurshin got up. "How much longer before we're in position?"

"Twenty-five hours, perhaps a little longer," Makayev replied.

Velikanov was shaking with rage and fear. Spittle ran down the side of his chin.

"You will confine yourself to the galley for the duration, Doctor," Kurshin told him. "When we return home, no mention will be made of your outburst. You have my promise."

"Fuck your mother," Velikanov shrieked, and he leapt forward to the trim tank controls, which would change the submarine's buoyancy and bring her to the surface.

Kurshin pulled out his pistol and fired a single shot, the noise impossibly loud in the confines of the boat, striking Velikanov in the face just below the left eye. His head snapped back, and he was thrown violently to the deck, instantly dead.

Makayev had instinctively stepped back, his right hand going to the pistol in his tunic. Kurshin switched his aim to the captain.

"We're going to calm down now," he said in a reasonable voice.

Lieutenant Raina, their sonarman, had rushed to the control center hatch, his pistol in hand, a grim look on his face as he surveyed the scene.

"Put your gun down, Lieutenant, and get back to your post," Kurshin said.

The young man was wracked with indecision.

"The doctor was out of control," Kurshin explained. "I don't want to kill your captain."

"Then you would never get to the surface, Comrade Colonel," Raina replied.

"Better to die here like this, then," Kurshin said softly. "We have our orders, which I intend carrying out so long as I am alive."

Makayev had withdrawn his hand from his tunic. "Put your gun down, Aleksandr Ivanovich. The colonel is correct. The doctor could have killed us all. There was no other way."

Raina stepped back a pace and lowered his pistol.

Kurshin lowered his automatic and holstered it. "Have you detected anything on the surface?" he asked.

"A few ships, mostly small freighters," Raina replied.

"Any other submarines?"

"No."

"Good," Kurshin said. He turned to Makayev. "I would like to talk to you and your missile man in the wardroom."

Makayev nodded. "Take care of the doctor for me, would you, Aleksandr."

"Yes, sir."

The captain hit the comms switch. "Aleksei, are you ready up there?"

"Just about, Captain," Lieutenant Chobotov said. "I've isolated the Tomahawk's firing circuits. I managed to get one of them on the transfer rack, but I'm going to need help getting her loaded into one of the tubes."

"Good," Makayev said. "Come back to the officers' wardroom and we will discuss it."

"Aye, Skipper."

P-3C ORION

The four-engine turboprop-powered ASW (AntiSubmarine Warfare) aircraft came in low, at under fifteen hundred feet, over the *Indianapolis*'s last known position. They had finally been given the go-ahead by Sixth Fleet Headquarters to come off her position-keeping station. Something was definitely wrong, and all the brass were definitely uptight.

Lieutenant Lawrence Weaver had throttled well back so they were doing significantly less than two hundred knots, giving the ship's sophisticated electronic sensing equipment plenty of time to do its job.

In addition to the ASQ-114 computer which instantly analyzed data from the aircraft's radar systems, she also carried infrared sensors and magnetic anomaly detectors that were able to detect a mass of ferrous metal well beneath the surface of the sea—providing conditions were right.

Weaver banked slightly to port as they passed over the spot. Below he could see the Liberian-registered freighter standing by what appeared to be the burned out remains of a fairly good-sized cabin cruiser. But there was no other boat visible. No submarine. No debris, so far as Weaver had been able to see.

He straightened the aircraft out and banked to starboard making a wide looping turn over the area, the sun well up in the eastern sky.

"What are you showing down there, Al?" he radioed to his ASW man in the rear.

"We've got the freighter and another smaller vessel, maybe a pleasure craft. We're also painting a much smaller boat, perhaps eighteen or twenty feet. Maybe an auxiliary. No machinery noises except from the *Lorrel-E*."

"How about our Mags?"

"Not a thing, Lieutenant. Looks clean below the surface."

Weaver glanced at his copilot, Lieutenant Peter Reiland. "All right, we're coming around for another pass. Look sharp on the Mags now. He's gotta be down there somewhere."

"Roger," Technical Sergeant Albert McLaren replied.

About a mile and a half out they were lined up again on the *Lorrel-E* and the *Zenzero*. Weaver throttled back a bit more and dropped them another five hundred feet, the big aircraft beginning to mush slightly. But Weaver was a good pilot, he knew what he was doing.

He took a cigarette out of his shirt pocket and clamped it between his teeth without lighting it. He had quit two years ago. Submarines simply didn't disappear off the face of the earth. It was either lying on the bottom, and for one reason or another their equipment wasn't detecting it, or it had bugged out.

Either was unlikely. Why would J.D. Webb do such a thing? There was no reason for it, no reason at all.

They came over the *Lorrel-E* and this time he banked hard to the starboard for another run.

"Not a thing, Lieutenant," McLaren said. "If she's down there, we're not painting her."

"That's a roger. We're coming around again, are we ready with our Mark 84?"

"She's loaded and ready for the drop on your mark."

"We're coming around on it. Stand by."

The Mark 84 was a Sippican SUS communications buoy. Barely fifteen inches long and only three inches in diameter, it was programmed with a simple message—in this case, ESTABLISH COMMUNICATIONS—and was tossed into the water from a ship or aircraft. As soon as it hit water it would begin transmitting the same message over and over again on pulsed 2.95 kHz and 3.5 kHz tones that a submarine was capable of detecting beneath the surface if she wasn't too far distant.

They came up on the *Lorrel-E* again. "Stand by," Weaver radioed, steadying out the P-3C. "On my mark . . . mark!"

"She's off," McLaren said.

Weaver increased the throttles and the aircraft began to climb as he swung wide to port again. "Stan, contact Gaeta, tell them we've had negative contact on our sensors and have sent down the buoy."

"Aye, aye, Lieutenant," Staff Sergeant Stan Raymond, their radio operator, said.

"And listen up, you guys, she still may be down there."

LORREL-E

Captain Stefano Parus smiled as he put down the radiotelephone, his brief conversation with the owners in Athens finished. "She is ours," he told his first officer, Rupert Brecht.

"I think there is someone else very much interested in that little toy," Brecht said.

Parus had heard the Orion passing overhead, of course. "Who are they?"

"U.S. Navy."

"Well, it's too fucking bad. We were here first, and we're claiming our salvage rights."

"It's not much . . ."

"Enough," Parus said, rubbing his hands together. "She's

a floating whorehouse. Who knows what we'll find aboard. Diamonds don't melt, and who cares if gold does. We'll scrape it off the deck.''

"Shit."

"Take her under tow, Mr. Brecht," Parus ordered. "If she's still too hot, put some water over her, we'll cool her down."

"We may need to put some pumps aboard."

"Then do it, and look sharp about it. If those bastards are interested enough to send out a search plane, they'll probably be sending out a surface ship. Won't be able to do much about it if we've got the little bitch in tow.''

COMSUBMED OPERATIONS

CINCMED Admiral Ronald DeLugio—his uniform blouse off, his shirtsleeves rolled up above his thick forearms, and his tie loose—paced the balcony above and behind the communications consoles. He was fuming, and when admirals were mad, especially this one, everyone around was on tenterhooks.

The P-3C on station had come up with nothing. So far there had been no reply from the communications buoy, nor had they detected any large mass of metal beneath the surface.

The *Lorrel-E* had contacted the Italian coast guard, claiming their right of salvage over the *Zenzero*, which they were granted, providing there were no survivors aboard. The *Lorrel-E* claimed there were none.

Admiral DeLugio stopped and turned back to Captain Reid. "I want you to get a message to the skipper of the *Lorrel-E*. Tell him that he is to remain on station with that cruiser until we can get out there to take a look at it. If he refuses, tell him that we will blow his vessel out of the water."

"Aye, aye, Admiral," Reid said. "Sir, what if he *does* refuse?"

"Ken, if that sonofabitch moves so much as ten feet, I want his vessel sunk. And that's a direct order."

Reid raised his eyes. "There would be hell to pay . . ."

"Don't I know it. What's the ETA for the *Pigeon* on station?"

"Not for another hour yet, sir," Reid said. "Are you sure about that order, sir?"

"Kenny, we're talking about an attack submarine, nuclear-armed, with a crew of one hundred twenty-seven men and officers. You're damned right I'm sure. J.D. surfaced in response to an SOS from that cruiser, and now he's disappeared. We're going to find out what happened. No one or nothing is going to stand in our way. Clear?"

"Yes, sir," Reid snapped.

41

WEST BERLIN

THE AFTERNOON WAS CLEAR AND SUNNY WHEN THE PAN Am flight from Athens touched down at Tegel Airport with a sharp bark of its tires and taxied over to the terminal.

McGarvey had known someone was following him from the moment he'd left the Lykabettos safehouse, but he had taken no particular precautions. In fact he had become obvious about his movements, keeping to the open squares on foot, and finally taking a taxi directly out to Hellinikon Airport.

He'd expected to see someone on the flight, an out-of-place face, eyes that were quickly averted as he passed. But if they'd been there, they were very good because he'd spotted no one.

Walking with the rest of the passengers down the jetway,

he was passed through customs without event. At this point
he was still traveling under his real name. It would have been
too risky, they'd decided, for him to use his Kurshin persona
anywhere far from the eastern frontier. The secret services
in every Western European country had a file on the Russian
KGB colonel. It would have unnecessarily complicated things
if he had been spotted using the Russian passport.

Berlin was soon enough.

Trotter had promised that he would be kept at arm's length
for everyone's sake. There would be no shadows, nor any
contact on either side of the East-West border. The setup
team in East Berlin who had arranged for his weapons and
equipment, as well as the apartment and automobile, had
already been cut out of the operation. They had no idea what
or who was coming. Nor had they displayed, according to
Trotter, any interest in knowing. They were professionals
who understood that in this business unnecessary knowledge
could oftentimes prove fatal. The fallout was going to be
terrific once Baranov went down. Lesser crises had tumbled
presidents and entire governments.

So, who knew he was in Athens? Who knew or suspected
that he would be traveling east? It was called "covering your
own back door." Before he went across he wanted to know
who was back there.

But no one had been on his flight, which meant that either
a message had been sent ahead, or whoever it was who'd
been following him would be showing up on the next flight.

Walking across the main entry hall, he checked the incoming flight board. The next flight from Athens, via Rome this
time, was due to arrive at 2:15, barely a half hour from now.

He took the stairs up to the mezzanine where he got a spot
at a stand-up table in the *bierstube* from which he had a clear
line of sight to the exit doors from customs.

If a message had been sent ahead, they would easily spot
him here. If someone was coming on the next flight, he would
spot them.

Sipping his beer he watched the comings and goings below
in the main arrivals hall. Most of them were ordinary people,

nine-to-fivers, some of them here in West Berlin on business, others with their families here on vacation.

His life had never been ordinary, certainly not his adult life, and often he found himself pining for something he could never quite reach. For a time when he'd lived in Switzerland, after he had left the Agency, he had tried for such a thing. But the Swiss Federal Police had set their watchdogs on him. Assassins, even retired assassins, were not to be trusted under any circumstances. The Swiss were pragmatic, they'd more or less left him to his own devices, so long as he kept his nose clean. But the moment Trotter had shown up with an assignment for him, his tenure in Switzerland was at an end. Nor could he ever go back, legally.

Too, he often thought about Marta Fredricks, the Swiss cop who'd been assigned to live with him so that they could keep closer tabs on his movements.

When he finally left Lausanne she'd told him that she had fallen in love with him. They had both known at the time that any life for them together would be impossible. Nevertheless he had telephoned her last year. They had talked for a few minutes, only that long, but he had been able to hear in her voice that she had gotten over him. She was on a new, exciting assignment. And besides, he told himself, she was Swiss. She would never leave her country. Her family and friends were all there. Her career, her life, was there. And there was absolutely nothing that he could offer her.

For instance, he thought, at this moment there would have been nothing for her to do except worry about him. It was a callous attitude, he knew, but he simply did not need that sort of excess baggage.

The Athens–Rome flight was on time, and fifteen minutes later the first of the passengers began streaming out of customs. McGarvey watched them closely, most of them nine-to-fivers, more ordinary people.

He had no real idea exactly what or who he was looking for, he just knew that when he spotted the face he would recognize it for what it was; either one of Trotter's people along to make sure that McGarvey did as he was told, or one of the opposition here with orders to kill the American assassin.

When Lorraine Abbott emerged from customs, he was totally unprepared for her, and he nearly dropped his beer stein.

"Oh, Christ," he said to himself.

He slammed his stein on the table, grabbed his single overnight bag, and hurried down the stairs, his movements studied and very careful. What he did not need now was to attract unnecessary attention to himself.

Lorraine had walked directly across the arrivals hall, her stride purposeful, so that McGarvey didn't catch up to her until she had reached the taxi ranks outside. He came up behind her, took her arm without a word, and propelled her to the next taxi in line, where he unceremoniously shoved her in the backseat, climbing in after her.

"The Hotel Berlin," he told the driver. It was one of the better hotels in the city, on the Ku'Damm. It was expensive but he figured she could afford it, and security there was reasonably good. Berlin was still a difficult city during the night.

Her eyes were wide, her nostrils flared with fright, and a little indignation. She started to say something, but he held her off with a fierce warning stare, and she sat back, her mouth set, her shoulders stiff.

They rode into town in silence. The afternoon was warm and lovely. Children were playing in the Tiergarten, and she smiled when she saw them.

A few minutes later they pulled up in front of the big, modern hotel. McGarvey paid the cabbie and inside directed Lorraine to the registration desk.

"Get a room in your own name, I'll be up in a couple of minutes."

"I've come this far, I'm not going to let you slip away . . ." Lorraine started to say.

McGarvey still held her arm, and squeezed it hard, a sharp expression of pain crossing her features. "Get yourself a room, you goddamned fool. I'll come up in a couple of minutes. Do it now!''

He let her go, then turned on his heel and walked directly across the lobby without bothering to look back. At the bell captain's desk, he handed over his bag for temporary storage, got his chit, and went into the bar of Berlin's famous Grill Restaurant, where he ordered a cognac and lit a cigarette.

So much for Yablonski's expertise, he thought angrily. But then the man had been sent out to protect her from harm. He wasn't in fact her baby-sitter in the sense that he was to watch for her to slip out the back door.

By now Trotter would be beside himself. The entire mission could be jeopardized by her presence here. But, he decided, it would be even worse if a fuss were to be made. She was here in Berlin, and this is where she would remain, out of harm's way (no one would expect her to be here) until he was finished.

He waited a full five minutes before he paid his tab, and in the lobby used a house phone to call her. She answered on the first ring.

''Yes?''

''Are you all right?''

''Yes.''

McGarvey hung up, crossed the lobby, and took the stairs up to the second floor where the hotel's ballroom and other meeting rooms were located. He waited for a couple more minutes, to make sure he hadn't been spotted, with someone else on his tail, then took the elevator up to the seventh floor.

She let him in immediately. He locked and chained the door.

''You followed me from Lykabettos,'' he said.

She was definitely frightened. ''I waited outside until you left, and then followed you out to the airport.''

''What in God's name are you doing here?''

''I came to . . . stop you,'' she said breathlessly.

''What?''

''You're going to cross the border to kill someone. I know it. I'm going to stop you . . . any way I can.''

McGarvey looked at her in open amazement. "You're an antinuclear activist, for Christ's sake."

"It just happened. But it's not so strange."

"For a nuclear physicist?"

"Less strange than you'd think," she said defiantly. "If need be, I'll go to the newspapers with this story."

McGarvey was shaking his head. "The only things that would accomplish would be your arrest and most likely my death."

"If you went across. But you're not going to do it."

"Yes I am."

"For what?" she cried, her voice rising. "Revenge. You're going to risk your life to kill a Russian spy who made a fool of you?"

"You can't possibly know how wrong, how dangerously wrong you are," McGarvey said. "I'm not going after Kurshin."

"Then who?"

"You don't want to know."

"Who?" she shrieked.

He was across the room to her in three steps. He took her by the shoulders and shook her like a rag doll. She wanted to cry out again, but she couldn't catch her breath.

"Goddamnit, Lorraine, don't do this to me. My life is on the line. So are the lives of a lot of other people."

She was shaking her head. "I can't let you do this, Kirk," she sobbed. "Please . . . oh, God, please."

"I'll telephone Trotter. He'll send someone over here to place you under arrest. He can do it, believe me."

"No."

"I'm trying to save your life, Lorraine."

"And I'm trying to save yours."

McGarvey let go of her shoulders and turned away from her. He stared at the telephone. Trotter would be in transit back to Washington, unavailable until tonight, or possibly tomorrow morning. There was no one else he could trust. If there was a penetration agent within the CIA, another of Baranov's men, calling Washington would place Lorraine in an impossibly dangerous position here. But he simply could not wait here with her. He was not going to turn his back on this assignment. Too many good people *had* died because of Baranov, and there would be others. This opportunity might never present itself again.

He walked across the room to the telephone and picked it up. The hotel operator came on a moment later. "Give me an outside line, please. I would like to make a transatlantic call."

"Yes, *mein Herr*," the operator replied.

Lorraine had come across the room. Tears were leaking from her eyes, and she was shaking her head. "No," she said.

McGarvey looked at her.

"I promise you, Kirk, I'll do whatever it is you want me to do. I swear to God."

"Operator?" McGarvey spoke into the phone.

"Sir?"

"I don't need to make that call after all. Thank you."

MOSCOW

Valentin Illen Baranov's black Zil limousine passed the Ukraine Hotel and headed down Kutuzovsky Prospekt at a high rate of speed. It was a few minutes after six in the evening, and the KGB chairman was on his way home. His security people rode in chase cars ahead of and behind his limo. The only other person in the Zil with him, besides his driver-bodyguard, was his personal secretary, Petr Nikolaievich Borisov, a young KGB major whose loyalty was beyond question.

The limousine's telephone burred softly. Borisov answered it.

"*Da*," he said, and he listened for a full thirty seconds before hanging up and turning to Baranov.

"What crisis now, Petr Nikolaievich?" Baranov asked. He

was a short, extremely stocky man, with a barrel chest, a thick bulldog neck, and a huge head. But his voice was as soft as a gentle wind through a graveyard, and his eyes always seemed to hold a hint of amusement.

"It is White Knight. He has attempted to make contact. Direct contact."

WHITE KNIGHT was the code name of Baranov's personal source in Washington. They'd worked together for a lot of years.

"What was he told?"

"To stand by for the usual procedure," Borisov replied. Despite his nearness to Baranov, even he did not know WHITE KNIGHT's true identity. Baranov shared that with no one.

"Very good," Baranov said, and he settled back in his seat. It was about McGarvey, he was certain of it. Considering what was happening at this very moment in the Mediterranean—did the CIA already know about the *Indianapolis*? —this call was extremely important.

Baranov's apartment sprawled over the entire top floor of a twenty-five-story apartment building a few blocks from where Leonid Brezhnev had once lived. His private study was directly in the middle of the apartment, with no windows to the outside. The room, and its telephone equipment, was as secure from eavesdropping, electronic or otherwise, as Soviet technical abilities could make it.

When he was alone, he made his call. It was answered on the first ring.

"It is me," Baranov said. "What is the matter?"

"It is McGarvey," a man said. There was no mistaking his voice. "He has been sent to East Berlin to kill you. It will happen on Thursday night, after the reception. He will be coming across the lake . . . actually beneath the lake."

Baranov smiled. "I will be most happy to finally come face to face with him. Thank you, my old friend."

"There is more."

"Yes?"

"The scientist, Dr. Abbott. She is missing."

"Any idea where she might have gotten herself to?" Baranov asked, very interested by this latest development.

"No, but it would be my guess that she's followed McGarvey, or tried to."

"Is there a thing, then, between them?" Baranov asked. Kurshin had mentioned something about it.

"I believe so. I thought you should know."

"Yes, thank you. Now, sit tight, my friend. No matter what happens in the next twenty-four hours or so, sit very tight."

"I know."

"No you don't," Baranov said softly. "But you will."

42

ASR *PIGEON*

No sign had been found of the *Indianapolis* despite eight hours of continuous searching in ever-expanding circles. The DSRV (Deep Submergence Rescue Vehicle) had been on standby mode from the moment they'd arrived on station, but with no target on the sea floor she had not been sent down.

There was debris, of course. The *Pigeon*'s sophisticated sonar systems had picked up the wreckage of what appeared to be an old ship, possibly even Roman, but so far they'd found nothing even approaching the mass of the submarine.

The *Lorrel-E*, still claiming her right of salvage, continued to stand by. Her crew had managed to cool the *Zenzero* down enough so that they were able to get aboard with several pumps to keep her from sinking. An explosion somewhere in the vicinity of the engine room had blown a small hole in her hull, but so far the pumps had been able to keep up with the flow rate.

The *Zenzero* would not sink, unless the pumps failed, but at this point she was unstable and could capsize at any moment, especially if the wind and seas were to pick up, which they were forecast to do sometime during the night.

Captain Parus was fuming. He had been on the radiotelephone almost continuously with the owners in Athens who in turn were trying to put pressure on the U.S. Navy through the Italian government.

"We've got company, Skipper," the radio on the *Pigeon*'s bridge blared.

Lieutenant Commander Charles Wells hit the comms switch. "What have you got, Jim?"

"Looks like a Hormone-B, coming in fast from the south-southwest," Lieutenant James Powers, their ESM (Electronic Surveillance Measures) officer, replied.

Wells picked up his binoculars, stepped out onto the starboard porch, and began scanning the horizon. The Hormone-B was the Soviet Navy's updated version of the Kamov Ka-25 search helicopter. She was used to provide a real-time data link for over-the-horizon targeting and mid-course guidance for missiles from Soviet guided missile cruisers. He had been warned that a Slava-class cruiser was in the area. They were probably coming for a quick look-see, which was to be expected.

He had it, low on the horizon and incoming very fast. It was definitely a Hormone-B, he could make out the chopper's unique triple-tail.

Back on the bridge, Wells hit the comms switch. "It's definitely a Hormone-B, Jim, which means the Slava will be somewhere just over the horizon. Are you picking up anything?"

"The chopper is scanning us, Skipper. But nothing from her mother ship."

"Right, keep a close watch. I'm sending up our helo to take a quick peek."

"Roger."

Wells picked up his red phone, which in this case provided him with a direct encrypted link with Sixth Fleet Headquarters. Kenneth Reid in operations answered.

"Ken, Charlie Wells here. You'd better let me speak with Admiral DeLugio."

"How's it look out there?"

"Nothing yet, but we've got company."

"Right. I'll get him," Reid said, and a moment later DeLugio was on the line.

"Is it the Slava?" the admiral asked without preamble.

"Yes, sir. One of her Hormone-Bs is incoming right now."

"We expected that, Charlie. What about the *Indianapolis*? Any trace?"

"Not a thing, Admiral. We've expanded our grid twenty miles out and ten miles in. Usual seafloor litter, but nothing to send the DSRV down for. The *Indianapolis* is just not here."

"Damn," DeLugio swore softly. "What about the *Zenzero*, Charlie, can you tow her?"

"Yes, sir. But Captain Parus is raising a lot of hell."

"I don't give a rat's ass, Charlie. Shoot the sonofabitch if he gets in your way. I want that cruiser back here as soon as you can bring her in."

"There's a danger she'll capsize under tow. I'd like to put a couple of men aboard to look around first."

"Do that. All we know so far is that J.D. responded to an SOS, and now he's missing."

"Yes, sir," Wells said glumly.

"If you find anything, anything at all, Charlie, let me know immediately. Have you got that?"

"Aye, aye, sir."

"All right, good luck."

"Sir, I'm sending a helo out to take a look at that Slava."

"Good idea. Scan the living shit out of them. Let them know we don't like them playing around on our turf."

"Yes, sir," Wells said and he hung up the red phone and turned to his executive officer, Lieutenant Tom Lawson, a lanky kid from Texas, who was just turning away from the ship's comms.

"The chopper is already airborne, Skipper," he said.

"Good. I want you to take an auxiliary over to the *Zenzero* and look around. We're going to tow her back to Gaeta this afternoon before the wind picks up."

Lawson's eyes narrowed. "We're giving up here?"

Wells nodded. "Looks like it. You'd better take Randy along."

Lieutenant j.g. Randy Tanner was the DSRV's skipper, and an expert on salvage.

"What are we looking for?"

"First of all I want to know if she'll survive the tow, but I want you to keep your eyes open for anything . . . anything at all."

"Sir?"

"The *Indianapolis* responded to an SOS from the *Zenzero*, and now she's missing. Just keep your eyes open."

"What about the *Lorrel-E*?"

"They won't give you any trouble, Tom. I can guarantee it."

"Yes, sir," Lawson said, and he turned and left the bridge as Wells picked up the radiotelephone.

"Get me the skipper of the *Lorrel-E*," he told his radioman.

ZENZERO

The pleasure cruiser was listing ten degrees to port, the twisted remains of her boarding ladder half submerged in the water. She rolled sluggishly in the three- to five-foot swells. All of her windows and ports had been blown out by the heat of the fire, and the paint on her hull was mostly burned off down to the waterline. Still, she was surprisingly intact for all of that.

Lawson and Tanner tied their small auxiliary to the boarding ladder and scrambled aboard. The hull and bulkheads were still warm to the touch from the fire, but no longer hot. The ship stank of burned diesel fuel, wood, fabric, and paint. Water dripped everywhere.

"I don't know what that Greek skipper wants with this wreck," Tanner said as they made their way aft to the broad opening into the saloon. "There's nothing left to salvage. The hull itself is probably warped beyond repair."

The afternoon sun slanted into the interior of the ship. All the wood paneling had been burned off the bulkheads, exposing the bare aluminum. The furniture was mostly ashes, and the deck had buckled upward in some spots at least eight inches.

A half a mile to their south the Hormone-B helicopter was hovering a few hundred feet above the water. Tanner, who was a much smaller man than Lawson (slightly built men were assigned DSRV duty), looked over his shoulder. "I wonder how much those bastards know?"

"Probably about as much as we do at this moment," Lawson replied. "Not a whole hell of a lot."

They went into the saloon. ·

"I'll check the flooding below," Lawson said. They could hear the steady roar of the gasoline-driven dewatering pumps below and smell the exhaust.

"Right," Tanner said, stepping carefully through the debris forward to the galley, radio room, and owner's stateroom, all of them mostly gutted.

There was nothing here. The crew of the *Lorrel-E* had already been aboard and they'd reported finding no bodies. *So what the hell had happened to the crew?* Tanner asked himself.

Turning, he went back into the saloon and was about to call Lawson when he spotted something half buried in the debris of what had probably been a long couch built over an air-conditioning duct.

He shoved aside the burned fabric and wooden frame, and then had to bend back a section of the ductwork to expose a small metal cylinder, perhaps a couple of inches in diameter and no more than eight or ten inches long. Whatever it was, it didn't belong here. It had apparently survived the intense heat because it had been protected by the bulk of the couch and the ductwork itself.

Tanner picked it out of the debris and brushing it off took it outside onto the afterdeck where there was more light.

Some lettering was stamped into the side of the cylinder. It took him a minute to clean enough of the dirt away to read what it said, and his blood suddenly ran cold.

"Jesus Christ," he swore softly. "Oh, Jesus . . ." Tanner spun on his heel. "Lawson," he shouted. "Tom, topside . . . on the double, man!"

COMSUBMED OPERATIONS

Reid handed the encrypted phone to Admiral DeLugio. "It's Wells. He sounds . . . shook up."

Now that the Soviet guided missile cruiser had shown up, Operations was alive with activity. Wells had sent out a helo, to which the Russians had made absolutely no response, so far. But they were walking a tight wire every time American and Soviet naval forces were this close together. Now, with a missing attack submarine on their hands, the Pentagon was nervous.

"What's the problem, Charlie?" DeLugio asked. "Is it the Russians?"

"No, Admiral, they're behaving themselves," Wells said.

DeLugio could hear that the man was definitely shaken. "Take it easy. Now, what's going on out there?"

"I think we've got very big trouble, sir."

"I'm listening," DeLugio said, his jaw tightening.

"I sent my exec and my DSRV driver over to the *Zenzero*. They just got back. Randy . . . Lieutenant Tanner . . . found something aboard. In the main saloon."

"Go ahead."

"It's a cylinder . . . small, thick-walled. There are markings. Christ, Admiral, the cylinder came from the Army's proving grounds in Dugway.''

Something clutched at DeLugio's gut. "Any idea what it contained?''

"Yes, sir. Labun. It's a nerve gas. The cylinder is empty.''

DeLugio closed his eyes. "Run it out for me, Charlie. All the way.''

"Terrorists, Admiral. I think the *Indianapolis* has been hijacked by terrorists.''

43

EAST BERLIN

MORE THAN ANY OTHER CITY IN THE WORLD, THE CAPITAL of the failing German Democratic Republic was a study in stark contrasts. In many respects it was very much like the Berlin before the war, yet there was an Eastern Bloc drabness to the streets and squat buildings.

The three-hundred-foot-wide boulevard, Unter den Linden, had been completely rebuilt from the rubble and was the showcase of Eastern Europe. It was colossal by any standard; along it a monstrous television tower with restaurant and observation deck rose high above the city.

Karl Marx Allee, Marx Engels Square, and Leninplatz (all roads led to Leninplatz) were shining and brand-new, filled with activity. Trolley cars ran on polished tracks. Bratwursts were wrapped in paper, not plastic. And there was absolutely no litter anywhere.

But East Berlin was a city of relative darkness. From almost anywhere in or around the city, you could see the night glow of West Berlin.

A couple of blocks off any modern street or square (and there weren't many of them) you were plunged backward forty-five years, to buildings that still carried the scars of the war. Windows bricked or boarded up. Narrow cobblestone streets. Machine gun holes in stone walls.

McGarvey, using his Kurshin identification, crossed into the eastern sector of Berlin on the Friedrichstrasse a few minutes after 6:00 in the evening. On the American side the officials were distantly polite, but on the DDR side, the soldiers were almost obsequious. His bag was not searched.

The cabbie dropped him off at the Palast Hotel, then turned and headed immediately back to the western sector. Inside, McGarvey had a drink at the bar, then headed on foot around the huge Alexanderplatz, where behind the *Sparkasse*—the savings bank—he found the little two-door Fiat Trotter had promised would be waiting for him, the keys in the tailpipe.

He had driven directly over to the working-class district of Prenzlauder Berg, parking the car on the street in front of a very shabby apartment block.

The flat that had been set up for him was on the third floor and looked down on the narrow street. It was well stocked with food, drink, and Russian-made clothing that was his size. A very old black-and-white television set squatted heavily on a small table next to the window, the antenna cable snaking through the window frame up to an aerial on the roof.

Changing clothes and grabbing a quick bite to eat, McGarvey left the apartment a little after 10:00, taking the Leninallee directly out of the city, a few miles to the east, before turning south toward the Grosser Müggelsee. As he drove, traffic light and in some areas nonexistent at this hour, he lit a Russian cigarette from a pack he'd found in the apartment.

It was half cardboard filter and tasted terrible, but it was Kurshin's brand.

It would be a full forty-eight hours before he came this way again. They had figured it would be too dangerous for him to bring his own weapon across the border, and there was no gun in the apartment. Two days and nights, however, was too long to wait, unarmed. Too many things could go wrong.

He came down through Tierpark and Lichtenberg, past the huge Pioneer Palace that the Russians had built not so long ago, crossing the Spree River once into Treptow and again toward Köpenick along the southern shore of the big lake.

This far from the city, the night was very dark, although still to the northwest he could make out the glow on the horizon that was West Berlin, and almost directly west he watched as a jetliner came in for a landing at East Berlin's Schönefeld Airport.

He was alone now. This time absolutely alone. There would be no help for him from any of the East German networks that the Agency maintained, nor would he be able to run for the American Embassy on the Neustadtische Kirschstrasse. He would be denied. At this point he was no longer an American citizen. He was a Russian. The Americans and West Germans would shoot him if he tried to force his way back, and the Russians and East Germans would certainly arrest him if they discovered he was an impostor.

But the prize was definitely worth the risk. Baranov was coming. And for that man McGarvey's hate burned like a supernova in his gut. It was a constant that he had lived with for nearly two years.

The Köpenick highway branched off, the larger road heading into the town, the much smaller road running north a few miles to the lake. The forest was thick here, the pine trees crowding in on the narrow highway.

McGarvey slowed down. Somewhere in the woods to the east he thought he could see lights, but then he lost them. He figured it was probably a house along the lakeshore. Baranov's retreat was directly across the lake, perhaps a mile and a half or two, yet already McGarvey was getting the old feeling of the man's presence. Baranov was a force, there was no denying that.

Near the water's edge the paved road ended in a gravel lane that ran completely around the lake. McGarvey stopped his car, switched off the headlights, and got out.

There was absolutely no sound here, except for the Fiat's idling engine, and his own footfalls on the gravel. He walked a few yards away from the car to a spot where he could see the lake through a break in the woods.

Across the water he could see the lights of a few houses on the north shore, but nothing moved on the lake. Thursday night he would take the boat halfway across, don the oxygen rebreathing equipment that was waiting for him, and swim the rest of the way underwater to the shore below Baranov's house.

He turned after a minute or two and looked back the way he had come. He was not being followed. Lorraine was safely back in West Berlin . . . or she was as safe as she could be anywhere. She would not have come across. She had not followed him this time. She had given him her word. He believed her . . . or he hoped he did.

Back in his car he drove without lights another half mile, finding the driveway back down to the small cabin and boathouse on the lake that Trotter had described for him.

He turned the car around in the narrow driveway, so that it was pointed back up toward the lake road, then got out and hurried down to the boathouse, where he held up in the darkness for a moment.

There was no one here. The night was still. Not even a wind rustled in the trees or rippled the surface of the lake.

Using the key Trotter had supplied him, he unlocked the boathouse and slipped inside. Immediately he could smell gasoline, rotting wood, and something else. Something old and musty.

He switched on his penlight. A small motorboat floated in its slip, tied to the narrow walkway. A wooden garage door covered the opening to the lake. There was virtually no possibility that his light would be seen by anyone on the north shore; nevertheless he moved quickly.

Stepping down into the boat he found the two weapons wrapped in plastic and stuffed in the bilge, along with another package that contained the Russian-made rebreathing equipment.

Pulling out the Graz Buyra, he loaded it, screwed the Kevlar silencer tube on the end of the stubby barrel, and cycled a round into the firing chamber.

No matter what happened now, he told himself as he re-locked the boathouse and hurried back up to his car, he would not be caught here in the eastern zone with his back against the wall.

WEST BERLIN

Lorraine Abbott had gone to the telephone three times with the intention of calling Roland Murphy in Washington and demanding that McGarvey be pulled off this ridiculous assignment. Each time, however, something stayed her hand.

It was late. Well after midnight. She sat smoking a cigarette by the window, looking down at the traffic on the Ku'Damm. Berlin, like any large city, never slept. The Ku'Damm was the busiest of all streets in the western zone. Here were the cabarets and nightclubs, the shops and boutiques, and the sex stores and theaters. Absolutely anything could be had on the Ku'Damm.

Except, she thought bitterly, salvation. But the fact of the matter was she had somehow fallen in love with a murderer. All of her rationalizations that he was no different from a soldier killing on orders in time of war had completely broken down for her. She was left, then, with the crazy idea that somehow she could change him. If she could stop him this time, there might not be another. His past, she figured, she could live with. It was his future . . . their future that she could not imagine.

She had been a pragmatist all of her life. Except for her science, most of her creativity seemed to have been stifled, especially in her relationships with people . . . with men. She had always been the odd lot out in school. She was good-looking, she understood this with no vanity, and yet she'd been told on more than one occasion that she was unapproachable.

"You're an intellectual snob," Lawrence Givens, her former fiancé, had said to her a year ago.

"Does it bother you?" she'd shot back.

"Not particularly. Because you and I are cut out of the same cloth. You're a good physicist and you know it. Just as I know that I'm a damned good surgeon."

"But?" Weren't there almost always buts?

"But I'm also a man. You might try being a woman. At least once in a while."

"Go to hell," she'd replied good-naturedly, but the comment had stung, all the more so for its truth. Larry was a snob, and she didn't like that aspect of his personality. For an instant she had looked into a mirror and had seen that she was a snob as well.

With McGarvey she felt like a woman all of a sudden. The story she had told him about the palm reader when she was a little girl was mostly a lie, but it had seemed right at the moment she'd told him. In a way it was a justification to herself for being with him.

Now she was frightened. Not only for him, but of him, and most of all she was frightened for herself, because she had no idea where she was going. He was a murderer. But if she forced her way into helping him she could very well be the cause of his death. She was a scientist, trained in analytical thinking. But this time she had no way out, so in the end she had been incapable of doing anything.

Someone knocked at her door, and she looked up, her cigarette hand stopped in midair.

"Who is it?" she called out, getting up and stubbing out the cigarette.

"We're from the consulate, Doctor Abbott," a man said. "There is a message for you from Mr. McGarvey. It's most urgent."

"Oh, God," she cried, and she rushed to the door where she hurriedly undid the security chain and twisted the dead-bolt.

The door was suddenly pushed open, shoving her backward nearly off her feet. She got the impression of two very large men barging into the room, their guns drawn, and then something was pressed against her face, the smell cloying in its sweetness, and she was drifting.

44

WASHINGTON

DIRECTOR OF CENTRAL INTELLIGENCE ROLAND MURPHY was on his way home when the telephone in his limousine burred softly. He reached forward tiredly and picked it up.

"Yes?"

"Eagle one calls. Authentication is alpha-alpha-seven-zero-niner."

Murphy's gut tightened. Eagle one was the president. The use of an authentication code meant a situation of extreme importance was in progress.

"Hold," Murphy said, fumbling with the leatherbound code book. He found the proper date and cycle. The code matched. "Zebra-two-seven," he gave the counter code, and the connection was broken.

He powered down the Lexan dividing window. His body-guard, Preston Luney, riding shotgun, turned around. "Sir?"

"Get me over to the White House, Preston. On the double. West gate."

They were just crossing the river on the Key Bridge. His driver jammed his foot to the floor and the big Cadillac shot forward past the slower moving traffic, squealing tires as he turned sharply onto the Whitehurst Freeway.

The president had so far withheld his authorization for McGarvey to hit Baranov. By now everything would be in place in East Berlin. Had something gone wrong? It was possible that McGarvey had been discovered in the eastern zone. The Russians, of course, would make a big stink of it. Big enough, he wondered, for the president to go to such extraordinary measures of using a coding system that had been designed to alert key people in time of war?

He didn't think so. Not that. Not yet. But what then? He had a bad feeling that the coming hours were going to be anything but pleasant.

They were admitted without delay through the west gate a few minutes later. It was just 8:00 P.M. Murphy's bodyguard went with him up the stairs and into the West Hall where they were met by one of the president's Secret Service people who took them without a word to the elevator just off Center Hall, and punched the down button.

"Is he in the situation room?" Murphy asked.

"Yes, sir," the Secret Service agent said, his jaw set.

In the sub-basement they were met by two more Secret Service people, who escorted Murphy across to the bomb-proof door, which opened immediately for him, and he stepped inside, the door closing with a heavy thump of finality. Luney waited in the anteroom.

The president was seated at the end of the long conference table, in shirtsleeves, his tie loose. To his left were Secretary of State James Baldwin, his dapper vest and suitcoat properly buttoned; and Director of the National Security Agency Sterling Miller, his leonine head bent over a thick report he was studying intently. Across from the president were Joint Chief

Admiral Stewart O'Malley, in uniform, and his J.C. Vice Admiral, Taylor Barnes. At the far end of the room two Air Force officers manned the communications and display consoles.

Murphy got the definite impression that they were in crisis here. It only bothered him that he'd heard nothing all day.

"We've got ourselves a hell of a problem this time, Roland," the president said, looking up.

Murphy slipped into his seat across the table. "What has happened?"

"Apparently someone has snatched one of our nuclear submarines."

The DCI was stunned into silence. His first thought was Baranov and Kurshin. But God in heaven, how was such a thing possible?

"My reaction exactly," the president said heavily. He glanced at Admiral O'Malley. "Give him the short version, Stewart."

"At 0300 Zulu yesterday morning, our attack submarine *Indianapolis* detected what she took to be a weak SOS signal from an Italian-registered pleasure vessel about one hundred miles off Sixth Fleet Headquarters at Gaeta. That was the last word we got from her. She simply disappeared without a trace . . . until thirty minutes ago."

"Where is she now?"

"Submerged and running at a high rate of speed," Admiral O'Malley said.

"East," the president interjected.

"Our SOSUS (Sound Surveillance System) network picked up her footprint as she was coming out of the Malta Channel into the eastern Med. But then we lost her again. We've got half a dozen Orions up now searching the immediate area."

"Any possibility this is a mistake?" Murphy asked, somehow knowing that it wasn't.

"No," the admiral said. "I know the skipper J.D. Webb personally. He's a good man. But there is more."

"Yes?" Murphy said, holding himself in check.

"We have the pleasure vessel that sent the SOS."

"What does her crew say?"

"No crew. The boat was sabotaged, burned, and very nearly sunk. We found the remains of an automatic Morse code transmitter, and a canister which we believe contained Labun—a nerve gas. It was stolen nearly a year ago from Dugway Proving Grounds in Utah."

"A canister," Murphy mumbled.

"That we've found. Seven were stolen."

"Terrorists?"

"Russians," the president said.

Secretary of State Baldwin sat forward quickly. "We don't know that for a fact, Mr. President."

"Terrorists do not have the expertise to hijack a nuclear submarine, Jim," the president shot back.

"What about the sub's crew?" Murphy asked.

"We think there is a very good chance they're all dead," O'Malley said. It was obvious he was having a difficult time holding his temper in check. A slight tic played at the corner of his right eye, and his knuckles were white as he clasped his hands tightly in front of him on the conference table. "From what we have been able to piece together so far, we think that whoever was manning the *Zenzero* lured the *Indianapolis* to the surface with the fake SOS. J.D. would have sent someone over to check it out. They were most likely overpowered, and somehow the . . . hijackers managed to send the other canisters of Labun across to the sub."

"Would that have killed the entire crew?"

The admiral nodded. "Unless Webb went to battle stations—which there was no need for him to do—the gas would have circulated throughout the boat's common ventilation system within seconds."

"Wouldn't it have also killed the hijackers?" Murphy asked.

"It would have dissipated in under a minute."

The information was staggering. Murphy was having a hard time digesting it.

"Have there been any indications that the Russians were

up to something like this, Roland?'' the president asked. Murphy could see in his eyes that he already knew the answer.

"Baranov and Kurshin," the DCI said. "They managed with the Pershing out of Ramstein." He turned back to Admiral O'Malley. "Would Colonel Rand have had access to information about the *Indianapolis*?"

"The sonofabitch knew it all," O'Malley blurted. "Her technical data as well as her patrol station schedule! And he sold us down the fucking river!"

"Nothing from our intercepts has given any indication that such a thing was in the works," NSA Director Miller said.

"They wouldn't," Murphy replied thoughtfully. "If Kurshin has the boat, he's obviously got a crew with him. They would have been brought out at least twenty-four hours before the actual hijacking. It's possible they left a track. Where did the *Zenzero* come from?"

"Naples," O'Malley said.

"Then they would have holed up either there or in Rome. Who's in charge in Gaeta?"

"Ron DeLugio. His intelligence staff is running it down in Naples right now."

"In the meantime the *Indianapolis*, with nuclear weapons aboard, is heading east," the president said grimly. "She can be bottled up."

"The Bosporus," O'Malley said.

"Goddamnit, Mr. President, if you go ahead with any sort of a blockade a shooting war could start," Secretary of State Baldwin said.

"It may already have started, Jim," the president said. "The *Indianapolis* is certainly capable of it. She will not, under any circumstances, be allowed into the Black Sea. Once she gets that far, we've lost her."

"We cannot sit still and do nothing," Admiral O'Malley said through clenched teeth.

"You've said yourself, Stewart, that the Soviet Navy is operating a portion of its Black Sea fleet in the eastern Med."

"The *Nimitz* and her support group will remain in the

area," O'Malley shot back. "The *Baton Rouge* and *Phoenix* will be standing by off the Dardanelles." They were both Los Angeles-class attack submarines, the same as the *Indianapolis*.

"With what orders, Admiral?" the secretary of state demanded.

"We'll attempt to communicate with *Indianapolis*."

"If there is no response?"

"We'll kill her."

Secretary of State Baldwin turned back to the president. "You can't authorize this, Mr. President. In the name of God . . ."

The president's expression tightened. "As I've already said, Jim, I will not allow the *Indianapolis* to reach the Black Sea. It's as simple as that."

"Then a shooting war will begin."

"That depends upon how badly they want her."

"How badly do we want her back?" Baldwin asked.

"That much," the president replied, turning again to Murphy. "Get your Rome station on it immediately. So far we've only got speculation; we need proof linking the *Zenzero* to the Russians."

"Yes, Mr. President," Murphy said.

"And, Roland?"

"Sir?"

"I don't care how you get it. Do you understand me?"

"Yes, Mr. President. But if it is Kurshin, working under Baranov's orders, then there is only one man for the job."

The president nodded. "Where is he now?"

"East Berlin."

"Can we get him out?"

"Yes."

"Do it. We'll reconsider that other matter as soon as this situation is resolved."

"What are we talking about now?" Secretary of State Baldwin asked, alarmed.

The president ignored him. "But at this point, I'm inclined to give my go-ahead. Wholeheartedly."

On Murphy's orders, Trotter had remained at the embassy in Athens to run interference for McGarvey should it become absolutely necessary. It was a long way from Berlin, but much closer than Washington was.

"Pull him out," Murphy said when he had Trotter on the secure phone.

"What's going on, General?" Trotter's voice came over the encrypted line with only the slightest of interference. "I was just about to call you."

"It's Kurshin—he's off and running again. There's no time to explain now, John. Just get McGarvey down to Naples. I'll have the package sent over to you, and you can hand-carry it down there to him. He'll be working with Admiral Ron DeLugio, who is CINCMED out of Gaeta."

"We're going to blow a lot of resources in East Berlin pulling him out," Trotter said. "And there's another problem."

"Go ahead," Murphy said, girding himself.

"It's Lorraine Abbott. She slipped away from Yablonski at the Athens airport."

"Why wasn't I told?"

"We weren't sure what was going on here, General. But we managed to trace her to West Berlin where she registered at a hotel."

"Did she follow McGarvey?"

"Evidently."

"Well, get her the hell out of there."

"She's gone."

"What do you mean, gone?" Murphy shouted.

"Her suitcase and things are still in her room. She's simply disappeared. I think it's a real possibility that Baranov's people snatched her. And you know what that means."

Murphy did. It meant simply that Baranov had somehow been tipped off that McGarvey would be coming across to assassinate him. It meant their worst fear—that there was a leak at high levels within the Agency—was true. Mentally he ran down the list of those who knew about the operation. It was depressingly small, and dangerous.

"Pull him out of there, John," Murphy said, making his decision. "But don't tell him about Lorraine Abbott."

"Christ," Trotter swore.

"You can say that again," Murphy replied.

45

EAST BERLIN

SOMETHING WOKE MCGARVEY FROM A DEEP, DREAMLESS sleep. He looked at his watch. It was a few minutes before five in the morning. From where he lay on the couch beneath the partially open window he could hear absolutely no sounds from outside, nor were there any sounds from within the apartment building.

He'd returned from the Grosser Müggelsee around midnight, and had listened as the building gradually quieted down for the evening. Background noise. He'd finally fallen asleep around two.

Sitting up, he looked out the window down at the street. A few automobiles and a small truck were parked along the curb as before. Nothing new. No one had come, and yet he felt a presence that was out of place.

Something.

Then he heard it again. A noise out in the corridor, as if someone had shifted his weight, the floorboards creaking slightly.

Snatching his gun, he slipped the safety to the off position and padded across the tiny living room to the door. Someone was out there. He was certain of it. For a single crazy moment he had a vision of Lorraine Abbott coming across the border, somehow finding this place and coming up here. But that was impossible.

Very carefully he switched the gun to his left hand and with his right eased the door lock open. He stepped aside, out of the line of fire in case whoever was out there shot through the door.

"*Wer ist?*" he asked softly.

At first there was nothing, but then something thumped softly against the door frame.

He stood flat-footed, listening, straining to make some sense of what was going on out in the corridor. He thought he might be hearing someone breathing heavily, but again he could not be certain.

Switching his gun back to his right hand, he twisted the doorknob and all of a sudden yanked the door open.

A very large, barrel-chested man dressed in workmen's clothes reared back from the wall against which he had been leaning. McGarvey got the instant impression that the man was in pain, and that he was terrified, and then he saw the blood staining the side of the man's coat, and the small hole in the fabric.

"McGarvey . . ." he breathed hoarsely.

No one else was in the corridor, and he didn't think they had made enough noise to rouse the building. Whoever this one was, he certainly wasn't the opposition. But he was definitely in trouble.

McGarvey stepped out into the corridor and, stuffing the big gun in his belt, helped the wounded man inside, easing him down on the couch. He closed and relocked the door, and then closed the window, drawing the curtains tight before turning on the small table lamp.

The man's complexion was deathly pale. It was obvious he had lost a lot of blood. His left arm hung useless at his side, and his eyes seemed to focus and unfocus. He was struggling not to lay his head back, but he would not remain conscious for very long.

"Hold on," McGarvey whispered urgently. He hurried into the small bathroom where he grabbed several bath towels, bringing them back and stuffing them inside the man's coat against the gunshot wound in his side, just below his left armpit.

"McGarvey . . ." the man whispered hoarsely. "You must get out of East Berlin. Tonight, before it is too late."

"Who are you?"

"Reinhardt Geiger," the big man stammered. "Lighthouse . . . I'm from the network . . . I was sent . . ." He was wracked with a spasm of pain that cut his words off.

LIGHTHOUSE was the Agency's most important network in East Berlin. It had been going on for a lot of years. McGarvey seemed to remember that the KGB's operation at the Horst Wessel Barracks and in the embassy itself had been infiltrated. The network was mostly workmen, building-maintenance people, along with a few pool typists and secretaries. Their product had never been spectacular, but it had always been steady.

"Who sent you?" McGarvey asked.

"My control officer . . . one name . . . he gave me one name. John Trotter."

McGarvey sat forward, his gut clenching. "What about Trotter? Is my operation to be called off?"

"You must get out of East Berlin immediately. They are waiting for you on the other side. Important . . . Trotter . . . very important."

"Who shot you?"

"They're waiting for you . . . on the other side. They are expecting you . . . Wedding . . . the Wedding Crossing."

"Was it KGB?" McGarvey asked urgently.

Geiger suddenly reared up and grabbed McGarvey's arm. "They know about me. They know I received a message. They will come here . . . McGarvey, you must leave immediately."

"You're coming with me . . ." McGarvey started to say when the breath went out of Geiger in a big blubbering spray of blood, and he slumped forward into McGarvey's arms. He was dead.

For a moment McGarvey just sat there, his thoughts racing in a dozen different directions, all of them down long, dark alleys. Trotter would have known how risky it was to use someone from LIGHTHOUSE to make contact. The network was important. It meant that whatever reason they wanted him out of East Berlin had to be of overriding importance.

Kurshin. The single name crystallized in his brain. He had gotten the data from Rand in Washington, and he had escaped. He was on the move again, his target still En Gedi.

He eased Geiger's body back on the couch and checked out the window again. Still nothing moved below. He had parked his car on another side street a block away. If he could reach it before the KGB showed up he figured he just might have a chance of getting free. But a bitter feeling rose up inside of him that once again he was going to have to back away from Baranov. Once again the man was safe. It was galling.

The streets of East Berlin were coming alive in the predawn darkness as delivery trucks began making their rounds, and early shift workmen headed to their offices and factories.

McGarvey sat in his Fiat on Wisbyer Strasse a block from the bright lights of the Wedding Crossing. In the five minutes he had been there he'd watched two cars and one panel truck crossing into the west. Nothing had come the other way.

He had taken the time to clean out the apartment, wiping it down for his fingerprints, though he could not be one hundred percent sure he'd gotten them all. He had also made certain that Geiger had carried nothing incriminating with him.

Whatever happened now, he supposed that LIGHTHOUSE would have to be closed down, its people pulled out. Again he was struck with the desperation that Trotter must have felt in order to take such extraordinary measures.

No one else had shown up at the apartment by the time he had left, nor had he run into any trouble on the short drive up here. But if there was to be trouble, it was going to happen at the crossing.

The big pistol was stuffed in his belt at the small of his back. It was uncomfortable driving with it like that, but if he needed the gun, he wanted instant access to it.

Putting the Fiat in gear, he eased out behind a truck that turned left on Schonhauser Strasse just before the crossing. He went straight ahead, slowing and stopping under the bright lights, as two soldiers came out of their shelter.

He passed out his Kurshin identification. Geiger had said nothing about it. But McGarvey understood that it was possible his cover had been blown.

"The purpose of your visit to West Berlin this morning, sir?" one guard asked. The other was looking at him, his eyes narrowed.

"That is none of your business, Sergeant," McGarvey snapped in German.

The guard stiffened.

McGarvey took out his KGB identification booklet and flipped it open. The guard recognized it immediately for what it was, and his attitude changed. So did the other guard's.

"I'm sorry, Comrade Colonel," the young man said, handing McGarvey's passport back. "You may pass."

"Of course I may," McGarvey barked sharply. "Now, be quick about it."

The soldiers stepped away, and without a backward glance, McGarvey eased the Fiat across to the West. The street opened up, and forty yards across the no-man's-land, he pulled up at the western barrier. This was the French sector of the city. Two French soldiers came out.

"Kirk McGarvey. You were expecting me?"

One of the guards glanced over his shoulder back at the guardhouse. In the semidarkness McGarvey could just make out the form of a man standing there. He nodded. The soldier turned back.

"Yes, sir. You are to drive immediately down to Tempelhof Airport. Someone will meet you at Operations Building B."

"Who?"

"I don't know, sir. But welcome back."

"Yeah," McGarvey said. "Thanks."

WEST BERLIN

Operations Building B was on the military side of the big airport in the American sector of the city. McGarvey was met in front by an Air Force captain who was not wearing a name tag. He had been expected; the call had come from the Wedding Checkpoint.

"What's this all about?" McGarvey asked.

"I couldn't say, sir," the captain said. "If you'll just come with me, we have a Learjet waiting on the apron."

"Where are we going?"

"Naples, sir. And they want you down there on the double." The captain seemed almost afraid to look too closely at McGarvey. "Do you have to take a pee or something first, sir?"

"It'll wait."

NAPLES

The morning sun sparkled brightly on the Bay of Naples as the Learjet came in over the water for her final approach, the Air Force captain handling the little plane as if it were a toy. As soon as they had touched down and had completed their landing roll, they turned onto a taxiway and headed toward a hangar on the private aviation side of the airport, bypassing customs and immigration.

John Trotter and another, much younger, heavier man, also dressed in civilian clothes, were waiting for him inside. By the time McGarvey had walked through the door, the Learjet was already heading over to the fuel pumps. The captain would be taking her immediately back to West Berlin.

Trotter was strung out, the other one was clearly impatient.

"Did you have any trouble, Kirk?" Trotter asked.

McGarvey looked pointedly at the other one.

"It's all right," Trotter said. "This is Lieutenant Commander Malcolm Ainslie. Naval Intelligence. He's in on the entire thing."

"Is it Kurshin again?"

Trotter nodded. "I think so." He looked toward the stairs at the back of the hangar. "We've got a place to talk upstairs. You've got a lot of catching up to do."

"Why here?"

"We figured we'd attract less attention out here than in town," Ainslie said. His accent was East Coast, almost British. He seemed competent, but McGarvey could see in his eyes that he was as shook up as Trotter, and very angry.

"Geiger is dead."

"Christ," Trotter swore. "Were you blown?"

"I don't think so. But it was KGB. He said they knew he had taken a message."

Trotter thought about it a moment, then shook his head. "It doesn't change anything. We need you here, Kirk."

There were a couple of mechanics working on an old Beechcraft, but no one paid them any attention as they went to the upstairs office, where another Naval Intelligence officer was waiting for them. McGarvey was introduced to Lieutenant Frank Newman, who would conduct the briefing. He had been hastily sent out from the Pentagon and had himself arrived only a couple of hours earlier. The same anger McGarvey had seen in Ainslie burned in Newman's eyes.

"Before we get started," McGarvey said. "Lorraine Abbott is in West Berlin."

"I know," Trotter said. "The Hotel Berlin. Yablonski wasn't expecting it."

"Our people in Berlin are taking care of it?"

Trotter nodded. "They're watching the hotel."

There was something not quite right in Trotter's answer, but McGarvey did not pursue it. He turned to the other two men. "What's Kurshin done this time?"

"He's apparently stolen one of our nuclear attack submarines and possibly killed her crew," Newman said. He was a short, very dark man with deep-set eyes and thick eyebrows. He had a six o'clock shadow.

McGarvey whistled, long and low. Whatever Kurshin was or wasn't, he definitely had balls.

"And now the sub is missing?"

"Not quite," Ainslie said. "She passed our SOSUS line last night out of the Malta Channel, but then we lost her again. But we do know that she's now in the eastern Mediterranean."

"Submerged?"

Ainslie nodded.

Newman picked it up from there, leading them from the moment the *Indianapolis* had surfaced in response to the apparent SOS from the *Zenzero*, until the Italian pleasure cruiser had been brought back to Gaeta, where Naval Intelligence had taken her apart, coming up with a second, badly damaged Labun canister and the remains of the automatic Morse code transmitter.

"The *Zenzero* was a decoy," McGarvey said. "They would have gotten the *Indianapolis*'s patrol station schedule from the disk Rand handed over to Kurshin."

"Somehow the bastards got the rest of the canisters aboard, and . . ." Newman let it trail off.

"Assuming everyone aboard was killed, how many men would it take to operate the submarine?"

Newman and Ainslie looked at each other. "Many of her systems are automatic," Newman said. "Ten good men could do it, if they didn't find themselves in a battle situation. Maybe less."

"Have we picked up any indications that that many Russians had come over in the past few days?" McGarvey asked Trotter.

"We're looking to Rome right now, Kirk. You'll be flying up there this morning, because we've run into a brick wall."

"The Russians have the *Indianapolis*," Ainslie said angrily. "There's no longer any doubt about it, nor is there any doubt what they've got planned."

"How do we know the Russians have it?" McGarvey asked. "John? Was Kurshin spotted?"

"No," Trotter said heavily. "Ainslie's people traced the *Zenzero* back to a yacht-leasing service here in Naples. The leasing agent was a man named Arturo Ziadora."

"We have him in custody now," Ainslie said. "He finally broke this morning."

"Kirk, we had the Soviet Embassy files sent down here from Rome. Ziadora didn't know names, only photos, but he positively identified the man who had leased the yacht as Yuri Semenovich Nikandrov."

"Pick him up," McGarvey said.

Trotter shook his head. "The Navy has been told hands off this time. Nikandrov is too important. He's the number-two *rezident* out of their embassy, and a special assistant to the Soviet ambassador."

"You want me to talk to him?"

Trotter nodded. "You have the president's word on this one. No restraints, Kirk. Do you understand? We must know what they are planning on doing with the *Indianapolis*. It's an act of piracy that could very well start a shooting war."

"I know what they're going to do with her," McGarvey said.

"So do we," Ainslie barked. "They'll try to take her through the Bosporus into the Black Sea. But we've got a nasty surprise waiting for them."

"No," McGarvey said. "Not the Black Sea. Farther east."

He looked at Newman. "How much of a crew would they need to set up one of her nuclear missiles and fire it at a land-based target?"

"While avoiding detection?" Newman asked rhetorically. "More than ten men. Maybe fifteen, or twenty. Navigators, attack center crew, boat drivers, engineers for the reactor, and of course the missile crew."

"I don't think Kurshin would have brought that many men with him. But if he did, the answers will be in Rome with Nikandrov."

"They're going to try for the Black Sea," Ainslie said.

"Israel," McGarvey said, stepping over to the desk on which a map of the Mediterranean had been spread out. The *Indianapolis*'s patrol station off the Italian coast was marked. "What speed is she capable of, submerged?"

"The book says thirty knots," Trotter answered.

"More like forty knots," Newman corrected him.

"If the *Indianapolis* broke out from the Malta Channel sometime last night we're not going to have much time," McGarvey said. He stabbed a finger at the island of Crete. "Can we set up a monitoring post here?"

Ainslie and Newman had stepped up beside him. "We have a SOSUS station nearby," Newman said. "It can be done."

"We'll know within a few hours then," McGarvey said. "If she turns north, she's headed for the Bosporus. If she continues east, her target will be En Gedi. But that'll depend on the number of crew she's carrying." He looked up. "Has the president spoken with Gorbachev?"

"Not yet," Trotter said. "He wants the proof first. But there's another problem we're facing here. The Soviet Navy's Black Sea fleet is running maneuvers south of Crete."

"The *Nimitz* and her task group are in the region as well," Newman said.

"Then we'd better hurry," McGarvey said. "Or a shooting war just might begin."

"I'm coming up to Rome with you," Trotter said.

"Has Lev Potok been notified?"

Trotter shook his head.

"Do it, John. Now. Because I'd be willing to bet anything that this is a continuation of Baranov's plan to hit the Israelis. This time we might not be able to stop them."

46

USS *INDIANAPOLIS*

IT WAS JUST NOON LOCAL TIME WHEN THE SEVEN-THOUSAND-ton submarine settled gently to the silty bottom of the Bay of Messini on the south coast of the Greek Peloponnisos. She listed a few degrees to port because of the sloping bottom here.

"We have seventy meters over our keel," Fedorenko called softly from his position beside Kurshin at the wheel.

"Nicely done," Captain Makayev said. "Secure the boat from all but essential systems." He hit the comms switch. "Sonar, what does it look like on the surface?"

"I'm tracking numerous small boats, probably pleasure craft, Captain. They're all over the place up there. It's like a circus."

"Good," Makayev said softly.

Kurshin turned and looked at Makayev and Fedorenko. They were both good men, he thought. In the past day and a half, he had developed a respect and trust for their expertise.

It was too bad, he thought, that in the end the reward they were expecting in Moscow would be nothing more than nine ounces. But then, as Baranov had unnecessarily explained, they could not afford to have so many witnesses. Like Dr. Velikanov, one of them sooner or later would say the wrong thing at the wrong time. It could not be allowed.

"We are deep enough here?" he asked Makayev.

"No one will see us from the surface, even from an airplane, even if they were searching here, which I do not expect they are."

"Are you sure?"

Makayev, like all of them, was tired. They'd been operating without sleep for nearly forty-eight hours since Rome. He was becoming irritable, but his control was marvelous.

He shrugged. "In this business, Comrade Colonel, one can never be sure. But even their ASW aircraft would not be able to detect our presence with their magnetic anomaly equipment, there is too much small-boat traffic on the surface for them to succeed. This is summer, the tourists will be at it all day."

Fedorenko had been doing something at one of the overhead control panels. He turned around. "They will be concentrating their search in the Aegean by now."

Kurshin looked at him sharply.

"Gennadi is correct, Comrade Colonel," Makayev said. "Their SOSUS equipment certainly detected our passage through the Malta Channel. We have already discussed this."

"They cannot know for certain that their boat has been hijacked."

Again Makayev shrugged. "It is elementary, I think. They will have found that little Italian cruiser by now . . . above or below the surface. They will know that something is amiss. They also know that our fleet is up there. If I were them, I would be thinking very strongly about the Bosporus."

It was practically the same thing Baranov had told him.

But the beauty of the operation was they could not be sure. Nor did Gorbachev or the Politburo know anything. If and when the president used the hotline to call Moscow, he would learn nothing. An investigation would be immediately launched, of course. But by that time the operation would have been completed. Israel would have been ruined as a military power in the region, and Gorbachev himself would fall.

Kurshin got up from his seat at the helm. "We'll load and drop the missile now."

Makayev glanced up at the chronometer on the bulkhead. "It is twelve hours before our rendezvous. Time now to rest."

"No," Kurshin barked. "We'll drop the missile first." He softened his tone. "In case something happens, Captain. In case the Americans get lucky."

Both Makayev and Fedorenko looked at him, their stares harsh. Finally Makayev unbent a little. "As you wish," he said. He turned and hit the comms switch. "Aleksei, are you ready for us?"

"Yes, Captain. I will need at least two men."

"We're on our way."

Makayev turned again to his *starpom*. "The colonel and I will attend to our little chore. Make certain that Aleksandr keeps a close watch on his sonar equipment, we do not want any surprises."

Fedorenko nodded.

"When we are finished we will have something to eat, and then get some rest. We have another long night ahead of us."

Kurshin followed Makayev into the attack center forward, and then through the hatch and down the ladder into the weapons control center.

Aleksei Chobotov stood just aft of the starboard torpedo tubes. Behind him was the weapons storage and transfer compartment. He had managed to pull one of the Tomahawk missiles out of its storage rack and position it over one of the tube slides.

It was large, much bigger than Kurshin had envisioned. At a length of twenty-one feet, in the nuclear warhead version, the missile weighed more than four thousand pounds.

"You have finished reprogramming the TERCOM (Terrain Contour Matching) system?" Kurshin asked.

Chobotov's eyes were shining. "If the disk you provided me was accurate, Comrade Colonel, the missile is ready to fire."

"What is the target?" Makayev asked.

Kurshin ignored the question. "All the seals are back in place?"

"Yes, sir. As long as she doesn't stay in the water too long, it should be all right. Of course there is no way to be certain, but fuck your mother, the Americans build fine equipment."

"What about the rocket motor?"

"It is actually a turbofan jet, Comrade Colonel, with a solid fuel booster. They will survive."

"And the nuclear warhead?"

Chobotov involuntarily glanced over at the sleek missile. He shivered. "It is armed."

"No danger of a radiation leak?"

"None."

Makayev had stepped past Kurshin. He reached up and tentatively touched the missile's casing. A look of mild surprise crossed his features. "It's warm."

"I noticed that too, Captain," Chobotov replied. "But there is no reason for it, except that our hands are perhaps cold."

Makayev turned back and nodded. "With good reason," he murmured. He looked at Kurshin, something in his eyes, and then nodded again. "Then let's get the bastard overboard."

Despite the fact they were working with unfamiliar equipment, Chobotov knew his stuff. He and Kurshin hand-guided the missile down onto its loading rack while Makayev operated the hoist controls.

It was automatically slid to a loading gate on the starboard side, where Chobotov switched the loading grapples to the uppermost of the three torpedo tubes, the inner door of which was already open.

The missile slowly slid into place, coming to rest with a soft click, and a whir of machinery as the rack was withdrawn.

Chobotov closed and sealed the door and, back at the auxiliary control board, pressurized the tube.

The comms speaker squawked. "Captain, I have an orange light on Starboard A tube."

"We're getting set to launch," Makayev radioed back. "Stand by."

"Roger."

Chobotov's right hand hovered over the button for the outer door.

"No chance that the missile's engine will fire?" Kurshin asked.

"No, sir. I switched that circuitry into the passive-locked mode. There is no chance . . ."

Kurshin stood just behind the missile officer. He reached up and shoved the younger man's hand against the button. There was a sudden whoosh of air, and the submarine shuddered very slightly.

Chobotov looked over his shoulder at him.

"There," Kurshin said. "She is on the bottom just like us."

ROME

McGarvey was a nonperson as far as the CIA's Rome station was concerned. It was a matter of insulation, Trotter had explained on the drive up from Naples.

"You were never there, Kirk, so no matter what happens there will be no retaliations against our people."

Trotter had dropped him off at a small hotel in the Aventine District and had gone ahead to the embassy where he made a few phone calls, gathered up the files he needed, and returned in the early afternoon.

McGarvey was tired. He had managed to get a couple hours of rest, but he kept hearing Lorraine Abbott's pleas that he not go ahead with his assignment. She was an idealist, and worse, she did not have all the facts. Nor would she ever. "It's a big nasty world out there," someone had told him once. "The fact of the matter is, no one really cares whether you live or die. It's up to you to make a difference."

But he cared, and he expected Lorraine did too. He didn't know, however, if they made a difference or not. Just now he felt as if he were squandering what little time was left to them. If Kurshin had the submarine he would act quickly. By bottling up the Bosporus, the Navy had told the Russians they were suspected. The situation would not last much longer. They were all sitting on a powder keg, and the fuse was short.

From his third-floor window, McGarvey watched Trotter come down the street. He stopped to admire something in a shop window, turned as if he was about to change his mind, then turned again and came directly across the street and entered the hotel.

McGarvey didn't move for a long minute. Traffic was normal below; the pedestrians passing did not seem out of the ordinary. By the time Trotter was at the door, he figured his old friend had come away clean, and he went to let him in.

"The *Indianapolis* has disappeared again," Trotter said, coming into the small room. He laid his briefcase on the narrow bed as McGarvey closed and locked the door.

"They should have been within range of the Crete SOSUS by now."

"I know. I just got off the phone with Admiral DeLugio. He flew out from Gaeta to set up a field command post. He wants some answers and damned fast."

"Can't say as I blame him," McGarvey said. "What about Nikandrov? What did you bring for me?"

"Good news and bad news," Trotter said. "It took some doing to come up with what we needed without tipping my hand. Jesse Lipton"—chief of the CIA's Rome station—"knows that something big is in the wind, so I had to sidestep him. The skipper of the *Lorrel-E* went public with his salvage claim. The press somehow found out that the Navy had sent out one of its submarine rescue ships and they've put two and two together. Lipton asked me point-blank if I was involved in the mess. I had to lie to him."

"It's better that he doesn't know," McGarvey said. "What's the good news?"

"That's not all the bad, yet, Kirk. You're going to have to sit tight here until after dark. Perhaps as late as midnight, maybe even longer."

"We might not have the time."

"Nothing we can do about it. The Navy is watching the region. The *Indianapolis* has to be sitting on the bottom somewhere between the Malta Channel and Crete."

"That's a lot of water, John. And if I remember my geography the Mediterranean drops to fourteen thousand feet in some spots. The *Indianapolis* can't go that deep, can she?"

"The Los Angeles-class submarines, from what I'm told, have a service depth of around fifteen hundred feet. Beyond two thousand or twenty-five hundred feet her hull would implode from the pressure."

"So if she's on the bottom somewhere, it's near land."

"There's a lot of coastline between Malta and Crete. But the Navy is looking."

"In the meantime what about Nikandrov?"

"That's the rest of the bad news," Trotter said. "He's holed up at the Soviet Embassy. His normal routine keeps him there usually until around six in the evening when he takes a car to his home in Magliana—a suburb about five miles south of the city."

"He can't be lured out into the open sooner?" McGarvey asked.

"Not without alerting Lipton that we're up to something. And if Nikandrov is indeed involved in this mess, he'll be keeping a close watch over his shoulder. The good news is that he's sent his wife and two children away for a holiday to Switzerland. And once he gets to his house he usually stays there."

"Alone?"

"He has a bodyguard," Trotter said. He opened his brief-case and took out a file that contained maps of the suburb as well as a dozen or more photographs showing a house that appeared to be located in the middle of a big park, as well as shots of Nikandrov himself, and another much larger man, with thick eyebrows and dark penetrating eyes. "Andrei Nikovich Zalenin. He's Special Service II muscle."

McGarvey stared at Zalenin's photograph. He looked like a tough sonofabitch. He would be highly trained and highly motivated, not only to protect the physical safety of Nikandrov, but to make sure his charge did not himself go astray. If need be, his orders would include killing Nikandrov rather than allowing him to fall into enemy hands.

"The Nikandrovs apparently settle down very early for Russians. Normally around ten or eleven in the evening. He's up around five in the morning, and back at the embassy no later than six-thirty."

"A hard worker."

"Yes," Trotter said. "I figure the best time for you to get in there would be around midnight, or even a little later. My car is parked two blocks from here. There are some things in the trunk for you. I'll take a cab back to the embassy."

"What about afterward?" McGarvey asked.

"Depending on what you find, or what the Navy might turn up in the meantime, we'll see."

"How about Baranov?"

Trotter gave him a hard stare. "It looks as if the president will give the green light. Murphy seems to think he's on the verge because of this *Indianapolis* thing. But we blew some very good resources getting you out of East Berlin. There's a better than even chance that they'll be expecting you. If you go back across, you could be walking into a trap."

"If I have the green light, John, I'm going ahead with it. In the meantime I want you to pull Lorraine out of West Berlin."

Trotter shook his head. "I can't, Kirk."

"Why?" McGarvey shot back.

"I've been told hands off."

Again there was something wrong with Trotter's answer, something McGarvey couldn't put his finger on—or didn't want to. "Have we got people watching the hotel?"

"Around the clock," Trotter said.

"What about Lev Potok, and the Israelis?"

A fleeting look of relief crossed Trotter's features. "That's up to Murphy. He's taken it to the president. They're going to have to decide what they're going to tell the Mossad."

"If it's Kurshin aboard that sub, and we both know it is, he won't be making for the Black Sea. His target has always been En Gedi. The Israelis have to be warned."

"It's out of my hands, Kirk. Murphy knows the situation and so does the president. It's up to them, not us."

"What about you in the meantime?" McGarvey asked.

"You're going to have to get out of Italy, immediately. I'll be working out something."

"Where do we meet when it's over?"

"Here. If the light is on in the window, it's safe. Otherwise we'll meet in the Piazza San Pietro."

"In front of the Vatican?"

"Right," Trotter said. "Watch yourself."

47

USS *INDIANAPOLIS*

THE ODOR THAT HAD BEGUN TO PERMEATE THE *INDIANAPOLIS* had gotten to all of them. No one had eaten very much, nor had they slept. Makayev had ordered the boat's heating system turned low, but it hadn't helped.

At sunset their sonarman, Lieutenant Raina, reported that activity on the surface had dropped off sharply. An hour later nothing moved above.

Everyone else had gravitated forward to the control center. The orders Kurshin had given them had only taken them this far. They all wanted off the submarine now.

Kurshin hit the comms button. "Lieutenant Raina?"

"Sonar, aye."

"Still quiet above?"

"Yes, Comrade Colonel."

Kurshin checked his watch. It was coming up on 11:00 P.M. local. "Keep your ears open. A twin screw vessel will be approaching our position within the next few minutes."

"From what direction?"

"Landward."

"What is her size?"

"Two hundred eighty feet," Kurshin said.

The others were looking at him. "Our rescue ship?" Makayev asked.

Kurshin nodded. "The *Stephos* out of Athens."

"Her crew?"

"Our people," Kurshin said. "They'll send divers over to put a collar around the missile and bring her aboard. Once that's done we'll go topside."

"That's a lot of water," Makayev said.

"Yes it is."

The captain looked around the control room. "What about this boat? Do you mean to leave her here? Sooner or later she will be discovered."

Kurshin stepped across the control room to the navigator's table. The others crowded around him. He stabbed a blunt finger at a spot about thirty miles to their south.

"The bottom drops rapidly here," he said. "More than three thousand meters. Well below what this boat's pressure hull can stand. Before we get off, you will set the boat to head to sea at a slow speed, diving at a shallow angle. This can be done?"

Makayev nodded.

"Within a couple of hours there will be very little left of her."

"They will find her hull, nevertheless," Makayev said. "They have the equipment and the technology. And now they certainly have the will."

"That will take time," Kurshin said. "By then we will be long gone."

"What about us?" the captain asked. "I don't think we're returning to Moscow just yet."

"No," Kurshin said. "Not just yet."

The comms speaker squawked. "Captain, I'm picking up that twin screw vessel."

MAGLIANA

McGarvey was dressed in black. Outside of the city, he had pulled off the secondary highway where he had blackened his face and pulled on a black watchcap. The clothing and equipment Trotter had supplied were first-class. Strapped to his left forearm beneath his shirtsleeve was a nine-inch, razor-sharp stiletto, and strapped to his chest was a suppressed .22 Magnum automatic—the same weapon the Army's Delta Force used. It was a very good weapon for head shots, reliable and almost completely noiseless. The gun could be fired inside a house, and people in the next room would not hear it.

He had spent the afternoon memorizing the maps, layouts, and photographs Trotter had supplied him with, and in the early evening he had managed to get a couple more hours rest.

He circled the town to the south, the Tiber River on his left, keeping off the main highways. It was nearly midnight and there was no other traffic. There was no moon, and a light cloud cover made the night very dark.

Nikandrov's place was situated at the edge of a good-sized public park just outside the city limits. McGarvey drove slowly past the gated driveway, catching a brief glimpse of the house through the trees. A few lights illuminated the front of the two-story building, but no lights had shone from the windows. The KGB officer and his bodyguard had apparently settled down for the night.

Or had they? McGarvey wondered, turning back toward the park. If Nikandrov had had a hand in Baranov's plan to take the *Indianapolis* he would have to be getting very nervous about now. He had sent his wife and children away. Was that merely coincidence? Or had it been the move of a man who expected trouble would be coming his way? McGarvey thought the latter was likely.

He left the car a half block from the park entrance and hurried back on foot, plunging into the dark woods that were crisscrossed with footpaths. During the day this would be a pleasant place to spend an afternoon. Peaceful, so different from the bustle of Rome just a few miles to the north. It was probably why the Nikandrovs had picked the place.

An ancient stuccoed stone wall, at least eight feet tall, topped with broken glass, separated the Russian's property from the park. Where the trees had grown close to the wall, their branches had been trimmed back. Foreign agents, especially men as important as Nikandrov, always tried to maintain a low-key lifestyle. They wanted no attention brought to themselves. They were always torn between security measures that would be obvious, and openness that could be dangerous. Nikandrov had his bodyguard, but was the perimeter of his property alarmed? McGarvey decided he would have to find out before going over.

Keeping well within the relative darkness of the woods, McGarvey followed the wall for nearly a hundred yards before it turned west. From his vantage point he had been unable to detect any wires, or any sign that the wall was being monitored by closed-circuit television cameras.

Just here it was very dark. The glow of the lights at the front of the house was only faintly visible. This was the back of the property. The most vulnerable.

He followed the wall for another twenty yards, finally finding what he had been looking for: a second gate. A narrow dirt road ran through the woods up to the gate. It was mostly overgrown with weeds and looked as if it hadn't been used in a long time.

Keeping low, he emerged from the woods and studied the hinges and locking mechanism on the old iron gate for a couple of minutes. Again he found no evidence that any type of alarm system had been installed.

Nikandrov was relying on the wall, and on his bodyguard, Andrei Zalenin.

Pulling on a pair of leather gloves, McGarvey quickly climbed up the gate, and at the top angled over to the wall, stepping carefully across the jagged broken glass and jumping lightly into the deep grass on the inside, rolling once and then quickly scrambling into the bushes.

He waited a full five minutes for any sign that his entry had been detected. Somewhere in the distance to the south he thought he heard the whistle of a riverboat, but it wasn't repeated, and except for the insect noises the night was quiet.

The rear of the property had been badly neglected and was heavily overgrown with weeds and brush. McGarvey reached the house in under two minutes, stopping at the edge of the driveway where Nikandrov's big Mercedes sedan was parked.

Taking off his gloves and stuffing them in his pocket, he studied the back of the house. No lights shone in any of the windows. It was believed that Nikandrov's bedroom was on the second floor. His bodyguard would most likely be very near. Perhaps in an adjoining room.

Emerging from the brush he raced across the driveway, held up for a couple of seconds, and then went silently up on the low veranda, flattening himself against the wall beside the back door.

Still there were no signs that his presence was known.

There were two locks on the door. Using a slender case-hardened steel pick, he had the first open in ten seconds. The second lock took a little longer, but at length he felt the bolt slip free.

Pulling the gun from its holster, he cycled a round into the firing chamber, switched the safety to the off position, and tried the door. It opened inward, silently on well-oiled hinges.

The darkened house smelled of cigarette smoke. McGarvey remained outside for several long beats. Someone had been just inside smoking a cigarette. Within the last minute or so.

Had they seen him coming up from the back? Had they heard him picking the lock? Suddenly everything seemed wrong. His internal warning system was in high gear. A trap?

He had started to turn away from the door when a large-caliber silenced shot was fired from behind him, the bullet just missing his head, knocking a big chunk off the masonry.

Instantly he swiveled back on his left foot, diving inside

the house just as a second shot was fired, this one ricocheting off the door frame an inch behind him.

They had obviously seen him coming. Zalenin must have circled around from the front of the house once he realized that McGarvey would be coming through the back door, hoping to catch him from the rear, as he had very nearly done.

By now they would have called for help. Time was running out. But they had to have been expecting him. How?

Zalenin's bulky form appeared for an instant in the doorway, and disappeared.

McGarvey, standing in the shadows across the room, held his fire. The Russian was a professional. He had provided a brief target, and when there had been no shot he would have to believe that McGarvey was either down, or was elsewhere in the house.

It was a mistake.

Zalenin appeared again at the doorway, hesitated for just a moment, then came in.

McGarvey fired two shots, the first catching the Russian in the face just below his left eye, the second hitting him in the throat, destroying his windpipe.

Still, the Russian managed to get off a shot as he fell backward, but it went wide, and he crashed back against the open door with a tremendous racket.

Any reason for stealth now gone, McGarvey turned and raced up the dark corridor to the foot of the stairs. Something crashed above as he took the stairs two at a time. At the top he paused for just a second. Nikandrov would probably be armed. He would know by now that something had gone wrong and would be panicking.

There were four doors at the far end of the corridor. One of them was open. From an adjacent door McGarvey could hear the soft but urgent tones of someone talking. Nikandrov was on the telephone calling for help. His eyes would be on the corridor door.

Turning, McGarvey stepped silently through the open doorway into what he suspected was Zalenin's room. The door into Nikandrov's suite was ajar.

In the very dim light filtering in from outside, McGarvey could see Nikandrov's bulky form, his back hunched, the telephone in his left hand, a big pistol in his right trained on the corridor door.

Moving silently on the balls of his feet, McGarvey made it across the room in three steps, pressing the barrel of his weapon against the base of Nikandrov's skull.

The Russian's words stopped, and he stiffened.

"Put the telephone down," McGarvey said softly.

Someone shouted something in the phone, but Nikandrov carefully replaced the handset on its cradle.

McGarvey reached around and took the Russian's gun, and tossed it onto the bed. "Zalenin is dead, and we do not have much time, Comrade Nikandrov."

"The police are on their way," Nikandrov said, his voice steady.

"So you will give me the answers I need very quickly or I will kill you."

"You are here to kill me anyway."

"That's possible," McGarvey said. "You rented the cruiser *Zenzero* from a leasing firm in Naples. Who was the boat for, besides Arkady Kurshin?"

Nikandrov said nothing.

McGarvey jammed the gun hard against the man's neck. "Valentin Baranov will not mourn at your funeral."

"Nor yours."

"Yours will come first, I can guarantee it. We have the boat, and we have two of the nerve gas canisters. We know that one of our nuclear submarines is missing. I'm telling you this because I want you to know how important this business is to us."

"I don't know anything."

"How many men besides Kurshin?" McGarvey said. "Five seconds. Four . . . three . . . two . . ." He began to squeeze the trigger.

"Six," Nikandrov suddenly blurted.

"Who were they?"

"I don't know their names. They came into Rome on Monday night. I put them up at a small hotel . . ."

"Navy?"

"Yes. But one of them was a doctor, I think. An alcoholic."

"Where are they headed?"

"I don't know. In this you must believe me. There is nothing else. I was told nothing else."

"But you knew about the nerve gas and about the submarine?"

"The gas, yes. One of our people brought it over nearly a year ago. But I swear to you I know nothing about any submarines."

"What else was put aboard the *Zenzero*, besides the gas and the Morse code transmitter?"

"Food," Nikandrov said. "Weapons."

"Nautical charts?"

"Yes, for the coast off Naples. No others."

In the distance they could hear sirens. It was time to get out. McGarvey stepped back away from the Russian. "When you talk to Baranov tonight, give him greetings from McGarvey. He'll know who I am."

"Fuck you," Nikandrov swore.

McGarvey stepped back into Zalenin's room, then turned and rushed out into the corridor and down the stairs. He should have killed Nikandrov. But the man had cooperated, and he wanted the message to get back to Baranov. The KGB chairman would understand exactly what he meant.

Besides, he had never killed a man in cold blood. Nor would he ever do so . . . except for Baranov. With that one, there were no rules. None whatsoever.

48

BAY OF MESSINI

THE *INDIANAPOLIS* HOVERED TWENTY METERS ABOVE THE bottom, her helm and diving planes locked on a course nearly due south with a down angle of a few degrees. The bottom sloped at a slightly sharper angle here to well over three thousand meters so that there was no chance the boat would ground herself before her hull imploded from the water pressure.

It had taken the KGB crew of the MV *Stephos* nearly two hours to find the two-ton missile and send divers down to it. They had lifted it carefully up to the surface where under the cover of darkness they had loaded it aboard the ship.

It was well after two in the morning. The others had already locked out and had swum to the surface using the British-designed emersion suits which were good to around six hundred feet. Only Kurshin and Captain Makayev were left aboard. They faced each other across the control room.

"All the internal compartments are open?" Kurshin asked.

Makayev nodded. "Except for the reactor spaces. I don't want to risk a leak from the core, no matter what the prize we're seeking, Comrade Colonel."

"It would have made it impossible for their rescue vehicles to approach the hull for a lot of years to come."

"Insanity," Makayev said sharply.

"This is war . . ."

"Yes, this is war. But not against the sea, Comrade Colonel. Even a man such as yourself must understand common decency." The captain looked away through the open hatches down the length of the boat, gloomy in the red light, the odor of death much stronger now that all the hatches were open. "Every man who wears a uniform understands contingencies such as these. And so do the families of these boys." He turned back and looked Kurshin in the eye. "We will sink this boat to hide the evidence of what we have done, Comrade Colonel. But I will not contaminate the sea with radiation poisoning, nor will I make it impossible for the Americans to discover the final resting place of this crew."

Makayev was weak like the others. Kurshin wanted to kill him, but at this moment it simply wasn't practical. He needed the captain to set the boat on its final dive, and he needed the cooperation of Makayev's missile man.

"You're correct, of course," Kurshin said with an apologetic smile. He shook his head. "It's just that . . . it's the enormity of the thing. I wasn't thinking straight."

Makayev seemed relieved that he wasn't going to have to fight about the issue. "I know, it's gotten to all of us."

"I'm sorry about Dr. Velikanov."

"He was affected most of all," Makayev said, softening even more. "But there was nothing else to be done, Arkasha. He could have killed us all."

Kurshin's jaw tightened. No one on this earth had ever called him Arkasha except for Baranov. No one. It was everything he could do not to kill this bastard here and now. But again he forced a tired smile. "I appreciate your understanding, Niki. I really do."

"Just so," Makayev said. "The lockout chamber has been recycled and is ready for us?"

"Yes."

"Good. Go forward then and fill up your suit. We won't have much time to get free of the boat before she accelerates to a dangerous speed. She could drag us down with her."

Kurshin hesitated, searching the other man's eyes for some hidden purpose. But with Makayev, he suspected, what you saw was what you got. It was why he was always in trouble. He did not know how to play the political game so important for survival in the Soviet Union. He did not know how to hide his true feelings, his real intent.

"Don't be long."

"I won't be, believe me."

The five-man lockout chamber was just forward of the conning tower. Kurshin had donned his hooded emersion suit and had filled it with compressed air which would give him enough buoyancy and breathing air to reach the surface. Suddenly the *Indianapolis* shuddered and began to move at a down angle.

A few seconds later Makayev showed up on the run, and Kurshin helped him with his suit, filling it with air even as the captain was closing the lower hatch, and seawater began to rise above their knees.

The boat was already going very fast by the time the pressure inside the lockout chamber had been equalized and the outer hatch opened. Kurshin was about to suggest they slow the boat down when Makayev bodily shoved him out the hatch.

The burbling water slammed his body up against the conning tower, and then he was tumbling end over end with absolutely no idea which way was up.

Something grabbed at his left arm, and he looked down as the submarine slid below them, the prop wash again tumbling him end over end.

Makayev was beside and slightly above him, and gradually Kurshin realized that they were rising toward the surface, and he had to remember to force himself to breathe regularly lest he get an embolism in his lungs.

He raised his head to look up, but couldn't see anything at first. The water all around them was pitch-black. Gradually, however, he was able to see a dark bulk off to the left. It would be the hull of the *Stephos*. And then they were on the surface, only a light chop bobbing them in the waves.

Kurshin pulled a small flashlight from his pocket and flashed it twice. Immediately they could hear the sound of a small outboard motor, as a rubber raft headed toward them.

He yanked his hood off and breathed deeply of the fresh night air, the smells of the sea and the nearby Greek coast pure and wonderful after the confinement of the submarine.

Makayev had pulled off his hood and he swam over to Kurshin. "That was very close," he said.

Kurshin looked at him. "I suppose you saved my life."

Makayev said nothing.

"Thank you, Comrade," Kurshin said as he thought about when the time would be best to kill the man.

USS *BATON ROUGE*

Fifty miles southwest of the island of Crete, the attack submarine *Baton Rouge* was in her drift mode on a heading of two-six-five, submerged at three hundred feet beneath the surface. Far to the north, in the Aegean, her sister boat the USS *Phoenix* was keeping close tabs on the approaches to the Dardanelles. They had been taking part in OPERATION LOOKUP with the CVN *Nimitz* when they had received orders to search for the *Indianapolis*.

At all costs, their orders had specified, the *Indianapolis* was not to be allowed anywhere near the Dardanelles. "Top priority is communications. If the *Indianapolis* does not respond, and if she continues to make an attempt to reach the Black Sea, she is to be considered hostile, and is to be killed.''

Commander Richard Keyser had surfaced his boat for clarification, and when it had come his orders had seemed no less incredible than before. He knew J.D. Webb. They were friends. If J.D. was attempting to steal his boat, there was a gun pointed at his head. Or he was dead. Keyser would have bet anything on it.

A few minutes earlier their sonar had picked up what very possibly was a submarine far off to their south. They had run at high speed for five minutes, and then had shut down to drift again.

''Conn, sonar,'' the comms speaker blared.

''Conn, aye,'' Keyser said.

''I have a definite fix on that target. Range eight thousand meters, bearing three-six-zero. It's changing left to right.''

The other submarine was directly ahead of them and was moving almost due south. ''Is it the *Indianapolis*, Randy?''

The comms was silent for a beat.

''Yes, Skipper, I'd be willing to bet anything on it, unless there is another Los Angeles-class boat in the area.''

''No,'' Keyser said. ''No chance it's Russian?''

''Not a chance, Skipper. She's definitely an L.A. class.''

''What's she doing?''

''That's the part that threw me at first. She's not making more than ten knots, but she's diving, on a constant angle.''

''How deep?''

''Sir, a thousand feet . . . belay that. She's passing eleven hundred feet now, and the angle of her dive has increased.''

Keyser looked at his exec at the chart table across the control room. ''What's it look like, Dean? Are they heading for the bottom?''

''Just about ten thousand feet here, Skipper. But they've probably picked us up; they may be trying to duck under a thermocline.''

''Then we're going after her. Give me turns for full speed.''

Keyser turned back to the comms. "Sonar, keep a sharp watch, I want to know when she levels out."

"She's still going down, Skipper."

"She'll level off. She has to."

The *Baton Rouge* accelerated smoothly, the angle on her planes down five degrees as she turned on an intercept course.

The Los Angeles-class boats had a service depth of around fifteen hundred feet, though they were considered reasonably safe a few hundred feet deeper than that. It had always been one of their problems whenever they came up against the Russian Alfa-class boats that were constructed of welded titanium. The Alfas were not only faster, they could dive to nearly three thousand feet.

Keyser hit the comms switch three minutes later as the *Baton Rouge* began to level off at one thousand feet. "Sonar, conn."

"Sonar, aye."

"What's she doing?"

"Skipper, she's passed eighteen hundred feet and her angle hasn't changed. I'm starting to pick up hull compression noises."

"Christ," Keyser swore. "Go active, ping him once, Randy, let him know we're here."

"Aye," Chief Petty Officer Randy Sparkman replied. Moments later they all heard the single pong.

"Anything?" Keyser radioed.

"Negative. I'm getting more hull compression noises. Skipper, she's just passed two thousand feet. I think . . . wait . . ."

Keyser turned on his heel and hurried aft to the sonar control center. Sparkman looked up and shook his head.

"She's breaking up, Skipper."

Keyser donned a set of headphones. It took him a moment or two to sort out just what it was he was hearing. But it was there. The *Indianapolis* was definitely breaking up.

"Give me another range and bearing."

Sparkman hit the active sonar, the pong reverberating

throughout the boat. "It's a scattered target, Skipper. She's losing all her air. Same range and bearing, but she's going down now. Straight down."

"Oh, Christ," Keyser swore again, ripping the headphones off. He hit the comms switch. "Dean, surface the boat. Emergency practices."

"Aye, Skipper."

49

MV *STEPHOS*

A BILLION POINTS OF LIGHT SPARKLED ON THE DEEP BLUE of the Mediterranean as the Motor Vessel *Stephos* raced east into the rising sun. She was a French-built hydrofoil, and when she rose up out of the water on full plane she was a sight to see. Capable of speeds approaching fifty knots, at this moment she was doing nearly that, leaving behind a creamy but curiously flat wake.

She was beautiful, her lines sleek, her hull and superstructure all white except for the huge red crosses on her port and starboard sides. Her expansive forward deck, however, was cluttered with what appeared to be big crates, all marked LEBANESE RELIEF ORGANIZATION. In actuality, the crates were a sham; they served to hide the Tomahawk missile securely cradled to her hastily assembled launching rack.

"Within ten minutes," Kurshin had been assured by KGB Captain Ivan Akhminovich Grechko, who skippered the *Stephos*. "We can have the crates stripped away, the missile raised and fired."

"You have done a fine job," Kurshin said.

Kurshin, Grechko, and Makayev had gone below to the captain's cabin where they sat around a low coffee table on which was spread a chart depicting the entire eastern Mediterranean from Greece to Israel.

Grechko stabbed a blunt finger on the chart at a point fifty miles north of Crete. They were just passing the eastern end of the island.

"We'll make the Carpathos Strait just south of Rhodes within the next ninety minutes. Puts us out in the open Med for the run to the north side of Cyprus."

Kurshin had been intently studying the chart. He looked up. Grechko and Makayev were watching him.

"What time?"

"We should be around the island Cape Andreas late this afternoon, and in position off the Syrian coast before nightfall."

Kurshin thought about it a moment. "We'll reduce speed later today, perhaps around noon," he said. "But I'll leave that up to you. The point is I don't want to close with the coast before nightfall."

"That makes sense." Grechko nodded his agreement.

"And then what, Comrade Colonel?" Makayev asked.

"We launch the missile, scuttle this boat, and take the auxiliary to the coast just north of Jeble where we'll be picked up and flown immediately to Tbilisi."

"Why Georgia?" Grechko asked. "There isn't much there except for peasants, factory workers, and old women."

"Because we're going to have to be hidden."

"For how long?"

"I don't know. Perhaps for a long time."

"Because of the target?" Makayev asked.

"Yes, Niki, because of the target."

"Where?"

Kurshin sat back. He decided that it was going to be a pleasure killing this bastard. "What if I said Tel Aviv?"

The color drained from Makayev's face, but Grechko was grinning. "That would teach those Jews a lesson," the KGB captain grunted. He was a roughshod man, with absolutely no class. He was ex-navy, though, and knew what he was doing here. "But you can't be serious, Comrade Colonel."

Kurshin had kept his eyes on Makayev. He shook his head. "We are not going to hit a civilian target." He sat forward again and drew the chart a little closer. "Here," he said, pointing. "En Gedi."

"What is there?" Makayev asked.

"Israel's stockpile of nuclear weapons. Their *only* nuclear weapons."

Makayev licked his lips. "They'd be deep underground. Beyond the damaging power of that missile, I think."

"You're correct. But the nuclear blast will contaminate the surface for a lot of years to come, rendering their weapons inaccessible."

Grechko was grinning again, his face like a death's head. "Destroyed by an American weapon. That is rich."

"But there's more, isn't there," Makayev said.

"What do you mean?" Kurshin asked.

"There are some politics involved . . ."

"You are a naval officer, Captain Makayev. Let's just keep it at that, shall we?"

"I don't like this."

"I don't care," Kurshin said coldly.

"What time do we launch?" Grechko asked softly.

"Midnight. We'll set it and the scuttling charges on a timer, giving us enough time to get clear. The missile will launch, and within sixty seconds the charges in the hull will blow and the *Stephos* will go to the bottom." Along with all but one of her crew, Kurshin thought.

SOSUS CONTROL CENTER, CRETE

Two miles west of the city of Iráklion, on Crete's north coast, the U.S. Navy's SOSUS control center was housed in a low cement-block building, adjacent to a small paved airstrip. Normally only a dozen men were stationed at the tiny station, but that number had more than tripled with the arrival of the CINCMED, Admiral DeLugio, and his staff.

An hour ago, McGarvey and an intensely worried Trotter had flown down from Rome. They stood now, facing the admiral, his intelligence officer, Malcolm Ainslie, and Frank Newman, the lieutenant the Pentagon had sent out, across the situation table.

"That's it, then," DeLugio said heavily. The flash message from the *Baton Rouge* had just been relayed through Gaeta. He passed it across the table to McGarvey. "God only knows what happened out there, but it looks as if your job is done."

"Are they sure it's the *Indianapolis*?" McGarvey asked as he quickly scanned the message. But then he had the answer.

"Yes," DeLugio said.

300638ZJUL
TOP SECRET
FM: USS BATON ROUGE
TO: COMSUBMED
A. INDIANAPOLIS BROKE UP BELOW 2500
FEET AT 0449 Z THIS DATE. LAT. 35-40.1 N,
LON. 22-11.8 E.
B. SONAR DETECTED LOS ANGELES-CLASS
FOOTPRINT DIVING ON A COURSE OF 183.
C. SONAR DETECTED NUMEROUS SOUNDS OF
HULL COMPRESSION FAILURE.
D. DEBRIS ON SURFACE DEFINITELY CAME
FROM USS INDIANAPOLIS. DESCRIPTIONS
AND SERIAL NUMBERS TO FOLLOW TEXT.
E. IT IS BELIEVED THAT ALL HANDS WERE
LOST.

McGarvey looked up from his reading. "She was heading south? Any possibility the *Baton Rouge* was wrong?"

"No," DeLugio said. "But at least you were correct in one thing, McGarvey. The *Indianapolis* was definitely not heading for the Black Sea."

"Nor Israel," Ainslie said.

"Admiral, how long before we can have the *Pigeon* on station?" Lieutenant Newman asked.

"Two days before we'll know anything. But it doesn't matter now. The politics are for the president to sort out. But the crew of the *Indianapolis* are all dead."

"There were only six of them," McGarvey said. "Plus Kurshin."

"It's the proof Washington needed. And with that small a crew it's no wonder they lost control of the boat." DeLugio shook his head. "The bastards. At least they lost."

"I wonder . . ." McGarvey muttered half under his breath as he studied the map board that formed the surface of the situation table. The others were talking, but their words flowed around him.

The *Indianapolis* had been tracked by the SOSUS network as she emerged from the Malta Channel about forty hours ago, and then she had disappeared. It had given her plenty of time to pass Crete and come very near Israel, though from what he had been told about the ship's nuclear missiles they could have been fired from nearly anywhere in the Mediterranean. The Tomahawk had a range of more than seventeen hundred nautical miles. From the spot where she had been hijacked off the coast of Italy to En Gedi was barely twelve hundred miles.

Kurshin would have had plans for his escape once the missile was fired. It had taken them this time to get ready.

But the *Indianapolis* had been heading south, not east, and she had been diving. A mistake on the Russian crew's part? Or, as the admiral suggested, had the boat simply gotten away from them? "It's not like driving a car. Running a boat of that size takes a well-trained, experienced crew," Lieutenant Newman had said.

Baranov was a man who left nothing to chance. And Kurshin was good. The very best. They were not stealing the boat, trying to get it into the Black Sea. They only wanted one of the missiles. The target was En Gedi.

He ran his finger north along the chart from the position where the *Indianapolis* went down, and suddenly it came to him.

Trotter had been watching him. "What is it, Kirk?"

McGarvey looked up. "Kurshin is not on that submarine," he said.

DeLugio and the others were looking at him.

"They killed the crew and took the boat here, to the Gulf of Lakonia or the Bay of Messini where they hid on the bottom for twelve hours or so."

"Why? What are you saying?" Trotter asked.

"Kurshin wanted one of the Tomahawk missiles. It's my guess they shoved it out a torpedo hatch, set the submarine on a southerly course, with a down angle on her planes, and got out through an escape hatch. Is that possible?"

Admiral DeLugio was nodding. "But why?"

"Could a Tomahawk be launched from the deck of a surface ship?"

"Yes . . ." DeLugio started to say, but then he had it too. "Christ. They had a mother ship waiting for them. They'll launch the missile and then get the hell out of there."

"Not off the Greek coast," McGarvey said. "They're heading east."

"Where?" Trotter asked.

"Someplace where they have friends. They're not out to commit suicide. They want to launch that missile . . . on En Gedi . . . and then have the chance to get away." McGarvey was studying the chart. "Syria or Lebanon would be my guess."

"That's a long ways across open water. They can't have made it yet," Ainslie said, his eyes bright.

"Tonight," McGarvey replied. "They'll launch sometime after dark."

"Then we've got them," Ainslie blurted. "It's not so easy

to hide a missile that size. And they'll need launching equipment. A ramp."

"It'll be hidden. Have we any satellites watching this end of the Mediterranean?"

"I don't know," DeLugio barked. "But we'll damned well find out."

"We're looking for any boat big enough to handle the missile, heading east," McGarvey said.

"There's a lot of traffic out there," the admiral said, "some of it Russian Navy."

"The missile won't be aboard a Soviet ship. The Russian Navy has nothing to do with this. It'll be a civilian ship. Something that moves fast, something that would not be challenged . . . something completely unlikely."

"We don't have the ships to check every vessel. Too much water out there, McGarvey," the admiral said.

"Bring me the pictures. I'll know it when I see it."

"I'll talk to Murphy," Trotter said. "The Israelis will have to be notified."

"Yes," McGarvey said, again looking down at the chart. "The problem is going to be approaching that boat. If we get too close, he just may say the hell with it and launch the missile anyway."

"What the hell sort of a bastard is he?" DeLugio snarled.

"I don't know yet," McGarvey said. "But I'm learning." He looked up. "Get those pictures."

50

MV *STEPHOS*

THEY HAD REACHED THE WESTERN COAST OF CYPRUS BY early afternoon, and Captain Grechko had slowed the boat down, bringing her off her hydrofoils so that she operated as a conventional craft.

In this mode she was capable of speeds around twenty knots, but they would still reach their launch position off the Syrian coast sometime around eleven, giving them plenty of time to set up for the shoot and get free.

The motion aboard was not so comfortable now as it had been before. The *Stephos* tended to wallow at times in the heavy swells coming from the southwest across the entire fetch of the Mediterranean, but no one was complaining; in less than twelve hours they would be on their way home.

Kurshin had taken over the captain's cabin and after their

meeting this morning he had managed to get several hours of deep dreamless sleep so that when he rose a few minutes after three he was fully rested. He stood in the middle of the room, his head cocked, listening to the sounds of the ship. Grechko had brought four KGB crewmen with him: an engineer, a loadmaster, and the two divers who had located the missile and had placed the collar around it. With Captain Makayev and his four-man crew, it made ten men aboard besides Kurshin.

Except for Grechko and his engineer, the others were resting. It had been a long two days and nights.

Kurshin picked up the phone and called the bridge. Grechko answered. "How does it look, Ivan Akhminovich?"

"We've got Cape Kormakiti off our starboard now, about fifteen kilometers."

"We're on schedule?"

"Of course," Grechko said. "We'll round Cape Andreas after dark. Everything is going as you wished, Comrade Colonel."

Kurshin heard a hesitancy in the man's voice. "Yes, what is it?"

"It's your submarine drivers. Makayev and the others have been huddled together since before noon. I don't like the smell of it."

"I'll take care of it," Kurshin said. He had been expecting trouble from Makayev.

"I'm coming down, we'll talk about it . . ." Grechko started to say, but Kurshin cut him off.

"No. I'll be topside in a minute. I want to check the missile. When I'm finished we'll have our little chat."

"As you wish."

"Yes," Kurshin replied, and he hung up. He stood beside the desk for a moment or two deciding on his options, and on the timing of his moves. Grechko was an ambitious man; he would go along with whatever happened. Makayev, however, was the weak link. Without his cooperation his missile man, Lieutenant Chobotov, would refuse to do what was necessary to ready the missile for launch.

Now was the time to resolve that issue and get ready for his ultimate solution.

He strapped on his shoulder holster and checked to make certain that his Graz Buyra was ready to fire, then went across the cabin to where he had stuffed his emersion suit in a locker. Pulling it out, he unzipped one of the leg pockets and withdrew the slender cylinder of Labun nerve gas, with its timing device attached to the release valve.

Two had been used aboard the *Zenzero*, and four aboard the *Indianapolis*. Neither Russian crew had bothered to count. It was their mistake.

Handling the deadly cylinder with extreme care, Kurshin removed the safety seal from the valve, checked his watch again and set the timer for eight hours. Pulling the four life jackets from a locker over the door, he gingerly put the cylinder inside and replaced the life jackets.

Before he left the cabin he looked around. At a few minutes after eleven this evening, this place would become a killing chamber. He nodded in silent satisfaction, and a smile crossed his features as he stepped out into the corridor and went topside.

On the foredeck, Kurshin ducked beneath the false crates into the space where the Tomahawk lay cradled in its launch ramp. Electric motors tied now to the ship's power system would raise the ramp to an elevation of twenty degrees, plenty to assure a good launch. Everything was in readiness except for the setting of the timing and firing circuitry, which only Lieutenant Chobotov was capable of doing.

Back out on deck, he looked toward the south where the mountains of the big island of Cyprus rose up in the haze-filled distance. So close now, he thought. And when it was finished he would not only have Baranov's gratitude, he would have the man's patronage . . . with that, anything was possible. Absolutely anything.

Grechko was alone on the bridge when Kurshin went up. The ship was being steered by an autohelm unit, her course and position determined by satellite navigation equipment.

"Are they still below?" Kurshin asked, closing the door.

Grechko nodded. "Rimyans is watching them." Rimyans was one of the divers.

"Are your people armed?"

Again Grechko nodded. "Are you expecting trouble over this thing?"

"Very probably."

"I thought so. What do we do?"

"Get your people up on deck. As soon as they're in place I'm going to call Makayev and his crew up to get the missile ready for firing."

"Do you think they'll cooperate?"

Kurshin gave him a hard stare. "They're navy, we're KGB. They'll cooperate."

Grechko's eyes narrowed. "But I think we'll need that lieutenant to launch the missile."

"Only to set up the firing circuitry," Kurshin replied. "Afterward he will be expendable. They all will be. Do I make myself clear, Ivan Akhminovich?"

"Perfectly," Grechko said softly, and he picked up the phone to call his crew.

Kurshin stepped to the forward windows and looked down at the crates strapped to the foredeck. The *Stephos* was an innocent ship on a mission of mercy. No one could tell otherwise without coming aboard. He raised his eyes to the sky. In the distance to the east he could see the contrail of a jet aircraft flying very high. Possibly an airliner, he thought. Possibly the Israeli Air Force. Possibly almost any kind of a jet. But not a spy plane. Those you never saw.

He had given a lot of thought to McGarvey over the past days. But now, for some reason, he was getting an uncomfortable feeling that somehow the man was watching him. Impossible, and yet the notion was there, at the back of his head. It was because of Ramstein, he supposed, that he was becoming jumpy. But McGarvey had managed the impossible then. How about now? He was a devil.

"Give them two minutes," Grechko said.

Kurshin turned back to him. "Do they understand what is required of them?"

"Yes, Comrade Colonel. As a matter of fact I had already discussed this very possibility with them. They know what to do."

"Good."

Grechko crossed the room, opened the door, and stepped out onto the bridge deck. A minute later he waved. "They are in place now."

Kurshin picked up the telephone and hit the button for Makayev's cabin. It was answered on the first ring by the captain.

"Yes?"

"Send Lieutenant Chobotov topside. I want him to ready the missile."

"So soon?"

"Yes, now."

The line was silent for a moment, but then Makayev was back.

"Yes, Comrade Colonel, we'll be right up."

Kurshin hung up the phone. There was no mistaking Makayev's tone, nor his use of the word—*we'll*. It was to be a showdown, and now. Again Kurshin grinned in anticipation.

"They're on the way up," he said out on the bridge deck.

"All of them?" Grechko asked.

"It would appear so. You cover us from here. But no matter what happens, Lieutenant Chobotov isn't to be harmed."

"I understand."

Kurshin reached the main deck just as Makayev and his crew showed up from below. They all carried sidearms. Grechko's men had hidden themselves, which was just as well because Makayev's people drew their weapons and spread out.

"We're taking over this ship," Makayev said.

"And then what, Niki?" Kurshin asked calmly.

"We're going to dump the missile, and then sail into Limassol on the south side of Cyprus where we'll turn ourselves over to the authorities."

"Why?"

"What we have done is an act of war, Colonel. We have decided that we will not compound this insanity by firing a nuclear weapon on any target . . . military or civilian."

"Have you lost your nerve then?" Kurshin asked, still grinning.

Makayev ignored the question. He looked up at Grechko standing on the bridge deck. "Where is your crew?"

Grechko smiled. "Shall I call them?"

"Yes."

"Very well," Grechko said, and at that moment the other four KGB officers, all of them armed with AK74 assault rifles, appeared on deck.

Makayev's men stepped back in surprise and shock.

"Put your weapons down now," Kurshin ordered.

Makayev was shaken, but he was a good man and he held his ground, his weapon pointed at Kurshin's chest. "I will kill you."

"And then you will die," Kurshin said. "And I think, Niki, that perhaps you love your life more than I do mine."

Still Makayev hesitated.

"If you cooperate now, you have my word that nothing will be said about this incident. Everything will be as before."

After several long seconds, Makayev finally uncocked the hammer of his automatic and stuffed the weapon in his holster. "Do as he says," he told his crew. One by one they holstered their weapons.

"A wise decision, Niki," Kurshin said.

Makayev looked at the KGB crew who still held their weapons at the ready. "Tell them to put down their guns."

"First I would like Lieutenant Chobotov to ready the missile. I need your fullest cooperation."

"All right," Makayev said heavily. "Do it, Aleksei Sergeevich."

Chobotov hesitated for a beat, but then broke away from the others and went with Kurshin around to the foredeck where they ducked beneath the false crates.

"I want it armed and set to fire at midnight exactly," Kurshin told him.

"What if something goes wrong, Comrade Colonel? I mean what if we are delayed for some reason in raising the launching ramp?"

"Nothing will go wrong; trust me, Lieutenant."

"Well, if these crates are not removed and the ramp isn't raised I wouldn't want to be within fifty kilometers of this ship," Chobotov said. He took a small flashlight from his jumpsuit pocket and handed it to Kurshin. "You will have to hold the light for me, sir."

"With pleasure," Kurshin said. "And believe me, you and your captain will get exactly what you deserve for this."

And very soon, Kurshin thought. Very soon.

It took the young lieutenant less than ten minutes to arm the Tomahawk's firing circuitry and install the timer onto the proper circuit board.

When he was finished, he replaced the access panel with its ten fasteners. "There," he said, turning around.

Kurshin had taken out his gun and had screwed the silencer tube on the end of the barrel. Chobotov opened his mouth to cry out when he realized what was about to happen, but Kurshin fired a single shot point-blank into his left eye, slamming him backward, his head bouncing off the deck.

Reholstering his gun, Kurshin turned and calmly ducked back out from beneath the false crates and made his way back to the afterdeck where Makayev and the others still stood at gunpoint.

Makayev looked beyond Kurshin. "Where is Aleksei?"

"Dead," Kurshin said. "Kill them."

Makayev reached for his gun, but Grechko's men opened fire, and Kurshin began to laugh.

51

SOSUS CONTROL CENTER, CRETE

TIME WAS RUNNING OUT FOR ALL OF THEM. IT WAS NEARLY six in the evening and still they had come up with nothing concrete. As someone around the situation table had growled, the stretch of the Mediterranean they were searching—from the eastern end of Crete to the coasts of Israel, Lebanon, and Syria—encompassed more than two hundred thousand square miles of water. Heavily trafficked water.

A special circuit had been set up linking the SOSUS center with the National Security Agency's Ft. Meade satellite reconnaissance service, over which KH-11 photographs came in a steady stream.

An SR-71 spy plane had been dispatched from its base at Prestwick, Scotland, downloading its first batch of photographs through a special satellite link. The second batch, taken two hours later, would show them relative movements when compared to the first, and were due to be transmitted at any minute.

Naval Intelligence units along with local CIA stations throughout Europe had enlisted the cooperation of Interpol in an effort to track down the leasing of any ships within the past few days to a week. Their reports were continuously added to the growing pile of data.

But this was summer. The Mediterranean was a playground for boaters from nearly every country in the world.

The CVN *Nimitz* and its task force continued to shadow the Russian fleet, of course, and the *Phoenix* and *Baton Rouge* continued to watch the approaches to the Black Sea on the off chance that they had been fooled into believing that the *Indianapolis* had actually gone down. It would be another full twenty-four hours before the ASR *Pigeon* was on station and they could send the submersible down for a firsthand look.

But by then, it would be too late.

Trotter had been on the encrypted telephone with General Murphy all through the late morning and afternoon. The Israelis had been fully assessed of the situation, and they had sent up the U-2 spy plane they had purchased from the U.S. Air Force some years back, and which had proved very effective for them. They had no capability of down-linking such photographs; instead, the U-2 had to be returned to its base, the film canisters unloaded, and the film processed and printed. The results of that first overflight were expected soon.

It had become a gigantic job of collation. Each possible target vessel had to be studied carefully to make certain it was of the proper size. But although the Tomahawk missile was heavy, it was only twenty-one feet long; it wouldn't take a very large boat to handle it. Assuming the missile was going to be fired sometime tonight, and from a spot somewhere within the vicinity of the Syrian or Lebanese coasts, there was another limiting factor. If the missile had been transferred from the *Indianapolis* in the early morning hours (and there

was still no proof of that), then it would take time to cross
the nearly eight hundred miles of sea. With each target, once
its speed was determined, they extrapolated backward, to see
if the vessel could have been off the coast of Greece at the
proper moment.

"That is, if they're going to fire the missile from that
close," Ainslie said.

McGarvey looked up from the situation table and rubbed
his eyes. None of them had gotten any rest, and all of them
were becoming edgy. Ainslie had been talking to Admiral
DeLugio, who looked and acted like a wounded bear on the
verge of going on a rampage.

"What are you saying to me, Mal?" the admiral growled.

"Just this, Admiral. We've got no guarantee that Mc-
Garvey is right. If I were this Kurshin, I would be getting
rid of the missile at the first possible opportunity. They've
been within firing range the whole time."

"They might have doubled back, is that it?"

"Yes, sir. By now they could be anywhere. Anywhere at
all. And once it gets dark we're not going to have a chance
in hell of finding them."

"What are you suggesting?"

"Convince the president to go public," Ainslie said after
a brief hesitation. "Gorbachev wouldn't dare go ahead with
it."

"It wouldn't work," McGarvey said.

They looked over at him. "Why not?" DeLugio demanded.

"Because Gorbachev and the Politburo know nothing about
it, that's why. This is a Baranov plot. It doesn't go beyond
him. And you can bet he's got his alibis. Whatever happens
or doesn't happen, his hands are going to be clean."

"Bullshit," Ainslie swore. "You've got this Baranov sonofabitch on the brain. The man is the head of the KGB, and
a Politburo member. Responsible men do not do these kinds
of things."

McGarvey laughed tiredly. "You don't know what you're
talking about."

"It's a goddamned vendetta. I've seen the report, McGarvey. You fucked up two years ago, and although you managed to stop the missile launch in Germany, you fucked up again by not stopping this Kurshin you're so hot to go after. And less than two months ago you fucked up again, nearly getting yourself killed in the process."

"Besides, his target is Israel, not the States, is that it?" McGarvey said tightly. He was beginning to lose his temper.

"Get out of here, McGarvey. We don't need your kind. You're nothing but a hired gun, and from where I'm standing it doesn't look like you're even worth a damn at that."

Trotter, who had been talking on the phone across the room, put it down. "Kirk," he called in warning.

"Admiral, call Admiral O'Malley," Ainslie said. "He can take this to the president. Before it's too late. And order this maniac out of here. This is a Navy matter. The CIA will just fuck it up."

McGarvey was around the big table in three steps. He grabbed a handful of Ainslie's uniform blouse with his left hand, the big Graz Buyra he had taken from the Grosser Müggelsee boathouse in his right, the barrel pressed into the soft flesh beneath the man's chin.

"Stand down, mister," DeLugio roared.

"I've come up against this sonofabitch before, Ainslie, and you're right, I did fuck up," McGarvey said through clenched teeth. "He wants to unseat Gorbachev and become party secretary himself. If Kurshin pulls this off for him, Baranov just may succeed, and then you and the Navy will definitely have a problem."

"Mister, that's a direct order," DeLugio was shouting, but McGarvey ignored him.

"But he's counting on assholes like you to help him do his work. Going public with this now will only delay our search, giving him plenty of time to do what he's set out to do."

Admiral DeLugio had snatched a .45 automatic from one of the Marine guards and he jammed the barrel into the back of McGarvey's head. "Lower your weapon now," he said.

McGarvey cocked the Graz Buyra's hammer. "Let me get on with my job, Admiral."

"We'll talk about it. First put down your weapon."

"He very nearly succeeded in Ramstein, and this time he managed to steal one of your submarines and kill her crew. He won't stop."

"Kirk," Trotter shouted again from across the room.

McGarvey did not divert his stare from Ainslie's bulging eyes. "We're not giving this up, John."

"Killing him won't do any good," a familiar voice said.

McGarvey glanced toward the door. Lev Potok and his number two, Abraham Liebowitz, both of them dressed in battle fatigues, stood there.

"Who in hell let them in here?" DeLugio bellowed.

"I did," Trotter said. "They're Mossad."

"Kirk, I know where your missile is," Potok said. "Or at least I think I do. We've got a chance now to stop him."

"The U-2 flight?"

"Yes. I've brought the photographs with me. But we need your information to make sure. And it will be dark very soon. We don't have much time."

McGarvey slowly lowered his weapon, uncocked the hammer, and holstered it. "Stay the hell out of my way, Ainslie," he said. "And put that goddamned gun down, Admiral."

DeLugio lowered the .45 after a beat.

Ainslie had staggered backward, rubbing at his throat. "Arrest this man! Now!"

"Shut the fuck up," Admiral DeLugio snapped. He turned to Potok and Liebowitz. "As you say, gentlemen, we don't have much time. Let's see what you've got."

A space was cleared on the situation table. Potok unsnapped his briefcase and quickly laid out a batch of photographs that the U-2 had taken on her overflight of the coastlines of Syria and Lebanon.

McGarvey picked up a magnifying glass and studied the images of a large boat with a white hull. A red cross had been painted on each side of her sleek hull. The foredeck was littered with crates. In one photograph he could make out the lettering.

Lieutenant Newman had picked up another magnifying glass and he too studied the photographs. When he looked up he shook his head. "Won't wash," he said.

"Why?" Potok asked.

"This is the Motor Vessel *Stephos*, right?"

Potok nodded.

"That's the Red Cross ship out of Athens that your people checked out, wasn't it?" Newman asked Ainslie.

At first the man said nothing, but a look from DeLugio got him started. "Yes. It's a legitimate Red Cross vessel."

"Did you have a chance to find out where she was sailing to?" Potok asked.

"No," Ainslie admitted. "She was a legitimate ship, and there just wasn't enough time to mess with it."

"Besides," McGarvey said, "we discounted her because of the timing. At twenty knots or so she wouldn't have been able to make it from the Greek coast, where we think the missile was transferred, this far east."

"At twenty knots," Potok said. He turned again to Ainslie. "Did your people tell you what kind of a ship this was?"

Ainslie was confused. "No . . . just . . ."

"It's a hydrofoil, Kirk," Potok said. "She is capable of doing fifty knots over reasonably calm seas, which is exactly what we have now."

"We didn't show that kind of speed."

"No, she probably got the hell out of there in a big hurry to put as many miles between her and the pickup point as possible, and when she was well clear she slowed down to normal speed."

"Christ," McGarvey swore softly.

"What we need to know is your best guess for the time of transfer. When was the missile taken off your submarine?"

"Sometime between midnight and two in the morning, as best we can figure from the track of the *Indianapolis* before she was spotted," DeLugio said.

Newman snatched up a pair of dividers, and quickly walked them across the chart, starting from a spot between the Greek bays of Messini and Lakonia, where they figured the missile had been offloaded, to the Syrian coast where the *Stephos* was now heading.

He looked up. "Bingo," he said.

Again McGarvey studied the photographs. "Still doesn't nail it down solid."

"Your missile is twenty-one feet long, is that right?" Potok asked.

DeLugio nodded.

"The pile of boxes on the *Stephos*'s foredeck would just hold it."

"Marked Lebanese Relief Organization. Still could be legitimate . . ." McGarvey started to say.

"We've checked on it, Kirk. They know nothing about it," Potok said.

McGarvey thought about it for a moment. It was just the kind of ploy Kurshin would be using. The man had been called the chameleon. He was always out in the open in plain sight, only you were never quite certain what you were seeing.

"How sure are you of this, Lev?" McGarvey asked.

"Now, just about one hundred percent. The Air Force is standing by. We can make a surgical strike . . ."

"No," DeLugio cut him off. "In the first place, if you hit the missile's fuel tanks and they blow, you'd be spreading radioactive material into the sea."

"And in the second place," McGarvey picked it up. "Kurshin will be waiting for something like that to happen. He might just decide to blow the missile the moment your jets came over the horizon."

"Killing himself," Potok said.

"I don't think he cares."

Potok started to say something, but then he nodded. "We've both seen him in action. You're right."

"We can have a unit of SEALS there within ninety minutes," the admiral said.

McGarvey and Potok were looking into each other's eyes.

"My people will do it," the Israeli said. "We've got the bigger stake . . ."

"Yes," Trotter broke in. "The target is their nuclear research facility at En Gedi. A lot of civilians could be killed."

No one else in the room except for Trotter and McGarvey knew the real nature of En Gedi, and Potok glanced at him gratefully.

"Have your SEALS standing by just over the horizon, Admiral," McGarvey said. "This fight belongs to me and Potok."

"No," DeLugio said.

Potok looked at him. "Either I have your word, Admiral, or my Air Force will make a first strike before you could move. We can be on top of that ship within eight minutes."

DeLugio was shaking his head. "This KGB officer of yours is not alone. He's at least got his crew from the submarine, and most likely a small crew that brought the *Stephos* out for the pickup."

"Probably not," McGarvey said.

"What are you talking about?" DeLugio demanded.

"It's Kurshin. He has the habit of killing his own people once they have served their purpose."

"Jesus."

"How long will it take you to get us out there, Admiral?" McGarvey asked.

"I'll get us there," Potok said. "We have three missile boats shadowing the *Stephos*. They're just over the horizon. We'll fly to Limassol, and from there by chopper out to our boats."

"It's our missile, goddamnit," DeLugio argued. "Neither of you knows anything about it. If it's armed, will you be able to disarm it?"

"He's right," McGarvey said after a beat.

"Me," Lieutenant Newman said. "That's why they sent me."

"All right," McGarvey agreed.

"And me," Ainslie said, stepping forward.

McGarvey's eyes narrowed.

"My job is naval intelligence, and I did get us this far. Let me do my job."

"What's the real reason?"

Ainslie's lip curled. "I'm an ambitious officer, McGarvey. I want to be there when you find out that you're wrong."

"Can you shoot?"

"I'm an expert."

McGarvey glanced at Potok, who shrugged. "You're on," he said. "Just don't get in my way."

"I'm calling in the SEALS," DeLugio said. "They'll be on standby status."

"But well off, Admiral," McGarvey cautioned. "If that missile explodes, it's not going to be very healthy around there. What about one of our submarines?"

"Twelve hours at least," DeLugio said.

"Then you'd better wish us luck."

52

MV *STEPHOS*

"ARE YOU JUST ABOUT FINISHED?" KURSHIN ASKED THE
two KGB officers in the dimly lit forward machinery space.

Rimyans, one of the divers, looked up, his dark eyes piglike
in his broad face. "We have the engine room to go. It'll be
another half hour, perhaps longer."

The other officer, Viktor Georgevich Budanov, reached up
out of the bilge hatch for a screwdriver. He looked at Kurshin.
"What's the matter, Comrade Colonel, are you getting nervous?"

"No," Kurshin replied, controlling his temper. It was just
9:00 P.M. Only a couple of more hours and these bastards
would be dead.

"Well, fuck your mother, but I'm nervous. We've got
enough plastique here to sink an aircraft carrier, and some-

times I get a little twitchy, if you know what I mean.''
Budanov laughed.

The *Stephos*'s engines suddenly changed pitch, and the
boat shuddered as she slowed down. Kurshin glanced over
his shoulder toward the ladder up. They were probably just
about on station. Soon now, he told himself.

"Get on with it then," he said, turning back to the other
two. "We're abandoning this ship around eleven o'clock. I
want everyone in my cabin a few minutes ahead of time.''

"Why?" Rimyans barked.

Again he controlled his temper. They had followed their
orders and had killed Captain Makayev and his crew, but
ever since that incident their attitudes toward him had changed
dramatically. Only Grechko had remained civil. They no
longer trusted him. And with good reason.

"Moscow is not so far from here, Comrade Lieutenant. I
would suggest you keep that in mind.''

Rimyans flinched, but he didn't back down much. "You
have our fullest cooperation, Comrade Colonel.''

"I want nothing more from you," Kurshin snapped, and
he turned on his heel and left.

The ship was starting to roll slightly as she slowed to a
complete stop. On deck he took the ladder up to the bridge.
One of the other divers, Nikolai Pavlovich Sokolov, was the
only one there. He was a thick bear of a man, with shoulders
that bulged out of his jumpsuit.

"Why have we stopped?" Kurshin asked.

"We're just about on station," Sokolov said languidly. He
wore a Makarov automatic pistol at his hip, and his AK74
was propped up against the helmsman's seat. "There is a
countercurrent here that will drift us into position within the
next hour or so.''

"Who told you to do this?"

"Captain Grechko, naturally.''

Kurshin stared coldly at him for several long seconds
"Where is he?"

Sokolov shrugged. "Below somewhere with Anatoli. Having something to eat, I think.''

Kurshin glanced out the forward windows. In the distance to the east he thought he might be seeing the dim glow of the city of Jeble. But unlike European cities, most Arab communities were relatively dark.

"Stay here," he told the KGB officer. "When we're on station let me know."

"Those are my orders," Sokolov said.

"Yes," Kurshin said, forcing a smile to his lips. "See to it that you keep a sharp watch." He left the bridge and, below, went back to the galley. No one was there, nor was the main saloon occupied.

Something was going on. He could suddenly feel it thick in the air. Pulling his Graz Buyra from its holster, he screwed the silencer tube onto the end of the barrel again and switched the safety off as he moved silently forward on the balls of his feet to his cabin door.

A light shone from beneath the door, and he thought he could hear someone murmuring something inside. The voices were too low and indistinct, however, for him to make any sense of what was being said. But the fact that they were in his cabin was indictment enough.

Holding his gun out of sight behind him, he opened the door and stepped inside. Grechko and Akensov were intently studying the chart on the low coffee table. They both looked up guiltily, Grechko's eyes flicking for just an instant to the life jacket locker above the door.

So they had discovered the Labun canister, and they knew what he was planning, Kurshin thought. It was just as well.

"We were just going over the chart," Grechko said.

"It's not far now," Kurshin said, smiling. He closed the door.

"How are Leonid and Viktor doing with the explosive charges?"

"They'll be another half-hour."

"Good. I'll be glad to get off this toy boat . . ." Grechko stopped in mid-sentence; something he'd seen in Kurshin's eyes reflected in his own.

"You know, don't you?" Kurshin said. "It's too bad."

Grechko suddenly reached for his pistol, but he was too slow. Kurshin brought his big weapon around and fired one shot, catching Grechko in the face, driving him backward against the couch. Akensov started to roll left, but Kurshin calmly switched aim and fired a second shot, this one catching the KGB officer in the side of his head just below his left ear, shattering his jaw and exploding inside his brain. He was dead before he hit the floor.

Neither of them had cried out, nor would the sounds of his two shots have carried very far outside the cabin. He didn't think there was much danger that the others knew what had happened here. Not yet.

For several long seconds he stood stock still as he weighed his new options. Again he was getting a bad feeling that somehow McGarvey was watching him; somehow, as impossible as it seemed, McGarvey was somewhere very near. The man was coming.

He looked at his watch. Barely five minutes had passed since Rimyans had told him they would be another half-hour getting the explosive charges in place. They would be occupied for at least twenty-five minutes. No reason for them to come topside.

He went out of his cabin and hurried back up on deck. The ship was dark. They had been running without lights for the past two hours. Holding the big gun in his right hand, he climbed awkwardly up the outside ladder to the bridge deck.

Sokolov was studying the readouts on the satellite navigation unit above the helm. He turned around when Kurshin came in. The instant he saw the gun he realized what was about to happen and he dove for the Kalashnikov rifle. Like the others, he was too late.

Kurshin fired one shot, this one catching the KGB officer in the forehead just above the bridge of his nose. The back of his head exploded in a mass of blood and bone, and he was flung against the bulkhead.

Now there were only two of them left. For the moment they were useful. But only for the moment.

Holstering his gun, he went into the radio room where it

took him a full minute rummaging around in the drawers and cabinet to come up with a flashlight and a small screwdriver.

Outside, he hurried down to the main deck, listened for a second to make certain that Rimyans and Budanov were not coming up, and then went around the port side to the foredeck, where he ducked beneath the false crates.

He had to hold the flashlight in the crook of his neck while he removed the screws from the missile's forward access panel. When he had it off, he reached inside and very carefully eased the timer away from its circuit board and shined the light on it. The liquid crystal display showed 168 minutes, 8 seconds before firing—just midnight. Using the screwdriver to turn the reset button, he cycled the mechanism to 48 minutes exactly. The missile was now set to fire at ten o'clock.

Replacing the timer with its circuit board, he quickly slid the access panel back in place and tightened the screws. When he was finished, he tossed the screwdriver aside, switched off the flashlight, and ducked back out onto the foredeck.

Still nothing moved. The ship, for all intents and purposes, was dead in the water.

Working carefully and methodically, acutely conscious now of the ticking clock, he began removing the straps that held the false crates in place. As each of the lightweight wooden boxes came free—exposing a section of the missile and its launching ramp—he tossed it overboard.

The work was not difficult, though the crates were bulky and the ship was rolling a little more than before. Even so, by the time he was finished he was sweating heavily.

Again he stopped to check his watch. It was coming up on 9:30. Rimyans and Budanov would be just about finished by now.

He yanked his pistol out of its holster, checked the safety, entered the midship's hatch, crossed the main saloon, and at the ladder into the hold and engine spaces, paused for just a moment. He thought he could hear them talking below. Careful to make absolutely no sound, he went down the ladder, and at the bottom, crept aft to the engine room door, which was open.

Rimyans, his back to the door, was saying something to Budanov, who was just crawling out from behind one of the big turbocharged diesel engines.

"Yes, Comrade Colonel, we are finally done," Budanov said, spotting him.

"Thank you," Kurshin said with a polite smile, and he shot Rimyans in the back of the head, driving him up against the desalinator panel.

Budanov cried out as he desperately tried to reach his own pistol, but Kurshin fired a second shot, this one taking the man's jaw off, and he crumpled in a heap and lay still in a pool of his own blood and shattered teeth.

Now he was finally alone. Exactly the way he had wanted it.

Back up on the foredeck, he hurriedly removed the three straps holding the missile onto the launch ramp, and then the waterproof plugs covering the turbojet's air intake and exhaust.

Standing back, he flipped the switch on the portable electrical panel that Grechko's people had set up, and the Tomahawk's launch ramp began to rise up from the deck.

OFF THE SYRIAN COAST

They made good time through the light chop, the heavily silenced one-hundred-horsepower Johnson outboard pushing the big rubber raft at thirty knots.

It seemed to McGarvey that it had taken them days to get to this point, yet it had been only hours. They had been flown aboard an Israeli Air Force C-130 to the British base outside Limassol on the south-central coast of Cyprus, where they had transferred to a Sikorsky SH-3D Sea King helicopter for the 150-mile run up the coast and then across the open water toward the Syrian coast.

They had been transferred by sling down to the deck of one of the Israeli gunboats standing by; the transfer had taken nearly a half-hour. Potok and McGarvey had gone first. By the time Ainslie and Newman were down, the gunboat skipper had finished his hasty briefing.

The *Stephos* was about twenty miles out, and drifting slowly east on the current. She was showing no electronic emissions, and the latest U-2 overflight had detected no lights. In fact, the U-2 would have missed her completely except for the infrared radiation coming from her diesel exhausts.

The Israelis supplied them with suppressed nine-millimeter automatics, stun grenades, night vision goggles and helmets, as well as tactical communications radios. In addition, they carried a single fifty-millimeter sniper rifle with night-spotting scope and one hundred rounds of ammunition.

"There could be twenty men aboard," the gunboat commander had told them. "And you can damn well bet they're highly trained and motivated. They'd have to be to come this far."

"I don't want your people making a move until we say so, or until you've lost all communications with us; is that understood?" McGarvey had said.

The skipper had glanced at Potok, who nodded. "You've got it."

In the rubber raft, their radios clicked once. "Copy?"

"Affirmative," Potok spoke softly into his radio. They were speaking in English because of McGarvey and the others.

"You should be about a mile out. She's lying five degrees off your starboard bow."

"I've got it," McGarvey said, suddenly picking out the silhouette of the *Stephos*. Something seemed odd . . . out of place.

"We have it," Potok radioed softly.

Then McGarvey understood what he was seeing. "My God," he said. He looked at Potok. "The missile is up in the firing position."

"You're right . . ." Newman started to say, when they

all heard the unmistakable sound of automatic-weapons-fire from the ship.

"That's a Kalashnikov," Potok shouted, and he opened the Johnson's throttle to the stops, the rubber raft surging ahead on a burst of speed.

53

MV *STEPHOS*

Kᴜʀsʜɪɴ ᴄᴏᴜʟᴅ ʜᴀʀᴅʟʏ ʙᴇʟɪᴇᴠᴇ ʜɪs sᴇɴsᴇs. Tʜᴇ sʜᴏᴛs had come from somewhere aft, and had raked the hull of the twenty-foot auxiliary launch that he had been about to lower into the water.

From where he crouched behind the now useless boat, oil and gasoline leaking from its pierced tanks, he peered into the darkness, looking for a movement, anything.

Who was it? Had Grechko hidden an extra crew member for just such a contingency? He didn't think so, but then the KGB captain had been no fool . . . only slow.

He glanced quickly at his watch. The missile was due to launch in less than twenty minutes. Was this then to be his fate? Was he meant to die here like this? He could not accept such a thing. There were so many projects Baranov had promised him.

"Together we will do great things, Arkasha," the KGB director had said. Kurshin could hear his words clearly. "We will have a great future, you and I."

There were rubber rafts aboard. He had seen the canisters up on the bridge deck. It would be a long haul to the Syrian coast, but he had been made to do even more difficult things in his life. It was possible. Anything was possible.

But who had come for him . . . ?

Then he had it. Budanov. He could see the man's jaw shattering, he could see him pitching onto the engine-room floor in his own blood. It had been a stupid mistake on his part, not making certain the man was dead. It was the only possibility.

"Viktor Georgevich," he called out softly. "Can you hear me?"

He thought he heard a gurgling sound, as if someone were choking on their own saliva.

Tensing his muscles he fired a shot aft, the bullet ricocheting off the metal superstructure, and then he leapt away from the protection of the launch toward a half-open door across the portside passageway.

Budanov's returning fire slammed into the boat, ricocheted off the deck, and blew the door off its hinges.

Kurshin cried out as he dove into the forward staterooms corridor. "My eyes! My eyes!" he screamed.

He pushed his way farther back into the relative darkness and raised his pistol. Moments later he heard the sounds of someone coming, and his finger tightened on the trigger.

He was hardly prepared for the apparition that suddenly filled the doorway, and he nearly missed his shot. Budanov, his entire lower jaw shot away, blood streaming from his half-destroyed tongue, stood there weaving on his feet, the big AK74 with night-spotting scope clutched tightly.

Budanov started to bring the rifle up, but Kurshin finally fired, the shot catching the KGB officer in the right eye, shoving him violently backward against the rail, his knees collapsing beneath him.

Kurshin rushed out on deck, where he stood over Budanov's body for just a moment. The man's left leg was twitching in death. Kurshin raised his pistol again and fired a second round into the shattered face.

"No mistake this time, Comrade," he said, smiling.

Now it was time to leave.

Turning, he raced to the ladder up to the bridge, holstering his pistol. Topside, he glanced down at the missile in its last few minutes of countdown to launch. Again he smiled.

"Succeed in this for me, Arkasha, and the world will be yours." Baranov's words came clearly to his ears. "Money, women, status, and prestige."

But he had never wanted any of those things. Always there had been only one constant in his life. Killing.

"Then you shall have that," Baranov had said, laughing. "The streets will run red with blood wherever you walk." Baranov had touched a finger to the side of his nose. "Believe in me, there is enough killing to be done in this world . . . even for a man with your appetites."

Kurshin found the two life raft canisters attached to the deck wings on either side of the bridge house. He quickly released the retaining straps holding the starboard-side canister down, and was about to toss it overboard when something hot and unbelievably hard slammed into his side, picking him bodily up off his feet and knocking him backward against the bulkhead.

He sat for several long moments, dazed, scarcely believing he had been shot. He looked down at his side. There wasn't much blood, but the bullet had passed beneath a rib and had exited out of the small of his back. He had been lucky.

Pulling himself half erect, he cautiously peered out over the edge of the rail, but he couldn't see a thing. The sea was pitch-black. He couldn't even distinguish the horizon.

Then he heard the sound of an outboard motor. Incoming. Very fast.

McGarvey. The single thought crystallized in his brain. The sonofabitch had come after all, and in a way Kurshin was glad for it. They would finish here, now, the two of them, one way or the other.

Keeping below the level of the rail, he scrambled back to the bridge door, opened it, and inside grabbed Sokolov's AK74 still leaning against the helmsman's chair.

Once again out on the starboard wing deck, he cycled a round into the firing chamber, keyed the night-spotting scope, and rose up. In one smooth motion he brought the scope to his eye, scanned the sea . . . finding, then missing, then finding again the rubber raft. He got a brief impression that there might have been four men aboard. The raft was very close, well within twenty-five yards.

He fired, keeping his finger on the trigger, playing the rounds back and forth across the rubber raft, which literally exploded under his fusillade. And still he fired, until finally the assault rifle's firing pin hammered on an empty chamber.

Slowly, stiffly, he rose up as he continued to scan the water with the scope. There was a lot of debris in the water, but he could not tell if there were bodies, or if anyone lived.

Raising the scope a little higher he scanned the surrounding waters, but he could see no other boats.

Against all odds he had finally triumphed. This made up for everything. Baranov would forgive his previous mistakes.

"The world is *my* will and *my* idea, Arkasha. Never forget this."

He laid the gun down and stood there for a long time wavering on his feet, his eyes coming in and out of focus.

Give yourself the chance, Arkasha. Minimize your risks wherever possible.

Stumbling to the portside wing, he released the other life raft canister and shoved it overboard. The instant it hit the water far below, the canister broke open and the raft began to automatically inflate.

He could not survive such a long fall into the water. Not now. Not wounded.

It seemed to take forever for him to climb down to the

main deck, and when he reached the bottom of the ladder he fell, pain raging through his body, nearly causing him to black out.

Pulling himself up again, he worked his way past Buda-nov's body, where he opened an electrical panel on the bulkhead and hit the switch that lowered the boarding stairs.

Ainslie was gone and Newman had taken at least two rounds in the chest. He was unconscious but still alive. Potok, wounded himself, had managed to inflate his life jacket, and he held on to the Pentagon man.

They had spotted the single figure on the bridge deck, and McGarvey had fired a quick burst from the sniper rifle. The man had gone down, but seconds later all hell had broken loose.

Potok looked around. "Kirk?" he called out softly.

There was no answer.

The *Stephos* had drifted down on them and now was barely fifteen yards away. Potok could clearly see the Tomahawk missile raised in its launch position.

They had come so close, he thought bitterly. And they had failed.

"McGarvey," he shouted.

But still there was no answer.

Kurshin stood at the head of the boarding stairs, his ear cocked. Had he heard a voice? Someone calling out? He held his breath to listen, but the night was silent.

There was no one. Even McGarvey could not have survived.

He started down. The fully inflated life raft had drifted with the current back down against the hull of the ship. Somehow he was going to have to paddle it away before the missile fired, and before the explosive charges below took the ship to the bottom.

Kurshin was halfway down the stairs when a dark figure suddenly rose up from the water and scrambled aboard. Blood flowed down the side of his face from a head wound, and as

he straightened up to his full height Kurshin could see that
he held a stiletto in his right hand. The holster strapped to
his chest was empty.

His eyes!

The knowledge exploded in Kurshin's head.

"You're the devil," he shouted.

"You knew that I was coming for you," McGarvey said,
starting up.

Kurshin backed up a step before he came to his senses.
The man wasn't the devil . . . he was nothing more than a
man. He grappled his pistol out of its holster and thumbed
the safety off. But McGarvey was too quick.

They fell back against the stairs, each of them scrambling
desperately to bring their weapons into play while holding
on to the railing. Kurshin managed to yank his gun hand free,
and he raked the barrel against McGarvey's skull with every
ounce of his strength, causing the American to reel away.

McGarvey was like an animal driven by wounded rage.
He recovered instantly, batting the gun away as Kurshin fired,
the shot going wide, and the automatic slipping from his grasp
and falling overboard.

An incredible pain stitched Kurshin's side, just below the
gunshot wound. He had a split instant to realize that he had
been stabbed—McGarvey's knife hand coming around
again—when he kicked out, the heel of his boot catching the
American full in the chest.

He turned and clambered on all fours back up the stairs to
the deck of the ship, mindless of his wounds.

At the top, he raced forward to Budanov's body where he
snatched up the man's Kalashnikov rifle, spun back on his
heel and fired off a burst just as McGarvey started to come
over the side.

The American either ducked or fell back, but Kurshin
didn't wait to see. He turned again and raced forward around
the superstructure to the foredeck where he flattened himself
against the bulkhead. His breath was coming raggedly, and
he didn't know how much longer he could hold on.

He raised his left wrist to his eyes and tried to focus on

the watch numerals. It was 9:55. The missile would fire in
five minutes.

He looked across at the Tomahawk elevated in its cradle,
barely ten feet away. When its engines fired he would die.
But he would have succeeded. He would have won. And that
was all that counted now, because in the end McGarvey would
be dead too.

McGarvey eased up again over the top of the rail and peered
down the length of the port-side deck toward the bow of the
ship. A man lay crumpled in a heap by an open doorway.
But it wasn't Kurshin.

Time. It always came down to a matter of time, he thought.
By now the missile was most likely in its countdown mode.
But the Russian would have set it to launch after he was clear
of the ship.

Or would he? Or had he been delayed? Or didn't he care?

Kurshin had called him the devil. They were two men cut,
in many respects, from the same cloth. Both of them were
killers. Only an accident of geography at the moment of their
births had determined which side they killed for.

But Kurshin had murdered his own people for expediency's
sake, hadn't he? Was there any difference between that and
what he himself had done? By his own mistakes he had caused
the deaths of a lot of good people. Their names and faces
were always with him.

Who then was the worst: the killer by commission or the
killer of innocent people by omission?

McGarvey pulled himself the rest of the way over the rail,
paused in the darkness for just a second, and then raced
forward on the balls of his feet toward the open doorway
halfway up the port-side passageway.

Kurshin reached around the corner and fired a quick burst,
raking the deck just as McGarvey ducked inside.

Without hesitation, McGarvey raced down the corridor to
the starboard side, where he flung open the door with a crash.
Then, careful to make no noise, he turned and hurried back
the same way he had come.

Kurshin would be watching the starboard-side passageway now. He hoped.

Nothing moved on the port side as McGarvey emerged from the doorway, and stepping over the body of a man whose face had been mostly shot away, he sprinted forward.

Sensing something behind him, Kurshin started to turn as McGarvey reached him, shoving him up against the bulkhead, the point of the stiletto beneath his chin.

"When is it set to launch?" McGarvey shouted.

Kurshin tried to struggle, but McGarvey increased the pressure on the stiletto, drawing a little blood.

"When?" he shouted.

Kurshin smiled. "Why don't we stay here like this and find out together? We have a lot to talk over, you and I."

"I'll kill you now!"

"Then we'll die together," Kurshin whispered. The moment the words escaped his lips he realized he had made a mistake.

McGarvey saw it in the Russian's eyes. The missile was going to launch at any moment.

"Sonofabitch," Kurshin shouted, and he gave a massive heave.

McGarvey was off balance and he stumbled backward, the point of the razor-sharp blade raking Kurshin's throat, opening up a five-inch-long gash that instantly spurted blood.

The Russian was incredibly fast. In four long steps he was across the foredeck and at the rail.

"No," McGarvey screamed, the sound nearly animalistic in its intensity. He threw the stiletto with every ounce of his strength at the same moment Kurshin disappeared over the side. A second later there was a big splash and then the night was quiet.

McGarvey turned and faced the missile. The countdown was started now.

He forced himself to calm down. To think it out. To remember something of what Frank Newman had told them.

Stepping forward around the base of the missile launcher, he found the control panel with its single switch. He flipped it, and the launch rack immediately began to descend. But slowly. Too slowly.

The Tomahawk's guidance system was in its nose cone, Newman had told them. There was a small access panel just a few inches from its tip.

But it was too high to reach yet.

Ten screws, Newman had said. It would take time to remove them.

He spotted the screwdriver lying on the deck, and he picked it up.

"If they've placed a timer circuit in the firing mechanism, we're going to have to first determine if removing it will cause the rocket to fire anyway," Newman had said. "It's possible they installed fail-safe devices. We'll just have to see."

The missile's nose finally came down within reach. McGarvey found the access panel and began taking out the screws one at a time, working as fast as he could. But his fingers were slippery with blood, his own as well as Kurshin's, and twice he dropped the screwdriver.

The last screw jammed. Not bothering with it, he jammed the blade of the screwdriver in the crack between the nearly loose panel and the missile's casing, and pried it outward. The screwdriver snapped, but the panel had come far enough open so that he could get his fingers beneath it.

He gave it one last heave, and it finally pulled away with a loud screech.

Directly inside the access panel he could see the timer mechanism, its counter switching to eight seconds.

Reaching in, he pulled it out, extending it delicately on its wires.

The counter switched to seven.

The interior of the nose cone was filled with circuit boards, components sealed in black boxes, and a rat's maze of wiring.

Six.

McGarvey tried to make some sense of it. "At the very least, we might try disconnecting the TERCOM unit, if we have the time," Newman had explained.

Five.

But there was no time. And Newman was dead, most likely. He'd taken at least two or three hits to the chest.

Four.

Of course if the missile launched now, in the down position, it would explode here aboard the ship.

Three.

Baranov would not have won, this time. But he would try again. Time was on his side. Time, patience, ruthlessness. There would be others to take Kurshin's place.

Two.

McGarvey reached inside the missile and grabbed a handful of wires. Still he hesitated.

One.

He yanked with all of his might, pulling the entire bundle of wires free from their connections to the various circuit boards.

The counter on the timer switched to zero. A tiny buzz sounded from somewhere within the body of the missile, and then the night fell silent, except for the gentle lap of the wavelets against the hull of the ship.

BOOK FOUR

54

THE WHITE HOUSE

THE PRESIDENT'S NATIONAL SECURITY ADVISER, GENERAL Donald Acheson, put down his telephone with a big grin. For just a moment or two he held himself in check, but then he jumped up, rushed out of his office past his startled secretary, and hurried down the corridor to the president's study.

Knocking once, he let himself in.

The president, seated comfortably in his favorite easy chair, was talking with the Senate majority and minority leaders. He barely glanced at Acheson, but he suddenly smiled.

"Well, I think that about wraps it up then," he said, getting to his feet.

Senators Reid and Hubbard were only momentarily startled. But they too got up, shaking hands with the president.

They gave Acheson a curious look as they left, but they said nothing.

"What have you got?" the president asked the moment the door was closed.

"We've beat the bastards. O'Malley just called from the Pentagon, he's on his way over with the full report."

"Thank God," the president said softly. "Was it Arkady Kurshin after all?"

"Yes, Mr. President. McGarvey killed him."

"Did we suffer any casualties?"

"Two killed, one of them a naval intelligence officer, and the other the staffer O'Malley had sent over."

"Did we take any prisoners?"

"Apparently not."

The president's jaw tightened. "Good," he said. "We'll have to invent a cover story, of course. Our two people were killed in an accident during a routine training mission. It's tough, especially for their families, but I'm definitely putting a lid on this entire business. And there *will not* be any leaks."

"Yes, sir."

"You say Admiral O'Malley is on his way over?"

"Yes, sir. He said he'd be here within twenty minutes."

"Get Murphy over here, and you'd better try to reach Sterling Miller at NSA. I'll give Jim Baldwin a call."

"Are we going to meet here or in the situation room?"

"Here will be fine," the president said. "What about McGarvey? Is he all right?"

"From what I understand he came out of it okay, Mr. President."

"Good. That's very good. We're going to need him."

The president made it obvious that he was switching off the recording equipment in his desk. No one in the room missed the significance of his action.

Admiral O'Malley had come over from the Joint Chiefs with the report on the "Incident," as they were calling it, and everyone had had a chance to read it.

"That's it, then," Secretary of State James Baldwin said,

looking up over the tops of his reading glasses. "A first-class job on McGarvey's part."

"It's Baranov, of course," the president said.

"We can't know that for sure," Baldwin replied. He looked to Roland Murphy for support, but the DCI shook his head.

"I can't agree. It's him all right."

"None of those bodies carried any ID that would link them to the KGB."

"Of course not."

"In fact there was nothing aboard that ship that in any way linked them to the Soviet Union."

"Aside from the fact they used Soviet-made weapons," Admiral O'Malley said.

"Readily available on the open market," Baldwin replied sharply. He looked this time to National Security Agency Director Sterling Miller for support. "Your people came up with no communications intercepts, nothing that would indicate an operation of this magnitude was being directed out of Moscow?"

"Nothing."

Murphy leaned forward on the couch. "You don't seem to understand, Jim, that this was a Baranov operation. The normal lines of communication between Moscow and the KGB's field stations would not have been used."

"Then there's no proof linking the Soviets to this . . ."

Murphy shrugged. "We may never have positive identification of their bodies, and Kurshin's wasn't found. But some of them were certainly the submarine drivers. The others brought the *Stephos* out to the rendezvous. The Tomahawk missile was on board. Its serial number matched the one aboard the *Indianapolis*. I don't think you can possibly argue that they didn't hijack the sub, kill the crew, steal the missile, and scuttle the boat. You can't deny that."

"I'm not denying anything, General, except for the fact we have no hard facts. Nothing that would stand up in a court of law. Nothing that the president could use to take to Gorbachev. There simply isn't that kind of hard proof here.

Kurshin was a fanatic, that's all. He managed to put together a crew who, as incredible as it still seems to me, managed to get away with this. Or very nearly managed to. But there is nothing concrete linking that act of piracy and international terrorism with Moscow.''

"He's right," General Acheson agreed. "But it doesn't alter the fact that we all know damned well that Baranov, with or without the consent of the Politburo, engineered this thing.''

"So what do we do about it, Donald?" Baldwin asked. "Exactly what is it you are suggesting?''

Acheson started to reply, but the president held him off.

"We'll get to that in just a minute, Jim. First we have two other aspects of this situation to consider.''

No one said a thing, but they all knew what was coming.

"The first, of course, is the Israelis. The cat's out of the bag, so to speak. The Soviets know that they have battle-ready nuclear weapons. They won't let that go. It's going to put Peres in a very difficult situation.''

"All they have to do is hold tight and keep their mouths shut," Baldwin said.

"Do you think they'll do that?''

"If they're smart," Baldwin said softly. "We can bring certain pressures to bear.''

"I'm not so sure it would work this time.''

"It damned well better, Mr. President, lest another can of worms is opened over there.''

"For instance?''

"The Soviets have a very good case for introducing nuclear weapons to the region, for instance. For another instance, Peres might finally listen to his military advisers and make a preemptive strike somewhere. Just to show their muscle.''

"Do you actually think that's possible?" the president asked.

"I do. They'll take whatever steps are necessary to protect their current advantage.''

A small glint of triumph crossed the president's eyes.

"Which brings us to the second consideration. Valentin Illen Baranov."

"Kurshin was his man, Mr. President," Murphy said. "There's no doubt about it."

"Nor do I feel that Baranov will give up so easily. He's a tenacious bastard."

"Gorbachev will take care of him," Baldwin said.

"I think it's gone beyond that, Jim," the president replied thoughtfully. "From what I've read he's consolidated his power over the past couple of years, ever since he brought Powers down."

"Something like that could not happen again, Mr. President," Murphy said with a tight jaw. Donald Suthland Powers had been one of the best directors of central intelligence that the Agency had ever known. Baranov had ruined him, and in the end had been at least the indirect cause of his death.

"Don't be so sure," the president said ominously.

"What are you suggesting, Mr. President?" Baldwin said, a dangerous edge in his voice.

The president's eyes never left Murphy. "Is he still in East Berlin?"

"Yes, Mr. President, through the weekend. Unless of course he reacts to the news that his latest operation has failed, and he runs back to Moscow. That's possible."

"Is it possible, General, to reactivate McGarvey?"

"I won't hear of this, Mr. President," Baldwin blurted. "With all respect, sir, we cannot sink to that level."

"Is it possible?" the president asked.

"Yes it is."

"What would his chances be?"

"This time, not very good. Baranov will know, or guess, that McGarvey is coming for him."

"Because of Dr. Abbott?"

"Yes, and because of the Powers thing. McGarvey, as you know, was involved."

"What about Dr. Abbott?" Baldwin asked.

"She was kidnapped from her hotel in West Berlin," Murphy explained. "We have good reason to suspect that it was Baranov's people who took her."

"Why? What use can she be to him, especially now?"

"Bait," Murphy said.

"For whom, for what?"

"McGarvey. He and Dr. Abbott . . . apparently have a thing for each other."

"Good Lord," Baldwin said. He turned again to the president. "Mr. President, if you mean to send McGarvey into East Germany to assassinate Baranov, then you will have my resignation as Secretary of State immediately."

"I won't accept it, Jim," the president said. "But I am sending McGarvey across. To rescue Dr. Abbott. We cannot simply abandon her."

"He's an assassin."

"Yes, he is."

"And Baranov, if Roland is correct, is waiting for him. Expecting him to come across."

"That's true as well," the president said. "Can he pull it off, General?"

"I honestly don't know, Mr. President. But I suspect that if anyone can do it, he can. He's motivated."

Baldwin was shaking his head angrily. "If it gets back to us, it could topple your administration."

"Well, it's my administration, Jim. And it's a risk I'm willing to take, this time."

55

CG WORDEN

THE 8200-TON LEAHY-CLASS GUIDED MISSILE CRUISER STOOD off about twenty miles to the west of the MV *Stephos*. The sun was just coming up over the eastern horizon. McGarvey squinted his eyes against the glare as the Sikorsky MH-53E Sea Dragon minesweeper helicopter came in low and slow.

From where he stood on the after bridge deck with Executive Officer Tom Nielson, he could see the Tomahawk missile in its sling fifty feet beneath the belly of the chopper.

Nielson, a tall lanky man with bright red hair and freckles, smiled grimly. "That's that," he said. He glanced over at McGarvey. "Hell of a job you did out there, sir."

McGarvey nodded, but he didn't take his eyes off the incoming helicopter. "Any word on the *Indianapolis* and her crew yet?"

"No, sir. The *Pigeon* won't be sending down the DSRV until later this morning. But it doesn't look good."

"No," McGarvey mumbled. None of it had looked good from the beginning. It had been a bloodbath from start to finish. The carnage aboard the *Stephos* was hard to comprehend. Kurshin's Russian crews had done their jobs, and their reward was a bullet in the brain. There will be no witnesses, Baranov had undoubtedly told Kurshin. And that's exactly what had happened.

Ainslie had been killed outright, most of his skull destroyed, and when they had gotten to Potok, half of his left arm blown away; Newman was dead and they had had to pry his body away from the Israeli's iron-hard grip.

Potok had been brought here to the *Worden* where the ship's doctor had stabilized his condition and had patched up his arm as best he could under the circumstances. As soon as the Tomahawk was safely aboard he would be flown up to Tel Aviv.

The comms speaker blared. "Mr. Nielson, is Mr. McGarvey with you, sir?"

"Aye, aye," Nielson said, keying the comms.

"Admiral DeLugio is on the radiotelephone, he would like to speak with Mr. McGarvey. Afterward, the captain would like you both in the wardroom."

"We're on our way."

The Sea Dragon hovered over the landing pad at the stern, and the loading crews were guiding the Tomahawk onto a mobile cradle. There was only a light swell running, and the crews were expert, so the transfer went smoothly. When the missile was finally down, McGarvey went with Nielson into the bridge, where one of the ratings handed him the telephone.

"Kirk McGarvey, is that you?" DeLugio shouted.

"Yes, sir."

"The Navy wants to thank you. Admiral O'Malley sends his personal thanks."

"Too little too late, Admiral," McGarvey said. He didn't feel much like celebrating. He wanted only to go to bed and sleep for a week, get roaring drunk, and fetch Lorraine Abbott from West Berlin—not necessarily in that order.

"But you stopped the bastards, McGarvey."

"Yes, sir," McGarvey replied. "Was there anything else?"

DeLugio hesitated for a beat. "Not from this end. But I have an urgent message for you from your boss. You're to meet with Trotter ASAP."

"There on Crete?"

"Negative. He's gone to Athens. He said you'd know where. We'll get you there this morning via Tel Aviv. The Israelis want to talk to you first. How's Major Potok?"

"I haven't talked to him since he came out of the operating room. But I'm told he'll live."

"Listen up, McGarvey," DeLugio said, a note of caution in his voice now. "As I've already said, you did a hell of a fine job for us out there. But you're going to have to watch what you say to the Israelis. They're going to want to know a lot more than you're authorized to tell them. That comes from the top, the very top. I hope I've made myself clear."

"Don't worry, Admiral, your secrets are safe with me. Besides, I don't know anything."

"I'm sorry, McGarvey," DeLugio said after another beat. "I take my orders too."

"Yeah," McGarvey said, and he hung up the telephone. He stood there for a long moment, looking through the forward windows toward the long bow of the ship. Time to get out now, he thought. But the job wasn't finished. Trotter was waiting for him. There was very little mystery about what he would say.

"Sir?" Nielson said.

McGarvey looked up. "Right," he said.

He followed the executive officer below to officers' territory. There was a lot of activity aboard the ship. The Navy SEAL unit that Admiral DeLugio had sent out was back from the *Stephos*, and Marine guards, sidearms at their hips, seemed to be everywhere.

Nielson knocked once on the wardroom door and then they went in. Lieutenant Commander Bruce McDonald was seated at the highly polished mahogany table with the *Worden*'s missile officer, Lieutenant Sam Nakajima.

They both looked up.

"Did you speak with Admiral DeLugio?" McDonald asked. He was a sharp, compact man with thinning, ash-brown hair.

"Just now," McGarvey said, taking a seat across the table from him. "How is Major Potok doing?"

"Just fine. In fact, better than we expected he would. He's awake now and he's asking for you. We'll be flying both of you up to Tel Aviv as soon as the Tomahawk is secure belowdecks."

"What about the *Stephos*?"

"The Israeli Navy has taken her under tow. They're taking her up to their Kishon Naval Base at Haifa," McDonald said. "And we owe you another debt of gratitude. The SEALS found and disarmed the Labun gas cylinder, as well as the explosives. It would have made quite a mess had they gone off." He shook his head. "Your Russian was some sonofabitch."

"Yes, he was," McGarvey said.

"This is probably no time to tell you this, Mr. McGarvey," Lieutenant Nakajima said. "But you were damned lucky. You pulled out the right wires. The *only* right wires. Had you grabbed the bundle a half an inch to the left, the missile would have exploded. It was the self-destruct circuitry."

"I didn't have much of a choice."

Nakajima shook his head. "Well, sir, you've got balls."

There was nothing to say.

"Are you hungry? Do you want something to eat before you go?" McDonald asked.

McGarvey shook his head.

"All right, then," the captain said, getting to his feet. He stuck out his hand. McGarvey got up and shook it. "I'll add my personal thanks, McGarvey. You did good."

"That's what they're paying me for, Captain. Thanks for your hospitality."

"I'll take you down to Major Potok in sick bay now, sir," Nielson said.

"We'll have you out of here within twenty minutes," McDonald said. "Good luck."

Below and farther aft, McGarvey was shown into Potok's room. The Israeli's left arm was in a cast from the shoulder down, and he looked pale and very drawn. But he was dressed and sitting up on the edge of his cot.

The Navy doctor with him was checking his eyes with a tiny light. When he was finished he straightened up and turned to McGarvey. "I've given Major Potok a stimulant that should keep him mobile for another few hours. But no longer. When he crashes he damned well better be in a medical facility."

"I'll see to it. Thanks, Doctor," McGarvey said.

The doctor glanced down again at Potok, and then he and Nielsen withdrew from the room.

"How do you feel, Lev?" McGarvey asked.

"Like *dreck*, but at least I'm feeling," Potok said. His voice was weak.

"They're moving you by chopper to Tel Aviv in the next few minutes. Apparently I'm to go with you. But you have to know from the start, Lev, that I'm not going to be able to tell your people very much more than they already know."

"We don't want much from you, Kirk. But we have something to say to you. Something . . . something very important. We owe you."

"But not now?" McGarvey asked.

"No. Not here. In Tel Aviv. There is a man who wishes to speak to you."

"Who?"

"I can't give you his name. Not yet. But what he has to say is critical. Believe me."

"I do," McGarvey said.

GROSSER MÜGGELSEE

The uncertain dawn came cool and gray. Lorraine Abbott stood at the window of her second-floor room looking down at the driveway. She was in East Germany, near a lake. She knew at least that much, as well as the fact that something had happened overnight. Something that was causing her Russian captors some consternation.

It was Kirk, she thought, and the certainty gave her a small measure of comfort.

A black Mercedes sedan had pulled up and two bulky men had gotten out. They were standing below now speaking with the short, heavily built man who had identified himself as Baranov. From what she could gauge of their actions, they seemed to be happy. They had received some good news, and her spirits sank again.

She turned away from the window. Her room was large and extremely well furnished, with a spacious, pleasant bathroom. Since her kidnapping and hasty trip across the border in the trunk of a car, she had been forced to remain here. She had not been mistreated; her meals came regularly and were very good. But she had not been given a radio or television, nor had she been allowed any reading material.

Most of the time she had spent with her ear to the wall or door, listening to what was going on in the rest of the house, or watching from the window.

Baranov had spoken to her only once, when they had first brought her here. He had merely introduced himself and promised that no harm would come to her. But in that brief exchange she had been struck with the man's charisma. He exuded a raw, but controlled, power. His eyes, she had decided, had the capability of looking inside of her. The experience had been chilling.

In the bathroom she splashed some cold water on her face, and then looked into her own eyes. They were clear, although she was frightened. Eventually they would have to let her go. Eventually they would have to take her back to West Berlin. Her major fear at the moment was that her release wouldn't come soon enough to stop Kirk from coming here first.

Now that she had met Baranov, and seen something of his organization—she had spotted at least three guards outside —she didn't think Kirk would have much of a chance against them.

Back at the window, she looked down at the driveway. The Mercedes was still there, but the men were nowhere in sight. She was craning her head to see toward the side of the house when the lock at her door clicked.

She turned as the door opened and Baranov entered the room, a gentle, almost wistful smile on his features, wrinkling the corners of his deep-set eyes. She thought he looked like the typical picture of a Russian peasant. Except for his power, which no peasant had.

"Good morning, Dr. Abbott, I'm happy to see that you're up. It's us early risers who do best in the world, don't you agree?"

Baranov's voice was soft and cultured, his English gently British in its intonations.

"When are you going to release me?" Lorraine demanded.

"Very soon now," Baranov said. "Your breakfast should be up in a minute or so. I thought I'd take this time to have a little chat with you. It seems a friend of ours will be showing up here soon."

Lorraine's blood ran cold. "Who is that?" she managed to ask, though her voice sounded shaky in her own ears.

"Kirk McGarvey, of course. He and I are very old friends. We go way back together. But of course I'm sure he told you this."

"How do you know he's coming here?"

"Oh, dear lady, I have my sources," Baranov chuckled. "You can't imagine."

"What do you want?" she suddenly cried. "Why are you doing this now?"

Baranov's eyes narrowed slightly. "What do you mean by 'this'? 'Now'?"

"You know damned well what I'm talking about. Whatever

little plan your killer, Arkady Kurshin, was supposed to carry out backfired on you. Kirk stopped him. Now there's nothing left.''

Baranov's jaw was tight. Lorraine thought she could almost hear or feel a thrumming vibration coming from him; as if a low-pitched string had been plucked within his body, or as if he were a high-tension line. For just that moment she felt as if she were very close to death.

She backed up against the curtains.

''What did he tell you in your little West Berlin love nest, dear lady?'' Baranov asked, his voice controlled. He advanced a pace. ''What little secrets did he whisper into your ear at the moment of consummation?''

''I don't know what you're talking about.''

''I think you do,'' Baranov said, advancing another pace toward her. ''And do you know what? You're going to talk to me this morning. You're going to tell me simply everything that you know.''

He took another pace forward. At that moment Lorraine stepped away from the window, all of her weight on her left foot as she kicked out with every ounce of her strength with her right, the toe of her low-heeled shoe connecting solidly with Baranov's groin.

The man didn't even flinch.

He reached out slowly, took a handful of her hair, and, as if he were gently leading a horse by its mane, led her across the room where, with his free hand, he slapped her face, knocking her nearly unconscious down on the bed.

56

TEL AVIV

THE MORNING WAS VERY BRIGHT, HEAT SHIMMERING UP FROM the tarmac as McGarvey and Potok hobbled down the Sea Dragon's aft loading ramp.

They had not said much to each other on the three-hundred-mile flight from the *Worden*. Potok had laid his head back and had closed his eyes. He was on the verge of collapse. "Just one more thing to do," he'd said.

McGarvey let his thoughts drift back and forth between Lorraine Abbott and John Trotter. It wasn't finished, of course, and would not be until Baranov was destroyed. He'd known that all along. He'd known it most acutely the moment he had seen the look of triumph in Kurshin's eyes. He'd thought he had won. There would be others like him, other handmaidens to Baranov. Sooner or later they would succeed.

He was filled with fear now; Baranov had become his worst nightmare, and Lorraine Abbott his greatest challenge. He had thought of both of them as Kurshin died.

But he was an assassin.

He would give Baranov death, or die trying. What could he give to Lorraine? He had nothing. Men such as he never did.

They had landed on the military side of Lod Airport. A fuel truck lumbered across the taxiway, toward the helicopter, at the same moment an army jeep raced over from the AMAN Headquarters building a half-mile away.

Potok's number two, Abraham Liebowitz, was driving. He pulled up at the base of the ramp, jumped out, and hurried around to them. He said something in Hebrew.

"In English," Potok said, straightening up.

Liebowitz glanced at McGarvey. "He's waiting for us. If you want, I can take care of everything. You should be in the hospital."

Potok shook his head. "No," he said. "We owe this man, Abraham. I'll see it through."

He helped Potok into the front seat, and McGarvey climbed in the back as Liebowitz got behind the wheel. He turned around.

"We have a plane standing by for you, Mr. McGarvey. As soon as we're finished here you'll be flown directly to Athens. In the meantime, is there anything I can get for you, or arrange?"

"No," McGarvey said. He was very tired, and it was difficult at this moment to keep his thoughts straight. But as they drove back across the field toward the collection of low cement-block buildings, he knew that what he had done hadn't been for Israel. It had been for himself.

In fact, he thought, turning that notion over in his mind, everything he had ever done had been for himself. Some inner need to prove himself, over and over again. To prove his strength, his virility, his loyalty, his honor. And again he was struck with the idea that there wasn't very much difference between himself and men such as Kurshin, other than their place of birth.

Someone had asked him once if he was proud of what he had done for his country. He had wanted to immediately say Yes, of course I'm proud. But something had stayed him. He hadn't known the answer to that question then, and he didn't know it now.

They pulled up at the rear of one of the three-story buildings and inside took the elevator up to the top floor, where Liebowitz ushered them into a small conference room.

A very short man, with longish white hair and hunched shoulders, stood looking out the window toward the U.S. Navy helicopter that had brought them in. He wore a shapeless dark suit, the collar of his white shirt on the outside of his jacket. When he turned around McGarvey was struck by the knowledge, understanding, and sympathy in the man's eyes. If there were an opposite of Baranov, this man was he.

"Are you up to this, Lev?" he asked.

"I want to see it through, sir," Potok said.

"Then sit down, please. Everyone."

They sat down across the bare table from him. A pair of fighter-interceptors roared across the field, and when the sound faded McGarvey thought he could hear his own heart.

"Do you know who I am, Mr. McGarvey?"

"Isser Shamir. Director of the Mossad," McGarvey replied. It was highly classified information in Israel.

Shamir inclined his head. "Just so. It would seem that the range of your knowledge is quite good. Good enough, I believe, for you to understand that I'm not given to idle boasting, false accusations, or rumors."

"I've heard that, sir," McGarvey said. He was beginning to get an uncomfortable feeling that he had not been brought here merely to be thanked. There was something else going on.

"Israel would like to offer you her gratitude. Twice now you have saved my country from something very terrible, each time at the extreme risk of your own life."

"There is no debt of gratitude, Mr. Shamir."

"Oh, but there is, Mr. McGarvey. And Israel pays her debts. Always." Shamir glanced over at Potok, and then back again. He seemed to be debating with himself, as if he were carrying an impossibly heavy burden that made any kind of a decision nearly out of the question.

"My government knows what is stored at En Gedi, Mr. Director. And so do the Russians."

"Yes. It will forever change the politics of this region. The age of our innocence—as bloody as it has been—is gone. That cannot be altered."

"That's a matter for the politicians, not for me."

"But you are not finished, I believe," Shamir said, watching him carefully. "Am I correct in assuming that you will make an attempt in the very near future on the life of Valentin Baranov?"

McGarvey held his surprise in check. "I can't say."

"This operation has the backing of your Agency and, I would suspect, even your president."

McGarvey said nothing.

"Such an operation would take planning. The need-to-know list will be quite small, nevertheless there are others who know what your orders are. The specifics of your orders."

"Even if that were the case, you know that I could not discuss it with you."

"There will have been some agonizing over this decision, I think . . ."

McGarvey got to his feet. "I'm sorry, sir, but I would like to leave now."

"As I said, Mr. McGarvey, Israel owes you a debt of gratitude. I would like to repay it now by saving your life."

"Please, Kirk," Potok said. "Sit down and merely listen to what we have to tell you. I promise you will not be asked to reveal anything sensitive to your government. You have my word."

"And mine," Shamir said.

"What do you want with me?" McGarvey asked, his voice tight in his throat. "What more do you want?"

"En Gedi was penetrated, Kirk," Potok said.

McGarvey turned to him. "By the Russians, yes we know this. They needed the proof and they got it."

"We thought he was one of us. He went by the name of Benjamin Rothstein. His real name was Vladimir Ivanovich Tsarev. KGB. He worked directly for Baranov."

"How did you find this out?"

"It's not important. Listen to me, Kirk. En Gedi was penetrated twice. Once by a man named Simon Asher. He died in the . . . vault, trying to sabotage one of the . . ." Potok cut it off, and he glanced at Shamir.

"Go on," the old man said softly.

"Asher was trying to sabotage one of our nuclear weapons. We think he may have been trying to set it off. We're not sure about that part."

"He worked for the Russians too?" McGarvey asked. It was typical of a Baranov operation. The man covered all of his bases. He never relied on a single line of action. Always there were many paths down which his people were directed.

"He had one connection with the Russians. With the same man who was Tsarev's control officer here in Israel. We didn't find that out until later. By then we had found out something else . . . something even more disturbing."

"Go on," McGarvey prompted.

"Kirk, we are very sure of our facts. I can't tell you how we came to know what we do, but it has to do with thousands of telephone intercepts, a records search that has taken us six weeks, and a complete search of . . . your own background. We checked your record, all the way from the day you joined the Agency until you were asked to resign after the incident in Santiago."

McGarvey's chest was suddenly tight. It felt as if all the air were being squeezed out of his lungs. "Is this how you repay your debts?" he asked sharply. "By spying on your friends?"

Shamir waved it off. "Our existence was and is at stake, Mr. McGarvey. And so now is yours, if you go up against Baranov without forewarning."

"What are you talking about?"

"Simon Asher worked for someone within the Central Intelligence Agency," Potok said.

McGarvey turned on him. "We would not have sent someone here with the intent of destroying your nuclear weapons and killing a lot of people in the process. Whatever we have done, it's not been that."

"I agree," Shamir said. "This man whom Asher worked for, also works for Baranov. He was another aspect of the plan to neutralize our ability to defend ourselves."

"How do you know?"

"I can't say," Shamir said. "But it is true." He took a folded sheet of paper out of his breast pocket and handed it across the table.

McGarvey didn't immediately reach for it. "Who is it?"

"We don't know for sure," Shamir said.

"You just said . . ."

"We have it narrowed to five names. Five men who could have caused what has happened over the past ten or more years. There are no other possibilities."

Still McGarvey made no move to take the piece of paper.

"You will not be allowed to take this list with you when you leave this room, Mr. McGarvey. And we will deny ever having had this conference with you. You must understand this."

Slowly McGarvey reached out and took the paper from Shamir's outstretched hand. He glanced at Potok, whose eyes were shining, and Liebowitz, who had looked away.

He opened the paper. Five names had been typed in the middle of the page. All the air left the room.

57

ATHENS

MCGARVEY LOST HIMSELF IN THE CROWDS OF HELLINIKON Airport. He had come in on what was treated as a diplomatic flight, and his passport and single bag had not been checked.

Instead of going directly out to the cab ranks, he had doubled back into the main international terminal, where he hung around for nearly a half-hour, watching over his shoulder.

Paranoia comes to every field officer sooner or later. But what happens when there's a reason for it? Then it's time, he'd been taught, to trust no one: friends, wives, lovers— none of them were free of suspicion.

It was a few minutes after three in the afternoon when he finally decided that he had come away clean, and he went down to the Hertz counter to rent a car. He had waited until the flight from London had touched down and its passengers had been released from customs so that the crowds were particularly heavy. His was just another face in the crowd.

You shall be known by your tradecraft. That bit of wisdom had been drummed into his head at the CIA's training facility outside of Williamsburg, called The Farm. When in doubt, change it, do the unexpected.

There were a lot of people around the car rental counter, some of them families, others businessmen anxious to get a car and be on their way. McGarvey allowed himself to be jostled in line until he got himself behind a man of the same general build and height, carrying an overnight bag over his shoulder, while shoving two heavy suitcases forward with his foot.

The man's passport wallet jutted out of a side compartment of the overnight bag.

Five minutes later, when they finally got up to one of the busy clerks and the man reached into his overnight bag for his identification, it was gone.

"Oh, bloody hell," he swore, his accent British. He unzipped his bag and frantically searched inside.

"Sir?" the young woman behind the counter asked with concern.

"What's the matter, old man?" McGarvey asked.

The Brit looked up. "My passport, money, identification . . . everything. It's gone."

"Maybe it's in one of your suitcases?"

"No, I just had it coming through customs. I must have dropped the bloody thing." He was extremely agitated.

"I thought I saw an information booth upstairs on the main floor," McGarvey said helpfully. "Maybe someone's turned it in."

"Right, mate," the Brit said, and he stepped out of line, snatched up his suitcases, and rushed off.

"Good luck," McGarvey said to his retreating figure. It would be nothing more than an inconvenience to the Englishman. His embassy would supply him with new papers, and no doubt his home office would arrange for funds.

Turning back to the clerk, he rented a Ford Taurus, and a half an hour later he was making his way through heavy traffic into the city.

As he drove he kept looking in his rearview mirror for any sign that he was being followed. But by the time he had reached the city proper he was convinced he was completely clean.

It was nearly five by the time he found a place to park the car near the Athens Academy off Venizelou Street. He had kept the nine-millimeter automatic that the Israelis had given him. He took it out of his bag, loaded it, and stuffed it in his belt at the small of his back.

Next he opened the passport wallet that he had lifted from the hapless Brit at the airport. The man's name was Gordon Gutherie, and he was from London. Besides his passport, the wallet contained eight hundred fifty pounds, about half that much in drachmas, a driver's license, half a dozen major credit cards, and a collection of various business cards, photographs, notes, and one slip of paper on which was written only a telephone number. From what McGarvey could gather, the man had something to do with Ford-Leland, some sort of an engineer or factory rep. Whoever, he was reasonably well heeled.

McGarvey took a moment to study the passport and driver's license photographs. They had been taken at two different times, and really didn't look like the same man. Nor did Gutherie look much like him. But at a busy border crossing at night it might work. He'd managed to cross other borders on much shakier documents.

Stuffing the passport wallet in his coat pocket, he locked up the car and walked, overnight bag in hand, down the block where he found a cab.

"Where in God's name have you been?" Trotter demanded, opening the door of the Askilipiou safehouse where they'd met the last time.

"Covering my ass," McGarvey said, coming in and dropping his bag on the couch.

Trotter closed and locked the door behind him, and then went to the window, where he parted the curtain and looked down at the street. "Do you think you were followed?"

"If there was anyone waiting at the airport for me, I lost them," McGarvey said, pouring himself a stiff cognac from the sideboard and drinking it. He poured himself another.

"Was it Arkady Kurshin? No doubts in your mind, Kirk?"

"No doubts," McGarvey said. "The man is dead."

"Have we got his body?"

"Not yet."

"For Christ's sake, Kirk, what happened out there? I've only been getting bits and pieces. And what in heaven's name did the Israelis want with you?"

"There's no time for that now," McGarvey said, turning away from the sideboard. "Is Baranov still in East Berlin, at the Grosser Müggelsee house?"

"Yes, but he's scheduled to leave sometime tomorrow morning."

"So far as you know, my equipment is still in place in the boathouse?"

"It should be. We've kept our distance from the Lighthouse network. Nothing much else we could do under the circumstances. But of course you wouldn't be able to use them in any event, nor will you be able to use the Prenzauerberg apartment."

"I'm going after him, John. Tonight. Can you get me to West Berlin?"

"We've got an Air Force VIP jet standing by for you. It's a three-hour flight."

McGarvey stared at his old friend for a long time. Whom to trust? He'd never really known in this business. But Trotter had always been at the top of his short list.

"What?" Trotter asked.

"How about Murphy? Has he gone to the president with this? Is that why you wanted me back here?"

Trotter nodded. "You've got the green light, Kirk. From the president."

"No mistakes now. I want this perfectly clear between us. My orders are to assassinate Valentin Baranov, the director of the KGB. Is that correct?"

"Yes it is. From the president himself."

"Who else knows?"

"What do you mean?"

"Besides the president, General Murphy, you, and me, who else knows that I'm going across the border tonight to kill him?"

"I don't know. The president's advisers, possibly the secretary of state."

"How about in the Agency? Is Larry Danielle in on it?"

"Yes, I'm sure he . . ."

"Van Cleeve?" McGarvey asked. He was deputy director of intelligence. "Phil Carrara?" He was DDO, Trotter's boss.

"Phil, yes. But I don't know about Howard. What are you getting at?"

Again McGarvey stared at his friend for a long time. They had been through a lot together; too much?

"Someone is selling us out to the Russians. Selling me. Baranov knows every move I make. They're the ones who would be in the right position to know."

"And me, Kirk," Trotter said. "Don't forget about me." His eyes were wide and naked behind his thick glasses. He looked like a scarecrow. His clothes hung loosely on his thin frame.

"Do all of them know the details of my crossing, and about the equipment at the boathouse?"

"Some of it. But you don't have to do this. Just say no, Kirk. Everyone will understand. Good Lord, you've certainly done your bit. You've saved their ass twice now—at Ramstein, and aboard the *Stephos*. They've got no right to ask for more."

McGarvey managed a slight smile. "But you and they were right all along, John. This is a vendetta. The man has to be destroyed, or else he will destroy us all."

"There are other ways. There will be another time."

"Have you still got the Kurshin identification? I can still use it. There's no way for Baranov to be certain yet that Kurshin is actually dead."

"I've got it, Kirk. But not now. Please. Especially not now for you!"

The half-smile left McGarvey's face. "What is it, John? What aren't you telling me this time?"

Trotter stepped back almost as if he were suddenly afraid of McGarvey. His face was contorted with dismay. "I'm sorry . . . I . . ."

"What is it?"

"Murphy told me to keep my mouth shut."

"This is us talking now, John. You and I. Come on."

"It's Lorraine Abbott," Trotter blurted.

McGarvey's heart skipped a beat. "She's at the hotel in West Berlin. Your people are watching her."

"No," Trotter whispered.

"Where is she?"

"We don't know for sure. Not yet."

"John, goddamnit, talk to me."

"Kirk, she disappeared from the hotel a few hours after you had gone across. We think that Baranov took her. She's probably at the Grosser Müggelsee house with him now. As bait."

A black rage threatened to engulf him, blotting out all reason and sanity. But he held on. "Why wasn't I told?" he asked, his voice low, menacing.

"It was thought that stopping Kurshin and recovering the Tomahawk missile were more important . . ."

"By whom, John? Who thought that?"

"The president. General Murphy."

One of the names dropped off the Mossad list of suspected penetration agents.

"Were you going to let me go across tonight without telling me, John? Has it gone that far?"

"No, I swear it. If I couldn't talk you out of crossing, I promised myself that I'd tell you."

McGarvey believed him, though he no longer knew if he believed *in* the man.

"I'm going across. I'll kill Baranov and I'll bring Lorraine back with me." McGarvey looked directly into Trotter's eyes. "If anyone gets in my way, John, *anyone*, I'll kill them too."

Trotter swallowed hard. He nodded.

"When Baranov is dead, I'll return to Washington and finish the job. And I don't care who you tell that to."

58

GROSSER MÜGGELSEE

IT WAS NIGHT. VALENTIN ILLEN BARANOV STOOD AT THE water's edge gazing across the lake toward the mostly dark southern shore.

His mouth was foul from too many cigarettes, and most of his outward passion had been spent on his attack against Lorraine Abbott. There would be no permanent scars, at least not on her delicate body, but the encounter would be something she would never forget for the rest of her life.

The fire, however, still burned brightly within his breast. The great destroyer was finally coming. He had received the telephone call less than an hour ago, confirming the fact that McGarvey had come to Athens and was presently en route to West Berlin. There was no doubt what his plans were. He would come across the border using falsified documents that would identify him as Arkady Kurshin. He could not know that his cache of equipment in the boathouse had been discovered and had been tampered with.

Yenikeev had filed down a crucial part within the rebreather's regulator valve, making it very likely that it would fail, and McGarvey would drown.

If, by some chance, the man survived that, and brought the AK74 ashore with him, he would be in for another surprise. Yenikeev had removed the assault rifle's firing pin, rendering it useless.

In a very large way, Baranov fervently hoped that McGarvey would make it this far. He wanted to see the man's face with his own eyes. He wanted to look at the devil at the moment of his death.

For thirty years Baranov had made his plans, had bided his time when necessary, and leapt forward when it was possible. From Mexico to Cuba, from Czechoslovakia and Hungary to Laos and Vietnam, from Poland to Afghanistan, his touch had been felt. At home he had patiently consolidated his power, his cause getting an unexpected boost when that moderate fool, Gorbachev, had become party secretary with his prattle about *perestroika* and *glasnost*. There were still enough men in positions of power within the Rodina who distrusted that bastard.

The shift of power would have happened this year. There would have been a bloodless coup.

Would have been . . . except for one man. Depending upon what was waiting for him back in Moscow, the takeover could be delayed for years.

But McGarvey was coming here. This very night. It was going to give Baranov the greatest of pleasures to spit in his face when he was finally dead.

A dark figure appeared out of the woods to his left. Baranov flinched and started to step back before he realized that it was Yevgeni Mikhailovich Kedrov, the chief of his six-man bodyguard contingent.

"Comrade Chairman, you have a visitor at the house," Kedrov called softly.

"Who is it?" Baranov demanded. He'd half expected some of those fools from the Horst Wessel to come out here. The conference had gone as he had expected it would, even though he had been preoccupied with his own thoughts.

"A Militia captain."

Baranov's eyes narrowed. "From where?" The Militia were the Soviet Union's civilian police.

"Moscow. He says he's come here on orders to arrest you, sir."

For a moment Baranov could hardly believe his own ears. But then everything fell into place for him. Of course the American president would have called Gorbachev after the debacle in the Med. There had been no proof linking that operation to the KGB . . . no hard proof, that is. But Gorbachev would have instigated an investigation nonetheless.

He glanced again toward the opposite shore.

"Keep a sharp watch here, Yevgeni Mikhailovich. He'll be coming across tonight."

"Yes, Comrade Chairman. But what about that Militia captain?"

"Not to worry. I'll take care of it. Who is up there with him?"

"Sergei."

"Where are the others?"

"Dmitri and Leonty are on the road by the gate. Gennadi and Rotislav are here in the woods with me."

The house was perched on the crest of the hill overlooking the lake. On the other side of the hill was a broad swampy area thick with underbrush and brambles.

McGarvey was coming, and he was coming from across the lake. There was no doubt of it.

"Keep your eyes open," Baranov said again and he started up the path to the house, its lights visible through the woods.

On the way up he felt in his jacket pocket for the reassuring bulk of his pistol, and he smiled. The fools had sent a Militia captain out here to arrest him. It was ludicrous. He would return to Moscow, all right, but under his own power and in his own good time. Once there, they would never dare to arrest him. The Lubyanka was a fortress in more than one way, with its many dark secrets. Once home they would not touch him. They could not.

A Mercedes 240D was parked on the driveway in front of the house. A man sat behind the wheel. Baranov angled over to the car. As he approached, the car door opened and the man got out. He looked young and very nervous.

"You are Captain . . . ?" Baranov demanded.

"No, Comrade. I am Lieutenant Lubyanov," the young man said.

The irony of the man's last name was rare just at this moment, but Baranov suppressed a smile. "Your captain is in the house?"

"Yes, sir."

"What are your orders?"

The young man was embarrassed. "Ah . . . we were sent to . . ."

"Never mind," Baranov said, smiling warmly this time to put the man at ease. "I will speak with your captain. We'll get this straightened out in no time at all."

Baranov turned and walked up to the house. He could feel the young lieutenant's eyes on his back, and it irked him. But his control was marvelous, as it had always been.

He was met in the main stairhall by Sergei Sergeevich Nemchin, one of his bodyguards.

"Where is he?"

"In your study, Comrade Chairman," Nemchin said. "I didn't know what to do with the stupid bastard."

"What's his name?"

"Rybalkin. Nikolai Petrovich. He's a captain with the Moscow District Militia."

"Here to arrest me?"

"Yes, sir," Nemchin said with a laugh, but he seemed just a little nervous about it.

"Stay here, Sergei Sergeevich, I'll handle the captain."

Nemchin nodded. His jacket was off, and a big sweat stain had darkened his shirt beneath his shoulder holster.

"Stay here," Baranov repeated, and he went back to his

study, hesitated for just a moment at the door, and then went in.

Militia Captain Rybalkin was a moderately built man with thick black hair, which was combed straight back, and a broad honest face. Baranov thought the name might be familiar; perhaps his father or an uncle worked in Directorate One headquarters out on the circumferential highway.

"Good evening, Captain," Baranov said.

Rybalkin had been standing at the window looking outside. He nodded grimly. "Comrade Valentin Illen Baranov, I have come to place you under arrest and return you immediately to Moscow for prosecution."

"I see," Baranov said. "On what charges?"

"Treason."

Baranov's breath caught in his throat.

"I am under orders from Special Moscow District Prosecutor Kuryanov. Sir, I wish no trouble from you or your men."

"Nor shall you have any, Comrade Captain, if indeed you are who you claim to be, and you do have the orders and proper authority."

Rybalkin pulled out his Militia identification and held it up for Baranov to see. Then he handed over a sheaf of papers which was the Bill of Arrest.

Baranov took it to his desk, where he put on his glasses and quickly read through the legal document that named him and Arkady Kurshin as co-conspirators in three indictments: adventurism, engaging in acts contrary to Soviet law, and engaging in activities likely to bring harm to the Soviet Union.

It was Gorbachev, of course. But he had had no direct hand in this. He had simply pointed a special prosecutor in the right direction and allowed his much-vaunted "rights of Soviet law" to go into action.

Baranov looked up. The Militia captain was watching him closely.

"Call Sergei in here, would you please, Captain?"

Rybalkin's eyes narrowed and he stiffened, his hand going instinctively to the gun at his side.

"I promised you no trouble, Captain, and I meant it. But if I am to leave with you, I will have to instruct my people what to do here."

"Very well," Rybalkin said. "We will also require Comrade Kurshin to accompany us back to Moscow."

"That, I'm afraid, will be impossible. Major Kurshin is dead."

"Who killed him?"

"The Americans, I think."

"Where is his body?"

"That I couldn't say, Captain. But it is not here."

Again Rybalkin hesitated. It was clear that he understood something was not quite right here, and that he was probably in some sort of danger. But his orders were official. They were his protection.

He turned and had started to open the door into the corridor when Baranov withdrew his pistol from his pocket, switched the safety off, cocked the hammer, and fired two shots. The first bullet smashed into Rybalkin's left lung a couple of inches from his spine, and the second entered his head just below his left ear, slamming him against the door, where his legs collapsed and he fell dead.

The door was shoved open seconds later by a white-faced Nemchin, his pistol in hand.

"It was a mistake, Sergei Sergeevich," Baranov said. "He hadn't come here to arrest me at all. I think he was here to assassinate me."

Nemchin's eyes went from Rybalkin's body to the gun in Baranov's hand. "Yes, sir," he said.

"He probably works for the Americans. His lieutenant is out in the car. Kill him."

Nemchin hesitated for only an instant, but then turned on his heel and raced down the corridor. Baranov could hear his steps in the stairhall and the front door being flung open.

He folded the Bill of Arrest and put it in his pocket as he came around the desk. It would turn out, he supposed, that these two had been gunned down by McGarvey. Unfortunate.

Nemchin was back moments later. Baranov met him out in the corridor.

"The car is gone."

"He must have heard the shots. Call Dmitri at the gate. Have him stop the car."

Nemchin grabbed the walkie-talkie from the hall table and keyed it. "Dmitri, are you there?"

"Is that you, Sergei?"

"Yes. That Mercedes that came up a few minutes ago is on its way back down. Stop it."

"We can't. We just let him through."

Nemchin turned to Baranov who had heard the exchange. "Shall we go after him?"

Baranov thought about it for just a moment, then shook his head. "No, we'll attend to it later."

"But, Comrade . . ."

"Later," Baranov snapped, and Nemchin blanched.

59

BERLIN

IT WAS A FEW MINUTES AFTER 11:00 P.M. THE WEEKEND was winding down and traffic in West Berlin was almost frantic in its intensity. It seemed as if the city was trying to have fun at a breakneck speed, perhaps because so many Berliners thought there might not be a tomorrow.

McGarvey sat in the backseat of a cab waiting to cross the frontier. There were two cars ahead of them.

He had picked up the same Fiat with the East German license tags from the Operations hangar at Templehof. No one had been around this time to greet him, or to ask him any questions, and the airbase gate guard had simply waved him through.

He had driven directly up to the British Sector of the city where he had left the car and his Kurshin identification in a car park on Kant Strasse a couple of blocks west of the main post office and tourist information center. Then he had walked down to the bright lights of the Ku'damm where he had caught a cab.

Baranov would know that he was coming tonight. And the man would know that he would be using the Kurshin ID. It made him sick to think how long this had gone on. All this time Baranov had been at least one step ahead of him because of the penetration agent in Washington. Christ, it was galling.

Sitting in the cab, watching the lights of the crossing and the East German border guards doing their jobs, McGarvey tried not to think in any great detail about Lorraine Abbott. Baranov had taken her for bait. As extra insurance to make sure McGarvey would show up.

He didn't think Baranov would have harmed her. Not yet. The man would wait until later. In a way she was going to be the spoils for the victor; if Baranov won, she would be destroyed. McGarvey had to wonder: if he killed Baranov, would Lorraine have any better chance for survival?

Border restrictions between the east and west sectors of the city were almost nonexistent, though identification papers were still being demanded and closely scrutinized.

When it was finally their turn, McGarvey wound down his window and handed out his Gutherie passport.

The border guard looked up sharply from the passport photograph to McGarvey's face bathed in the harsh violet glow of the big lights.

"Do you have another form of identification? Something else with your photograph on it?"

"Bloody hell," McGarvey swore, but he dug out the driver's license and handed it out.

The guard studied it for several seconds. One of the other guards walked over and looked at the passport and driver's license and then studied McGarvey's face.

"Shake a leg, would you be so kind, chaps? I'm thirsty," McGarvey said. He feigned a little drunkenness.

"Where are you going at this hour?" the one guard demanded.

"The Palast Hotel, where the hell else would I be going?"

"Let me see your reservations," the guard asked. He looked on the seat beside McGarvey. "Where is your luggage?"

"I've got no reservations, you silly bugger. Don't you understand? I want a drink. A drink! When I'm done I'll be returning."

The West Berlin cabbie had turned in his seat. He didn't look happy. "Please, sir, I wish no trouble. Perhaps you should go back now."

"Where did you pick him up?" the guard asked the cabbie.

"The Ku'damm, where else?"

The guard nodded, hesitated just a moment longer, then handed the papers back to McGarvey. "See that you stay out of trouble, Herr Gutherie. You wouldn't find our jails pleasant."

McGarvey slouched down in his seat as they were waved through and the cab headed into the east zone. It was a matter of hard Western currencies, of course. The East Germans were allowing practically anything to attract American dollars, British pounds, or especially West German marks into the country. And who knew, maybe a strong-arm bandit would mug him. At least the money thus gained would find its way into the economy.

EAST BERLIN

This side of the city was much darker than the West, though traffic was about the same. A few minutes later the cabbie dropped him off in front of the modern Swedish-built hotel. McGarvey paid his fare and stumbled into the hotel, crossing the lobby and entering the relatively crowded bar.

He ordered a cognac, drank it down, then left the hotel, walking away without looking back.

It was possible that the border guards might have called the hotel, and that the security people there would be watching for him. They had been suspicious of the poor photographs in his passport and driver's license, and of his attitude.

A police car, its blue lights flashing, raced past as Mc-Garvey ducked into the darkness of a doorway. He watched until it turned a corner two blocks away, and then he hurried east, away from the Unter den Linden and the other well-lit main streets.

Four blocks away he found what he was looking for in a neighborhood of apartment buildings. The streetlights here were out at both ends of the tree-lined block and very few lights shone from any of the apartment windows. A lot of cars and small trucks were parked on both sides of the street, all of them in the shadows beneath the thick trees.

The doors of the fifth car he tried were unlocked. It was a small Renault, fairly new and in reasonable condition. In under sixty seconds he had the ignition lock out of its slot in the steering column, thus releasing the locking pin, and had scraped three wires bare, twisting two of them together. When he touched the third against the pair, the motor came to life.

For just a second before he pulled away from the curb and drove off he had the feeling that he had somehow slipped into the edge of a powerful whirlpool, and that he was being inexorably sucked down toward the center in ever-accelerating spirals.

But it was too late for second thoughts. It had been too late for a long time now.

GROSSER MÜGGELSEE

The night was pitch-black beneath a deepening overcast. A cool wind had sprung up from the northwest, bringing with it the odors of dampness, decaying wood, rotting vegetation.

McGarvey had hidden the car a quarter of a mile away from the boathouse on the lake's south shore. He stood now in the dark woods looking down at the driveway and the house, and beyond it the boathouse on the water's edge.

Nothing moved except the tree branches in the wind and the wavelets lapping against the shoreline. Nor were there any sounds, or any hints that someone was here waiting for him.

Yet he sensed danger all around him. On the way out of the city he had intended to write this place off. The penetration agent had told Baranov that he would be coming. He would also have told the man about the equipment that had been left here.

But of the five men on the Mossad's list of suspects, did all of them know every operational detail? Did all of them know about this place, and what had been left here for him?

He had to find out, and yet he was sick with apprehension about what he would discover here.

His pistol in hand, McGarvey moved quietly from tree to tree, working his way through the woods parallel to the driveway until he came to the final clearing up from the lake and the boathouse.

Again he stopped for a few seconds, his every sense straining to detect the presence of someone else. But there was nothing.

Keeping low, he stepped out from behind the bole of a tree and raced across to the boathouse. He hurriedly unlocked the door and stepped inside.

The boat was still there. Outwardly it seemed as if nothing had been disturbed since the last time he had been here.

Holstering his gun, he stepped down into the boat and pulled out the packages containing the rebreathing equipment and the assault rifle.

Had someone been here? Did Baranov know about this place, these things?

Who to trust? Always in the end it came down to that. Trust no one and your job becomes impossible. Trust the wrong person and you're dead.

Holding the tiny penlight in his mouth, he unwrapped the

AK74 and quickly field-stripped it, finding his answer in less than twenty seconds.

"Christ," he swore softly.

The firing pin had been removed from the rifle.

Maybe it had come like that. Maybe someone in LIGHT-HOUSE had been tricked. Maybe someone else had an ax to grind.

He shook his head. He knew who it was, just as he supposed he had known for a long time. It was no easier seeing it confirmed here and now.

Laying the gun back in the boat, he climbed up on the dock and let himself out of the boathouse. There were a few lights across the lake. Perhaps the answers, or more accurately the reasons, were there.

Perhaps there would be nothing for him. Perhaps there never had been.

60

THE WHITE HOUSE

THE PRESIDENT SAT IN HIS STUDY WAITING FOR ROLAND
Murphy to arrive from CIA headquarters. It was the Mc-
Garvey thing, and he was glad that Jim Baldwin wouldn't be
here to listen in.

He glanced at the clock on his desk. It was just about 8:00
P.M., which meant it was coming up on midnight in Germany.
By now, if everything was going right, McGarvey would be
across the border.

But Murphy had sounded shaky on the telephone. "Time
is of the essence, Mr. President."

"I'll have Don Acheson standing by."

"No, sir. I think this is something you should consider on
your own. Or at least hear me out, and then afterward . . .
well, sir, you're the president."

"Yes," the president had said.

He turned and looked out the bowed windows into the rose garden. During his brief tenure as DCI he had thought that his was the most difficult job in the world. He knew better now. The difference was that anyone except for the president was allowed to make a mistake.

Ten hours ago he had called Party Secretary Gorbachev on the hot line. Had that been a mistake? Had he given away an advantage?

The Soviet leader had a lot more experience, and he had proven himself to be an adept, capable administrator. But he was one tough sonofabitch across the bargaining table. And he understood the balance of power as well as or better than anyone in government anywhere.

"A situation has developed that you should be aware of, Mr. President."

"Yes, Mr. President, what is it we can do for each other?"

"A number of Soviet naval and, we presume, intelligence officers have been killed in an incident off the coast of Syria a few hours ago. One of them has been identified as Major Arkady Aleksandrovich Kurshin."

"I see," Gorbachev said, a hard edge to his voice.

"Major Kurshin and ten other men, whom we are assuming worked with or for him, managed to steal one of our cruise missiles. They were about to launch it when they were stopped. All of them are dead."

"What was the target of this missile?"

"I think we can safely assume it was somewhere within Israel."

"And the bodies of these Soviet citizens?"

"They have been taken to the morgue at the military hospital in Tel Aviv. Once autopsies have been performed, I believe the intention is to turn them over to your government."

There was a longish pause on the line. When Gorbachev came back his voice sounded very guarded and even tired. "I will admit to you, Mr. President, that I had no knowledge of this. I assume your intelligence is accurate."

"I believe so."

"Then I will find out what has happened. The Soviet government does not engage in acts of terrorism."

"Nor does my government."

Again there was a heavy silence on the line for a second or two.

"Elements of your Sixth Fleet appear to be engaged in a search and rescue mission, Mr. President. Is there any connection between that activity and this alleged act of terrorism?"

"Your Black Sea Fleet is also in the region, Mr. President. I would sincerely hope that there is no connection. We would take that very gravely."

"Yes," Gorbachev said. "Moderation, Mr. President."

"And caution, Mr. President."

The intercom on the president's desk buzzed. Had it been a mistake calling Gorbachev? If it had been, it was his own, and he would answer for it. He flipped the switch. "Yes?"

"General Murphy is here, Mr. President."

"Send him in."

Murphy came in a moment later. He looked worn out. It was as if he had aged ten years in the last couple of days.

"Good evening, Mr. President," he said, crossing the room.

"General," the president said, motioning him to a chair. "You said time was of the essence."

"Yes, sir. And it may already be too late."

Something clutched at the president's gut. "What's the situation?"

"I've had our people in Moscow keeping their ears open ever since this . . . situation came up. It was they who learned about Baranov's movements in and out of Moscow, and it was they who came up with what little information we had on Arkady Kurshin."

"They've been discreet? Especially in view of the present circumstances?"

"Yes, Mr. President, they have taken extra precautions. I

just learned that two Moscow Militia officers were sent to East Berlin with orders to arrest Baranov.''

The president stiffened. "Are you sure of this, Roland?"

"Yes, sir."

"What are the charges?"

"Treason."

It was Gorbachev. The man had been as good as his word. But this now changed everything. "McGarvey will have to be recalled."

"I agree, Mr. President. If he happened to run into those two cops, and something should happen . . ."

"Yes. I want him out of there immediately."

"I've sent John Trotter to West Berlin to see what can be done."

"What are you saying to me, Roland? What's to be done is to recall him. If you have to use another network inside East Germany, then do it. Just get him out of there."

"That's just it, Mr. President, we're not sure he's in East Germany. He was supplied with Russian identification papers to make his crossing easier. He also had an automobile with East German plates. The car has not crossed into East Berlin."

"Nor has anyone using the papers McGarvey was issued?"

"No, sir."

"How do you see this, Roland?"

"He's either decided not to cross for the moment, for whatever reason. Or he's already gotten across using another set of identity papers, in which case he has effectively put himself out of reach."

The president felt the cold thrill of fear in his chest. "Why would he have decided to change plans like that?"

"He has a habit of doing things his own way, Mr. President. But I don't know his reasons in this instance."

61

GROSSER MÜGGELSEE

THE LIGHTS IN THE HOUSE WERE OUT. BARANOV STOOD IN the mostly dark stairhall, well away from the open front door, listening to the night sounds. McGarvey was out there somewhere, he told himself as he stared down toward the lake.

He was coming. The great destroyer was coming. But he was late.

Baranov glanced at his watch for the fifth time in as many minutes. Nemchin, standing across the hall at the window, glanced over at him.

"Perhaps he will not be coming after all, Comrade Colonel."

It was well after midnight. Baranov looked up, a tight little smile on his features. "Oh, he will be here, Sergei Sergeevich."

"How can you be certain?"

Baranov's smile deepened. "Because he and I have had this appointment with each other for a number of years now. He won't fail to keep it."

"Perhaps he's drowned in the lake, Comrade Colonel. We won't know until morning when we can send a boat out."

Baranov had considered that possibility. But the more he thought about it, and about McGarvey, the more he was certain that the American would not be destroyed so easily. He is like a fox, that one. Sly. More clever than a Russian.

There was an old peasant proverb: The Russian is clever, but it comes slowly—all the way from the back of his head.

McGarvey wasn't like that. He was a man of action. A man who well understood and accepted his destiny. In that way he was much like Arkasha. Only better.

He was coming all right.

"Keep a sharp watch," Baranov said. "I'll be down in a minute."

Nemchin nodded as Baranov turned and went upstairs to Lorraine Abbott's bedroom. The upstairs hall was in deeper darkness, but when he opened the bedroom door he could see her pale figure in the dim light filtering in from outside.

She was nude, and she lay spread-eagle on the bed, her ankles and wrists tied to the bedposts. He had taped her mouth so that she could not cry out, and he had patiently calmed her down, giving her the instructions, he'd told her, that would save her life.

"Move so much as a muscle, Doctor Abbott, and you will die," Baranov had said.

He remained at the doorway, not wishing to approach any closer. It was possible, the thought had crossed his mind, that she might wish to kill herself in an effort to kill him.

Working patiently and very carefully, he had strapped ten ounces of plastique explosives to her thighs, the edge of the gray, puttylike material just touching her pubis. The plastique was wired to a small battery through a simple contact switch that he had taped to the small of her long, slender back.

If she moved, the plastique would explode, blowing the entire bottom half of her torso away.

If McGarvey got this far, he would want to help her. But the moment he did so the woman would certainly die, and he would at least be severely injured, if not completely incapacitated.

"I trust that you're comfortable, Doctor," Baranov said softly.

She looked at him, her eyes wide, her body held rigidly still. She was a believer.

"It shouldn't be long now. He will be here soon. And I sincerely hope that he will be able to see you like this."

Her eyes blinked and Baranov had to laugh.

"Be careful, little one, unless you mean to kill yourself this soon." She was a good-looking woman, he decided. McGarvey had very good taste.

She was blinking her eyes rapidly.

"Do you want to talk to me, is that it?" Baranov asked gently.

She blinked her eyes again.

"I think not. The time for talking is past. Now it's time for dying."

It had taken McGarvey thirty-five minutes to circle the lake, keeping to the narrow forest-service tracks through the woods. Only when he had to cross the Spree River did he risk driving on the main highway, and he got off it at the first possible chance.

He sat now in the Renault, its lights out, its engine ticking over softly. The dirt track ended in a rough-hewn log barrier beyond which was only darkness. Three times he had tried to head back down toward the lake, but each time the road he had used had ended in such a barrier.

Baranov was here, though. He could almost feel the man's presence in the night air.

"I'm coming," he said to himself. "And you damned well know it, you bastard."

Farther in the distance he thought he could make out the bulk of a dark hill rising up. Evidently a ridge separated the lakeshore from the approaches to this side. Only the single road which led directly east from the main highway cut down toward the lake, giving access to Baranov's house. And that road would be guarded.

But it didn't matter. None of that mattered now. McGarvey's hate burned brightly within him, like the terrible fire of an open-hearth furnace; unquenchable.

From where he sat, the house would be almost straight across the ridge, perhaps half a mile away. The night was pitch-black. He could see no lights anywhere, not even the glow from Berlin or from Schönefeld Airport just a few miles to the south.

Switching off the car's engine he got out, careful to make no noise as he closed the door. He stood there sniffing the air and listening for sounds. But the night was still, the air heavy and damp.

There was no other way. He would have to make his approach from this side.

He took off his jacket and laid it on the hood of the car, then calmly checked his pistol. It was fully loaded, and he had an extra clip of ammunition in his pocket, along with the stiletto strapped to his left forearm.

How many people did Baranov have with him? Four, six, perhaps eight or ten? They would have night-spotting scopes and assault rifles. But they would not be expecting him to come this way. They would be watching the lake.

He smiled grimly as he reholstered the automatic at the small of his back and climbed over the log barrier. He had been waiting for this moment for a long time. And he suspected Baranov had been waiting for it too. The final confrontation.

The ground sloped sharply downward for about five feet, and at the bottom McGarvey stumbled into icy water over his knees. At first he thought it was a drainage ditch, but as he slogged through the underbrush he soon began to realize that he was in a swamp. This part of the terrain was probably lower than the level of the surface of the lake, so it could never be properly drained.

Sharp brambles tore at his hands and face, and mud sucked at his feet, making it nearly impossible to continue in some spots. Several times he had to backtrack or go left or right around dense thickets or much deeper water.

It was possible, he thought at one point, that there would be no way for him to reach the house from here. It was even possible that he would get himself lost out here and wander around until dawn.

Twice he tripped and fell headlong into the water, but gradually the land began to rise up and become less wet so that he was able to make much faster progress, finally pulling himself up out of the swamp, muddy and bleeding, forty-five minutes after leaving the car.

One thing was certain, he told himself as he held up for a few moments to catch his breath, he would not be able to take Lorraine back this way, no matter what condition she was in.

He pulled the pistol out of its holster, ejected the clip, and cycled the slide back and forth several times. The gun was wet and muddy, but it would still function. Replacing the clip, he levered a round into the firing chamber and then started up the steep hill toward the crest about a hundred feet above.

Near the top he dropped down and crawled the rest of the way on all fours.

The house was large, broad balconies wrapped around both sides to the front. It stood on a flat spot against the side of the hill about fifty yards below where McGarvey lay in the darkness. He could see the driveway leading back toward the highway to the west, and below, the lake and in the distance the opposite shore.

No lights shone from the house, nor could he detect any movement, anything that would indicate someone was down there.

But there would be one or two men somewhere on the driveway, and certainly a couple down by the lake waiting for him to come across. Which left the house. Baranov was there, but how many others were with him? There was no way of knowing.

Crawling on his stomach, he worked his way down the hill toward the back of the house.

Once he thought he heard the squawk from a walkie-talkie, and he held up. But the noise wasn't repeated, and he continued.

Baranov saw him.

He had gone into the breakfast room at the back of the house on some instinct, and he spotted a movement on the hill. Turning, he hurried back to Nemchin in the stairhall and grabbed one of the AK74s.

"I think he's coming from over the hill. Radio Yevgeni and Rotislav, tell them to get up here on the double. But no noise."

"Yes, Comrade," Nemchin started to say, but Baranov had spun on his heel and was racing back to the breakfast room.

Keeping well back away from the window, Baranov raised the assault rifle to his shoulder and keyed the image intensifier. At first he could see nothing other than the gray shapes of the trees.

But then he had him! It was McGarvey. There was absolutely no doubt of it in his mind.

"You sonofabitch," he mumbled half under his breath. "You magnificent sonofabitch." What he wouldn't give to have such a man working for him. Kurshin had been good, but this one was the very best, bar none.

"Is it him, Comrade?" Nemchin asked softly at his shoulder.

"Yes. Did you get Yevgeni and Rotislav?"

"They are on their way. Do you have him in the scope?"

Baranov keyed the image intensifier again. McGarvey had

disappeared. For a frantic second or two he scanned the hill-side, finally picking the American out again nearly at the bottom of the hill, barely twenty yards from the back of the house. There was no possibility that he could see inside, and yet Baranov instinctively stepped back a pace.

"I have him."

"Then fire, Comrade Chairman. Kill him now. Get it over with."

"Not yet."

"This is a dangerous game we are playing. With all respect, Comrade . . ."

"No," Baranov said, turning around. "He's here to kill me, but he's also come for the woman. I mean to give him both."

"Then I can no longer be responsible for your safety."

"You never were."

"I don't understand, Comrade."

"I want to talk to him, Sergei Sergeevich. Before I kill him and his whore. That is all you must understand."

"Do you mean to allow him here, inside the house?"

"Of course," Baranov said, brushing past Nemchin and heading for the stairs. "But he will never get out of here alive. I promise you."

Nemchin remained in the breakfast room for just a moment, but then he followed Baranov.

"Believe in me, that's all I ask," Baranov's words floated back to him. "That's all I've ever asked."

At the base of the stairs he watched as Baranov reached the top and disappeared. He raised the walkie-talkie to his lips. "Yevgeni, you'd better get up here on the double. McGarvey has arrived, and I think Baranov has lost his mind."

"Hold on," his walkie-talkie squawked. "We'll be there in a minute."

Nemchin suddenly felt a presence above him, and he turned. Baranov had come back to the head of the stairs. In the very dim light Nemchin thought that the man's face looked like a death's head.

"Comrade . . ." he started to say when Baranov raised his pistol and fired one shot, a sudden starburst exploding inside of his head.

"Believe in me," Baranov whispered, but Nemchin was dead.

62

GROSSER MÜGGELSEE

MCGARVEY HEARD THE GUNSHOT AND HE HUGGED THE ground, thinking for just a moment that he'd been spotted and they were shooting at him.

But when a second shot didn't come, he rose up and peered into the darkness. At first there was nothing to be seen except the back and east side of the house, the driveway to the highway, and the path down to the lake.

Something terrible had happened in the house. All he could think of was that Lorraine was down there with Baranov.

He jumped up and raced the last few yards to the back corner of the big house, where he flattened himself against the rough brick wall.

He switched his pistol's safety to the off position, cocked the hammer, dropped down below the level of the stone balcony, and started in a dead run toward the front of the house.

Someone was coming up from the lake. He heard them at the same moment he came out around the balcony.

There were two of them.

McGarvey raised his pistol and fired three shots in rapid succession, getting the impression he had hit at least one of them. Then he ducked back behind the stonework just as someone opened fire with an AK74 on full automatic, chips of stone and mortar dust flying everywhere.

As soon as the firing stopped, McGarvey extended his gun arm around the corner and fired three more shots.

A man cried out on the path across the driveway, and then the night fell silent again.

Leaning against the wall, McGarvey quickly ejected the nearly spent clip of ammunition from his pistol and rammed the new one home.

Counting to three, he leapt out away from the balcony, swinging his gun left to right as he dodged and zigzagged his way across the driveway.

Both of them were dead. He could see their bodies from where he had reached the protection of the edge of the woods. Both of them were dressed in dark clothing, and both had been armed with assault rifles. One of them, his face a mass of blood, lay on his back at the end of the path. The other one had taken at least two hits in his chest, and he too lay on his back, tangled in the low underbrush.

There would be others. These two had come up from the lake, where they had been waiting for him to come across. There would be someone coming up from the driveway at any moment. And at least Baranov was in the house.

But what was the first shot? He couldn't understand.

The driveway remained empty. McGarvey crouched in the darkness watching so intently for someone to come up from the highway that he nearly missed the third Russian coming from the lake.

He heard a slight noise behind him and to his left, as if

someone had stepped on a twig and then stopped in their tracks.

It saved his life. He looked over his shoulder, spotted the dull ruby glint of a night-spotting scope illuminating him, and rolled left, dropping to the ground.

The Russian opened fire with his assault rifle, the rounds slamming into the tree just inches behind McGarvey, and kicking up the dirt as he rolled over and over again.

He looked up at the last possible second as the Russian raced across the path swinging the rifle up again into firing position, and he snapped off two shots, the first going wide, the second catching the man in the chest just below his sternum, driving him backward, the weapon clattering to the ground.

Where were the others?

McGarvey remained for just an instant where he lay on the ground, listening for the sound of others coming. But once again the night had fallen silent.

He was in an exposed position here, not only from someone in the house, but from anyone coming up the driveway. He leapt to his feet and raced back across the clearing to the front of the house, where he held up at the foot of the four steps which rose to the front veranda.

Why wasn't someone else coming? Why hadn't Baranov or his people opened fire from the house?

What was the sonofabitch waiting for?

McGarvey scrambled up the steps where he flattened himself against the wall beside the open door. Inside, the stairhall was in darkness, but he had enough of his night vision to see the figure of a man lying at the foot of the stairs, a walkie-talkie lying beside his body.

The man was dead. It was obvious from the angle at which his head was bent, and the way his left leg had folded up beneath him.

He had been killed by the single shot McGarvey had heard. Who the hell was he, and who had shot him? This was making no sense.

Girding himself, McGarvey rolled through the doorway, feinted left, and then raced directly across the hall to the side of the staircase.

Still nothing moved. Still there were no sounds. Still no one opened fire.

Perhaps, he thought, Baranov had already gone. Perhaps these were only the staff.

He looked up the stairs, trying to penetrate the deeper darkness in the corridor above.

Baranov was here. McGarvey could feel his presence in the house, like some dark, forbidding, evil spirit. He was here all right, waiting.

Moving soundlessly on the balls of his feet, McGarvey started up the stairs, taking them one at a time, testing each step before he put his full weight on it, his every sense searching out ahead of him for the presence of the man.

At the top he stopped again. A door was open at the end of the corridor. But except for the rectangle of dim light filtering out he could see nothing.

He held his breath to listen. There was no sound . . .

But then he heard a single pistol shot somewhere outside in the distance. He half turned; a fusillade of gunfire came from a long way off, perhaps down the driveway somewhere.

Someone else was coming here. Suddenly there was no time.

"Baranov," he shouted, rushing down the corridor toward the open door. "You sonofabitch!"

He pulled up short just at the doorway and laid his head back against the wall. The firing outside had stopped. The silence was ominous.

"Baranov," he shouted again, and he rolled left through the doorway, nearly firing on instinct alone at the man standing across the large room.

"Hello, Kirk," Baranov said gently. He was aiming his pistol at Lorraine.

McGarvey took it all in within a split second: the gun in Baranov's meaty paw, the cords binding Lorraine's wrists and ankles, the C4 taped to her thighs. She was blinking her eyes but she wasn't moving.

"I wanted the time to talk to you," Baranov said. "But it's no longer possible." There was something wrong with him, in the way he held himself, in the almost furtive look in his eyes.

"You heard the gunfire. Someone else is coming for you," McGarvey said, finally finding his voice. Just another half-ounce of pressure on the trigger of his pistol and the man would be dead.

"So it would seem. And now the advantage is once again yours. I'll trade you Doctor Abbott's life for mine."

"No," McGarvey said. Now that he had come to this point his rage was gone, leaving in its stead a deep aching weariness. He looked into Lorraine's eyes. He had tried to warn her. God, why wouldn't they listen?

"You won't throw her life away merely to kill me. We will meet on another day."

"We'll just wait here for a little while."

"For those others to come?" Baranov asked, nodding toward the door. "Do you know that they are policemen here to arrest me?"

"Good."

"I won't allow that to happen, McGarvey. Not now. Not yet."

"You don't have any choice."

"I'll shoot her."

"And then I'll shoot you."

Baranov shook his head. "The plastique will blow and she'll die. Is that what you want?"

Lorraine had closed her eyes. She was beginning to shiver. McGarvey looked at her again. She was one of the innocents. For some reason they were attracted to him, like moths to an open flame with the same fatal consequences. I'm sorry, he wanted to tell her. But it was too late for that now.

"That's up to you," McGarvey said, turning back to Baranov. "But you're not leaving this room."

"Why?" Baranov asked. "You're not so different from Arkasha. I've watched you develop. I've seen what you are capable of doing. Do you want money? Position? Power? What? Name it and it's yours."

McGarvey shook his head, but said nothing. In a large way, of course, Baranov was right. But there had to be reasons, there had to be sanity. He had to be able to believe in that much.

"Why?" Baranov asked again. "Because of Powers? Because of those officers in Germany, or the crew of the submarine? Is this for revenge?" He was agitated.

"Yes," McGarvey said softly, his voice barely a whisper. *And for myself,* he thought. *What I've become because of men like you.*

"You're the loyal soldier, is that it? The dedicated intelligence officer. Fuck your mother, you stupid bastard, all these years you've been betrayed. Did you know that?"

"We'll wait . . ."

"His code name is White Knight. He has worked with me for years."

"Which makes him a Russian patriot."

"He's a traitor . . ."

"And you're going to hand him over to me. You're going to kill him. It'll be his reward for long years of service."

"He betrayed you," Baranov argued. "If we all die here he will go on. Someone will take my place. Others will fall . . . innocent people . . . he is very good. You can't believe . . ."

McGarvey raised his pistol so that it was pointing directly at Baranov's head.

"No," the Russian cried. "Believe in me! I will kill her!"

Lorraine's eyes were still closed. She was shivering even more.

"There is no time!" Baranov screeched. "McGarvey!"

"Then go," McGarvey said, stepping away from the doorway. He did not lower his gun.

Hope flickered across Baranov's eyes. "Put your gun down."

"Go," McGarvey growled. "While you still have the chance."

Baranov's gaze shifted to Lorraine, whose shivering was steadily increasing. "I want your word, McGarvey. I don't want to be shot in the back."

"You have it. Now get out of here."

"What about White Knight? He is . . ."

"Go while you can," McGarvey roared.

Baranov quickly edged his way across the room while keeping his gun trained on the bed. At the open door he looked into McGarvey's eyes. "You're not so different," he said. He spun on his heel and disappeared out into the corridor.

Without hesitation, McGarvey stepped out the doorway after him and fired two shots in rapid succession, striking Baranov high in the back and in the base of his skull, driving him forward.

"I lied," McGarvey said softly.

Baranov tried to rise up, blood streaming from his wounds.

McGarvey took a few steps closer and fired a third time at point-blank range into the back of the Russian's head, slamming him back down.

He fired again. And again, the bullets pumping into Baranov's inert form. And still he pulled the trigger until the ejector slide stopped.

The director of the KGB was dead. Long live the KGB.

McGarvey let the empty pistol fall from his hand. Outside, several cars raced up the driveway and screeched to a halt in front of the house.

He turned and went back into the bedroom. Lorraine, her eyes wide, was looking at him.

"It's finished, my darling," he said, approaching the bed.

She had stopped shivering, but she was blinking her eyes frantically.

"He's dead," McGarvey said.

Someone entered the stairhall and started up the stairs. There were a lot of them. He could hear them shouting back and forth, and could hear the squawk of their walkie-talkies.

"Nothing will happen to you now," McGarvey told her. He reached down for the tape across her mouth. "I promise you."

Her nostrils were flared, and a low moan formed at the back of her throat.

"It's all right . . ."

They were in the corridor, and someone came to the open doorway. He shouted something in Russian.

"We're Americans," McGarvey said in English. He had hold of the edge of the tape. Lorraine moaned again, her eyes nearly bulging out of their sockets.

"Put your hands over your head immediately, or I will open fire," the man in the doorway shouted in English.

She was trying to tell him something. With her eyes. What?

"Now!" the Russian shouted.

McGarvey let his eyes go down to the C4 taped obscenely to her thighs. Wires led from the plastique to a small package, which he figured contained the battery and firing mechanism. A second pair of wires ran beneath her left leg and disappeared.

"God in heaven," McGarvey breathed, his body going rigid.

"Put your hands up . . ." the Russian ordered.

"Listen to me," McGarvey called out, his eyes locked into Lorraine's. "There are explosives taped to this woman's body. I think they're wired to some sort of a pressure switch."

The Russian at the doorway said nothing.

"Do you understand me?" McGarvey called, not daring to raise his voice.

"Yes, I do. Now step away from the bed very carefully." McGarvey hesitated.

"Do as I say, Mr. McGarvey, I have a demolitions expert with me. Please step away from the bed."

"It'll be all right," McGarvey whispered to her. "Believe me." Slowly he moved away from the side of the bed and turned to the men crowded in the doorway.

"Get out of here, we'll take care of it," the Russian said.

He looked very young. He held a big automatic in his right hand.

"I'll stay," McGarvey said.

"Did you kill Baranov?"

"Get your demolitions man in here, goddamnit! Now!"

"Did you kill him?" the Russian asked implacably.

"Yes, you sonofabitch. Now get your man in here."

"Good," the Russian said. "You can stay." He turned. "Get Valeri up here on the double."

63

EAST BERLIN

"HOW DID YOU KNOW MY NAME?" McGARVEY ASKED THE
Russian cop.

"I wasn't sure it was you. But we'd been told that you
were on the move, and that you had an old vendetta with
Chairman Baranov."

It was just dawn. They sat in the back of a panel van,
downtown near the Brandenburg Gate. The sodium vapor
lights were pale against the gray morning sky.

"He was a very bad man, Mr. McGarvey," Lieutenant
Lukyanov continued. "We had come to arrest him. My captain thought he would return with us, but I disagreed."

"Even if he had, he wouldn't have stood trial," McGarvey
said tiredly. He looked at Lorraine shivering in the corner.

She was all right physically, but Baranov had done something to her. Something terrible. It was still in her eyes, and he supposed it would always be there.

"Perhaps you are right. In any event it is a moot point now." Lieutenant Lukyanov glanced at Lorraine. "She will be okay?"

"I don't know."

"What about you?" Lieutenant Lukyanov asked, turning back to McGarvey. "You are a spy. You do this sort of thing all the time. I sincerely hope that you do not show up on Soviet soil again."

"This is Germany."

Lieutenant Lukyanov smiled thinly. "I'm just a simple policeman, not Spycatcher." Spycatcher was a KGB agent in popular Soviet fiction.

McGarvey returned the smile.

Lieutenant Lukyanov reached across him and opened the side door. "Go," he said. "I cannot drive you across, but you and Dr. Abbott will not be hindered. And I believe someone is waiting for you."

"You're a long way from Moscow."

"And you from Washington, Mr. McGarvey. Go in peace."

"We're in the wrong business for that," McGarvey said.

They shook hands and he stepped down out of the van. Lieutenant Lukyanov helped Lorraine out, and McGarvey had to hold her to keep her from falling. She was shivering again.

The lieutenant slid the door closed, the van backed away from them, turned and drove off, leaving them standing there alone.

With the morning, traffic had begun to build up on both sides of the border. Still holding Lorraine tightly, McGarvey led her down the broad sidewalk past the remains of the East German sentry complex, none of the soldiers paying them the slightest attention, only an occasional face turning their way from one of the vehicles waiting to cross.

"It's all right now," he said softly in her ear.

At first she didn't react. He didn't know if she had even heard him. But then, as they walked, she slowly turned her head and looked up at him.

"It's over," he said. "We're almost there."

"Don't leave me, Kirk," she whispered.

"I won't."

WEST BERLIN

John Trotter got out of the back of a dark red Mercedes sedan. He looked thinner to McGarvey, his features more gaunt, the planes of his face more sharply defined.

"We need to get her to the hospital," McGarvey said.

"Has she been injured? Is she hurt?" Trotter asked in alarm. He looked and sounded completely strung out.

"I don't know, but I want someone to look at her. We'll stay for a couple of days, if need be."

Lorraine clutched tightly at his arm as he helped her into the back seat of the car.

"I'll be there," McGarvey told her. "I'm not going anywhere. I promise."

She looked into his eyes for a moment, until hers began to cloud over, and she finally allowed herself to sit back and release his arm.

McGarvey got in beside her, and Trotter climbed in the front seat. Their driver was a young man in a dark blue windbreaker.

"The military hospital at Tempelhof," Trotter said. "And shake a leg."

"Yes, sir," the driver said, and they pulled away from the checkpoint and headed south through the city.

Trotter turned in his seat. His eyes seemed very large and damp behind his thick glasses. "I didn't know what to think when we got the call from the police barracks in the east zone."

"What are you doing here, John?" McGarvey asked.

"Murphy ordered me up here to see if I could extract you

somehow. We got word that a warrant for Baranov's arrest was about to be served . . ." Trotter's eyes got a little wider. "You ran into them?"

McGarvey nodded.

"What in heaven's name happened over there, Kirk? What about Baranov . . . did you . . ."

Lorraine let out a little cry, and she tried to burrow her way into the corner.

"Later," McGarvey said.

"Kirk?"

"Later."

If it was easier for a camel to pass through the eye of a needle than it was for a rich man to enter the gates of heaven, McGarvey wondered what it would be like for an assassin. Or a traitor.

Trotter had taken over one of the offices in the hospital while McGarvey had taken care of Lorraine. The doctor had given her a sedative and she was finally resting.

"She'll sleep for twenty-four hours at least."

"What about afterward?"

"I don't know, Mr. McGarvey. It will depend in a great measure on her capacity for shock. It's different for everyone."

"She's a strong woman."

"Then I suspect she'll recover just fine. But it's going to take time. Do you know what happened to her?"

"Not yet."

"Well, whatever it was, it overloaded her brain. It tore her down to a point where she was nothing. She may need help to bring her back."

McGarvey had nodded. "She'll have it," he said, but riding upstairs in the elevator he wondered if he would be capable of helping himself, let alone her. What was his own capacity for shock? He had never known. Perhaps he would find out at last.

Trotter was just putting down the phone when McGarvey entered the office.

"That was Murphy. He wants us on the first plane back to Washington. Kirk, I couldn't tell him what happened over there because I don't know myself. He's hopping mad. He wants some answers."

"Baranov is dead," McGarvey said, watching his old friend's face. They had been through a lot together. All the way back to the early days, even before Santiago, and before the Carter Administration had practically emasculated the Agency.

Trotter flinched. He licked his lips. "Did you kill him?"

"Yes."

"From a distance, Kirk? With the rifle? With your pistol from the beach? How . . ."

"I shot him in the back. After I had given him my word that I wouldn't do it. He believed me."

Trotter's mouth was open, but no sounds were coming out.

"It was a trade, John."

"For what?"

"For my life, for Lorraine's, for a . . . name. But I cheated him. I lied."

"What name?"

"Our penetration agent. White Knight."

"Ah," Trotter said after a beat, but the sound was less of a word than it was merely the release of the deep breath he was holding. He half turned away and looked out the window.

"He was willing to throw the man's life away without compunction. It meant nothing to him," McGarvey said.

Again there was a silence between them.

"How long had you known?" Trotter asked at length.

"Known what, John?"

"That it was . . . me."

McGarvey's heart sank. "I hadn't. Not until this moment."

Trotter turned back to him, his face suddenly twisted in a grimace. "But you said he named me!"

"I lied," McGarvey said softly. "To him, to you."

"Then you have no proof!" Trotter cried. He fumbled in his jacket for his gun, his movements frantic and unprofessional.

But then he'd never been an assassin, McGarvey thought, watching his old friend. Trotter had been a good cop and a tough, extremely capable administrator. But he'd not been a killer in the sense of one who pulls a trigger.

Trotter pointed the pistol at him with a shaking hand. It was a .32 automatic, deadly enough at this range.

"Why, John? Can you tell me that?"

"You wouldn't understand."

"I'd like to try."

"You don't know anything. You're nothing more than a paid killer. An assassin. A tool to be used for those disgusting but sometimes necessary jobs. Like a shovel to pick up dog shit. Nothing more."

"Was it for power? You're an ambitious man. Was that it?"

Trotter's lip had curled into a feral snarl. "You killed the man. You've been up against him. You tell me! He could not be resisted. Not that one. When he wanted you, you came. When he held a dance, you did the jig."

"He was just a man."

"You had to shoot him in the back. You couldn't face him."

"What did he promise you? The directorship of the CIA? Did he have that power?"

"His power was unlimited. Even when we were young . . ."

A revelation slipped into place in McGarvey's mind. "You knew him from the beginning? Is that it, John? Maybe in college? Maybe he got to you in the service? Where, John? When? How?"

"In Germany in the fifties. Before the Wall. He was there. We all were there. And he promised me heaven and earth. He was capable of it, Kirk. God, he was capable of anything."

"But it went bad somehow?"

"He wouldn't keep his word. So I sent you after him. He knew I would. I mean, he knew I'd send someone after him, but he didn't know how good you were. And all the time we were still communicating with each other. He was telling me his plans and I was telling him about you. Goading him. Daring him.''

"But he nearly had you killed at the safehouse in Falmouth.''

"But I had you, Kirk. I've always had you, while he only had Kurshin. And Kurshin was no match for you, was he?''

McGarvey lowered his head. "But you were my friend, John.'' He turned toward the door. "I trusted you. As a matter of fact you were the only one I ever trusted.'' He didn't think Trotter would shoot him in the back.

"You were a fool,'' Trotter spat. "Turn around.''

McGarvey shook his head and swayed forward on the balls of his feet as if he were about to collapse. He had to reach out with his left hand to steady himself against the door frame. The movement masked his right hand going to his left sleeve.

"Turn around.''

"John,'' McGarvey cried in real anguish. He spun around and in one swift movement threw the razor-sharp stiletto sidehanded with every last bit of his strength, the blade burying itself in Trotter's chest at the same moment he fired.

The shot caught McGarvey high in the chest, slamming him back against the door, and he was falling, it seemed, forever into a deep, bottomless pit.

64

THE ISLAND OF SÉRIFOS

SOMEONE WAS COMING. MCGARVEY HAD BEEN FEELING IT
for several days. He stood on the catwalk of the lighthouse,
looking back toward the village, watching the man in khaki
trousers and short-sleeved shirt make his way up the path.

He had not thought their isolation would last, but he had
hoped they would be left alone at least through Christmas.
Lorraine was downstairs fixing their lunch. From time to time
the sounds of her singing drifted up to him. She was on the
mend, but it was too soon, damnit. Far too soon for her.

Summer had given way to a lovely fall in the Aegean Sea.
Each day was as sparkling and warm as the day before, and
time had begun to take on an ethereal quality.

Trotter's bullet had missed McGarvey's lungs, and within

ten days he had been allowed to leave the hospital at Tempelhof.

Lorraine had remained at his side for the entire time, his injury seemingly working to bring her out of her deep state of shock, though she would not talk to anyone about what had happened to her at the Grosser Müggelsee house.

Lawrence Danielle, the deputy director of central intelligence, had come to West Berlin on the day before McGarvey was discharged, and they had talked for nearly six hours, the story finally emerging that Valentin Baranov had been killed in an automobile accident, and John Trotter had committed suicide, just as his wife had done nearly six years earlier.

"John was a difficult man," Danielle said. "Everyone knew that. In fact, we all used to think that his ambition would be his downfall one day."

"But there was never any proof," McGarvey said. It still hurt.

"No, but then he and Baranov had had years together to perfect their operation. He was a lot like Kim Philby. There was no real proof that he was a traitor either, not until he disappeared from Beirut and showed up in Moscow."

"It's easy for men like him, is that what you're saying?"

"Even you can't imagine how easy it is," Danielle said, getting to his feet. He patted McGarvey on the arm. "What can we do for you, and for Dr. Abbott?"

"Just leave us alone, Larry. That's all."

Danielle looked at him oddly. "I don't know if that's possible, but I'll see what I can do." He turned and walked across the room. At the door he had stopped and looked back. "By the way, McGarvey, the president sends his thanks."

The man on the path was much closer now, and McGarvey finally recognized him. He uncocked the hammer of his Walther PPK, switched the safety to the on position, and went downstairs.

Lorraine was just coming from the kitchen to call him down for lunch as he was putting the pistol in the hall cabinet. Her eyes widened and she stopped in her tracks.

"What is it?" she asked.

"It's General Murphy. He's down on the path."

Her eyes went questioningly to the cabinet.

"I wasn't sure who it was at first. I didn't want to take any chances."

"Isn't it over yet, Kirk?"

"I'd hoped so."

She glanced toward the veranda overlooking the sea. "I don't know if I could handle . . . anything else."

"You won't have to. I promise you," McGarvey said.

"I will . . . someday," she said, her voice soft, wistful. "At least I think I will." She turned back to him. "You gave me my life, darling, don't let them take it away from me again."

"I won't. I promise you. Believe me." He made no move to go toward her. In the weeks they had been here together they had not touched. He had told himself that when she was ready, he would know it. She wasn't ready now. Perhaps she never would be.

She shivered, as if someone had walked over her grave. "I'll lay out an extra plate," she said, and she turned and went back to the kitchen.

McGarvey couldn't imagine why the DCI was coming here, unless it was out of morbid curiosity to see his battle-wounded troops. But he and Lorraine had been friends for several years. McGarvey thought he would know better than to bother her now. Unless there was something else. Unless there were more complications.

He went out to the stone bridge just as Murphy reached the bottom of the path.

"Where's your bodyguard?" McGarvey called out. He found that he was angry again.

"I left him in the village," Murphy said without breaking stride.

"Aren't you afraid I'll shoot you?"

"Will you?"

"I'm an assassin."

Murphy stopped a few feet away from McGarvey and looked at him critically. "I'm not the enemy, remember?"

"I didn't think John Trotter was either. And he was my friend."

Again Murphy seemed to study him. He shook his head. "My opinion of you hasn't changed, McGarvey. You're still a dangerous man."

"But a necessary evil," McGarvey said, remembering Trotter's words.

"Yes . . ." Murphy started to say when his gaze went beyond McGarvey. "Hello, Lorraine," he said.

McGarvey glanced over his shoulder. Lorraine had come to the door.

"What are you doing here, Roland?" she asked.

"I've come to take you home."

"Not yet."

"Mark O'Sheay has been asking about you, and your lab wants to know when you're coming back."

"I'm not ready for that. I don't know if I'll ever return. Maybe . . . someday."

"Listen to me, Lorraine, you can't stay here. Not with him."

"He saved my life."

"He nearly got you killed," Murphy said. "Come back with me while you still have a chance. For God's sake, you're a scientist. Think, Lorraine!"

But she was shaking her head. "Not yet, Roland, please."

Murphy started forward, but McGarvey blocked his path. "Go back to Washington, General."

"Not without her," Murphy said.

"You don't understand," McGarvey snapped.

"I think I do. It's you who doesn't realize where this is heading. You don't know, or you don't want to admit to yourself, what danger she's in, being this close to you."

"Go!" McGarvey shouted, stepping back a pace. His thoughts were getting tangled.

"What you did for us was magnificent. No one is denying that. Your country owes you a debt of gratitude. But for God's sake, let her go!"

"I can't," McGarvey cried.

"You must!" the general shouted.

"Stop this!" Lorraine screeched.

A gull cried overhead, then swooped down the face of the cliff behind them to the sea.

"Please," Murphy said softly.

Lorraine said nothing.

After a beat, Murphy took a deep breath and let it out slowly, a look of defeat and genuine pain in his eyes. "I'll wait for you in Athens for twenty-four hours in case you change your mind."

"I won't," Lorraine said.

Murphy's gaze shifted again to McGarvey. "If you have any decency in you, let her go. She doesn't belong here with you. You know that. You must." He hesitated a moment longer, and then turned and headed back up the path.

McGarvey stood there for a long time, conscious only of his own beating heart, and of the conflicting emotions of hate, and rage, and impotence filling his mind.

What had he become, and when had it happened?

He couldn't say, nor did he think he would ever want to know for certain. The past no longer mattered, only the future.

It was very late, well past midnight. McGarvey lay on his back in the front bedroom, his windows open to the sea.

All afternoon he and Lorraine had avoided discussing Murphy's visit, just as in the past weeks they had stayed away from talking about Baranov and everything that had happened since En Gedi.

As was their routine, they had gone to bed early, each in their own room, each with their own thoughts and hopes for the morning.

He listened to the sounds of the sea below as he struggled to sort out his thoughts. He had given Lorraine her life, but, as Murphy had suggested, was he now keeping her from it? He loved her, that much he knew. But was it killing her?

He closed his eyes, and immediately he began to see faces, one after the other, floating in a dark void. He knew all of them intimately, as only an assassin could. They were his victims. The men he had killed over the past nine years. *My name is Legion, for we are many.*

"There is something missing in you," his sister had told him once, a long time ago. "Some deep hole that can never be filled."

He heard a rustle of fabric at the doorway and he opened his eyes. Lorraine stood there in her nightgown, her body outlined in the starlight filtering in from outside.

"Baranov is really dead?" she asked softly.

"Yes," McGarvey replied.

She shuddered. "He made me . . ."

"You don't have to do this, my darling."

"Kirk, he made me believe in him," she said. "He sat with me on the bed and he talked to me, nothing more. He told me things I didn't know were possible . . . about himself, about the world, about . . . me. And in the end I believed everything he said to me, and everything that he could ever say."

McGarvey's heart was aching not only for her, but for himself.

"Even though I knew he was wrong, I couldn't help myself. He took *me* away from me, and replaced it with his own soul."

"He's dead . . ."

"Yes," she cut in. She raised a hand to her heart. "But now he's dead inside here as well."

Slowly she slipped the nightgown off her shoulders and let it fall to the floor. She stepped away from it, her body shimmering.

"I believe in you, Kirk McGarvey. And now I want you to make love to me."

She came to him, and as he took her into his arms, he knew what had been missing all of these years—all of his life.

No one had ever believed in him.

MOSCOW

The connection was imperfect.

Lieutenant Colonel Vasili Semonovich Didenko sat in his nondescript office on the third floor of the Lubyanka, holding the telephone tightly to his ear.

Was it possible? he asked himself. Could it be possible?

"I want you to come in," he said. "It will take me a few days to arrange something, and in the meantime I want you to go to ground. Do you understand?"

. Didenko, who was the newly promoted chief of the KGB's Department 8 of Directorate S (Illegals)—the department that used to be called Viktor, for Mokrie Dela (Wet Affairs)—had been a student of Baranov's. A gifted student. He saw now, for the first time, at least one portion of his future.

"Can you hear me?" he shouted into the telephone. The connection between Moscow and Damascus was never very good, but this evening it was worse than normal.

"Tell me where you are, I can help you."

Didenko listened closely to what the man was saying. He was not only listening to the words for their meaning, but listening for a weakness. But there was none. There never had been.

"What are you saying to me?" Didenko shouted. "Fuck your mother, you cannot be serious. You need me . . ."

But the connection was broken.

Didenko slowly hung up the telephone. He sat in his dimly lit office for a long time before he got his coat and left the building. On the way across to the parking lot he pondered the other's last words.

"I've become a floater. When I want blood I'll call you. This time, you bastards, I won't let you fuck me up."

A preview of

CROSSFIRE

by

DAVID HAGBERG

Available
June 1991
from Tor Books

— PROLOGUE —

March 6, 1945
Golfo San Matías, Argentina

THE SUBMARINE WAS NEARLY SILENT AND MOSTLY IN DARK-
ness because her batteries were low. A short, wiry man,
dressed in black leather trousers and a heavy white turtleneck
sweater, stepped through an oval hatchway into an after storage compartment between the diesels and rear torpedo room.
He stopped and held his breath to listen. He was certain he
had heard something. Metal against metal, a scraping noise
somewhere below. Between the deck and the tanks.

For several long seconds he remained where he was, listening, but the sounds did not come again. His imagination?
They were all tired, strung-out, nervous. It was the end now,

and everyone on the crew understood what that meant. It was finally getting to them.

Captain Ernst Reiker continued through the compartment, his soft-soled boots making no sound on the grillwork of the deck. The torpedo room hatch was partially closed. He pushed it open on its well-oiled hinges and looked inside. The compartment was barely lit by a single dim red bulb over one of the torpedo tubes. The air stank of unwashed bodies and machine oil, laced with the alcohol used as propellant for the torpedoes.

The four men housed back there were all asleep in their hammocks suspended over the stored torpedoes. One of them snored softly. They were good men—boys, actually. Several of them, in his shorthanded crew of thirty-nine men and officers, had hardly begun to shave. It was a shame, because none of them would see the fatherland again. The war was over. Germany had lost. Once they ditched the boat and went ashore, they would have to remain on Argentine soil. There wouldn't be many other places in the world where, as Nazis, they would be accepted.

More's the pity, he thought; in the short time they'd been together as a crew, he'd come to admire them for their naïve trust in him and for their tenacity under difficult conditions.

He took one last look, then turned and retraced his steps through the engineering spaces. It was very late, time to get some sleep himself now that his daily inspection tour was completed. Yet he doubted that he would be able to shut down his brain as easily as had his teen-aged crewmen.

Reiker, at forty-four, was old for the German submarine service. Most of his peers had either died in the war or had been promoted to command fleets or battle groups from desks in Berlin or Bremerhaven. But he'd been turned down for such promotions because of something in his past, in his background. It was something he'd always denied, but it was no use. He'd gone as far as he could possibly go. Much farther than he should have.

All along he had known, of course, that there would be no honor for him at the end, though, ironically, his last orders to bring the submarine across a hostile sea had been loaded with words such as devotion to the fatherland, honor, heroism. But this time there would be no medals to be had. No marching bands. No cheering crowds at the docks. And he'd known it.

But he was a German officer, bound by his oath to the Führer to continue even though the war was over. There were no more battles on the North Atlantic to be fought, nor was there anywhere for him to take his boat and crew. No home port.

So many *but*'s, he thought as he stepped through the hatch into the red-lit control room. So many *if*'s. So many questions . . . with no answers.

"Captain on the conn," his second officer, Lieutenant j.g. Lötti Zigler announced. The sonarman, helmsman, and diving officer all came briefly to attention.

"At ease," Reiker said tiredly. "Anything yet?"

"No, sir," Zigler said.

"Where's Dieter?"

"At the periscope."

Reiker crossed to the ladder and peered up into the attack center. His first officer, Lieutenant Dieter Schey, his cap on backward, was hunched over the handles of the periscope.

"See anything, Dieter?" Reiker called. He was too tired to climb up and look for himself.

Schey, who was only a few years younger than Reiker but looked about twenty-five, turned away from the eyepiece and shook his head. The hair on his head was blond, but his beard had come out medium brown. "Nothing. No lights, no movement . . . in the bay or ashore. We might as well be parked at a desert island."

Reiker looked over at the nav station where a stool had been set up for their one passenger, RSHA Major Walther Roebling, who had come aboard with their cargo. He had brought with him a letter signed by the high command, giving him and the Reichssicherheitshauptant—the Reich Central Security Office—complete authority over the submarine and her crew. The secret service officer had spent nearly all of his waking hours perched on the stool, watching the control room crew at work, and tracking their position across the North Atlantic and then south across the equator. He wasn't in his customary position now.

"Where is he?" Reiker asked Zigler.

"He hasn't been here all night, Captain. Not since dinner."

"Ernst, let's put up the snorkel and run the diesels," Schey called from above. "No one will hear us, and we need the electrical power."

"Just a moment," Reiker said. Something was nagging at him. Something was wrong. He could feel it. Something about the major.

"Call his quarters," Reiker told his second officer.

Zigler picked up the interphone and punched the proper number. After a half-minute he looked around and shook his head. "He doesn't answer. Shall I go check?"

Reiker reached up and hit the comms button. "Major Roebling to the control center. Major Roebling to the conn, please."

He turned again to Zigler. "If he isn't here within sixty seconds, I want the boat searched for him."

"Aye, aye, sir."

Reiker climbed up into the cramped attack center and took Schey's place at the periscope. At first he couldn't make out much of anything. But gradually he began to distinguish between the dark shoreline and the even darker water. There was no moon tonight, and the sky was partially covered with clouds. He was able to see an occasional white line of surf breaking on the narrow, rocky beach, but nothing else. His first officer was correct. There were no lights, no signs of any human activity whatsoever, toward land or out to sea.

"What's with our little spy?" Schey asked softly at Reiker's elbow.

"This is our supposed rendezvous point, Dieter," Reiker said, making a second 360-degree sweep. "For twenty-four hours we have remained at periscope depth, waiting for someone to show up. Still nothing."

"Maybe they were delayed."

Reiker looked away from the eyepiece.

"No one thought it would end so soon," Schey said. He shrugged. "So badly; for us, that is."

"Why isn't he up here, Dieter? Why hasn't he ordered a party ashore to find out what has happened?"

"His orders . . ."

"His real plan, perhaps," Reiker murmured. Most of the mysterious cargo they'd taken on at Bremen was stored beneath the deck plates in the after storage compartments where he thought he'd heard the noise.

"You think the little bastard is up to something?" Schey asked.

"I think I would like to ask him that. Tonight."

Schey nodded grimly. "In such a fashion that he will not lie to us."

"Yes."

"What is all the commotion?" Major Roebling called irritably from below.

Reiker looked down into the control room. "Come up here, Major. I think you'll want to take a look at this."

Roebling, who was a slightly built man with the pasty complexion of one who'd spent too much time underground in bunkers, narrowed his eyes. "What is it, Captain?"

"I think it may be our contact at last."

"Impossible . . ." Roebling said quickly, then cut himself off.

"Nevertheless, you should come have a look for yourself, Major."

Roebling started up the ladder and Reiker and Schey exchanged glances. Schey lifted his sweater slightly, exposing the butt of his Luger.

"Now, what is this you are seeing?" Roebling barked angrily. "I am in no mood for your silly little games tonight."

Reiker nodded toward the periscope. "See for yourself."

Roebling studied the captain's eyes for a moment, then bent over the periscope and looked through the eyepiece. Schey took out his pistol.

"I don't see a thing," Roebling snapped, then he looked

up into the barrel of Schey's pistol. His eyes widened. "Are you mad, Schey? Put down your pistol. Now. Immediately."

"First we would like to have a little talk, Major," Reiker said.

"You're a dead man," Roebling growled.

"But you are not the one holding the pistol at this moment," Reiker said. "Zigler," he called below.

"Aye, aye, sir."

"From which direction did Major Roebling come just now?"

"Aft."

"Your quarters are forward," Reiker noted.

"I was in the crew's galley. We were out of coffee forward," Roebling said.

"Zigler," Reiker called again.

"Aye, aye, sir."

"Send someone forward to check out the major's compartment. Search it, and let me know what you find."

Roebling was glaring at Reiker, the raw energy of his hate strong enough to be a nearly palpable force in the cramped quarters.

"Yes, sir."

"And then send a party to the after diesel storage compartments. Break into the cargo we took on at Bremen."

Roebling tried to push forward, but Schey jammed the barrel of the gun into the major's face, and he stopped.

"Sir?" Zigler called up, evidently confused.

"Break into the cargo. Open some of the boxes. I want to know what it is. Now. On the double!"

"Do you understand what you are doing?" Roebling asked through clenched teeth.

"The war is over, Major," Reiker said. "Or very nearly so. We all know this. Which means there is nowhere for me to go, nowhere for me to take my crew. I would like to know if there is anything in the cargo you brought aboard that would be useful for us."

"It is for the Reich. You have your orders."

"There is no longer any Reich. So whatever you brought

aboard at Bremen is now for you. I would like to know what it is. I would also like to know what you were doing back there a little while ago. It was you I heard belowdecks.''

"You sonofabitch, you have your orders—''

Schey roughly shoved the major up against the escape trunk hatch, and jammed the pistol barrel so hard into his forehead that the front sight broke skin and a thin trickle of blood ran down between the man's eyes.

''It is my captain you are talking to, Major. With respect now, please, or I will splatter your brains all over the bulkhead behind you.'' Schey was grinning. He'd been waiting for such a moment ever since they'd left Bremen.

For the first time Roebling appeared to doubt his own safety. He looked from Schey and Reiker to the open hatch leading down to the control room.

''What has happened to your rendezvous?'' Reiker asked.

''I don't know. He was delayed. Maybe he is dead. I don't know.''

''What are your orders in such an event?''

''I am to hold the boat here for a full forty-eight hours.''

''And then?''

Roebling said nothing.

''We're waiting,'' Schey warned.

''Captain,'' Zigler called from below.

Reiker looked down into the control room. Zigler was holding a small rucksack open.

''He has an Argentine passport under a different name,'' Zigler said. He sounded excited. ''There is money here, American dollars, I think, and some civilian clothes. A notebook.''

''Going someplace?'' Schey asked casually.

Roebling's eyes had grown wide, and he was swallowing repeatedly, his Adam's apple bobbing.

''Captain, his bag was stuffed in a message buoy.''

''Waterproof,'' Reiker said. ''You were planning on abandoning the boat. Here? Tonight?''

Roebling held his silence.

''Answer the captain,'' Schey demanded.

Roebling almost seemed to be holding his breath now, as if he were waiting for something. Reiker tried to see into the man's eyes, tried to probe what was in his brain. Something was happening, or was about to. He had been getting ready to abandon ship. And he had been in the cargo spaces. . . .

Reiker's gut suddenly tightened. He hit the comms button and screamed into the microphone. "Get out of the cargo spaces! Now! This is the captain! Get out of there!"

Three explosions, one after the other, rocked the boat, sending Reiker sprawling off balance and nearly through the open hatch.

Schey was stunned for just a moment, but it was enough for Roebling to snatch the pistol out of his hand and shove him back.

Sirens were sounding all over the boat.

"Emergency stations, emergency stations!" Reiker was shouting into the comms.

"Have Zigler toss my bag up here," Roebling ordered. "Now!"

"Flooding aft of the main battery compartments," a crewman radioed desperately. "We can't handle it back here!"

"Seal the boat!" Reiker shouted. "Blow all tanks and prepare for emergency surface procedures!"

"My bag!" Roebling demanded, keeping the pistol trained on Schey.

Zigler tossed it through the hatch, and Roebling snatched it. He opened the escape trunk hatch, grinned as he stepped inside, and then slammed it shut, dogging it down. Immediately the hiss of water filling the trunk became audible.

"Captain, all after tanks have lost integrity. The explosions must have damaged them," Zigler shouted.

There was pandemonium below in the control room. Everyone knew that the boat was going to the bottom, that there was no saving her. But at least the crew forward of the battery compartments would be safe in watertight spaces. Some of them would have access to escape trunks once they reached the bottom, some two hundred fifty feet below the surface.

Schey stepped across to the escape trunk hatch and dogged

it down so that Roebling would not be able to get back into the submarine. Then he reached up and shut off the master valves, cutting off the escape trunk's water supply. With the trunk only half filled, the major would be stuck inside until they let him out, or until he suffocated for lack of oxygen.

Someone was screaming something on the ship's comms, and water was pouring into the control room as Reiker and Schey scrambled down from the attack center. Already the boat was listing nearly twenty degrees to starboard, and she was definitely down at the stern.

"Shut that hatch!" Reiker screamed.

Zigler, shaking his head in fear and disbelief, was bracing himself against the list. "We can't!" he cried. "All the hatches have been sabotaged! We're going down for sure!"

Reiker and Schey immediately slogged their way to the after hatch and put their shoulders to it, but it wouldn't budge. The hinges were frozen.

The water in the lower half of the control room was already chest deep, and as the boat continued to roll to starboard, sparks flew from a control panel and the lights suddenly went out, plunging them into darkness.

All through the forward compartments of the boat Reiker could hear his men screaming, crying out in blind panic. But it was over. In a few short moments they would be dead.

He looked up toward where the attack center hatch would be, though he could not see it in the total darkness, and felt at least a small measure of satisfaction. Roebling would die too, the precious Reich's cargo, the cargo that was to have saved the war effort, the cargo he'd been honor-bound by his oath to deliver to this shore, going down with him.

The water was cold as it came up over Reiker's head, and his main regret was that he would never see his wife and child again.

THE BEST IN PSYCHOLOGICAL SUSPENSE